SCAVENGER ALLIANCE

ABOUT THE AUTHOR

Janet Edwards lives in England and writes science fiction. As a child, she read everything she could get her hands on, including a huge amount of science fiction and fantasy. She studied Maths at Oxford, and went on to suffer years of writing unbearably complicated technical documents before deciding to write something that was fun for a change. She has a husband, a son, a lot of books, and an aversion to housework.

Visit Janet online at her website www.janetedwards.com to see the current list of her books. You can also make sure you don't miss future books by signing up to get an email alert when there's a new release.

ALSO BY JANET EDWARDS

Set in the Hive Future

PERILOUS: Hive Mind A Prequel Novella

TELEPATH

DEFENDER

Set in the Game Future

REAPER

Set in the 25th century Portal Future

SCAVENGER ALLIANCE

Set in the 28th century Portal Future

The Earth Girl trilogy:-

EARTH GIRL

EARTH STAR

EARTH FLIGHT

Related stories:-

EARTH AND FIRE: An Earth Girl Novella

EARTH AND AIR: An Earth Girl Novella

FRONTIER: An Epsilon Sector Novella

EARTH 2788: The Earth Girl Short Stories

HERA 2781: A Military Short Story

JANET EDWARDS

SCAVENGER ALLIANCE

SCAVENGER EXODUS 1

CHAPTER ONE

I was the only person who saw the aircraft arrive in New York, and I didn't realize what it was at first. I'd just stepped out on to the roof of the Americas Parliament House, when I noticed the small speck in the dawn sky.

Logic told me there was no need for me to worry about anything overhead. I was standing on top of the highest building in the area, so should be perfectly safe from the gliding attacks of the local predators. The crisp carpet of snow under my feet was an extra reassurance, since none of those predators would be out hunting while the temperature was below freezing point.

I still stopped to stare upwards and make sure this was only a bird. My years in New York had taught me that letting down your guard, even for a second, could get you injured or killed.

I couldn't work out what species of bird this was, but it was definitely far too high in the air to be anything dangerous. I forgot about it, fixed my eyes on where the blue, planet Earth flag was proudly silhouetted against the rising sun, and gave the distinctive, right hand on heart salute of the Earth Resistance.

My regular morning ritual completed, I would normally go back inside, but today I lingered with my eyes fixed on the Earth Resistance flag, brooding on the ominous fact that today was my eighteenth birthday. My position in the Resistance had been uncertain ever since my brother left, and turning eighteen would probably make my life even more difficult.

I was reluctant to go back indoors in case I found my worries becoming harsh reality, but the icy January wind was finding its way through my layers of clothing, and triggering an ache in the left arm that I'd broken last summer. I sighed, turned back to the door to the stairs, and then remembered the strange bird and gave a last glance upwards.

I was startled to see the bird was much closer now, vastly bigger than I'd thought, and didn't look like any kind of living creature I'd ever seen. It took me a moment longer to work out this had to be an aircraft. I'd heard people talk about how such things were commonplace centuries ago, used for long distance travel in the days before the invention of portal technology, but I'd imagined them having wide flapping wings rather than stubby, rigid structures.

The aircraft must have come from behind Fence, flying casually over the vicious wire that protected the respectable citizens from undesirables like me, but why? The last of the citizens had abandoned New York in 2389, withdrawing to their new settlements the summer before I was born, so what had brought them here now?

I stood there for another couple of minutes, watching the aircraft fly straight overhead and across the Hudson River to skyscraper-crammed Manhattan. It stopped there, hung motionless in the sky like a hovering bird of prey for a few seconds, then slowly dropped vertically downwards and vanished behind one of the buildings.

An enemy aircraft had landed in our city! I forced myself out of my stupor, ran back inside, clattered down the narrow flight of stairs, and then came to an abrupt halt as I saw the man walking down the corridor ahead of me. He had his back to me, just an anonymous shape in a thick, hooded coat, but the flickering lights of the gun tendrils on his right hand and wrist showed this had to be Donnell. Now that Kasim was dead, Donnell was the only person here with an Armed Agent weapon.

I hesitated. Given my dubious situation, I normally gave messages to one of Donnell's officers rather than approaching him directly myself, but he needed to hear this news at once.

"Sir!" I hurried up to him.

Donnell tugged down his hood as he turned to face me, and I saw his eyebrows lift in surprise.

"I just saw an aircraft!" I said. "It landed over the other side of the river in Manhattan."

Donnell frowned for a moment, and then shrugged. "I can't believe the citizens have suddenly started flying aircraft after all these years. It must be some off-worlders checking the art galleries and museums for anything worth salvaging. Forget about it, Blaze."

"Forget about it?" I repeated his words in shocked disbelief. The idea of the citizens trespassing in our territory had been bad enough, but the thought of off-worlders coming here and taking whatever they wanted was even worse. "But we're the Earth Resistance. It's our duty to stop the off-world colonies leeching resources from Earth. It says so in our charter!"

Donnell ran his fingers through his thick brown hair, with its scattering of silver strands that added distinction to his legendary good looks. "That's true, but I wrote that charter over thirty years ago, back when there were still a couple of billion people living on Earth. Everything is totally different now."

There weren't billions of people living on Earth now, there were probably less than a hundred million, and only just over seven hundred of us here in New York, but I thought that made it even more important to defend our rights. Angry words burst out of me. "We should still go to Manhattan and..."

Donnell lifted a hand to stop me. "Calm down, Blaze."

I was horrified to realize I'd been shouting at Donnell. I hastily shut up.

"You mustn't tell anyone else about the aircraft," Donnell continued. "Everyone in the Resistance would react like you, wanting to get their revenge on the off-worlders who bled our home world dry of resources to found their bright new colony worlds, while the members of the other divisions are even more bitter about the way those bright new worlds refused entry to anyone with a criminal record. Whatever I said, the whole of the alliance would go racing off to Manhattan, and that could get us all killed."

His attitude suddenly made sense to me. "You're worried the off-worlders could have advanced weapons?"

"That's one problem. The other is that it's nearly two months since the winter fever hit us. Only a handful of people recovered in time to go out hunting and fishing before the last blizzard. Now everyone's finally well again, we have to focus all our efforts on getting more food before the next blizzard arrives, because we've nothing left to eat."

Donnell's words shocked me. I'd known we were short of food, there had been strict rationing for weeks, but... "The food reserves are gone?"

"We'll be eating most of the remaining food for breakfast."

"I didn't realize that," I murmured.

"I discussed the situation with the leaders of the other four divisions. We made a joint decision not to frighten people with the truth, because we didn't want anyone heroically heading out into the blizzard and getting themselves killed in an attempt to get more food. I'm only telling you about this now so you'll understand why I'm asking you to forget about that aircraft. However wrong it feels to let off-worlders ransack Manhattan, we must hunt food rather than invaders today. We have children to feed."

I nodded in reluctant acceptance.

"It's not as if we'll ever risk going to Manhattan for supplies again after that disastrous trip last summer," Donnell added. "Anything left there is going to rot away and fall apart, so the off-worlders might as well take whatever they want."

I winced at the mention of that trip to Manhattan. I considered myself lucky to have escaped with nothing worse than a broken arm, because one of Donnell's officers had been killed.

"I won't tell anyone about the aircraft, sir, but if it takes off when everyone is out hunting then they'll all see it."

"It doesn't matter if people see the off-worlders leaving. They won't be able to fly after them."

There was a moment of silence after that. I thought our conversation was over, and was about to leave when Donnell spoke again.

"Happy birthday, Blaze."

He'd remembered my birthday! I gave him a wary look. "Uh, thank you, sir."

"It's time that we discussed your future."

Panic stabbed at me. What did Donnell mean by that? Did he feel that my eighteenth birthday marked the end of his debatable responsibility for me? I waited in tense silence to hear what Donnell would say next, but his attention had shifted to something behind me. I turned and saw Machico, the eldest of Donnell's officers, was coming down the corridor towards us.

Machico gave me a single inquisitive look before speaking to Donnell. "There's a problem downstairs, oh beloved leader. Some of the Manhattan division men started jeering at Queens Island division, and Queens Island naturally retaliated. Luther was eager to flaunt his officer powers, and waded into the middle of the argument before the rest of us could stop him."

He paused. "The good news is that Manhattan and Queens Island instantly stopped throwing insults at each other. The bad news is that they started ridiculing Luther instead."

I frowned, distracted from my own worries by concern for Luther. All the other divisions hated each other, so an argument between any of them was likely to turn violent, but the feud between Manhattan and Queens Island was particularly bitter. Luther was barely nineteen, and had only been an alliance officer for five months. I could understand him wanting to prove himself, but it would have been wiser for him to let a more senior officer deal with the situation.

Donnell groaned. "I'd better go and remind the troublemakers that my officers have the support of my authority as alliance leader."

The two of them turned to walk off down the corridor. I stayed where I was, but Donnell glanced back at me and waved his hand in a beckoning gesture. I chased after him and Machico, catching them up when they stopped by the big steel door that led to the main staircase.

"If I can deal with this problem quickly, then we'll be able to continue our talk," said Donnell.

I was even more nervous now. If Donnell wasn't letting trouble between the divisions distract him from discussing my future, then he must have something grimly serious to say to me.

Donnell put his hand on the security plate, and lights flashed as the plate checked his handprint. The door slid aside, and we went down six floors worth of stairs. When we reached ground level, Donnell yanked aside the heavy curtain that blocked the doorway ahead, and we left the Resistance wing of the building for the warm, smoke-scented air of the huge central reception hall.

In theory, this whole area was common ground and safe for everyone. In reality, each of the other four divisions had staked their claim to the corner of Reception by the entrance to their wing of the building, while the Resistance had an area in the centre of the room.

At this time in the morning, the members of each division should either be in the long queue for food, or sitting at the tables in their own areas and eating breakfast. Instead, half of them were on their feet and laughing. The target of that laughter was standing right in front of us, with two Manhattan men on one side of him and two Queens Island men on the other.

Luther usually had an air of calm self-confidence, but now his expression verged on panic. I could understand why. One of the Manhattan men taunting him was Cage, and I knew from personal experience how dangerous Cage could be.

"I've told you twice now to go back to your own areas," said Luther. "I'm an alliance officer, so you have to obey my orders."

"I'd no idea you were an officer, Luther," said Cage, in a voice of maliciously exaggerated innocence. "I must have missed hearing that wonderful news."

"I remember Donnell announcing Luther's officer appointment months ago," said the other Manhattan man, Shark, "but I assumed it was a joke. What has Luther ever done to earn an officer position?"

Luther ran his fingers through his black hair, obviously uncertain how to respond. I'd had a crush on Luther's good looks for a while back when I was fifteen. My feelings had survived a few months of his unrelenting indifference towards me, before being annihilated by a two-second encounter on the stairs. I was walking upwards, when Luther came dashing down past me, pushing me aside with a casual command that the traitor's sister should get out of his way. I'd heard that sort of remark plenty of times before and since, but it had been especially painful coming from him.

I didn't have a crush on Luther any longer, but I couldn't help sympathizing with him at this moment. I knew exactly what was happening here. Luther had become an officer five months ago. The other divisions had given him a relatively easy time back then, because his father, Kasim, had been Donnell's deputy and the only other person with an Armed Agent weapon. Now that Kasim had died from the winter fever, the worst of the division men had decided his son would be vulnerable prey, so they were circling him like wolves.

Luther finally opened his mouth to speak, but one of the Queens Island men called out from behind him.

"Of course Donnell wasn't joking. Kasim's son just has to whine for whatever he wants and he's handed it on a silver platter. It's the same thing that happened six years ago with..."

Donnell shouted from where he was standing next to me. "That's enough!"

The laughter round the room abruptly stopped. Shark and the two Queens Island division men turned and walked rapidly back to their own areas, but Cage lingered to give another mocking laugh at Luther before sauntering off with insolent slowness. As he approached the Manhattan corner, the bulky figure of Wall, leader of Manhattan division, strode forward to meet him. The glower of displeasure on Wall's dark face would have made any other Manhattan member tremble, but Cage's smile didn't falter.

I frowned. Cage had challenged Wall's leadership of Manhattan years ago. That challenge had failed because Wall was a strong, well-liked leader, but Cage's self-assured smile made me worry that he was planning a new leadership bid.

Donnell turned to me for a split second. "It seems we'll need to leave our talk until later, Blaze."

I didn't have time to reply before he and Machico hurried off to talk to Luther. I was left worrying about my own situation again, mentally replaying my conversation with Donnell about the aircraft, and cursing my stupidity for arguing with him. Donnell had remembered my birthday and was planning to discuss my future with me. My behaviour could be the last straw that made him discard me from the Resistance.

The cooking smells were tormenting my empty stomach, so I headed for the back of the room, automatically making the necessary detours to avoid trespassing on any other division's territory. Nobody would consider a girl like me a genuine threat, but going too close to their area would still bring retribution down on my head.

I joined the line of people queuing at the food table, and now I wasn't just worrying about Donnell's words, but uncomfortably aware of the leaping flames of the cooking fire as well. As the line slowly moved, I shuffled forward in turn, getting even closer to the makeshift hearth and chimney that had been built against the wall. I felt my hands begin to tremble and clenched them into fists. It was over six years since I'd escaped the London firestorm and come to New York as a refugee, but the sight and sound of flames still triggered bad memories.

The queue moved forward again. There were only three people ahead of me now, then two, then one, and finally I reached the table with its steaming cauldrons. I waited as my ration of soup was carefully ladled into a bowl and handed to me, then turned, eager to escape from the cooking fire, but found someone blocking my path.

"Hello, Blaze," said Cage.

CHAPTER TWO

I froze, my nerves jangling as I remembered the last time Cage had cornered me by this fire. I had only been eleven years old back then, a naive new arrival used to London's population of only a couple of hundred people, none of them a threat to me. Overwhelmed by the number of strangers in New York, struggling to learn the host of new rules, faces, and divisions, I'd made the foolish mistake of walking into Reception when none of the rest of the Resistance were there.

Cage had noticed me walking past the cooking fire, seen my fear of it, and couldn't resist the opportunity to entertain himself and his friends with some casual cruelty. He grabbed me from behind, and was dangling me upside down over the flames, making jokes about someone called Blaze being scared of fire, when Donnell arrived and forcefully intervened. Cage had kept a wary distance from me ever since then, so why was he confronting me now?

The answer had to be that today was my birthday. Cage suspected that turning eighteen would change my situation. He'd come to remind me that he still held a grudge over the incident by this fire, and make it clear that losing the protection of the Resistance would leave him free to take his long awaited revenge.

I tried to reassure myself that Cage could only frighten me with words this time – he surely wouldn't risk attacking me in full view of the whole alliance – but my panicking mind wasn't totally convinced. I glanced round, weighing my options if Cage did make a grab for me. Flight or fight? To escape past Cage, I'd have to move perilously close to the flames, and Cage knew exactly how I'd feel about doing that. As for fighting... Cage was twice my size. I wouldn't stand any better chance against him now than back when I was an eleven-year-old girl.

"Hello, Blaze," Cage repeated, giving me the smug smile of a man who believed he was handsome. I thought he was fooling himself. Cage's muscled figure and blond hair might have made him attractive ten years ago, but now he was in his mid-thirties, that blond hair was receding, and he had unflattering lines carved into his face that betrayed his bullying nature.

"Hello." I muttered the response while studying the size of the gap between him and the fire. Was it possible to squeeze through it without getting burnt? Could I even force myself to try when my head was filled with memories of choking smoke and my mother's dying screams?

"Now you're eighteen, I think it's time for us to come to an agreement," said Cage.

I stared at him in confusion. "What agreement?"

"The obvious one." He must have seen the bewilderment in my face, because he shook his head. "I thought you were more intelligent than this. Kasim's death from the winter fever has left Donnell short of an officer, and I'm willing to marry you on condition I get the vacant position. The arrangement could work extremely well for both of us. You'd get a powerful husband. I'd get increased status. Think about it."

"No!"

I said the word instinctively, stupidly, before I could stop myself. The smile vanished from Cage's face, and he leaned forward. I could feel his angry breath against my cheek as he whispered close to my ear.

"Do you really think you'll be able to pick and choose between a dozen offers? If you do, then I suggest you go and take a long hard look at yourself in a mirror. Donnell split up from your mother before you were born, and nobody believes you're his daughter, not even Donnell himself."

I backed away, but Cage instantly took a step forward to

close the gap between us again. His mouth was touching my ear now, so there was no way to avoid hearing his words.

"When you arrived here with your brother and the other refugees from London, everyone could see the boy was the living image of Donnell in his youth, but there was a suspicious resemblance between you and the London division leader."

"I look like Ice because he's a distant cousin of my mother."

"You look like Ice because he's your real father," said Cage, "but Donnell is a generous man so he publicly accepted both you and your brother as being his children. Given what happened a couple of weeks later, Donnell must have bitterly regretted that generosity. He's not the sort of man to go back on his word, so he's never actually denied you're his daughter, but he's shown no more interest in you than in any of the other Resistance children."

Cage laughed. "Now you're eighteen, Donnell will be eager to get rid of his embarrassing problem, but even the biggest bribe won't tempt many men to marry the plain-faced sister of a traitor. You'd better agree to my offer before I change my mind."

He straightened up, laughed again, then turned his back on me and stalked off. I stood there numbly for a moment, wondering if the people in the food queue had heard his words. No, surely they couldn't have done. Cage had pitched his voice too low for that.

I forced myself to move, scurrying past the fire to the centre of the room, and the safety of the group of tables belonging to the Earth Resistance. My best friend, Hannah, was sitting at our regular table. I saw her look anxiously at me, and pat the vacant chair next to her, but I wasn't going to endanger her by dragging her into a conflict between me and Cage.

I went to an empty table instead, put down my bowl, and spread my hands flat on the table top to stop them trembling. I'd made a dreadful mistake by the cooking fire. Agreeing to marry Cage was unthinkable, but I should have at least pretended I'd consider it. Instead, I'd flung a flat refusal in his face. Cage had already had one grudge against me, and now I'd handed him another.

I looked round for Donnell, and saw he was talking to Machico. I faced forward again. Those few moments by the fire must have really shaken me to make me consider asking Donnell for help. For over six years, Donnell and I had had a tacit agreement. I could remain a member of the Resistance, but neither of us would mention certain subjects. How my mother died. What my brother did. What I didn't do. The issue of whether Donnell was really my father.

I couldn't break that agreement and start making personal demands on Donnell now, especially after he'd said those ominous words about discussing my future. I'd have to find a way to deal with Cage myself.

There was a sickening moment as I wondered if Donnell's words were connected with Cage's offer of marriage. If Donnell knew about that and wanted me to accept Cage, then...

No! I couldn't believe that. I *wouldn't* believe that. Donnell would never push any girl into marrying a man like Cage. These two things had happened at the same time, but only because they'd both been triggered by my eighteenth birthday.

I stood there for a few seconds longer, with the scent of food making my stomach nag at me, then finally sat down at the table and began eating my soup.

CHAPTER THREE

As I scraped the last trace of soup from my bowl, Donnell began calling out the names of those who'd be in his hunting group. I felt a stab of uncertainty as I heard him say Cage's name, but told myself there was nothing significant about that. It was too dangerous for Donnell to let each division send out its own hunting party – the long-running feuds between them were bound to lead to one division's group "accidentally" shooting at another – so he split the men from each division between hunting parties led by himself and his officers.

Everyone knew those hunting parties were carefully randomized daily, so each man would get his turn at having the prestige of being in Donnell's group, but that didn't stop the chosen ones from giving gloating looks at those less fortunate. Donnell's officers each shouted out names in turn after that, with the exception of Luther, because he hadn't started leading hunting groups yet.

There was the traditional mockery of the man who was last to be called, then we all fastened our coats and put on hats and gloves. The men moved towards the glass-walled entrance area at the front of Reception, collected their bows and knife belts from tables, and headed out through the side door we'd been using ever since the main doors jammed shut four years ago. The women trailed after them, collecting their own knives and mesh fish bags. We had no groups to organize, because we all had our regular fishing spots, working in pairs for safety reasons.

Behind us came the children under twelve and the elderly, who'd be scrabbling in the snow for the genetically modified wintereat that was our main vegetable supply. It would be a miserable task in the freezing cold, but they wouldn't have to go further than the old front lawn that was our vegetable garden, and they'd be taking turns to shelter indoors. The children would have a couple of hours of school lessons, while the adults either taught them or cared for the babies and those too sick to work at all.

I just hoped there was still some wintereat left for them to find. Created a couple of centuries ago from the genes of a dozen parent plants including potatoes and cabbage, wintereat was designed to grow incredibly fast all year round in a huge range of climates, but nothing could make much progress when it was buried under snow.

The second I was outside, the wind chilled me despite my thick coat and boots. Up on the roof, the snow had been less than ankle deep because the wind kept blowing it away. Down here, it came to well above my knees, and was far deeper where it had drifted against walls. A gaggle of jubilant small children, rejoicing at being outdoors again after suffering three long days of extra school lessons during the blizzard, fought their way to the half-smothered row of portals by the front wall of the building. They started weaving their way in and out of the massive, upright rings.

"Dial it! Dial it! Portal, dial it!" they chanted. "We're ordering you by Newton. We're commanding you by Einstein. We're conjuring you by Thaddeus Wallam-Crane!"

I wondered how they'd react if one of those portals flared to life in response to their ritual game. It would never happen though. Two hundred years ago, Thaddeus Wallam-Crane invented portal technology. For the next century, people routinely stepped through portals to travel between neighbourhoods, between cities, even between continents, and then came interstellar portal technology. That gave humanity the stars, and started the great exodus from polluted Earth to new, unspoilt colony worlds scattered across hundreds of distant star systems.

Now Earth was semi-abandoned, and the only people left here

were the few who wouldn't or couldn't leave. I counted as both. I was a member of the Earth Resistance, so I'd never leave Earth, and none of the new colony worlds would accept me anyway.

My parents had probably travelled by portal a thousand times during their youth. I'd used a portal only once, when fleeing from the London firestorm to the safety of New York. My memories of that were a confused mixture of unconnected fragments. The acrid scent and taste of the choking smoke. The sight of the panicking faces of the other refugees crammed into the room that would be either our escape route or our coffin. The sound of Ice's voice shouting instructions, and my own frantic sobbing. The feel of my brother's arms clutching me tightly against his chest as he carried me through the glowing circle.

My brother and I had made it to safety, but we'd lost our mother to the London firestorm. Two weeks after that, my brother left, and the next day the lights on every portal in New York went out. The children playing here would never see a working portal, and I'd never see my brother again.

I forced away the painful memories, turned my back on the dead portals, and watched the leading men start breaking a path through the snow. They used long poles to test the ground ahead of them before stepping on it, and the straggling line of people behind them carefully followed in their footsteps.

This whole area had been redeveloped when the Americas Parliament complex was built here, so its buildings and paths were some of the newest in New York, but they'd had no maintenance for at least five decades. Every year the paths grew worse as cracks widened and ruts deepened, but the real danger was from broken or missing maintenance covers over old drains and tunnels. We'd marked the worst of the hazards with red flags, but new ones appeared all the time.

The women were following the men now. I joined the line myself and started plodding slowly towards the river. Hannah was my fishing partner. I couldn't see her ahead of me, so I turned to look behind, and spotted her distinctive blue hat. I edged cautiously to one side to let people walk past me, and stood waiting for her.

Hannah spoke the second she reached me. "Blaze, why didn't you come and sit with me at breakfast?"

I pulled a face. "Because Cage cornered me by the cooking fire, and I said something that made him very angry. I couldn't come and sit with you straight after that. If Cage is planning to take revenge on me, and I remind him you're my friend, then he could come after you too."

Hannah seemed more worried about me than scared for herself. "Why did he corner you, and what did you say to him?"

I was aware of the other women giving us curious looks as they went by. "I'll tell you all about it when we're alone."

Hannah frowned. "I suppose that's best, but... Are you all right?"

"I'm perfectly fine."

"No, you aren't. I can hear your voice shaking."

I stepped back onto the path, and we started moving again, with Hannah behind me. "That's just from the cold," I called over my shoulder.

She gave a single explosive sound of disbelief. "Hah!"

We trudged on through the snow. Once we reached the river, the two women directly in front of me moved out of line. The path turned to follow the riverbank now, and more women left the line as we passed one fishing spot after another.

There were only the men, Hannah, and me left when we reached the featureless back wall of a squat, single-storey, grey building, wedged into the small gap between what had once been two matching apartment blocks. A fire last summer had reduced one of those apartment blocks to a burned out shell, and a heap of its fallen, blackened rubble had blocked access to the fishing spot I shared with Hannah. The only way to reach it now was to use a ladder to climb over the flat roof of the grey building.

The men split up into several groups, each of which headed off in a slightly different direction. Donnell was leading the first group. I thought I saw him glance back at me, but it could have been just my imagination.

I turned back to the building and found the ladder was missing. Hannah and I had left it leaning against the wall after our last fishing trip, but it must have blown over in the blizzard. We had to grope in the snowdrifts to find it and lift it back into place.

Hannah climbed the ladder first, and I tossed our bags up to her before climbing up myself. There was an awkward moment when I pulled myself up on to the snow-covered roof – I was still nervous of trusting my left arm to take my weight – but Hannah was standing ready to make sure I didn't fall. After that, we just had to walk across the roof, step down onto first a high wall and then a rather lower concrete block, to reach a long, narrow pier jutting out into the river.

The grey building had one tiny window facing the river, and a door that sagged on its hinges but still grudgingly opened and shut. Hannah and I fetched the equipment we kept stored inside the building, baited hooks and set out our fishing lines at the end of the pier, and then put up a small tent. The moment we were sitting inside it, Hannah started questioning me.

"So what happened between you and Cage at the cooking fire?"

Hannah and I had been born within a few months of each other, and been best friends growing up in London. After we came to New York, and I'd lost both my mother and my brother, we'd become even closer than before, and I shared all my worries with her.

"Cage suggested marrying me," I said.

Hannah gave me a wide-eyed look. "Seriously?"

"I can hardly believe it either. Donnell has an officer vacancy now that Kasim is dead, and Cage seems to think marrying me will get him the position." I wrinkled my nose. "Chaos knows why he'd think that. Donnell's not taken any interest in me for six years, so there's no reason for him to hand out rewards to my husband, and he couldn't make Cage an officer anyway. The alliance rules specifically state that Donnell can only choose his officers from among the Resistance members, because none of the other four divisions trust their rivals to help run things."

"Cage must be planning to leave Manhattan division and join the Resistance when he marries you," said Hannah.

I shook my head. "You know Cage can't leave Manhattan. At

least, he can't leave Manhattan and expect to keep breathing. Donnell would never force anyone to stay in the Resistance against their will, but the other divisions demand absolute loyalty for life, and kill anyone who breaks their allegiance."

"The division leaders give permission for a woman to move if she marries someone in a different division. Wall might extend the same permission to Cage if he thought Cage would stay secretly loyal to them." Hannah's voice had a cynical note. "Manhattan would love the idea of one of Donnell's officers favouring them."

I thought that over. "That's true, but Donnell's officer appointments have to be confirmed by two of the other division leaders. Even if Wall voted in his favour, Cage would still need to get another division leader to support him, and how could he manage that?"

I didn't wait for Hannah to answer, just shrugged and kept talking. "Not that it matters. I've already told Cage I'm not marrying him."

"You turned him down right away?" Hannah frowned. "That was a bad idea. Cage won't react well to an instant rejection."

I groaned. "I know it was a mistake. I should have been tactful about it, pretended to consider Cage's offer for a while before saying no, but I instinctively blurted out a refusal. Cage was furious about it. He said..."

I hesitated, reluctant to repeat Cage's angry words. I didn't care about his reference to my brother and calling me plain – I knew I wasn't one of the prettiest girls in the alliance – but I'd hated him saying that Donnell wasn't my father.

"He said some very unpleasant things." I skipped over the details.

Hannah lifted a hand to her mouth, and chewed nervously on her gloved forefinger. "You made Cage angry. He can be very dangerous when he's angry. Remember the story about how he got his nickname."

I winced. That story dated from before the last of the citizens had left New York. Cage had only been sixteen back then, but he'd trapped one of the citizens and put the man in a cage. The tales of what happened after that had given me nightmares when I was younger.

"I saw you arrive in Reception with Donnell this morning," said Hannah. "Had you been talking to him?"

"We had a short conversation."

"What about?"

Donnell had ordered me to keep the aircraft's arrival secret, so I dodged the question. "I'd been on the roof with a good view of the weather."

"If you told Donnell about you offending Cage, do you think he'd step in to protect you?"

I didn't want to frighten Hannah, but it would be cruel to let her build up false hopes. "I don't think I can count on that. Donnell mentioned my birthday, and said he was going to talk to me about my future."

Hannah made a sick, gagging noise. "That sounds like a warning. Is Donnell going to discard you from the Resistance?"

I tried to keep my voice calm and confident. "He just said that he'd talk to me. It needn't mean anything bad."

"It's not likely to mean anything good though, is it?" Hannah chewed on her gloved finger again. "If Donnell does discard you from the Resistance, none of the other divisions will be eager to accept a girl with a broken arm."

"My broken arm has healed perfectly," I said.

"No, it hasn't." Hannah made an exasperated clicking sound with her tongue. "It's still hurting you."

"My arm sometimes aches a little," I admitted, "but that's just a temporary problem because of the cold winter weather."

"It doesn't matter if it's temporary or not," said Hannah. "If Donnell discards you from the Resistance, you'll have to beg for membership of one of the other divisions. Their leaders will hold your brother's actions against you, and a badly healed arm will be an extra reason for them to decide against taking you in."

She paused. "You could be left fighting for survival on the fringes of the alliance, Blaze. You don't understand how hard that would be. I do. I lived that life for two years in London."

I was tempted to say that I did understand. Eleven years ago,

Hannah's father fought Ice for the London division leadership, lost, and died of his injuries. The next day, Hannah and her mother were formally expelled by Ice. I'd watched every struggle they went through in the next two years, because I sneaked off each day to visit Hannah, taking her scraps of food and other oddments.

Watching someone else going through something wasn't the same as experiencing it yourself though, so Hannah was probably right that I didn't understand.

Hannah pulled a pained face. "After my mother was killed in that stupid accident, I would have starved to death, but you talked your mother into pleading my case with Ice. He let me rejoin London division, but took every opportunity to make it clear I was its most unwelcome member. When we arrived in New York, and Donnell wanted you and your brother to join the Resistance, I was terrified. I knew Ice wouldn't let me stay in London division without you."

My mind conjured up the memory of Ice's unreadable face, the emotionless tone of his voice, and the exact words he'd used as he spoke to Seamus and me that day. "Your father has invited you both to join the Resistance, and the three New York divisions have said that you must accept that invitation. They've agreed to give house room to us homeless beggars, because they know having more people will give everyone a better life, but they won't tolerate Donnell's children staying with us in case it makes him favour London division over them."

Whenever I remembered that day, I always got caught up in the pointless loop of thinking through what happened next, and wondering if there was anything I could have done to make things end differently. I should have realized there was something terribly wrong about Seamus's behaviour. I'd known that he hated our father for abandoning him as a child. I'd expected Seamus to resent being forced to move to the Resistance, but we were welcomed with open arms as Donnell's adored children, and Seamus seemed to revel in being the centre of attention.

I hadn't thought that was strange at the time. I'd been awed to meet my legendary father at last. I'd believed Seamus felt the same way, but he hadn't forgotten his old anger. In fact, he had a new and even more bitter grievance against Donnell, thinking our mother would still be alive if Donnell had taken his family with him to New York years ago.

Seamus was just hiding his feelings while he gathered the knowledge he needed to take his revenge for our mother's death. Two weeks after our arrival in New York, Seamus left, and the next day every portal in New York died. Three hours after that, Donnell and I had a blazing argument where we both said impossibly destructive things to each other, and we'd never risked talking about anything personal ever again.

Hannah's voice dragged me out of the painful past. "It was a huge relief when you persuaded Donnell to make me a trial member of the Resistance, but then there was that trouble with your brother and..."

She shook her head, and her voice changed from anxious to despairing. "I tried so hard to please Donnell and the rest of the Resistance after that, but they were suspicious of both of us, treating the slightest mistake like a crime. If Donnell discards you from the Resistance, then I won't be in any position to help you, Blaze, because he'll discard me as well."

I opened my mouth to say something reassuring, but closed it again. Hannah was right. Her position in the Resistance was even more precarious than my own. There was a grim silence before Hannah spoke again.

"Do you think you could persuade Ice to take us back into London division?"

"I doubt it. Manhattan, Queens Island, and Brooklyn were furious about Seamus sabotaging the New York portal network. They put part of the blame on Donnell for being gullible enough to trust him, but most of their anger was targeted at London division for bringing a traitor to New York. Ice had to grovel for months to stop the whole of London from being expelled from the alliance with nothing but the clothes on their backs."

"But your mother was Ice's cousin," said Hannah. "You're the only relative he has left now. Surely that must mean some-thing to him."

"Ice doesn't seem to have ordinary feelings."

There was a long silence before Hannah spoke again in a mournful voice. "Everything would be so different if you only looked more like Donnell."

Her words echoed what Cage had said at the cooking fire, hitting me hard in my most vulnerable spot. I hadn't met my father at all until I was eleven years old, and we'd hardly spoken since then, but my life had still been built on the fact I was the daughter of the legendary Sean Donnelly, founder of the Earth Resistance. If that wasn't true, if I wasn't the girl I'd always believed I was, then who was I?

One of the fishing lines gave a sudden jerk. "Fish!" I shouted, eager for an excuse to escape this conversation.

A shoal of fish must have arrived, because a flurry of activity on the fishing lines kept us busy for a while. When things calmed down again, I kept the discussion to neutral topics. By the afternoon, we were both feeling so dreadfully hungry, that we talked about nothing but food, debating our chances of getting a decent meal to eat tonight. We were catching some fish, so the other women should be successful as well. It was less easy to predict the men's hunting luck, which could vary wildly from one day to the next. There was only a faint chance of them bringing home one of the deer that sometimes strayed into New York, but they should get some geese. Hopefully there'd be wintereat leaves, and perhaps even baked roots as well.

Finally, we heard a piercing whistle blowing one short note, then a longer one, and another short. That was Natsumi at the next fishing spot, signalling that it was time to pack away the fishing gear and head back.

By the time we'd got everything into the building, and carried the net bags of fish over the roof, my left arm was aching badly from the combination of hard work and cold. I tried to hide the problem, but Hannah must have seen some betraying sign, because she insisted on carrying more than her share of the bags as we followed the path to where Natsumi was waiting with her sister, Himeko.

"Blaze." Natsumi greeted me with her usual brief nod, and ignored Hannah entirely.

The four of us continued along the path in total silence. Natsumi and Himeko had been members of the Earth Resistance since the day it was formed, and were unrelentingly hostile to me for being the traitor's sister, and to Hannah for being my friend. I sometimes made an effort to make polite conversation with them, forcing a few grudging sentences out of them in return, but I was too tired to try it today.

The wind had eased now, but as the other fishing pairs joined us in turn, it started snowing, large wet flakes that hovered on the edge of turning to rain. By the time we'd reached the Parliament House, my coat was dripping wet, and there was a chill, damp feeling across my shoulder blades.

As we went in through the door, Hannah and I shook the water from our coats, then unbuckled our knife belts with hands that were stiff and clumsy from the cold, and carefully placed them on the table reserved for the Resistance knife belts.

Two women came bustling over to collect our fish bags. I'd just handed them mine, when I saw their faces suddenly change. They seemed to be staring past me at something.

Confused, I turned to look behind me, and saw the door was opening again. Three figures came through it, strangers dressed in matching, hoodless, blue and black outfits. For a second, I was too stunned to think, but then I realized these people had to be from the aircraft I'd seen that morning.

I was face to face with the off-worlders, the enemy!

CHAPTER FOUR

There was total silence as everyone gathered round to study the off-worlders in their fancy clothes. I spared only the briefest of glances for the woman, and the slightly built boy who couldn't be much older than me, focusing my attention on their leader. He was a broad-shouldered man with light brown hair, almost exactly the same age, height, and weight as Cage.

I saw people shuffling aside to let Donnell through the crowd. He walked up to stand facing the off-worlders, and I was stunned when it was the boy rather than the man who stepped forward to meet him and started talking.

"We apologize for the intrusion," he said, pronouncing his words with odd precision. "Our aircraft was damaged when we landed across the river, and we saw the smoke from your fire so we headed here. We'd be grateful for food and accommodation until the weather improves and we can make our way to the nearest settlements."

There was a shout of laughter from over to my left, and I heard Cage cruelly mimicking the boy's accent. "Their lordships apologize for the intrusion. They'd be grateful for food and accommodation."

"We should eat them, not feed them," Shark joined in the attack. "We could use the meat."

The off-worlders drew closer together, and I saw the boy's head turn rapidly to left and right as he searched for the speakers among the hostile faces surrounding him.

"Quiet!" shouted Donnell.

"We should keep the woman alive though," said a voice from directly behind me. "We could have a lot of fun with her."

Donnell whirled round, stepped past me, and I heard the crack of a fist meeting bone. By the time I looked over my shoulder, his target was lying on the floor clutching his jaw, and everyone was backing away from them. I hastily scampered backwards myself.

Donnell watched the man on the floor for a moment, to check he wasn't planning to get up and continue the fight, then looked slowly round the faces in the crowd. "When I say be quiet, I mean it."

He pointed the finger of his right hand as he said the last words. That might have been just for emphasis, but the lights of the gun wrapped around his right forearm were flashing at high speed, warning it was at alert status. Everyone froze, barely daring to breathe, as Donnell walked back to the three tense figures in blue and black, and paused in front of the woman.

"Pretty." He touched her cheek fleetingly with one hand, before turning to face the crowd. "The off-worlders could prove valuable. No one lays a finger on any of them, especially the woman. Understand?"

There were hasty nods in response.

"I'll take them to the Resistance wing for questioning," said Donnell. "Luther, you're coming with me. Machico, you're in charge here."

The two of them came out of the crowd. Luther went to stand next to Donnell, while Machico looked round with a relaxed smile on his weathered face.

"Today's thrilling entertainment is over, people."

Everyone turned and started drifting away. I was the only one standing still now, my brain struggling to adjust to what had happened. The enemy wasn't just at our gates, but inside them, and Donnell... The way he'd just acted towards that woman seemed completely out of character. Everything I'd been told by others, everything I'd seen for myself, confirmed that Donnell had never been attracted to anyone since his relationship with my mother broke down. Could he really be interested in an off-world leech?

I stared at the group heading for the stairs, Donnell in the lead, the three off-worlders behind him, and Luther bringing up the rear. The woman looked about twenty-two or twenty-three, and yes, she was pretty even with her blonde hair wet and straggling limply against her head, but...

Donnell glanced over his shoulder. "Blaze! You're coming with me too."

Me? Included in this? I was too bewildered to move for a second, then pulled myself together and hurried after the group, catching them up as they went through the curtain to the Resistance stairs. As soon as the heavy material fell back into place behind us, the woman started talking.

"I don't..."

"Hush!" said Donnell sharply. "It's dangerous to talk here with only a curtain between you and the mob."

The woman frowned and went quiet, but the boy waved his hand urgently at the man. "Yes, but Braden injured his leg on the way here. He needs to see a doctor."

"I wish we had a doctor here, but we don't," said Donnell. "What sort of injury is it? Can you make it up the stairs, Braden? You'll be much safer up there."

"It's just a cut." Braden rolled up one leg of his blue and black outfit, to show a bloody gash in his right calf. "I can manage the stairs."

We headed up to the sixth floor, moving slowly since Braden was limping. Donnell opened the security door, we went through into a grey corridor, and the door closed behind us. I usually felt a wave of relief as I entered the top floor of the Resistance wing, the safest place in the Parliament House, but this time we'd brought an unknown threat with us.

Donnell paused to speak to the off-worlders. "When we first occupied this building, my technical expert, Machico, spent six weeks getting full control of the security system. Only my most trusted Resistance members have access to the top floor of our wing, so you'll be safe here."

I flushed with pleasure at the comment about trusted Resistance members, then realized Donnell had probably forgotten all about me when he said it. He'd given me, my brother, and Hannah neighbouring apartments up here when we first came to New York. My brother had only lived here for two weeks, and a few months later Hannah was unjustly accused of stealing from the sixth floor supply rooms and moved down to an apartment on a lower floor, but I still had my original rooms.

"Luther, we need a medical kit," said Donnell.

Luther dashed off into a storage room, while Donnell led the rest of us to his conference room. He pulled out one of the chairs from around the circular table for Braden to sit down.

Luther arrived with the medical kit a moment later, and Donnell knelt down to clean Braden's wound with some alcohol and tie a bandage round his leg. The boy frowned as he watched this, as if he thought the treatment incredibly primitive.

"Don't you have regrowth ointment?" he asked.

"We used the last of our ointments and medicines three years ago." Donnell stood up. "This is a straightforward cut, and I don't think it needs stitches, but I'll get Nadira, our best nurse, to check it when she's off duty later this evening."

"Thank you," said Braden.

Donnell gestured at the other chairs, and we all sat down. I'd never done more than peek through the door of this room before, so it felt strange to sit down in a chair at Donnell's side, and even stranger that an off-worlder woman was sitting on the other side of me. I glanced at her, and saw her hands were clenched tightly together on her lap. I realized she was terrified, and felt a traitorous moment of sympathy.

The off-worlder boy had taken a chair opposite me. I took my chance to study him, still finding it hard to believe he was the leader of these three. His hair was a nondescript brown, and his face wasn't classically handsome, but he had an anxious, strained expression in his eyes that caught my attention. I revised my estimate of his age up a little, but not by much. He could be nineteen, but I doubted he was twenty.

"Before we get started," said Donnell, "I'd like you to place any weapons you're carrying on the table. I'd rather not be driven to uncivilized measures like searching you."

"We didn't bring weapons," said the boy. "It didn't seem necessary when we were only expecting to spend a few hours in an empty city."

"Today hasn't gone according to plan for either of us," said Donnell bitterly. "Let's move on to some introductions. I'm Donnell. The young man on my left is one of my officers, Luther. The girl on my right is my daughter, Blaze Donnelly."

My head snapped round to look at Donnell. He'd called me his daughter for the first time in six years. Had he meant to do that, or...?

"Your name is Donnelly?" The tone of the boy's voice changed, as if he was reciting something he'd memorized. "When the last of the two hundred and one worlds in the Alpha sector star systems opened for colonization in 2365, the Earth Loyalist Party came to power and blocked further colonization. Five years later, the Expansionists won the key vote that allowed the colonization of Beta sector to begin."

The boy leaned forward eagerly. "Sean Donnelly organized the militant arm of the Earth Loyalist Party in an escalating series of protests about the drain of Earth's resources and population to other worlds. When those failed to achieve any change in the United Earth Government's colonization policy, Sean Donnelly formed the Earth Resistance and took up arms to... You're *that* Sean Donnelly?"

Donnell nodded. "Yes, I'm *that* Sean Donnelly. For an off-worlder, you seem incredibly well informed about Earth's history."

The boy looked oddly wary. "I'm good at remembering things I read. My name is Tad, and these are Phoenix and Braden."

"The polite response would be to say that I'm pleased to meet you," said Donnell, "but frankly I'm not. I was already struggling to keep things under control here, and your arrival has made the situation far worse. You must have noticed that the people downstairs aren't pleased to see you. In fact, most of them would like to kill you."

"I don't understand why they want to kill us," said Braden. "We haven't done anything to hurt them."

Donnell pulled a face. "Those people would argue that you off-worlders haven't just hurt them, but destroyed their lives. Try looking at things from their viewpoint. They've spent the last few decades fighting for survival on a depopulated ruin of a world, watching loved ones die in stupid accidents or from the lack of basic medicines, while knowing that the people who wrecked Earth were living in well-fed comfort on planets in distant star systems. They hate you for that, and by our rules I've no right to protect you from their anger."

Phoenix's eyes widened in alarm. "You can't let that mob kill us!"

"When you walked in the door, I had to make a split second decision on how to react, whether to let you get lynched or try to protect you. I decided to do my best to keep you alive, but I'm not going as far as shooting my own people to do it, so I'll need your cooperation."

Donnell paused. "As I said, I've no right under our rules to protect you, but people will accept me doing it if they think I'm interested in one of you as a future partner. Given my past history with relationships, that future partner has to be you, Phoenix."

She shook her head. "I can't possibly marry you. I'm in a committed relationship with a woman on another world."

Donnell sighed. "I'm not really planning to marry you, Phoenix. This is just a pretence aimed at keeping the three of you alive. No one will harm my future wife, and I can extend some of that protection to Tad and Braden if we claim they're..."

He broke off his sentence and studied Tad and Braden. "Sadly, I don't think anyone will believe those two are your brothers, so we'll have to settle for them being your distant cousins."

"Oh." Phoenix frowned in thought for a second. "Well, so long as we're just pretending..."

"You have my word on it," said Donnell. "If I explain the plan to my officers, and get them to drop a few hints about my feelings, then it shouldn't take more than an occasional gesture in public to convince people."

I'd been utterly bewildered by Donnell's behaviour downstairs, but now it made sense. Donnell wasn't interested in Phoenix, he'd just been acting a part to stop the off-worlders from being murdered. I still didn't understand why Donnell had included me in this meeting though. I caught Luther giving me a confused glance that showed he didn't understand it either.

Donnell turned to Tad. "Now where are you from, why were you fool enough to come to New York in this weather, and how did you break your aircraft?"

"We're from Adonis," said Tad.

Adonis! I blinked. Cage had been quite right with his mocking comment about "their lordships". Settled nearly a century ago, Adonis had been the first and worst of the leeching colony worlds, grabbing huge amounts of Earth's resources to make itself into the richest of the new worlds, famous for the wealth of its aristocrats.

I looked at Tad with fresh eyes. He wasn't just any leech, he was a lord of leeches. I folded my arms and glowered at him, and he threw an anxious glance in my direction before speaking again.

"We're a team from the Adonis Institute of Cultural Heritage. We portalled from Adonis to Earth America Off-world on a routine museum retrieval mission. We'd been warned that none of the portals in the New York area were working, so we brought an aircraft with us to fly here, but we'd no idea there'd be snow."

Donnell gave a despairing roll of his eyes towards the ceiling, Luther's dark face was filled with amusement, and I couldn't help laughing aloud.

Tad gave me another look, one of embarrassment this time, and hastily continued with an edge of self-justification to his voice. "The inhabited continents of colony worlds were all chosen to have mild climates, so we don't have snow in winter."

He paused. "When we arrived at Earth America Off-world, we had to be vaccinated against Earth diseases and go into quarantine. We were only released from quarantine two days ago, and it was impossible to fly in yesterday's blizzard, but there was a clear sky this morning. There was no problem with the flight itself, or even the landing, though the snow was far deeper than we expected. It was when we came out of the museum..."

"My fault," said Braden.

"It wasn't your fault," said Phoenix.

"No, it wasn't," said Tad. "The wind was gusting very strongly, so it was perfectly sensible of you to move the aircraft closer to the skyscraper for shelter. That huge sheet of glass falling on it was pure bad luck."

Both Luther and I laughed this time.

"You were extremely lucky that glass landed on the aircraft instead of one of you," said Donnell. "It must be over sixty years since anyone bothered to do any maintenance work on the Manhattan skyscrapers, so pieces often fall off them on windy days. The ground over there is littered with glass, masonry, even whole windows, but you wouldn't have seen the debris when it was covered in snow."

There was a short silence before Tad spoke again. "We saw the smoke coming from this building, so we headed for the Unity Bridge to get across the Hudson River and come here."

Donnell looked at Braden. "How did you hurt your leg?"

"Hole."

"He fell into it and cut his leg on something." Tad expanded on Braden's depressed, single word reply. "The hole must have been at least waist deep, but it was hidden by snow."

Luther put his hand over his mouth, to smother yet another laugh at the off-worlders' incompetence, but I didn't find this funny. I'd seen too many people hurt in similar accidents.

"Again, you were extremely lucky," said Donnell. "The hole could have been much deeper. There are places where you can fall straight down into cellars or underground storage tanks. Did you find what you were looking for in the museum?"

"No," said Tad. "Someone must have already collected it."

"A big disappointment for you. Will your institute be sending another aircraft to rescue you?"

"They can't. Most of the old aircraft have broken down, and

they can't be repaired because the Earth factories that made replacement parts closed down decades ago. Ours was the only aircraft still in working order that had detachable wings. You need to remove the wings to get an aircraft through a freight portal, so..."

"I see." Donnell drummed his fingers on the table for a moment. "I'm not risking sending people to escort you to Fence in winter, so you'll have to stay here until the spring."

"What's Fence?" asked Phoenix.

"The defences protecting the citizens' settlements to the south-west of New York," said Donnell.

"We don't need an escort," said Tad. "When the snow melts, we can make our own way south-west."

"Really?" Donnell gave a disbelieving shake of his head. "You've only been in New York for a few hours, and you've already destroyed your aircraft and injured one of your party, but you think you'll make it all the way to Fence without any problems?"

Tad frowned.

"The mere fact you think you'd be better off travelling after the snow melts, tells me you'd be dead long before you reached Fence," added Donnell.

"What's wrong with the snow melting?" asked Tad. "Surely we could travel faster without it?"

"Yes, but there are predators in New York," said Donnell. "They've all taken shelter from the cold at the moment, but they'll come out to hunt as soon as the temperature rises above freezing point."

"Nobody warned us about predators." Tad exchanged glances with Phoenix, and groaned. "I suppose you're right that we can't travel alone. So, what's the situation here? If these people are the remnants of your Earth Resistance forces, where did all the children come from, and why are you finding it so difficult to keep things under control?"

Donnell grinned. "When a large number of men and women are together for over thirty years, you tend to get children. As for me struggling to keep things under control... That's because it isn't just the Earth Resistance here."

He leaned back in his chair. "I formed the Earth Resistance to fight in a last desperate attempt to save our home world. Our first attacks were aimed at the interstellar portals, but those were difficult targets. The problem wasn't so much that the Off-worlds on all continents were heavily guarded, but that their interstellar portals were in constant use. We'd no wish to kill random groups of men, women and children, so we decided to target the United Earth Government instead. We came up with a plan to occupy the United Earth Regional Parliament complexes on all five continents. We succeeded in the Americas, Europe, Africa and Australia. We messed up in Asia when..."

He shrugged. "Well, past mistakes don't matter now. During the first year, there were several attempts to throw us out. We lost Australia, but we held on in the Americas, Europe and Africa. By the second year, the United Earth Government had stopped bothering us. With law and order breaking down in the cities, the Regional Parliaments preferred to meet in safer locations anyway."

I frowned. I didn't understand why Donnell was explaining so much history to the off-worlders. They only needed to know the basic fact that we shared this building with four other divisions, and those divisions included some very violent criminals.

"I had to evacuate my people from Africa in 2380 because of massive flooding in Lagos," continued Donnell. "That left the Earth Resistance split between London and New York. Both cities were rapidly emptying back then, with people either leaving for colony worlds or moving to rural areas. The remaining citizens were fighting off gangs of looters, and putting up barricades to defend their neighbourhoods, but we had surprisingly little trouble. Most of the citizens sympathized with us, while the looters didn't want to tangle with an organized group of fighters."

I was growing increasingly bewildered by this. I remembered the odd way Donnell had acted downstairs, pretending that he was attracted to Phoenix. Was the same thing happening again? Was Donnell giving the off-worlders all this information for a reason I didn't understand?

"The real problems started when London was officially abandoned in 2382," said Donnell. "When the authorities shut down the power and water supplies, the last of the citizens pulled out to join the new settlements in small towns. I sent all of my people who weren't on record as political criminals to join them. Any chance of the Resistance halting the collapse of Earth was long gone by then, so I felt anyone with the chance of salvaging a decent life for themselves should take it. The looters were left stuck in an empty city, running out of food, and attacking my remaining people to steal their supplies. I portalled over to London myself to..."

"Portalled?" Tad interrupted, leaning forward eagerly. "Our information was wrong and you have working portals after all? But in that case, we can just portal back to America Off-world."

"We *had* working portals," said Donnell. "We also *had* access to the Earth data net. Past tense. Please let me finish explaining."

"Sorry," said Tad.

"I managed to convince both sides that they had to work together to have any hope of survival," said Donnell. "A few months after that, the United Earth Government ordered a new blanket security block on the portal network. Only people on a newly created register of reputable citizens could use the portals, and of course Earth Resistance members weren't on the list. We could get round that by breaking into the control box on an intercontinental portal and hardwiring it, bypassing the DNA security checks to get illegal manual access."

Tad made an odd squeaking noise. "But hardwiring a portal is horribly dangerous. If you make a mistake, what arrives at the other end isn't... human."

Donnell nodded. "It was only worth the risk for vital trips. I'd got married by then, and wanted to stay in London anyway, so I left my deputy in charge of New York. Seven years after London was abandoned, the whole situation was repeated in New York. I had to risk portalling back here to negotiate another alliance with the New York gangs. I expected that to only take a few months, but things were far more complicated than they'd been in London."

I felt deeply uncomfortable listening to Donnell talk about how he'd left London and my mother. No, I wasn't just uncomfortable listening to it, I was angry. Donnell had never discussed this with me, but he was happy to tell every detail to total strangers.

"There wasn't just one New York gang to deal with," said Donnell, "but a dozen, and they all hated each other. Every time I thought I had the situation under control and would be able to portal back to my family in London, another major problem flared up."

Donnell suddenly turned his head and looked directly at me, an oddly intent expression on his face. I hastily stared down at the table.

"Ah," said Tad. "So some of the people down there are criminals."

"Exactly," said Donnell. "To make things even worse, we lost access to the Earth data net a week after I arrived in New York."

"You mean the United Earth Government put a security block on that too?" asked Tad. "There might be ways to work round that."

I heard the sound of movement, looked up warily, and saw Donnell had stood up and gone across to the ancient wall vid next to the window. He pressed the button to turn it on, but nothing happened. He sighed, hit the wall next to it, and the screen flickered into life and showed two words. "No signal."

My grandparents had had magical technology imbedded in their heads that linked their brains directly to the Earth data net, giving them instant access to information and moving images of people, animals and amazing places. My parents had had to use wall vids to get that information, and see those images with eyes instead of their minds. I had never seen them at all. Since before I was born, the wall vids had only displayed those two words. "No signal."

"Oh," said Tad. "No, there's no way to work round that. When you turn on wall vids, they automatically connect to the local data net to get their operating software. If they can't get a signal, they're just useless pieces of electronics."

Donnell sat down again. "I've no idea what happened, but we woke up one morning and every vid and comms device in New York was complaining about having no signal. London had the same problem. That didn't just cut us off from the outside world, but severed our communications between London and New York as well. We were reduced to writing notes to each other and throwing them through a portal."

He grimaced. "That made everything far more difficult, and was totally disastrous in some situations. Words said in anger may eventually be forgiven, but written ones never fade away."

Donnell turned to give me that intent look again. I didn't dodge his gaze this time, but I could feel myself blushing, and was relieved when he turned back to face the off-worlders. There was a brief pause before Donnell spoke again, suddenly dropping his detailed explanation to rush forward in time to the present in three short sentences.

"I never went back to London. Six years ago, it was hit by a firestorm, and we had to risk portalling everyone from London to safety in New York. All the New York portals stopped working two weeks later."

I was trying to work out what was happening here. Why had Donnell introduced me as his daughter, and given me those strange, meaningful looks? Had all that detail about him leaving London for New York really been for the benefit of the off-worlders, or had Donnell been telling me what went wrong between him and my mother?

If that was true, then what did that comment about words said in anger mean? Was that just about Donnell and my mother, or was it also about Donnell and me? Was he finally raising the subject of our cataclysmic argument, and hinting that we could somehow fix what had happened between us? It seemed a weirdly indirect way to do it, but given we'd avoided talking to each other for the last six years...

"If all the portals stopped working at once," said Tad, "the fault has to be at the main New York portal relay centre. Possibly a power failure. The global portal system has its own dedicated power supply, totally independent of everything else, so it wouldn't have been shut down when the city was abandoned. If one of the power links at the relay centre has burnt out, it could be simple to repair."

My fingers curled in tension, and I looked up anxiously. If Donnell had really meant that explanation for me, if this was his way of tentatively broaching the forbidden subjects of the past, then the last thing we needed was a discussion about how Seamus had destroyed the New York portal relay centre.

"It's not simple," snapped Donnell. "The main New York portal relay centre exploded into several hundred thousand pieces."

"Oh." Tad looked crestfallen.

"This explanation would go a lot faster if you'd stop interrupting me," added Donnell.

"Sorry," said Tad, for the second time.

"After a few fights, splits, and mergers, the New York looters finally settled down into three rival divisions," Donnell continued. "When the refugees arrived from London, the London Resistance and the New York Resistance merged together fairly well after a few initial ego clashes, while the London looters remained as a separate division."

He paused. "So now I've got just over seven hundred people on my hands, but they're divided between five almost equally sized, fiercely independent divisions. The only reason the Resistance is notionally in charge of the alliance is that all the other four divisions hate each other, and any bid for power from one of them is instantly opposed by the other three. It's hard enough keeping the peace at the best of times, but we've been rationing food for weeks so everyone's very hungry and short tempered."

"When we crossed the Unity Bridge, I saw there were fish in the river," said Tad. "Is the food shortage because you've no way to catch them, or because pollution has made them too toxic to eat?"

"There was a big clean up of the local rivers when the United Earth Americas Parliament moved to New York," said Donnell, "and pollution levels have dropped even further since the city was abandoned. Even the unpredictable weather patterns are easing. It's a struggle to grow vegetables here – centuries of building, demolition and rebuilding have left the soil full of rubble – but the local fish and wildfowl are plentiful and perfectly safe to eat."

Tad nodded. "So the problem is that you don't store food for the winter."

Donnell's patience cracked. "Of course we store food for the winter! Do you think we're complete fools?"

"Sorry," said Tad, for the third time.

Donnell took a moment to calm down before speaking again. "A lot of rooms in this building were filled floor to ceiling with stasis boxes preserving old documents. We threw out the papers, and used the stasis boxes to store food reserves. Combined with our regular hunting and fishing, those are normally enough to last us through the winter, but two months ago we were hit by some sort of fever."

He sighed. "Since then, everyone has either been sick themselves or caring for those who were ill. Over thirty people died from the winter fever, including Luther's father, my best friend and deputy, Kasim. People have only just recovered enough for me to risk sending them out hunting again, and our food reserves are almost gone."

He gave Tad a pointed look. "The last thing I needed was you three marching in and demanding food. Never do that again. We'll feed you when we can manage it, but everyone here has been hungry for weeks."

He paused. "I also need to point out that I've been using some words you'd be familiar with to explain past events, but the word looter is considered an insult round here. You must never use that word, or call people criminals, you say scavengers. You never refer to gangs either, you say divisions. Remember that please. I've had to punch one person already today because of you, and I'm getting too old for fist fights."

"We'll try not to cause any more trouble, but why are you punching people when you're Armed?" Tad pointed at the gun enveloping Donnell's right wrist, its glowing tendrils snaking across the back of his hand and up his arm. "That's one of the specialist weapons carried by elite Military Security agents. You were never in the Military, let alone in Military Security, so how did you manage to get one of those? They were designed to bond to their owner for life, self-destructing when he or she died so the weapon could never be stolen."

"Kasim gave it to me. He was a Military Security Armed Agent himself, and he stole an unbonded weapon for me before he defected to join the Earth Resistance." Donnell gave a dismissive wave of his hand. "Yes, I'm Armed, but that doesn't mean I can go round killing anyone who disagrees with me."

Tad blinked. "I wasn't suggesting you should kill people. I just didn't understand why you'd need to punch them."

"I got into the habit in the early days," said Donnell. "The other divisions have always settled their status disputes with fights. Originally, those fights involved weapons like knives, but the rate of injuries and deaths was terrifying, so I talked the alliance into banning fights with weapons. Once it was just fist fights, throwing the odd punch myself earned me respect and was a fast way to make a point. I admit being Armed gives me a huge advantage, because very few people risk hitting me back, but I still don't want to get dragged into any more fights on your behalf."

Donnell stood up, and we all hurried to stand up as well. "That's enough explanations for now," he said. "When I've time, I'd like to hear a news update on how the rest of humanity is getting on, but right now I need to concentrate on keeping this small part of it peaceful. I'll give you accommodation up here to keep you safe. Please don't abuse my trust by roaming round and trespassing in random rooms. My daughter has a right to privacy in her own bedroom."

Tad looked embarrassed. "We wouldn't dream of..."

Donnell kept talking over the top of him. "And don't leave this floor without an escort. The other divisions each have their own wing of this building, and they'll kill you if you accidentally wander into their territory."

He turned to Luther. "Organize some bedding and less

distinctive clothes for the off-worlders, and then find them some rooms. There should be a few with working plumbing over in corridor B6."

Luther nodded, and led the three off-worlders out of the room. I was about to leave too, when Donnell spoke again.

"It's time we had our talk, Blaze. I could use a drink, so let's go to my apartment."

I was sick with tension as I followed him down the corridor. Donnell surely wouldn't tell me to leave the Resistance straight after introducing me as his daughter, but what else could he want to discuss? Were we finally going to talk about our relationship, my mother, and perhaps even my brother?

CHAPTER FIVE

Donnell pressed his hand to the key plate beside his apartment door, and led the way into a room where luxurious armchairs surrounded a stained card table littered with crumpled paper cups. It was six years since I'd been in this room. It had been a mess back then as well.

Donnell swept the cups into a bin, tossed an old coat off an armchair onto the floor, and waved at me to sit down. I remembered curling up in that armchair on my first day in New York. My mother was dead. My whole world had gone up in flames. My hands were burned from touching a red-hot door. I was a huddled ball of misery, crying in pain and despair. Donnell had knelt on the floor next to me, murmuring comforting words, and gently dabbing some ointment on my hands that magically took away all the pain.

I'd been too lost in anguish and shock to appreciate it fully at the time, but for two precious weeks Donnell had been a real father to me. All through my childhood in London, people had told me stories about him – everyone except my mother who never even mentioned his name. I'd built up a fantasy image of my legendary father over the years, and the reality had been less heroic but far more human and caring.

Those two weeks had ended in disaster, but I'd been hanging on to the memories for years now, replaying each moment in my head until I wasn't sure how much was true and how much my own embellishment.

Now I sat down like a dignified adult, and watched nervously as Donnell went across to the single huge window, picked up a fresh paper cup from the stack on the windowsill, and poured amber liquid into it from a half-empty bottle. He sipped it and gave a groan.

"I know I shouldn't drink on an empty stomach, but..." He glanced at me. "Do you drink our apology for whiskey yet, Blaze?"

"No, sir." I helped run the stills that made the stuff, but never drank more than the odd test sip myself. I wished I was more like my father in a lot of ways, but I'd no desire to copy his drinking.

"Very wise. It's filthy stuff that stinks of sour wintereat." Donnell came and sat in a chair facing me. "Do you think it's possible for you to stop calling me sir?"

I gave him an anxious look. A few of Donnell's oldest friends called him Sean. Everyone else either called him Donnell or sir. In my case, there was the awkward question of whether he'd expect me to call him Donnell or Father. I couldn't afford to get that wrong, so I'd have to make sure I didn't call him anything at all.

"Yes, sir," I said. "I mean, yes."

"You had an encounter with Cage this morning."

I gave Donnell a startled look. "I didn't know you'd seen that."

"I didn't see it myself. I've had two officers watching the food queue for trouble ever since we started rationing. Vijay and Weston were on duty this morning, and told me that Cage had spoken to you by the cooking fire. What did he say to you?"

I hesitated before speaking. "Cage said you had a vacancy for an officer. He seemed to think that if he married me..."

"He could fill that vacancy." Donnell finished the sentence for me. "Well, naturally Cage would make his move today. I told him I didn't want you to marry anyone until you were at least eighteen, and he's taken me at my exact word."

Donnell's comment terrified me. "You knew Cage was planning this? You want me to marry him?"

Donnell looked startled. "Chaos, no. I realize I haven't been much of a father to you, but you surely don't think I'd marry you off to someone like Cage?"

I felt relief that was oddly mixed with guilt at ever doubting Donnell's reaction.

"It all started that day by the cooking fire when you were eleven," he continued. "It was only two days after your brother left. I was in my room, an emotional mess and more than a little drunk, when Weston came to tell me there was trouble in Reception. I headed down there, and I could hear your screams before I even entered the room."

I'd done a lot of screaming that day. I'd tried to keep my head, stay calm while Cage was dangling me over the fire, but then one of Cage's friends tossed a log into the flames. A batch of sparks flew up into my face, and I went into a blind panic, battling to get free by gouging at Cage's arms with my nails.

Cage hadn't liked his victim fighting back, and reacted by lowering me even closer to the fire, so the trailing lengths of my hair caught fire. Utterly desperate at that point, I bit his arm savagely, and he flung it sideways to free himself. I was sent flying, landed on the ground dangerously close to the fire, and was frantically crawling away from the scorching heat when Donnell arrived on the scene. I could still remember the sound of his voice shouting at Cage, and the thuds of the punches that followed.

"I hit Cage hard that day," said Donnell, "but you did him far more damage than me. The whole of the alliance was making jokes about a child biting him for months afterwards."

People were still making jokes about me biting Cage even now. The bite had got infected, and left a scar when it finally healed, so Cage still had the teeth marks of an eleven-year-old girl on his left forearm.

Donnell sighed. "The laughter and public humiliation destroyed Cage's chances of taking the leadership of Manhattan from Wall."

I was shocked. "I thought Wall had already defeated Cage before I bit him."

"Both Wall and Cage encouraged people to believe that version of events. Wall because he didn't want people knowing how close he came to losing his leadership position. Cage because he'd rather people thought he was defeated by a powerful man than a little girl."

Donnell shook his head. "I knew the truth though. Wall admitted it to me himself. The leadership of Manhattan was hanging in the balance when Cage held you over that cooking fire and you bit him. Wall warned me that Cage would blame you for his failure, and I knew he was right. I'd seen two of Cage's enemies die suspiciously convenient accidental deaths, I was afraid you'd be next, and decided the only way to keep you safe would be to shoot Cage."

I blinked.

"Machico talked me out of that. He said people were already blaming me for my son's actions, so shooting someone, even Cage, could make the whole alliance fall apart. I settled for having either Kasim or myself guarding you for every second of the next few days, but then Cage came to me and apologized for attacking you."

I blinked again. "Cage apologized? But he never apologizes for anything."

"It was more of an excuse than a real apology. He made some ridiculous claim that he'd only picked you up because he was worried you were dangerously close to the cooking fire. He intended to move you to safety, but his good deed went wrong when you panicked and bit him."

I choked in disbelief. "Cage claimed he was moving me to safety? I wasn't anywhere near the fire until he carried me there and dangled me over the flames."

"I knew you'd been traumatized by the London firestorm, so you wouldn't have willingly gone near the cooking fire. My first impression was that Cage was acting apologetic to put me off guard while he looked for a chance to take his revenge on you, but then he told me his real reason. He'd lost his bid to take the leadership of Manhattan, but thought of a new idea for gaining power. Marry you and become an alliance officer. The man has such a vast ego that he believed I'd eagerly welcome him as a future son-in-law."

I was stunned. "You mean Cage suggested marrying me when I was only eleven years old?"

"In fairness, Cage didn't expect or want to marry a child. His idea was that I should announce the engagement, and he'd move to the Resistance and become an officer immediately, but wouldn't marry you until you were sixteen years old."

Donnell grimaced. "My instinct was to tell him to go pollute himself, but I knew that would be like painting a target on your back. Instead, I gave him a very carefully worded answer, avoiding actually saying that I agreed to the marriage, but letting him assume it. I told him there couldn't be any formal arrangement until you were at least eighteen though. I made the point that I'd led the arguments in favour of the alliance rule that no one could marry until they were eighteen years old, so announcing my daughter's engagement when she was only a child would make me look ridiculous."

He gave a humourless laugh. "Cage agreed his plan should wait until you were eighteen. From then on, all I had to do was drop an occasional hint about the future to keep you perfectly safe from him. Cage would never harm you while he saw you as his path to power."

For six years, I'd been convinced Cage hated me because of the scar on his arm, and wondered why he hadn't lifted a finger against me. Now I finally understood. Cage's ambition was stronger than his desire for revenge.

Donnell took a sip from his cup. "Cage was constantly stirring up trouble. I thought he'd either get himself killed in a fight, or be caught committing one of his murders disguised as 'accidental deaths', long before you were eighteen. I underestimated his cunning. Cage stayed regrettably alive and well. At one point, I thought he was going to be diverted into making another try for the Manhattan leadership, but he didn't."

"My impression is that Wall's grown more popular with his division members over the years."

"Yes. Wall's led Manhattan since the start of the alliance. He was firm to the point of brutality in the early days, but he's mellowed over the years. He still has his harsh moments dealing with troublemakers, but he's generous enough the rest of the time, and almost over-indulgent with the children. Not just the ones he calls his nephews and nieces, but the other Manhattan children too."

I kept carefully quiet. Wall had had several girlfriends over the last decade or two, and accumulated about a dozen children. He had an odd habit of referring to them as nephews and nieces rather than sons and daughters, possibly because he'd never married any of their mothers, but they were all openly acknowledged and loved. I'd often envied them.

Donnell didn't seem to notice my silence. "I'm guessing you told Cage you wouldn't marry him."

I gave a nervous nod. "I don't understand how Cage expects to get two division leaders to vote in favour of him becoming an officer. I'm not even sure that Wall would vote for him after all the trouble he's caused in Manhattan."

"I think Wall might be tempted to vote in favour of Cage becoming an officer just to get him out of Manhattan division," said Donnell. "More urgently, how did Cage react to you refusing his offer of marriage?"

"He said some unpleasant things. He ended by saying I'd better accept his offer before he changed his mind."

"He's not taken your answer as final then," said Donnell. "That's good. I suggest we build up his hopes for a while before dashing them."

I frowned. "Surely that will make him even angrier in the end."

"Definitely," said Donnell, "but I want to delay a confrontation with Cage until the spring. The alliance is in an unhappy mood after the deaths from winter fever, the food rationing has made me unpopular, and losing my deputy has weakened my position."

He pulled a face. "Did you hear what that Queens Island man said to Luther this morning? The bit about Kasim's son not having to earn anything, and it being the same thing that happened six years ago? That wasn't just an attack on Luther, but on me over what happened with Seamus."

I tensed at the mention of my brother, but Donnell was already shaking his head and moving the conversation on.

"People are discontented, and the arrival of the off-worlders has made the situation even more explosive, so the last thing I need right now is yet more trouble."

I felt my stomach lurch in panic. It sounded as if Donnell was struggling to hold the alliance together. If he lost control, what would happen to us all?

"It will be much easier for me to deal with Cage in the spring when people are well-fed and happy again," continued Donnell. "We just need to keep him quiet until then. Cage is the type to think your opinion on your future husband doesn't matter nearly as much as mine. I can have a word with him tomorrow, say that he took you by surprise, but I'll talk you round over the next few months."

He paused. "If Cage approaches you directly again, try to give him the idea I'm pressuring you to accept his offer. You're reluctant but will eventually give way."

"I'll try, but I don't think I'll be very convincing."

Donnell laughed. "I didn't think I was very convincing when I hinted I was agreeing to his plan, but Cage believes the universe exists for his personal benefit. If things appear to be working out how he wants, then he won't question it."

He was silent for a moment as if thinking something through. "The only person I've ever told about my arrangement with Cage was Kasim. I don't think it's necessary to start involving my other officers now. Apart from anything else, it would be disastrous if the truth slipped out."

Donnell stared down into his cup. "Everything is so much more difficult without Kasim. It's hard to believe he's really gone. I still half expect to walk into Reception and find him standing on a table, telling a whole mob of people one of his ridiculous stories about the long ago days when he was working undercover as a Military Security agent."

I forced a smile. "Back when I was eleven, I actually believed the story Kasim told about him having cosmetic surgery so he could go undercover as a horse."

Donnell gave a bellow of laughter and raised his paper cup in a toast. "To you, Kasim! You ran things in the Americas for the seven years I was in London, you were my right-hand man through all the chaos when the citizens abandoned New York, and for the next eighteen years you were always there guarding my back. You were my best friend and one of the finest men on this planet. Life will never be the same without you."

He gulped down the last of his drink, crushed the cup between his hands, and hurled it towards the waste bin. I looked at the raw emotion in his face, and didn't dare to say anything, just waited in silence until he finally started speaking again. This time he was talking to me rather than a dead man.

"Kasim is gone. I have to come to terms with that and promote one of my officers to the deputy position, but I'm not sure who to choose."

I stared at him. "Everyone's been assuming that Machico will be deputy now."

"Then everyone's wrong," said Donnell. "Back in 2375, I put Machico in command of our attempt to occupy the United Earth Parliament complex in Asia. Mac wasn't just a technical expert, but my tactical advisor as well. I thought he'd rise to the occasion, but he panicked when the shooting started. The only reason his party got away without being slaughtered was because Vijay took over command himself."

I frowned. "I knew the attempt in Asia failed, but not that it was Machico's fault."

"Only a few people knew about it, and I asked them to keep it quiet. I'm sure you understand you mustn't repeat that story, or talk about any other things you're told in confidence."

"I understand."

"Machico lost all faith in his own leadership abilities after that," Donnell continued. "He'll give me plenty of advice, especially when I don't want to hear it, but he barely trusts himself to lead a hunting party and absolutely refuses to let me make him deputy alliance leader. Machico says that I need to choose a much younger deputy anyway. Someone who'll succeed me as leader one day, so people know the future is secure."

"That's a good point."

"I've been thinking about the succession for years. Originally, I had this naive idea that your brother would come to join me when he was eighteen, take his place beside me and Kasim, and…"

Donnell shook his head. "That plan went up in flames when London burned. Over the last seven years, I've appointed three young men as officers. Aaron, Julien and Luther. What do you think of them? Do you see any of them as a possible future alliance leader?"

I was stunned. "Why are you asking me?"

"I get plenty of comments on my officers from the men in the other divisions, but I'd like to know what the women are thinking as well. You all go fishing together, so you must hear a few comments."

"Surely you should be asking Natsumi about this. The women of the other divisions go to her with their concerns. Not because she's Machico's wife, but because they know she'd be an officer herself if the other divisions allowed you to have female officers."

"That's why I'm asking you instead of Natsumi. The women are careful what they say to her, because they know it will be passed on to me. They won't have been so guarded about what they say in front of you."

That was perfectly true, I thought with an edge of bitterness. There'd been no reason for anyone to worry about me repeating things to Donnell in the last six years, since we'd hardly spoken.

"What do the women think of Julien?" asked Donnell.

I hesitated. Julien was a fair-haired, stocky man in his early twenties. He'd been an officer for almost two years now. His authority was accepted, but he wasn't popular, and the women felt he wasn't in control of his drinking. I wasn't sure how to say that given Donnell wasn't exactly in control of his drinking either. "They have concerns about Julien."

"Aaron?"

I was on much safer ground here. Slim, dark-haired Aaron was quiet but popular. "Aaron's been an officer for seven years, and built up a reputation for being fair and dependable. Everyone has confidence in him."

"Aaron is fair and dependable, but seems to have no desire to be my successor as alliance leader. I tried dropping a few hints to him last week and got nothing in response."

"Remember that Aaron's wife died of winter fever only three weeks ago. He loved her very much, so he's still deep in mourning, and focused on caring for his baby daughter."

"That's true. What about Luther?"

I hesitated again. I'd heard a lot of withering comments about Donnell favouring Kasim's son too much. I couldn't say that to Donnell though, because it would sound as if I was jealous of his affection for Luther. Chaos, of course I was jealous of his affection for Luther.

"The women mostly comment on Luther's good looks."

Donnell seemed to be studying me closely. "He's a handsome boy. I had the impression you found him attractive yourself."

I felt myself flush with embarrassment. "I had a childish crush on Luther for a while when I was younger. I didn't realize you'd noticed that."

Donnell shrugged. "Well, if you hear anything else about my junior officers or the deputy leadership, then come and tell me. You'll have plenty of opportunities to talk to me now, because I'm putting you in charge of the off-worlders."

I blinked. "What? Why?"

"I included you and Luther in the meeting with the off-worlders because I didn't dare to leave either of you in Reception. The situation was volatile enough already without the division men tormenting Luther, and I didn't want Cage approaching you again."

Donnell grinned. "Including you turned out to be surprisingly useful. If you hadn't been in the meeting, I might have been fooled by Tad's tale of being on a routine museum retrieval mission. I want you guarding him so you can keep doing exactly what you did in the meeting."

I didn't understand this. "What am I supposed to keep doing? I didn't do anything in the meeting."

"Yes, you did. You laughed at Tad. You wounded his pride. The boy was so desperate to convince you he wasn't a total fool, that he gave away the fact the museum retrieval story was a lie."

"It was a lie?"

"Oh, yes. Those three must be from Adonis, they speak Language with its unmistakable accent, but there was nothing routine about them coming here. The fact they had to be vaccinated against Earth diseases tells us that none of them have been to Earth before, and they didn't come to do a random sweep of old paintings or historic artefacts. When I asked if they'd found what they were looking for, Tad said the word 'it'."

Donnell shook his head. "Think about what that implies. One item. Adonis sent a team to Earth to retrieve a specific single item. More than that even, they sent their last precious working aircraft with detachable wings as well. What can possibly be that important?"

I thought of all the things I'd ever found in abandoned buildings. Jewellery, clothes, pictures, toys, the discarded trivia of millions of lives, were scattered everywhere in New York. All of it had once been special to someone, but I couldn't think of anything vitally important to off-worlders.

"I've no idea."

"Nor do I," said Donnell. "Whatever it is, it's very small, and Tad's got it in his pocket right now. When I asked about it, his hand unconsciously moved to check it was safe, but he wasn't worried when I mentioned the possibility of us searching him. That means we could see the item, hold it in our hands, and still not know what it was."

He shook his head again. "There's no point in trying to force answers out of people when you don't even know what questions to ask. We're in no hurry, those three can't go anywhere without our help, so we'll try the alternative approach of being friendly. If we talk to them as much as possible about random subjects, then they'll be pushed into talking too. In the end, they'll either give away their secret by accident, or decide they trust us enough to tell us about it."

I thought that through. "Isn't there a risk that we'll give away secrets as well?"

"If the off-worlders stay with us for months, they'll learn most things about us anyway. Besides, Seamus gave away the only secrets that really mattered years ago."

That was true. "Shouldn't we at least keep the off-worlders locked up?"

"Certainly not. Those three are civilized people from Adonis, conditioned from birth to obey the proper social rules of behaviour. If we lock them up, then we become the enemy, and they'll feel perfectly justified in telling lies, stealing, even attacking us. Instead, we turn their social conditioning against them. Treating them as our welcome guests means they'll feel obligated to behave well towards their hosts. They're already off guard, seeing us as civilized like them, and feeling grateful to us for protecting them from the mob downstairs."

"I understand," I said, not really understanding at all.

"We'll give them jobs that split them up, and regularly pair each of them with one of us. I can spend time with Braden, and Natsumi with Phoenix, but I'm sure Tad is the real key to this. He can't be more than nineteen years old, but he's the leader of those three, and my guess is he's very, very important. He's totally defenceless here, his life literally in my hands, but he still kept interrupting me when I was talking. That makes him either incredibly brave, ridiculously stupid, or someone used to always being the highest status person in any group. He's oddly well informed as well. Did you notice that?"

"Yes," I said eagerly, because this time I knew exactly what Donnell meant. "When Tad heard your name, he started talking about the formation of the Earth Resistance. His voice was different then, as if he was reciting something he'd learned by heart."

"I could believe Tad had done some research before coming to New York," said Donnell, "and learned about the Earth Resistance occupying this building, but why would he have studied enough details about me to know I'd never been in the Military? Young Tad is a mystery, Blaze, and you're the perfect choice for getting information out of him. Make friends with the boy so he lets down his defences. Get him to talk to you. Keep laughing at him, because that stings his pride. Take note of anything he says that seems strange."

I didn't want to pretend to be friends with my enemy, but I did want to please Donnell. I gave a reluctant nod of acceptance.

"You can start by taking the off-worlders down to dinner this evening," said Donnell. "I'll send some of my officers to sit at your table. I'm afraid it's likely to be a difficult situation."

We'd be eating at a table in the middle of Reception, while surrounded by people who'd like to murder the off-worlders. Yes, I thought that could definitely be described as a difficult situation.

CHAPTER SIX

When I went to collect the three off-worlders from their rooms and take them down to dinner, I found them standing together in corridor B6. They were wearing the same sort of scavenged winter clothing as the rest of us now, but the mere fact they were strangers would still make them painfully conspicuous in Reception.

I had every intention of being friendly to Tad, but his first words seemed carefully chosen to anger me. "Can't we eat up here instead of going back downstairs with the looters?"

"Donnell told you not to use that word!" I snapped at him.

Tad frowned. "I thought it wouldn't matter when I was talking to you."

"You thought wrong! I don't like you using that word, or that sneering tone of voice, to describe people like me and my mother."

He gave me a startled look. "But you belong to the Resistance, not..."

"My mother belonged to London division," I said coldly. "She had convictions for looting and arson, but don't you dare criticize her for that. My mother didn't belong to a privileged Adonis family like you. She was born on an Earth that was falling apart, and being in the wrong place at the wrong time was enough to make her a criminal."

Tad tried to speak. "I'm sorry that..."

I hadn't finished what I wanted to say, so I raised my voice and talked over him. "I lived in London with my mother for the first eleven years of my life, so you can count me as a looter too. I only came to New York, and joined the Resistance, because of the London firestorm. I was lucky and escaped through the portal to New York, but my mother was trapped in a burning building and..." My voice was betraying far too much emotion, so I let my sentence trail off into nothing.

"I'm deeply sorry for making ignorant assumptions," said Tad.

"We're all very sorry," added Phoenix.

Braden nodded hastily.

There was an awkward silence for a minute. I finally forced myself to speak in a calmer voice. "Nobody is allowed to bring food upstairs. When the rationing started, some people were giving their own rations to their children."

"That's understandable," said Phoenix.

"It's totally understandable," I said, "but it stopped those people from making a proper recovery from winter fever, and we need everyone in a fit state to hunt for food. There were cases where people had their food stolen from them as well. Donnell had to make a strict rule that everyone eats downstairs where he can supervise things."

We started moving down the stairs after that. Tad kept his mouth shut until we reached the second floor, but then the strain was too much for him and he started yapping again. "Donnell said that the authorities had shut down the city power and water supplies, but I noticed you still have power to run the security system."

"For political reasons, the United Earth Regional Parliament complexes were designed to be leading examples of environmental efficiency," I said. "The building walls, windows and roof all absorb solar power, and there are some other special features intended to save water. Not all the new ideas worked out well – we had to dig a whole new drainage system five years ago because the old one kept clogging up – but Machico has managed to keep most of the systems functioning."

"It's chilly in here," said Tad, "but it would be even colder if the only heat source was the fire downstairs. I suppose you're using the solar power to heat the building. You haven't got working lights though, and the water in the bathroom was freezing."

Donnell wanted me to get Tad to talk, which was obviously going to be the easiest job in the world. The boy was positively addicted to the sound of his own voice.

"We only put the lights on when it's fully dark outside," I said. "We can't afford to waste either power or water. Rainwater is collected in tanks on the roof, and if those run dry then we have to carry water up to refill them."

We'd reached the ground floor now. I pulled aside the curtain and led the way into the dimly lit Reception. The sound of voices abruptly stopped, and a mass of shadowy figures turned to stare at us in silent menace.

I instinctively looked round for Donnell, spotted him standing nearby with Machico, and was reassured enough to keep walking forward. As I joined the end of the queue by the cooking fire, Aaron arrived to stand next to me. I glanced over my shoulder and saw Tad, Phoenix, and Braden were behind us, while Julien and Luther had appeared to act as rearguards.

I faced forward again, trying to look calm and confident. Most people were already sitting at tables and eating, so I only had to endure a short wait in the queue by the cooking fire before I was handed a generous plate of food. I wondered why we were eating so well tonight. Had the hunting been particularly successful, did Donnell feel we all desperately needed a decent meal, or did he think there'd be less trouble about the off-worlders if everyone had full stomachs? I decided it was probably a combination of all three reasons.

I moved aside, glad to put more distance between me and the flames of the cooking fire, but still aware of the ominously silent crowd that was watching us. Aaron got his plate, and came to stand with me as the off-worlders were given their food. The portions handed to them were smaller than other people were getting, but I wasn't going to argue about that.

Tad, Phoenix and Braden joined us, there was another short delay while Julien and Luther got their food, and then I led our group to an empty table in the Resistance area.

As we sat down, the ceiling lights flickered on. Despite the fact they were on a low setting, the room instantly seemed much brighter. Whispers of conversation started up, gradually building to normal volumes, and people finally stopped staring at us and went back to eating. I noticed one person still had her eyes on us though. Hannah was sitting alone at our regular table. I pulled a face of apology at her, and she gave a resigned shrug in return.

The usual jugs of water, stack of paper cups, and jumble of plastic cutlery were in the centre of the table. Phoenix picked up one of the jugs, and poured out cups of water. She put one in front of Tad, but he didn't seem to notice. He had his head turned away from her, staring at the cooking fire.

"That fire is built in a marble depression next to the wall," he said. "Was it originally an ornamental pool?"

"Maybe," said Luther.

Tad seemed upset about something. "You've clearly added the chimney. It seems to be made of metal circles stacked on top of each other. Am I right that those metal circles were portals?"

I grabbed a plastic fork from the centre of the table, and stabbed a piece of baked wintereat root. "Yes, the chimney is made of portals welded together. It sends the cooking fire smoke into a blocked-off stairwell at the back of the room and up to the roof. Having that stairwell blocked off is a bit inconvenient, because it means we can't access the upper central floors from Reception, but it was the only way to deal with the smoke problem. Anyway, we can still reach those upper floors from each wing of the building."

"But..." Tad waved both hands in a despairing gesture. "You destroyed the portals!"

I took a full minute to savour my first mouthful of food before replying. "There are plenty more if we need them. New York is full of useless, dead portals."

Tad sighed, and finally noticed the cup of water that had appeared in front of him. He picked it up and stared suspiciously into it.

I saved time by answering the inevitable question before he

asked it. "We filter and boil all the drinking water. It's perfectly safe."

Tad nodded and took a cautious sip. "Where do you get the paper cups and plates?"

"There are whole warehouses full of them," said Luther. "Everything edible rotted away years ago, but we've got enough paper cups to last us centuries."

"But why not use real glasses?" asked Tad. "Surely there are warehouses full of those too?"

I was irritated by his tone of voice. "Because someone would have to wash real glasses, and we're short of hot water, but more importantly because people could break real glasses and use them as weapons in a fight."

"That must be why you have plastic cutlery as well." Tad finally turned his attention from our cooking arrangements to the food on his plate. "What is this meat?"

"It's not human meat if that's what you're worried about," said Julien. "When someone suggested eating you three earlier, it was a joke." He thought about that for a moment. "Probably a joke, but it's true that everyone is very hungry."

I saw Phoenix's hands tense in fear. "The green stuff is wintereat," I said hastily, "and the meat is a mixture of goose and duck."

"Phoenix is a vegetarian," said Tad. "Do you have any cheese or...?"

"Shut up!" snapped Phoenix.

Tad gave her a look of sheer, open-mouthed, disbelief.

"We're not on Adonis now, Tad," said Phoenix, in a savage voice. "Stop annoying these people with your questions, and stop asking them for things they haven't got. They don't have doctors. They don't have food grown in vats. They don't have livestock, or milk, or cheese. They can't have many crops in the middle of winter. In fact, they barely have any food at all, so you will shut up while we gratefully eat whatever they've generously given us."

She dug a fork into a piece of goose and pointedly ate it. Braden had given her a single, startled glance when she first told Tad to shut up, and then kept his eyes firmly on his plate during the rest of her outburst. I'd still been adjusting to the fact that Braden wasn't the leader of these three. Now his eagerness to stay out of their argument made it clear that he wasn't even second-in-command.

There was a short silence before Tad spoke again. "Am I really that bad?"

"Totally insufferable," said Phoenix. "You've a horribly superior way of asking questions that implies nobody else knows anything. Like the paper cups. Did you really think these people hadn't thought of using real glasses?"

There was a mixture of apology and defensiveness in Tad's voice now. "You've never complained before."

"I knew it wasn't your fault. You've had everyone grovelling to do your bidding since the day you were born because..." Phoenix broke off her sentence, and gave a wary look around the table. "Anyway, I had to put up with you being annoying on Adonis, but you can't behave like that here. You can stop doing my talking for me as well. If I wanted to mention being a vegetarian, I could have said it myself, but you decided to say it for me. You do that sort of thing all the time."

She turned to Braden. "Don't you agree?"

Braden gave Tad a panicky look.

"You can speak freely," said Tad.

Braden evidently didn't want to speak freely, because he took refuge in drinking from his cup of water instead.

Tad frowned. "Phoenix, you must tell me if I'm being annoying in future."

"It'll be my pleasure," she said.

There was dead silence while we continued eating. I noticed Luther was staring at Phoenix with an odd expression on his face. I couldn't work out whether he was attracted by her strikingly long, blonde hair, or appalled by the way she'd ranted at Tad. Julien had noticed Luther's interest in Phoenix too, and elbowed Aaron to draw his attention to it.

Aaron just gave a grunt in response. I'd witnessed Aaron's helpless agony as he sat by his wife's side and watched her die, and it was obvious from his look of grim depression that he was thinking of her now. I saw him cast a wistful glance at where brightly coloured blankets covered an area of floor next to the Resistance tables. The crèche ran there from dawn until late evening, and Aaron's daughter was among a group of toddlers playing with a heap of multi-coloured toys. I'd have been there tonight myself, taking my turn on evening crèche duty, if Donnell hadn't put me in charge of the off-worlders.

We finished our meal. I was standing up, collecting the dirty plates and cutlery into a pile, when I heard the sharp soaring note of a violin from behind me. I instantly dropped the stack of plates back down onto the table, and turned to see Donnell stepping into the empty space by the cooking fire. He opened his mouth, and the violin went silent again to let his golden voice sing the first line alone.

"Some men were fickle and some left through greed."

Everyone in the room turned to face him. I'd brought my bag along with me in case this turned out to be an entertainment evening. I pulled it out from under our table, and scrabbled hastily inside for the long thin flute case.

"Some fled through fear and some out of need," sang Donnell.

From all around the room, a tide of small children came scurrying to sit on the floor in front of Donnell. I thrust the plates aside so I could perch on the edge of our table, and held my flute poised at my lips as he sang the third line.

"But we who remain will prove faithful indeed."

The violinist stepped forward to stand next to Donnell, the downward sweep of his bow giving me my cue. My flute and a dozen other instruments took up the melody, while everyone else joined in singing the last line of the chorus.

"Earth is our heart, our home world!"

Donnell sang alone again for the verses, but everyone joined in for the choruses. I noticed Tad turning his head to look for the scattered musicians. During the third chorus, he shook his head and muttered.

"It's incredible. The tension in this room was so strong you could have cut it with a knife, but now..."

Luther laughed. "That's the legendary Sean Donnelly for you. The Earth Loyalist Party recruited him when he was only fourteen. They thought they were getting an innocent boy singer with a passionate love for Earth. They rapidly discovered that Donnell had his wild side, but the passionate love for Earth was real. Donnell became the image of the Earth Loyalist Party, grabbing the hearts of everyone who heard him sing."

He paused. "My father always claimed it was Donnell's looks, voice, and songs that delayed the opening of Beta sector for five years. My father was Donnell's best friend though, so he might have been exaggerating his influence."

"No, he wasn't exaggerating at all," said Tad. "Back home on Adonis, people both hate and admire Sean Donnelly for what he did. Of course, the delay in opening Beta sector for colonization didn't harm our worlds in Alpha sector. I expect there's far more hatred than admiration in the star systems of Beta and Gamma sectors."

After the final chorus, Donnell waved an arm to beckon another singer forward, and then strolled over to stand between me and Phoenix. He spoke in a low voice, and I stopped playing my flute to concentrate on his words.

"Phoenix, this is where I touch your hair for the benefit of all the nosy people watching us. All right?"

She nodded in response, and Donnell caught a strand of her hair, casually twisting it round his right forefinger.

"That song you sang was the Earth Loyalist Party's *Anthem to Earth*," said Tad. "Is it true you wrote it yourself?"

"It's true that I stole a centuries-old Irish tune, one almost forgotten since the imposition of an official common Language, and created some mangled new lyrics for it."

"They still sing it on Adonis," said Tad, "but they've changed the words a bit."

Donnell laughed. "They'd have to in the circumstances."

The current song ended. Donnell glanced round to watch the next change of singers, and then faced us again. "You three off-worlders will have to learn a lot of things very quickly if you want to stay alive here. The most important of those things is how much people resent you taking our food. We urgently need to show you'll be working to contribute as well. Phoenix, you'll go fishing with the women. They work in pairs, so I'll partner you with Natsumi, the wife of one of my officers."

"Thank you," murmured Phoenix.

"Tad, the men usually go hunting with bows," said Donnell, "but you shouldn't be with us long enough to learn to hit a moving target with an arrow. It'll be far more productive if you go fishing with the women, but partnering you with any other man's wife or daughter could spark trouble, so I'll send you with Blaze."

Oh joy, I thought. Donnell was sending Tad fishing with me, so I could get him to talk. Get him to talk? The hard bit would be managing to say a word myself. I'd probably be deaf by the end of the first day!

Out of pure awkwardness, Tad picked this moment to just nod instead of saying anything.

"Braden, you're a real problem," continued Donnell. "The second you arrived, all the men took one look at your muscles and instantly started calculating their chances of beating you in a fight."

Braden shook his head in bewilderment. "Why would they think I'd want to fight them? I'm a pacifist, I don't believe violence is ever justifiable, so I've never done any combat sports. I just enjoy lifting weights at the gym."

Braden spent time lifting weights for fun. That said a lot about how different life was on Adonis. People here in New York didn't lift weights for fun; they were far too busy carrying heavy loads as part of the daily battle to stay alive.

"It wouldn't matter what you wanted," said Donnell. "They'd force you into a fight so they could build their status by beating you. Since you're an off-worlder, there's a danger they wouldn't follow the alliance rule of stopping when you're helpless on the ground. It could easily escalate into someone kicking you to death."

I heard a faint squeak from Phoenix. Braden looked terrified.

"I'll have to put you in my own hunting party and keep a

personal eye on you," said Donnell. "You won't be any use with a bow, so you'll have to help by retrieving arrows and birds. Is your leg well enough for that?"

Braden nodded eagerly.

Donnell finally dropped the strand of Phoenix's hair. "We've survived the tricky moment of you three eating your first dinner in public without any trouble, but people are drinking our homebrewed whiskey now. Blaze had better get you safely back upstairs before anyone has time to get drunk."

Donnell turned and walked off towards the fire, and the rest of us stood up. I noticed Tad was giving me a puzzled look. "Is something wrong?" I asked.

"I was just wondering why you keep your hair so short," said Tad. "Most of the other women here seem to have long hair."

Phoenix sighed. "It's Blaze's hair, Tad. She decides how long or how short she wants it, and she doesn't have to explain those decisions to you."

"Sorry," said Tad.

I picked up one pile of dirty plates, while Braden picked up the other, and Phoenix collected the used paper cups. Tad gave them a confused look, belatedly seemed to think about helping to clear things away himself, and picked up the plastic jugs.

"The jugs stay on the table," said Julien. "Some people like to water their whiskey. Chaos knows why."

Tad hastily put the jugs down again. I led the three off-worlders to the nearest waste bin, and dumped my pile of plates into it. Braden copied me.

Over by the cooking fire, the singing had ended. Vijay and his husband, Weston, came forward to do one of their comedy routines.

"In 2206," Vijay began, "Thaddeus Wallam-Crane invented the portal."

All three off-worlders turned sharply to look at him, Phoenix still holding her stack of cups.

"That made him hugely respected by everyone on Earth," continued Vijay, in an impressive imitation of Machico giving a school lesson.

"That made him hugely powerful," said Weston.

Vijay turned to glare at him. "No talking in class!"

The gathered children all gurgled in delight, but I had a sad moment of mourning. Traditionally, the Vijay and Weston double act had always been followed by Kasim telling one of his ridiculous stories about his time as a Military Security agent. Perhaps I'd hear people repeat those stories one day, but it wouldn't be the same as listening to Kasim. He hadn't just told the stories, he'd played with words as he did it, using their variety, rhythm, and beauty to make his own sort of music.

"When people asked what he wanted for his hundredth birthday, Thaddeus Wallam-Crane decided he wanted a flying pig," said Vijay solemnly. "Everyone was eager to please him because they respected him so much."

"Because they were scared of him," interjected Weston, shivering theatrically in fear.

"I told you, no talking in class!" Vijay snarled at him. "The problem was that there weren't any flying pigs, but people didn't want to disappoint Thaddeus Wallam-Crane because they respected him so much."

"Because they were scared of him," said Weston, doing his terrified act again.

Vijay gave him an exaggerated look of annoyance, took a cloth from his pocket, and tied it round Weston's head, gagging him.

Vijay turned to face his audience of children again. "People decided to create a genetically modified flying pig because they respected Thaddeus Wallam-Crane so much."

Weston made desperate muffled noises from behind his gag, and the children burst out laughing.

The three off-worlders seemed fascinated rather than amused by the act. I tapped Phoenix's shoulder, pointed at the waste bin, and she hastily dropped the paper cups into it.

I led the way on towards the Resistance doorway, and hesitated when I saw Cage was blocking my way. I felt my usual instinctive panic at the sight of him, but told myself I was perfectly safe. Donnell and all six of his officers would be watching us.

Cage came to stand just a fraction too close to me for comfort, and gave me a friendly smile that made me even more nervous. "I hope you've been thinking about our conversation earlier, Blaze."

I remembered Donnell's instructions. I should give Cage the idea that Donnell was pressuring me to accept his offer. "Donnell has spoken to me about it."

Cage's smile widened. "I'm pleased to hear that." He abruptly turned and walked away.

"Wasn't that the same man who made fun of my Adonis accent?" asked Tad.

"Yes," I said. "That's Cage of Manhattan division. You asked about my hair earlier. When I was eleven years old, I had long hair trailing past my shoulders, and Cage set it on fire. Now I keep my hair short so he can never do that again."

I glanced back at the Resistance tables, saw Donnell was looking anxiously at me, and gave him a nod in response. His face relaxed, and he turned to look at where Aaron was collecting his daughter from the crèche. They walked towards him, Aaron holding Rebecca by the arm, and slowing his gait to match her short, uncertain steps.

As they reached Donnell, Rebecca held out a chubby, infant hand towards him in a demanding gesture. He laughed and leaned down to let her grab on to his finger. I felt an odd stab of pain, hastily turned my back on them, and led the off-worlders through the curtain into the safety of the Resistance wing.

CHAPTER SEVEN

When I went up to the roof to salute the Earth Resistance flag next morning, I found the snow under my feet was slushy. I frowned. The warmer weather would tempt the predators into coming out to hunt, and I'd be fishing with Tad instead of Hannah. I'd have to be careful the fool didn't get me killed.

I scurried back inside to get the off-worlders and escort them down to breakfast. I found the three of them standing outside Tad's door. They were already wearing outdoor clothing, and seemed to be deep in conversation. I caught the end of a sentence from Phoenix, her voice heavy with sarcasm.

"... and remember how well *that* worked out."

At that point, she noticed me, pulled a face at the other two, and fell silent. All three off-worlders turned to look expectantly at me.

"Breakfast," I said, in what I hoped was a cheerful, pleasant voice. I knew I'd made a complete mess of things last night, snapping at Tad instead of being friendly to him. I was determined to do better today.

I answered half a dozen questions from Tad on the way downstairs, and greeted Aaron, Julien and Luther with my best smile as they came to meet us in Reception. I was struggling to keep smiling as we went to join the food queue though. The wind had changed direction to one that didn't suit our makeshift chimney, so small clouds of smoke kept hiccupping back into the room. It stung my eyes, and the acrid scent triggered bad memories of struggling to breathe, while the sounds of people screaming and the roaring of flames filled my ears.

Tad turned his head to stare at the cooking fire too, though his attention was on the chimney rather than the smoke and flames. From the look on his face, he hated that chimney nearly as much as I hated the fire.

We collected our breakfasts. It was soup again, but thicker than yesterday. I was disconcerted when Aaron, Julien and Luther only escorted us as far as our table, before hurrying off to sit with Donnell and his other officers. I told myself there was no reason for me to worry. They had to organize this morning's hunting groups, but they'd be back to help me within seconds if anyone tried attacking the off-worlders.

"Blaze, where will we be fishing today?" Tad interrupted my thoughts.

I gave him an irritated look. "Yesterday, you said that you came across the Unity Bridge to get here from Manhattan, and you noticed the river had fish in it. Make a wild guess where we'll be fishing."

Phoenix laughed, and I heard a strangled sound from Braden.

Tad spoke in an overly dignified voice. "It seemed possible we'd go sea fishing."

I pointed out the blindingly obvious. "The sea is much further away."

"What kind of fish do we want to catch?" Tad asked.

I stared at him in disbelief. "Anything edible."

"You'll need to tell us about the predators Donnell mentioned," he said.

I groaned. "I will. *After* I've eaten my breakfast."

"I just..."

"Tad," Phoenix said sharply. "You remember you said I should warn you when you were being annoying? Well, I think you're annoying Blaze right now."

"I apologize," said Tad.

As I ate my breakfast, I was vaguely aware of a whispered exchange between Tad and Phoenix. Most of it was so quiet I couldn't make out the words, but then Tad spoke in a more audible, wounded tone. "But why doesn't she like me?"

I felt guilty. Donnell wanted me to be friendly to Tad, and trick him into betraying his secrets, but I was failing miserably. A second later, a crash to my left made me swing rapidly round in my seat, looking anxiously for a threat. I spotted a table lying on its side over in the Manhattan division area, and children running to get clear of where two angry men were standing, confronting each other. The first punch had barely landed before there was a shout from Donnell.

"Enough!" He strode towards the fighters, right arm outstretched, and the red targeting light of his gun flashing. "If you must settle your argument with a brawl, you can do it this evening in the Manhattan wing. This isn't the time or the place."

The Manhattan division leader, Wall, stepped forward to meet him. "Agreed. I'll deal with it."

Donnell walked away, while Wall turned to glower at the guilty parties. The two men immediately moved to stand with their backs to each other, in the accepted manner of acknowledging a fight wasn't over but merely postponed. I noticed Cage was standing suspiciously near them, and the odd smile on his face made me wonder if he'd somehow triggered the fight. Whether he had or not, the situation seemed under control now, so I returned to eating my breakfast.

There was a tense whisper from Phoenix. "Was that fight about us?"

I felt the same reluctant sympathy for her that I'd felt yesterday. "No, that was just a Manhattan division status dispute."

There was silence for the next couple of minutes. As soon as we'd finished eating, I stood up, fastened my coat, and put on my hat and gloves. The off-worlders copied me, and stood waiting expectantly as I stared thoughtfully at them.

"Is something wrong?" asked Tad.

"It's important to wear the right clothes in this weather. Those look like good coats. Your boots should be a little too big so you can wear extra socks for warmth."

"We're all wearing extra socks," said Tad.

I nodded. "Show me your hands."

The three of them held out their gloved hands for inspection, and I checked them in turn. "It's vital that your gloves are waterproof and tight fitting. If you have to keep taking them off to do jobs like baiting fishing hooks, then you'll get frozen fingers. Phoenix, you need gloves two sizes smaller than these, while Braden needs a warmer hat."

"People have been very generous giving us these clothes," said Braden hastily. "I'm not complaining about the hat."

"Finding you better hats and gloves isn't a problem," I said. "We've got vast stores of all sorts of clothing in Sanctuary."

"What's Sanctuary?" asked Tad.

"There are six wings to this building. Each of the five divisions has its own wing, and we use the spare one, Sanctuary, for hospital and storage areas. I'll find someone to stay here with you while I get the gloves and hat."

"Can't we go with you?" asked Phoenix nervously.

"That would be dangerous," I said. "Sanctuary is common ground like Reception, but people still wouldn't like you going in there. Remember that everyone here thinks of off-worlders as thieves and leeches. If you enter Sanctuary, even with me as an escort, you could be accused of planning to steal from our stores or harm the patients in our hospital area."

Braden looked appalled. "Why would anyone think we'd harm a patient in hospital?"

I sighed. "People are very defensive about the safety of patients in hospital because of something that happened in the early days of the alliance. A Manhattan man sneaked into the hospital area, and strangled an unconscious patient belonging to the Queens Island division. The murderer was caught in the act and executed, but Manhattan and Queens Island have had a bitter feud about it ever since."

I went over to the table where Donnell was sitting with his officers. "I need to get a couple of oddments from stores. Can someone sit with the off-worlders for five minutes?"

Everyone pointed at Luther and he groaned. "Why do I always get stuck with the menial jobs?"

"I had to do them when I was the newest officer," said Julien smugly. "Now it's your turn."

Luther frowned at him. "I wish you'd stop rubbing my nose in the fact you've been an officer for longer than me."

"And I wish you'd stop undermining my leadership authority in my hunting party," said Julien.

"Are you still sulking about yesterday?" Luther sounded exasperated. "I just made a few helpful suggestions."

"I'm not just talking about yesterday," said Julien. "I keep getting stuck with you in my hunting party, and you regularly contradict my orders. It seems as if you're intent on destroying the division men's respect for me."

"I told you that I was trying to help." Luther was on the edge of shouting now. "You use the same tactics day after day."

Julien glared at him. "I use the same tactics because they work. We're trying to outsmart geese, not..."

"Quieten down!" Donnell interrupted them. "I can't have my officers arguing with each other in front of the division men."

There was a grudging silence.

Donnell turned to Julien. "The reason I've been sending Luther out with your hunting party on most days, Julien, is that you're closest to his age and I thought you two were friends. It clearly isn't working well, so I'll take Luther in my own group in future."

"I should be leading a group myself," said Luther. "Now my father's dead, there are only seven of us left to lead the regular six hunting parties, and Machico's the first to admit that he isn't a gifted hunter."

"I'm a completely inept hunter," agreed Machico cheerfully. "There's also the point that I've got more than enough work on my hands keeping the electrical and plumbing systems in this building working, without leading hunting parties as well."

Donnell's other two senior officers, Vijay and Weston, had been watching the argument in silence, but now Vijay spoke. "Be very careful, Sean. Remember what happened the last time you overworked Machico. By sheer coincidence, your apartment plumbing and lighting were the first to break down."

Donnell ignored them. "It won't be long before Luther's leading hunting groups and you can go back to your technical work, Mac."

"You should let me take a group out today." Luther's voice held a sulky note.

"I know you're finding the situation frustrating," said Aaron, in soothing tones, "but every new officer has to wait a few months before leading hunting parties."

"You and Julien only had to wait three months," said Luther. "I've been waiting five."

"You have to wait until you've gained the respect of the division men," said Julien. "Aaron and I achieved that in three months. Given your progress so far, you'll be lucky if you manage it in three years."

"Julien, stop stirring up trouble," said Donnell. "Luther, you have to wait a bit longer to lead hunting parties because the division men are targeting you after your father's death. You aren't to blame for that. In fact, the truth is that their attacks are aimed at me as much as you. Now go and join the off-worlders."

Luther muttered something inaudible, and slouched over to join the off-worlders.

Weston laughed. "Vijay and I have both had helpful hints from Luther on how to improve our failings as hunting group leaders. I'll be interested to hear Luther's thoughts on your faults, Sean."

I didn't wait to hear Donnell's reply. There were three curtained doorways on each side of Reception. The centre curtain on one side was marked with a blue planet and led to the Resistance wing. The centre one on the opposite side was marked with a red cross and led to Sanctuary. I hurried through it, paused for a moment to stamp on a few cockroaches by a leaking water pipe, and then took the left turn that led to the big outdoor clothing storeroom.

The storeroom door was sticking as usual, and I was wary of yanking at it too hard in case I hurt my arm, but it finally creaked open. Hanging rails of coats lined the walls, and there was a group of huge plastic containers in the centre of the room that held smaller items. I started sorting through a box of gloves, quickly found one that was perfect for Phoenix, but had to hunt for another couple of minutes before I found its partner.

Finding a hat for Braden was much easier. I thrust the gloves and hat into my pockets, and headed out of the room, but froze when I saw the male figure standing in the corridor with his back to me. I'd have happily walked past anyone else, secure in the knowledge that the inviolable law protecting the safety of people in the hospital area extended to the neighbouring supply rooms as well, but this was Cage. If he caught me alone in here, he was bound to pressure me about his offer of marriage, and there was the hideous possibility that he'd try to kiss me.

I backed into the clothing storeroom again. I could hear the sound of footsteps approaching, so I looked round frantically for a hiding place, but couldn't see anywhere easy. In desperation, I fought my way behind one of the rails of coats, and crouched down in the narrow gap between it and the wall.

I held my breath as I heard the door creak. Cage had come into the room! I daren't risk peeking through the coats to see what he was doing, but it sounded as if he was pacing round the room. Did that mean he'd seen me come in here and was searching for me?

The sound of movement stopped, and there was dead silence. I was sure Cage hadn't gone, so I stayed huddled against the wall. There was a minute or two of silence before I heard the creak of the door again. For a second, I thought that was Cage leaving, but then I heard footsteps unnervingly close to me. Cage hadn't left the room, so someone else must have come in.

Cage's voice spoke from the other side of the heavy winter coats. "I've done what you wanted. In return, there'll be a point where you cast your division leader vote as I wish."

"You said you'd ask for a small favour," said a petulant voice that I recognized as belonging to Major, the leader of Queens Island division. "Controlling my division leader vote isn't a small favour."

Cage laughed. "It's a little late to argue the price for my help now, isn't it? You're already unpopular with your members. If I tell them about our arrangement, then you'll lose your position as leader."

There was a choking noise of disgust, and the sound of the two men leaving the room.

CHAPTER EIGHT

I didn't know exactly what Cage and Major had been talking about, but it was clear that Cage had done something that gave him power over the Queens Island division leader. If they caught me here, they'd know I'd overheard their conversation. I could imagine that situation ending in me suffering a fatal accident, so I stayed in my hiding place behind the coat rack for several minutes longer, before wriggling free and making my way cautiously out of Sanctuary.

When I was safely in Reception, I hurried back to the Resistance tables. I wanted to tell Donnell what I'd heard, but he'd already started calling out the names of people in his hunting group, so there'd be no chance of me talking to him in private until the evening.

Luther was standing by the off-worlders' table. He gave me an impatient look as I rejoined them. "What took you so long?"

I'd been feeling sorry for Luther, remembering how devastated I'd been when my mother died and picturing him just as grief stricken over his father's death, but I resented his withering tone of voice.

"I had trouble finding matching gloves."

Luther shook his head as if he couldn't believe my stupidity, and hurried away. I glanced round for Hannah, saw she was sitting alone at our regular table again, and beckoned her over to join us. She stood up and came towards me, an odd expression on her face.

"I'm sorry I couldn't sit with you this morning," I said.

"Everyone knows Donnell's appointed you to stand guard on the off-worlders," said Hannah. "Obviously that means you have to sit with them during meals rather than with me."

"Yes." I hesitated, worried by her oddly monotone voice. "Have you been told about the change of fishing partners?"

"Natsumi said the off-worlder woman will be fishing with her, and the boy with you, so I'm to go fishing with her sister, Himeko."

Hannah's voice still had that flat note to it. I could tell something was badly wrong, and wanted to ask her what it was, but I couldn't speak freely with an audience listening to every word I said. "I need to give the off-worlders a quick survival lesson outside. Can you come with us and watch my back?"

Hannah nodded, and the off-worlders hastily stood up. Hannah didn't seem in the mood for chatty introductions, so I just recited everyone's names before leading the way towards the side exit. Marsha was sitting by the row of knife and bow tables as usual. I noticed the winter fever had left its mark on her, adding extra grey streaks to her hair, but she greeted us with one of her usual wide, tranquil smiles.

I had mixed feelings about Marsha. I admired the way she'd survived after being rejected by all the divisions, and gradually carved out a position of power for herself, but I wasn't happy about the way she used that power. I was always careful to be polite to her though. Marsha's smiles were misleading. Despite her friendly act, she was notoriously easy to offend, and could be an implacable enemy.

"Marsha, we'll need knife belts for the off-worlders, please."

"I have some ready on the Resistance table."

I turned to the off-worlders. "Marsha is custodian of the knives and bows. You have to collect your knife belt on your way out and return it immediately you come back in. I shouldn't need to explain why Donnell doesn't want people wandering round Reception carrying knives."

Tad was studying the array of multicoloured knife belts on the table next to him. "These all have exquisite miniature paintings on them. Do you do these paintings, Marsha?"

She aimed her smile at him, but I noticed her eyes were coldly hostile. "Yes. I paint personal tags on each bow, belt, and knife, to make sure they can't be accidentally confused or deliberately swapped for different ones. All of the personal tags are unique, and nobody here has the skill to copy my paintings."

"Each division has their own table," I said. "The Resistance table is at the end nearest the door." I went over to it and picked up my own knife belt.

Tad was still looking nosily at the first table. "These belts all have two paintings, and one is always a clock face."

"You're looking at the London table," said Marsha. "The clock face is their division tag. Manhattan has a skyscraper, Queens Island has a boat, and Brooklyn has a bridge."

Tad frowned. "There's a Staten Island in New York, but not a Queens Island."

For an off-worlder, Tad seemed to know a surprising amount about the geography of New York, and he was demonstrating that knowledge at the most tactless moment possible. Marsha's smile didn't falter, but I knew she'd hold that innocent question against him.

"Queens Island was formed by several divisions merging." I tried to move the conversation on to a safer topic. "The Resistance tag is the blue planet Earth, but Donnell and his officers have a white circle instead to show they have a duty to act with impartial fairness to everyone in the alliance."

"That can't be easy. Do they manage it?"

"Mostly. If anyone is unhappy about an officer's ruling, they can refer it to Donnell. Everyone knows he's scrupulously fair."

Tad glanced at the belt I was buckling on over my coat. "I see your personal tag is flames, Blaze."

"Yes," I said tersely. I hated the fact that Marsha had painted flames on my belt, constantly reminding everyone of my fear of fire, but I wasn't the only one in this situation. Many of Marsha's tags had an edge of cruelty to them, and no one, however powerful, was safe from being a target.

If I was annoyed by my personal tag, then Cage must be totally infuriated by the one he'd had on his belt and bow for the last six years. It showed a set of teeth marks that perfectly matched the scar I'd left on his arm.

Cage was too clever to risk complaining to Marsha about it though. She chose her tags to highlight something about your general reputation, so attempting to get one changed always did more harm than good. It focused the attention of the whole alliance on whatever you wanted forgotten, and one annoying painted tag could be replaced with something even worse. If I ever hinted that I didn't like the flames on my belt, then they'd probably be replaced by a reference to my brother.

Tad watched Hannah pick up her belt. Inevitably he made a tactless comment about that one as well. "I see there's a hand for your personal tag, Hannah, but there's no division tag."

She glared at him. "I've no division tag because I only have trial membership of the Resistance."

"Oh." Tad took a hasty step backwards. "Sorry, I didn't mean to…"

Phoenix hastily intervened. "I've found what must be our belts. Three of them marked with a star for off-world." She laughed and held one out. "I think this one must be yours, Tad."

He took the belt, and looked at the open mouth next to the star. "That's a bit unfair."

Phoenix ignored him. "The belt with the limping man must be for Braden since he's hurt his leg." She handed the second belt to Braden, who accepted it without comment.

"That means this one is mine." Phoenix picked up the third belt and tried it for size on her waist. "I don't understand the tag though. It looks like a crown."

"That's because Donnell finally seems to be thinking of marrying again." Hannah's tone was acidly resentful.

Phoenix's face flushed with embarrassment, and I felt horribly uncomfortable. I wanted to reassure Hannah that Donnell was only faking an interest in Phoenix, but I couldn't repeat things I'd been told in confidence.

I hid my confusion by stooping to grab some net bags from the heap on the floor. I handed them to Tad and Phoenix, and saw their noses wrinkle in disgust at the stink of fish.

"Let's get outside now," I said.

I headed through the door and the others followed, the off-worlders still buckling their knife belts round their waists. The snow outside was melting fast, and water was dripping from the row of portals. I led the way past the vast glass front of Reception, and turned to study the end wall of the building.

"I don't understand how there can be predators in New York," said Tad. "Didn't people get rid of all the dangerous animals on Earth centuries ago?"

"There were a few left," I said, "and they are increasing in numbers now, but the real problem in New York is from off-world creatures. Falling stars."

"Off-world creatures?" asked Phoenix. "How did they get through the interstellar portals to Earth, Blaze?"

"They didn't *get* through the portals. They were *brought* through them to be zoo exhibits. In the confusion of huge numbers of people heading off world, some falling stars got loose."

"I've never heard of an alien creature called a falling star." Tad seemed surprisingly annoyed that he didn't know every single life form on hundreds of colony worlds.

"When the temperature is below freezing, all the falling stars find shelter and go dormant. Today things are warm enough for them to wake up and come out to hunt. There's one of them." I pointed out a bright scarlet patch on the wall.

"It looks too small to be dangerous," said Tad. "Do they have poisonous bites, or stings, or..." He watched me pick it up and let his words trail off. "Evidently not."

The falling star was almost big enough to cover my right hand, the scarlet contrasting with my black glove. "We call them stars because they look a bit like an Earth starfish with six arms. We call them *falling* stars because of the way they hunt. If you look closely, you'll see there are suckers underneath the arms. They use those suckers to climb up the side of buildings. They don't seem to have proper eyes, so maybe they hunt through scent or sound. Whatever the method they use, when they spot their prey they let go of the building, and spread out flaps of skin between their arms to slow their fall. Watch!"

I tossed the falling star into the air. It fought to get itself the right way up, and glided towards the wall.

"It looks a bit like an old-fashioned parachute," said Tad.

The falling star landed neatly at the base of the wall, and reverted to starfish form to start climbing up it again.

"As you just saw, they can control their fall," I said. "They silently swoop in, land on top of their prey, and smother it. After it dies from suffocation, they sit on the corpse for hours, slowly eating away the flesh with their digestive juices."

"It's a starbird from Danae in Alpha sector!" Tad seemed hugely relieved to have worked this out.

I shrugged. "Maybe."

"They live on the sides of cliffs on Danae, so I can see they'd like the sides of buildings here," he continued, "but they're perfectly harmless. They hunt the local equivalent of mice."

"The people who brought them to Earth thought they were harmless too," I said. "An alien creature that came in lots of different colours, and looked pretty floating through the air. They were ideal novelties to entertain the public. Easy to breed too."

I pulled a face. "Then they got loose, and they bred in the wild on Earth as easily as in the zoos. That was when people learned something new about them. Apparently there isn't much iron in their diet on their home planet, and that limits their growth. Once they're free in a city, they can feast on pure metal, growing far larger."

I turned and looked across at the other side of the river. "The falling star I just showed you is one of last summer's hatchlings." I pointed towards Manhattan. "Take a look at the grey thing gliding between those two skyscrapers."

"Is that as big as I think it is?" asked Tad, in a stunned voice.

I nodded. "The adult falling stars in New York don't just hunt mice. They hunt people!"

CHAPTER NINE

"But why didn't the United Earth authorities do something?" asked Tad. "As soon as they found out the falling stars were dangerous, they should have hunted them down."

"They tried," I said. "The problem was the falling stars had escaped from zoos in New York and Cairo, and both cities already had large abandoned areas controlled by criminals. When the authorities realized they couldn't deal with the falling stars themselves, they tried importing a natural predator of the falling stars from their home planet, and let some of those loose in New York and Cairo. Small, blue, flying lizard things."

Tad blinked. "The authorities had a problem with one alien creature loose on Earth, so they let loose a second one! That was pretty... desperate."

"Perhaps, but it worked beautifully in Cairo. When the lizards attacked as a group, they could kill even the biggest falling stars. It didn't help the situation here in New York though, because the lizards all died of cold in their first New York winter. The falling stars found their ideal home on the skyscrapers of Manhattan, and have been steadily increasing both their numbers and size. When I first arrived in New York, they rarely glided across the river to bother us, but now they're a constant threat."

Tad started asking another question, but Phoenix interrupted him in a strained voice. "We don't need to know details about how this happened, Tad, or how people tried and failed to deal with it decades ago. We *do* need to know how we fight those things. If one of them drops on me, what do I do?"

Chaos take it, I was starting to admire Phoenix. She'd been used to a safe, secure life on Adonis. Now she was among hostile strangers, faced with the prospect of having to hunt for food while falling stars were hunting her. She was clearly scared to death, but she was working hard to adapt and survive. I'd feel far safer if I was going fishing with her today rather than Tad.

"If a falling star catches you off guard," I said, "then you won't be in a position to do any fighting. It won't just be covering your head, but most of your body as well, pinning your arms to your sides. That's why we always work in pairs when we're outside. Falling stars hunt solo, so if you're caught then your partner is still free to do the fighting."

I pointed at the scarlet falling star that was slowly creeping up the wall. "The brain and central nervous system of a falling star are in the middle of its back. If you stab it there a few times, it will go into spasms and release its prey. If you keep stabbing it, then it eventually dies."

I turned to Braden. "If your objections to violence prevent you from fighting falling stars, you'd better say so right now before you get someone killed."

"Fighting to save a human life is ethically justifiable," said Braden earnestly. "Fighting to take a human life is not. Don't you agree?"

I lived in a world where verbal arguments often turned into physical fights. I'd never spent much time worrying about the ethics of that, because I was too busy staying alive. I ignored the question and drew my knife from my belt.

"You want to stab the falling star, but not injure the person being smothered. That's why Marsha's job with the knives is so vital. She grinds the blades to exactly the right length, slightly longer than a man's thumb. If a falling star is big enough to be a threat to a human being, then your knife will stab deep into the middle of it but not come out the other side."

Tad, Phoenix and Braden all drew their knives and studied them. Tad and Braden put their knives back in their sheaths after that, but Phoenix kept hers out.

"In theory, it sounds simple," I said. "In reality, it can get totally chaotic. The person being smothered has to try to keep perfectly still, which takes a lot of self-control when you're suffocating, but panicking and rolling around can make your partner miss the middle of the falling star. If they stab somewhere thinner by accident, they won't just hurt the falling star but you as well."

"So if you're the one doing the stabbing, it's vital to aim for the centre," muttered Braden.

I nodded. "Once the falling star starts flailing its arms, you stop stabbing for a moment to let the trapped person get free. Ideally, they'll join in the fight after that and help kill the falling star, but they're usually too busy being sick."

I turned and started heading back to where the groups of men were standing outside the building. Tad, Braden and Hannah followed me, but Phoenix glanced back at the baby falling star.

"Shouldn't we kill that one?"

"There's no point. It's too bright a colour to survive the winter. Falling stars are cannibals, killing and eating smaller ones of their own kind, and some Earth creatures hunt baby falling stars as well. The ones that make it to adult size are always a colour close to that of the buildings around here."

Tad gave a paranoid look upwards. "I thought all the darker patches on that wall were the concraz ageing, but..."

"Most of them probably are," I said, "but sometimes one is a falling star."

Phoenix reluctantly put her knife away, and we walked on.

"If someone gets hurt in a fight with a falling star," I added, "there's a whistle attached to your knife belt. You blow that to call for help. Three short blasts, three long blasts, three short blasts."

"Like the old Morse code signal," said Tad.

I was startled. "How do you know about Morse code?"

Tad and Phoenix exchanged glances. "I came across it in a history text," said Tad. "Braden is going to be with a whole group of men who know how to fight falling stars. Wouldn't it be better if Phoenix and I were each with at least two people who knew what they were doing as well, rather than just one? At least for the first couple of times we go fishing? I'm worried I'll mess things up and you'll get hurt."

"I'm pretty worried about that too," I said, "but Donnell told you the reason for it last night. We have to show people that you aren't just leeching food, but helping hunt it, and bringing along someone extra to nursemaid you would scream the fact you're a burden."

The depressed grunt from Tad seemed to mean he accepted that.

"Braden's belt is already tagged with the limping man symbol," I said grimly. "If you and Phoenix get warning tags as well, then there'll be real trouble."

"Are the knife belt tags really that important?" asked Tad.

"They're incredibly important," I said. "You shouldn't have asked questions about personal tags because that upsets people. You shouldn't have asked about Queens Island's name in front of Marsha either."

Tad gave a bewildered wave of his hands. "Why not?"

"Because Marsha was the leader of Staten Island division before it merged with Queens. There are two different stories about what happened back then. One version says Marsha's people deliberately betrayed her and left her behind because they'd had enough of her vindictive nature. Another says that Queens had promised to accept Marsha, but changed their minds when they found out that she'd injured her leg in the fighting at the citizens' barricades and it hadn't healed properly."

I shrugged. "I've no idea which is true, but Marsha was left without a division. A few months later, someone was attacked by a falling star and badly injured by their partner's knife. There was a huge argument about whether the partner had chosen a knife that was too long by accident or on purpose, and Marsha offered to take full responsibility for the knives in future."

I pulled a face. "She was risking her life doing that, because she had no division leader to speak in her defence if she made a mistake and someone got hurt. It took Marsha a long time to get everyone's full trust, more time to build up the tradition of the painted tags on the knife belts, but now she holds a powerful position as the judge of the reputation of everyone in the alliance. The personal tag on your knife belt sums up her verdict on you. No one wants to offend her in case they find something especially embarrassing painted on their knife belt, or even one of the warning tag symbols like the limping man."

Phoenix looked even more anxious than before. "Braden has the limping man painted on his knife belt. You say that's a warning? Of what exactly?"

"The limping man means people think you aren't contributing your share," I said. "It's a warning that you need to change your ways quickly or very unpleasant things will happen."

"Very unpleasant things," repeated Braden nervously. "Aren't we under the protection of the Resistance?"

"Yes, but the alliance rules on general justice still apply to you." I sighed. "You need to understand how our justice system works. Each division has the absolute right to deal with internal problems however they wish, but anyone committing crimes against people outside their own division is subject to the general justice rules. Those were originally intended to stop any division sheltering someone who attacked or stole from people in other divisions, but any alliance representative could use them to call general justice against you for taking food without contributing."

Tad frowned. "Who are these alliance representatives? The division leaders?"

"Each division has eight alliance representatives. The Resistance representatives are Donnell and his officers."

"You mean that any of thirty-two people in the other divisions could demand we were put on trial, and Donnell wouldn't be able to stop it?" asked Phoenix, in a shaky voice.

"Donnell has to follow the alliance rules," I said, "but it would take more than one alliance representative to get you put on trial. Any call for general justice has to be supported by at least four more representatives, including representatives from two other divisions, before things move on to a formal trial."

"But there'd be plenty of representatives eager to support a call for general justice against off-worlders," said Phoenix bleakly.

"I'm afraid that's true," I said.

Hannah broke her silence to join in the conversation. "You don't need to worry about general justice, Phoenix," she said, in a resentful voice. "You'll be perfectly safe as long as you keep Donnell interested in you. It's Braden and Tad who are really in danger. People will only allow them a few days to start contributing before..."

She was interrupted by a voice speaking next to us. "Have you finished instructing the off-worlders, Blaze?"

I hastily turned to face the figure swamped in a thick coat. "Yes, Natsumi."

"I hope they haven't been causing you any trouble." Natsumi's hood and scarf covered almost all of her face, so I could only see her alert, dark eyes, but her voice sounded surprisingly friendly.

"No, everything is fine."

"If you have any difficulties with the boy during the day, then use your signal whistle and I'll come at once."

"Thank you," I said, confused by her sudden concern for me.

"Braden, you should join Donnell now," Natsumi added, in glacial tones. "Phoenix, come with me."

Braden hurried to where a group of men were gathering round Donnell, and Natsumi and Phoenix walked away. I saw all the men and women were outside now, and the children were spilling out of the doorway to join them, running to start playing their game with the portals.

"Dial it! Dial it! Portal, dial it!" their ritual chant began. "We're ordering you by Newton. We're commanding you by Einstein. We're conjuring you by Thaddeus Wallam-Crane!"

I headed towards the crowd, with Tad walking on one side of me and Hannah on the other. I could see Hannah glaring across me at Tad, but he was watching the children playing with the portals. Hannah gave up on him, and turned her attention to where Phoenix was standing next to Natsumi.

"Phoenix doesn't look that pretty to me," she muttered. "I

always thought that Donnell was too busy being in love with a planet to really care for a woman, but if he wants to marry again, then he should choose one of the Resistance rather than an outsider."

"Forget Phoenix." I caught Hannah's arm, tugging her far enough away from Tad that we could have a whispered exchange in private. "Something is obviously worrying you. What's going on?"

She gave a startled laugh. "I should be the one asking you that. Everyone's gossiping about how Donnell's been calling you into meetings and putting you in charge of the off-worlders."

"Oh," I said. "I didn't realize anyone had noticed."

"Of course they've noticed! There are dozens of rumours flying around. Most are about the female leech, but there are some about you as well, and why Donnell is stopping you from fishing with me."

She looked at me expectantly. I hesitated, unsure what to say. Donnell had made it clear that I mustn't repeat anything I'd been told in confidence. That meant I couldn't tell Hannah about what had happened in the meeting with the off-worlders, or how Donnell had ordered me to try to get information out of Tad, or the situation with Cage.

"Oh," I repeated, and glanced across at where Tad was waiting, an anxious expression on his face.

"So are the rumours true?" demanded Hannah. "Has Donnell decided to recognize you as his daughter again?"

"Things do seem to have changed, but I daren't count on Donnell going as far as publicly calling me his daughter."

Hannah's face hardened. "I think Donnell has already said something to the Resistance inner circle. Yesterday, Natsumi was ignoring both of us, but today she was fawning over you and worried about your welfare. She's still ignoring me though. Does that mean the other rumour is true as well? Is Donnell sending you fishing with an off-worlder to stop you being friends with me?"

I blinked. "Why the chaos would people think that?"

"Because Donnell has never liked me," said Hannah bitterly.

"That's why he's never made me a full member of the Resistance. It doesn't help that my knife belt is still tagged with the thief's hand. Even the leech boy noticed it."

She gave a frustrated shake of her head. "I made one perfectly innocent mistake when I was twelve years old. How much longer do I have to keep paying for it?"

"I know that tag is unfair." I glanced over my shoulder, saw the men had already headed off down the path, and the women were forming a ragtag line and moving after them. "We have to go with the others now, but don't worry. I promise to talk to Donnell and sort this out."

"You could ask him to make me a full member of the Resistance as well," said Hannah eagerly.

"I'll do my best."

I sprinted back over to Tad, and we both hurried to join the end of the line of people. I saw Hannah running ahead of us to join Natsumi's sister, Himeko, and frowned. Hannah was right that Natsumi's change of behaviour was deeply significant. The older Resistance members were fiercely loyal to Donnell, modelling their attitude to me on his. Donnell had been ignoring me since my brother's betrayal, so the Resistance had ignored me too.

If Natsumi was being friendly to me now, then it must mean that either Luther had spread the news about Donnell calling me his daughter in that meeting, or Donnell had used that word again in front of others of the Resistance. That was good news, because it meant the whole of the Resistance would be eager to make me feel welcome among them again. The problem was that if the Resistance believed Donnell wanted to split me up from Hannah, they'd be equally eager to make her feel *un*welcome.

I'd promised Hannah I'd sort this out, and I'd have to do it quickly.

CHAPTER TEN

Tad and I followed the line of people walking along the river path. The nearby buildings had looked uniformly neat when coated with snow. Now that was melting, revealing the stark differences between buildings still in good repair and the ones with disintegrating roofs, those covered in ivy and the ones still with clean glass, concraz, concrete or stone facades. I was still worrying about Hannah's situation, and Tad was unnaturally quiet. We'd reached the riverbank before he finally spoke.

"I've been stupidly arrogant. I thought I knew about everything, but I'm totally ignorant of your life and your world, and that ignorance could get you killed. Please tell me when I'm doing anything especially foolish."

I couldn't see his face, because he was taller than me and currently staring up at the sky, but his voice was shaking.

"For a start," I said, "you'd better watch your feet, not the sky. There's a big hole in the path ahead and you don't want to break your ankle."

Tad hastily looked down, saw the hole that was half filled with slushy snow, and walked round it. "Sorry. I was watching for falling stars."

I laughed. "There's no need to do that while we're with a huge group of people. If any falling star made the mistake of attacking us, it would be dead in seconds."

Tad shook his head. "I'm useless."

Women gradually dropped out of line as we passed the

fishing spots, and I gave Hannah a wave as I saw her leaving with Himeko. I stopped walking when Tad and I reached the familiar grey building.

"Our fishing spot is on the other side of this building," I said. "It's the furthest from home, and we have to climb over the building to reach it, but it's worth the effort because there's a pier jutting out into the river. Once we're on that, we're safe from falling stars. They don't risk attacking anyone close to water because they can't swim."

As Tad and I headed for where the ladder was leaning against the wall, I heard a mocking male yell from behind us. "Good fishing, ladies!"

I expected Tad to turn his head to look behind us, but he didn't. Perhaps even he had the sense to realize that any reaction would invite more trouble.

"You go up the ladder first," I said, "then wait on the roof while I come up to join you. Keep an eye out for falling stars while you're up there. They won't be on the burned out building, none of them are a dark enough colour to hide on that, and they find it hard to climb ivy-covered buildings like the ones further along from here. That means they'll be coming from the undamaged apartment block."

Tad glanced at the blackened building. "When did that catch fire?"

"Last summer. It was very hot, and a lot of buildings caught fire."

Tad started climbing the ladder. "The remaining shell of the walls doesn't look very safe."

I laughed. "Nothing in New York is very safe."

Once Tad reached the top of the ladder, I tossed him the bags, and climbed up to join him. I felt nervous pulling myself onto the roof without Hannah standing by to help me, but my left arm didn't complain about taking my weight, and a minute later we were safely on the pier. I fetched the fishing gear from the building, showed Tad how to set out the array of fishing lines near the far end of the pier, and then put up the tent.

Once we were sitting inside that, I started feeling intensely uncomfortable. It was only a small tent. That had never worried me and Hannah, but now I was wedged in a tight space with a male, invading, off-world leech.

I inched as far away as possible from Tad, waited nervously to see if he'd spread himself out to take up more room, and reluctantly had to give him some credit when he left the gap between us. It was still a relief when the first fish took the bait. I left the tent to show Tad how to reel it in and use the long-poled landing net to bring it up to the pier level.

"Is it low tide at the moment?" Tad peered over the wooden rail. "It's a long way down to the water."

"Don't lean on that rail!" I said sharply. "The wood has gone rotten in places, and falling in the river in midwinter is a really bad idea."

Tad hastily straightened up.

Once we'd caught three more small fish that we could just pull up on the end of the line, and one surprisingly large, striped bass that was a real struggle to get into the landing net, I decided Tad was competent enough to be left in charge of the fishing lines. I went round to the other side of the pier to try throwing the cast net into the river.

I loved the moment of excitement as you pulled the cast net back up with the rope, never knowing if it would be limply empty, contain a single squirming fish, or you'd been lucky enough to sweep up a passing shoal that could feed a dozen hungry people for a day. This time there was just a single small fish. At a different time of year, I'd have tossed it back into the river, but we needed every mouthful of food.

Tad had turned to watch me. "Can I try throwing the net?"

"No, there are far too many jagged bits of wreckage at the bottom of the river. If you throw the net in the wrong place, or let it get swept away by the current, then it will be ripped to shreds."

There was the sound of a distant whistle. One long, one short, one long. A pause and then the same pattern was repeated. I took out my own whistle to reply. One long blast, one short, one long. I waited a moment, and blew the same pattern again.

Tad frowned. "What was the whistling about?"

"It's just the regular roll call. Every couple of hours, the letter K gets echoed down the riverbank to check that everyone's all right. If you don't hear from anyone at the next fishing spot in the line, then you whistle Q and go over to see if they've got a problem, but we're the end of the line so..."

I broke off, because there was another burst of whistling, far longer and more complicated this time. Natsumi was asking if the off-world leech was giving me any trouble. I replied that he was working hard.

"I'm not a leech," said Tad, in a deeply offended voice.

I laughed, and made a mental note of the fact Tad hadn't just heard about Morse code, he knew the signals for all the letters well enough to understand a complex message.

After the mid-morning roll call, the day settled down into something almost like a routine day fishing with Hannah, except that I had to do most of the work of two people as well as answering a string of questions from Tad. Just after the big thrill of the mid-afternoon roll call, there was a sudden chorus of bird alarm calls, and a flock of geese flew up into the air from somewhere just downriver of us. They formed up into trailing v-shaped skeins before flying away.

"Did a hunting party disturb those Canada geese?" asked Tad.

I blinked. "How do you know those are Canada geese when you've never been to Earth before?"

"There's a zoo on Adonis with animals and birds from Earth." Tad hastily changed the subject. "I suppose we don't get a midday meal because of the food rationing."

I added the geese comment to my mental list of strange things about him. "We don't have a midday meal on short winter days anyway. If it wasn't for the food rationing, we'd have had a much bigger breakfast though."

"I'm sorry," said Tad. "I shouldn't have said anything. I'm sure you're even more cold and hungry than I am."

There was a weary edge to his voice. Tad had never gone hungry before, never known cold like this, never even seen snow until he came to Earth, but he'd been working as hard as he could today and this was the first hint of complaint.

"You can go in the tent for a while," I said. "It's always much warmer out of the wind."

Tad went to sit inside the tent, but peered out at me. "You need to take a break too."

I hesitated, but Tad had left as much space as possible for me, there was no action on the fishing lines, and I was frozen. I went to sit next to him, and he instantly started asking yet more questions.

"Why do the men hunt with bows instead of guns? There must be some guns in New York."

"There are, but they're all useless without their activation codes. The gun control laws of the last two centuries insisted on all guns being security locked to their owners."

"Modern weapons are highly sophisticated," said Tad, "but it should be possible to make a basic gun like the ones used centuries ago."

"It is possible, but there's the risk of a homemade gun exploding in your face, and the problem of finding or making ammunition for it. Why bother when we've plenty of modern hunting bows? They're far more effective than homemade guns, and you can endlessly reuse the arrows."

"That's true," said Tad. "There seems to be a strict rule here, that the men hunt with bows and the women go fishing. Donnell doesn't seem to have any female officers either. Neither of those things make sense to me. Women have been on equal terms with men for centuries."

"Sometimes it only takes one or two people in a position of power to reverse centuries of progress," I said gloomily. "When the New York alliance was first set up, there were nine divisions including the Resistance. The other divisions had been fighting each other for years. They didn't trust each other to run things, so they put Donnell in charge of the alliance, but he had to follow rules decided by a majority vote of all the division leaders. When someone proposed a rule that women couldn't use bows, the leaders of four divisions voted in favour and five against."

Tad asked the obvious question. "If the majority of the division leaders voted against that rule, why do you have it now?"

"Because four of the divisions were a lot bigger than the others back then, so the Resistance, Manhattan, Brooklyn, and Queens got a double vote. The Resistance voted against the rule, but the other three double votes were in favour."

"So the end result was that the rule was passed by seven votes to six," said Tad. "I assume they also voted to prevent women from becoming officers."

"They didn't openly exclude women from becoming officers. In theory, Donnell can choose any Resistance member to be an alliance officer, but two of the other division leaders have to vote in favour for the appointment to be confirmed."

"And they won't vote to confirm any female officers."

"Exactly. They always use the same argument to justify that. Donnell's officers have to lead hunting groups. Women can't lead hunting groups because they can't use bows. Therefore women can't be officers."

I shrugged. "During the first year of the alliance, the smaller divisions gradually merged with Manhattan, Brooklyn and Queens. Two of those smaller divisions had female leaders, but one lost her leadership position when her division merged with Brooklyn, while Marsha was excluded entirely when Staten Island merged with Queens. After that, there were only a handful of women among the alliance representatives, and since fishing was regarded as lower status than hunting with bows they were gradually replaced by men."

"So that's how you ended up in the current situation," said Tad. "Excluding women from using bows was also a way of excluding them from holding positions of power. This all happened over eighteen years ago. Hasn't Donnell tried to change the rules on bows?"

"He's tried twice. Once after the last of the New York division mergers. Those left the alliance with four divisions of roughly the same size, so each leader had just one vote. Manhattan, Brooklyn and Queens Island all voted against women using bows."

"And the second time?"

"The second vote was soon after London division arrived. Ghost had just taken over the leadership of Brooklyn, and had a totally different attitude to their old leader. The Resistance and Brooklyn voted in favour of women using bows, but London's leader voted with Manhattan and Queens Island against it. I think that was partly because London division were refugees, their position was horribly weak, and Ice was worried that voting to change existing laws could trigger a backlash against them."

I paused. "Once one of the division leaders takes a position on something, he sticks to it. The leadership of Queens Island has changed since then, but their new leader, Major, is even more fervently opposed to women using bows."

"I expect he's scared the women would be better archers than him."

I laughed. "That's probably true. Major boasts about the draw weight of his bow, and can fire arrows a very long distance, but he's barely mediocre when it comes to hitting his target. The finest hunter in the alliance is Ghost. He hasn't got the muscles of the other division leaders, but he's a fast and accurate archer, and he got his nickname from his incredible ability to sneak up on his prey unnoticed."

"You said that you spent the first eleven years of your life with your mother in London division. Was that very bad?"

"What life is like within a division is almost totally dependent on the division leader," I said. "Ice got his nickname because he never shows emotion. That makes some people nervous around him, but Ice keeps strict order in his division. Bullying, disobedience, or troublemaking are dealt with instantly and harshly, no matter who is involved. People who follow his rules and work hard get protection and good treatment."

"A total dictatorship, but a fair one," said Tad.

"Yes. You can tell Ice is a good leader, because London division arrived here empty-handed, but they're on equal terms with the other divisions now. You can tell he's well liked, because he's led London division for three decades. It's possible to seize the leadership of a division with only a handful of key men helping you, but you can't hold onto it for more than a couple of years without widespread support."

Tad was silent for a minute or two as if he was thinking

something over. "So when Donnell went to London, he married your mother, but she stayed in London when he returned to New York. You escaped the firestorm and came to New York when you were eleven years old, but your mother died."

He paused. "My father died when I was only six, so I can understand how you felt back then, and why you hate privileged off-worlders like me."

I felt strangely guilty that I couldn't tell Tad he was wrong about me hating him. In between the maddening arrogance, and the annoying questions, there were moments like this when the boy was quite human and likeable.

Tad shook his head. "You shouldn't have to live like this, Blaze. When Braden, Phoenix and I leave in the spring, we could take you with us to one of the colony worlds. You could have the sort of decent, civilized life that you deserve."

I stared at him in disbelief. "You seem to have forgotten that I belong to the Earth Resistance."

"I realize that any colony world would be reluctant to accept an Earth Resistance member, especially Sean Donnelly's daughter, but I know some powerful people so I should be able to..." Tad seemed to notice the look on my face at this point, because he let his sentence trail off.

"So you're offering to use your influence to get me a place on one of your bright new worlds?" My brief liking for Tad changed to fury, and I glared at the leech. "And what favours are you planning to ask in return for your generosity?"

Tad looked horrified. "Nothing," he said hastily. "I wouldn't dream of trying to bribe a girl into..."

I wasn't listening to him. I was outraged that Tad thought I was like my brother, that I'd turn traitor and betray everything and everyone to grab at the chance of a place on a new world.

"Whatever your plan is," I ranted at him, "there's one big flaw in it. I'm not interested in your bribe because I'd never leave Earth. You may not think much of this planet, Tad. First people ruined it with centuries of over-population and pollution, then they callously ran off and left it, but this is the home world of humanity and some of us love it!"

Tad cowered, pressing himself into the side of the tent to create more distance between us. "Please forget I ever suggested you going to another world. I assure you I wasn't trying to bribe you to be... affectionate to me. I was just worried about how difficult and dangerous your life is here in New York."

Affectionate to him? I realized I'd got things completely wrong. Of course Tad hadn't been assuming I'd turn traitor like my brother. Tad didn't know how Seamus had betrayed us to the off-worlders in exchange for a place on one of the new colony worlds. Tad didn't even know I had a brother.

"I apologize," I said, in a much calmer voice. "I didn't think you were trying to bribe me into sleeping with you. I overreacted because I care about Earth, and because what you said reminded me of something bad that..."

There was a sharp movement from one of the fishing lines. "Fish!" I said, and crawled hastily out of the tent.

There was a brief distraction while we reeled that fish in, and put new bait on the hooks, then Tad spoke again, choosing his words with paranoid care. "I accept you want to stay on Earth, but there must be better places to live than in New York. Couldn't you come to Fence with us and join one of the settlements there?"

I shook my head. "When the last of the citizens left New York, a lot of them withdrew to those settlements behind Fence. They won't have forgotten how they fought a losing battle to defend their neighbourhoods from the looters, or how some of their friends died on the barricades. They wouldn't let a looter's daughter into their settlement, they'd shoot me!"

"We wouldn't have to mention your mother," said Tad. "We could just say you were from the Resistance."

I groaned. "The citizens would shoot me for that too."

"But your father mentioned sending Resistance members to join the citizen settlements."

"The citizens used to let Resistance members join them so long as they weren't on record as political criminals," I said. "That all changed when they found out the Resistance had formed an alliance with the old criminal gangs. Allying with the citizens' bitter enemies meant we became their enemies too, and..."

I broke off my sentence because something was moving high above us on the undamaged apartment block.

"Look!" I pointed. What had seemed like just another aging piece of concrete on the side of the building had detached itself, and was gliding steeply downwards. "Falling star on an attack run!"

CHAPTER ELEVEN

Tad put down the fishing line that he'd been reeling in, and looked upwards.

I saw the falling star bank slightly, turning to the left. "It's not coming for us or the other fishing pairs," I shouted. "It's after something on the other side of the building. Come on!"

I climbed onto the concrete block, then the wall, and finally the roof. I ran across to the other side, and checked Tad was following me before heading down the ladder. I arrived on the ground, waited impatiently for Tad to catch me up, then ran along the front of the burned out apartment block.

As I rounded the corner, I nearly fell over a heaving, grey mass on the ground. Whatever the falling star had been hunting, it had caught it.

"Get your knife out!" I yelled.

I grabbed my own knife from its sheath, fell to my knees next to the falling star, and started stabbing its centre. A moment later, Tad was hacking away with his knife as well. For a few seconds, there was no reaction from the falling star, then its tentacles started lashing out. One of them hit me hard, knocking me sideways into the slushy snow, and Tad turned his head to look at me.

"Are you all right?"

"I'm fine. Kill it!"

The falling star had released its prey now. I ignored the pathetic heap of wet, black fur, picked myself up, and rejoined the attack. For another minute, we battled to dodge the flailing tentacles and stab the centre of the falling star, and then it abruptly went limp. Tad kept stabbing it until I pointed out the obvious.

"It's dead."

Tad stood up, and made a retching noise as if he was going to be sick. "What's that dreadful smell?"

"Digestive juices. If you think this is bad, imagine what it's like for the prey being smothered in them."

"Oh yes." Tad turned to look at the black-furred object that was lying on its side, gasping for breath. "Is that poor cat all right?"

He stretched out a hand towards the cat. It struggled to its feet, flattened its ears against its head, and hissed at him. I laughed.

"I thought cats were kept as pets," said Tad, in a wounded voice.

"The ones round here have been feral for generations."

Tad watched the cat stagger off into the building. "It could have shown a bit of gratitude for us saving its life."

"Forget the cat," I said. "We keep some carts in the entrance to the intact apartment block. We'd better get one and load up the falling star, so it's ready for us to collect after we've finished fishing. Now most of the snow has melted, there shouldn't be a problem getting the cart along the path home."

I headed for the building, and gestured at the carts. "We'll use the nearer one because it has the best wheels."

"Why do we want to take the falling star back to...?" Tad broke off and groaned. "Please don't tell me that we're going to eat it."

I grinned at him. In the last few minutes, my emotions had swung wildly between liking Tad and loathing him, and now fighting a common enemy had made him, at least temporarily, my ally. "They try to eat us. Why shouldn't we eat them?"

"The stink!"

"You have to drain the digestive juices, soak the falling star in water for twenty-four hours, then skin and boil it. By the time you've done that to a baby falling star, there's nothing left to eat, but a big one like this has plenty of meat on it."

Tad collected the cart, and pushed it back to where we'd left the falling star. I eyed it dubiously. This was one of the biggest falling stars I'd ever seen. Tad might be able to lift half its weight, but I couldn't.

"We'll have to cut it in two pieces to get it onto the cart," I said.

It took us a quarter of an hour to hack through the leathery skin and get the pieces of falling star into the cart. I was ready to drop from fatigue by the time we'd got back over the roof to start fishing again, and desperate to hear the whistled signal from Natsumi that would order us to head home.

When the longed-for whistle finally sounded, we still had to pack up, and then struggle over the roof yet again, this time with the extra burden of bags of fish. When we reached ground level, I looked dubiously at the cart with its heavy load of falling star pieces, and then at the heap of fish bags.

One of us was going to have to push the cart along the badly rutted path home, while the other carried the fishing bags. Pushing the cart would be an equal strain on both arms, and my left arm was already painful. If I carried the bags, I could take most of the weight on my right shoulder.

"Tad, you'd better push the cart."

He started picking up the fish bags.

"I said you'd better push the cart," I repeated. "I'll carry the bags."

Tad piled the fish bags on top of the cart. One fell off, but he picked it up and wedged it between a couple of falling star tentacles. "I can take the fish bags as well. You've had to do most of the work today, showing me how to do everything, and you look exhausted."

I hesitated. "You'll find it difficult pushing that cart without overloading it as well."

Tad got the cart moving. "I'm much stronger than I look."

I stopped arguing. I didn't like accepting help from an off-worlder, but Tad was right about me being exhausted.

"I've been doing weight training at the gym for the last year," Tad added. "That's how I met Braden."

I blinked. Yesterday, Tad had claimed that he, Phoenix and Braden were a team working for the Adonis Institute of Cultural Heritage. Now he'd just let slip the fact he'd met Braden at the gym.

The cart juddered to a halt and tipped sideways, one of its wheels firmly jammed in a hole in the path. I turned to help Tad free the cart, but saw him casually lift it out of the hole himself. Whatever else he was lying about, it was true that he was much stronger than he looked.

I saw Natsumi and Phoenix standing on the path ahead of us. Natsumi gave a nod of approval at Tad pushing the over-loaded cart.

"I'm glad to see you're making the leech work hard for his food, Blaze." She gestured at Phoenix. "You can take charge of this one too."

Phoenix instantly moved to stand by my side, and I heard her give a faint sigh of relief. Our group walked on down the path to where three more figures in heavy coats were waiting. One of them was Himeko, but I couldn't see Hannah.

"Why isn't Hannah with you, Himeko?" I asked anxiously. "Has there been an accident?"

Himeko shrugged. "No. Hannah decided to go back with a couple of the other women."

Hannah hadn't been hurt then, but I still frowned. Phoenix had clearly had a grim time fishing with Natsumi. Judging from the cold tone of Himeko's voice, Hannah would have had a bad day as well, bad enough that she'd chosen to head back with another fishing pair to escape from Himeko.

Tad, Phoenix and I moved on with the others. Phoenix was pale and silent, while Tad was too breathless to talk. When we finally reached the Parliament House and went inside, he stopped pushing the cart and groaned.

"We weren't the only ones to get a falling star then," he said. "I thought we'd done brilliantly, but..."

I turned to look at a row of carts by the wall, each half-buried in the unwieldy bulk of a falling star. Fifteen of them. Sixteen with ours. I was torn between delight at the sight of so much potential food, and anxiety that sixteen adult falling stars had come across the river from Manhattan to attack us in a single day.

During my first year in New York, we'd only killed one or two large falling stars a week. The number had gradually increased since then. Last year, the record in a single day was ten falling stars, and now it was sixteen. Would we reach the point where falling stars didn't just make life difficult and dangerous for us, but totally impossible?

I tried to concentrate on the positive thought that this was a huge boost to our food supplies. "We did well," I told Tad, "which is far safer for you than doing brilliantly. People would be grumbling if you hadn't brought back your share of food, but they wouldn't like an off-worlder outdoing them either."

Marsha was on duty by the door as usual. Phoenix and I handed our knife belts to her, but Tad was still staring gloomily at the carts. Marsha pointedly held out a hand towards him. "Knife."

"Sorry." He hastily unbuckled his belt and handed it over. "I forgot."

She shook her head. "You must never, ever forget. Only Donnell and his officers are allowed to carry weapons on common ground. If anyone caught you wearing your knife belt in Reception, they'd be entitled to kill you and claim self defence."

Marsha limped away to put the knife belts with the others lying on the tables, waiting to be cleaned and locked away for the night.

Tad gave me an uncertain look. "She was joking, wasn't she? People couldn't kill me just for forgetting to hand in a knife belt."

"Yes, they could," I said. "That rule is vital. There are back doors to every wing of this building. Each division can smuggle anything they like in through them, so they'll all have vast numbers of hunting bows, knives, swords, and chaos knows what else in their private storerooms. If we let people carry those weapons on common ground, then a casual fight could escalate into a mass bloodbath."

Several women arrived, grabbed the fish bags, and wheeled our cart to join the others. I saw Hannah standing over by the Resistance tables, and was reminded that I must talk to Donnell about her as soon as possible. He didn't seem to be in Reception at the moment, but Aaron and Braden were walking towards us. I noticed Braden's limp was much worse than it had been at breakfast.

"Can you take charge of Braden now?" asked Aaron. "I've got another job to do."

I nodded, and Aaron went hurrying off.

"How is your leg, Braden?" I asked.

"A little sore after so much walking."

"I'll ask Nadira to check it again after..."

I was interrupted by a sudden outbreak of jeering. I turned and saw Rogue of Queens Island division being dragged through Reception by a group of ten men.

CHAPTER TWELVE

Rogue was in his mid-twenties, with black hair in dreadlocks that hung past his shoulders. He was a muscular man, but stood no chance of resisting the ten men forcing him across the room.

"What's going on?" Phoenix asked in an anxious whisper.

I pulled a face. "You remember what I told you about general justice rules?"

"You mean he's..."

Phoenix let her words trail off as a girl stepped forward from the Queens Island division area. That was Rogue's girlfriend, Raeni, a year or so younger than him, her hair and skin even darker. She called out his name in a tense voice, saying the single word as if it was a question. Rogue glanced at her, and gave an odd shake of his head, before being dragged outside.

I sighed. I didn't want to watch this, but the off-worlders probably needed to see the punishment. It was the only way they'd really understand how important it was for them to prove themselves useful.

Rogue was briefly out of view, then appeared again as his captors dragged him to the post positioned outside the glass-walled front of Reception.

"Why are they tying him to that post, Blaze?" Phoenix had an edge of panic in her voice. "What are they going to do to him?"

I was too worried about what was happening outside to answer the question. A general justice punishment squad included two men from each division. Normally the two men from Rogue's own division would be trying to protect him from the others, making sure they were the ones to tie him to the post. Instead, they were pointedly standing well away from him, letting the two men from Manhattan division, their most bitter enemies, enjoy the chance to tie up a man from Queens Island.

I frowned. When general justice was called against someone, there was always a delay of a week to gather evidence, so Rogue's trial had been held during the last blizzard. The whole of the alliance had watched as his division leader, Major, had refused to speak in his defence.

Now it was obvious that Major had ordered his men not to defend Rogue during the punishment either. The Queens Island division leader had a reputation for that sort of underhanded, vicious behaviour when he was displeased with one of his people. I deeply pitied everyone who had to live under his rule.

Rogue was totally helpless now, tied to the post with his arms behind him. The Manhattan men laughed at him, and one of them grabbed hold of Rogue's hair, yanking his head brutally backwards, and leaned in close to whisper something in his ear. Why wasn't one of Donnell's officers out there supervising this situation?

Then I saw Aaron stroll up to join the group of men. He must have already been outside, but blocked from my view by the wall of the building. He said something to the Manhattan men, and they moved away from Rogue. I relaxed. Aaron would keep this under control.

"What are they going to do to him?" repeated Phoenix.

"They're punishing him by using him as bait," I said.

Tad looked horrified. "Bait? For falling stars?"

I nodded.

Rogue was alone at the punishment post now, face tense, eyes desperately looking upwards. The men were chatting cheerfully to each other as they watched and waited. The off-worlders watched too, caught in a sort of horrified fascination.

"They won't actually let the falling star eat him, will they?" asked Braden.

"No," I said. "The punishment squad always move in and kill

the falling star, but how fast they do that depends on whether they have a grudge against the person being punished and want to see them suffer. That's why Aaron's out there. If the squad waits dangerously long to attack the falling star, Aaron will start killing it himself."

There was a short silence. "The sun is setting," said Tad. "Falling stars don't attack in the dark, do they?"

I shook my head.

"Maybe he'll be lucky and nothing will happen," said Phoenix.

"It's better if he does get attacked," I said. "His sentence isn't for a length of time but for three falling stars."

Phoenix's face twisted as if she was going to be sick. "You mean they'll keep tying him to that post until he's been attacked three times?"

"Yes," I said. "Rogue's trial was held the day before yesterday, but this is his first evening at the punishment post. There was no point in putting him out there when the temperature was below freezing, because the falling stars wouldn't attack."

"What did he do to deserve so inhuman a punishment?" asked Phoenix.

"He stole food," I said. "Rogue was one of the first to get the winter fever, so among the first to recover as well. He was out hunting and..."

My words were drowned out by cheers. The top half of Rogue's body was now covered by a massive, grey falling star. I started counting seconds.

"Why isn't anyone helping him?" Phoenix's voice was breaking down into sobs.

As she asked the question, the group of men finally moved in, and their knives swiftly dispatched the falling star. The men dragged it off Rogue, and I saw his head go back as he frantically gasped for air, then forward again as he was violently sick. His hair was drenched with the digestive juices of the falling star, and he looked as much a beaten wreck as the cat Tad and I had saved earlier.

"He still has to go through that two more times?" Phoenix bit her lip. "That's barbaric."

"On Adonis, you use the civilized method of punishing crimes by locking the culprit up in prison." Donnell's voice came from behind her. "There's no point in debating whether that's better or worse, because it's not an option for us. We can't lock people up in prison when we need everyone working to help us survive."

We'd been so busy watching events outside, that none of us had noticed Donnell arrive. Now we all turned to face him.

"The other divisions like using this for general justice punishments," he added, "since it has the benefit of getting us extra food. They often use it as a punishment for their internal problems too. If I managed to stop it, they'd only replace it with something worse."

"What could possibly be worse than what's going on out there?" Phoenix pointed at the glass wall.

"Phoenix, your name tells me you were born on Adonis," said Donnell. "Do you know what happened in Earth's cities after the barricades started going up?"

"I've heard the stories about the fighting on the barricades, and what happened to citizens who were captured. You mean some of the people here were at the barricades doing those terrible things?"

Donnell nodded. "And some of the citizens happily telling those stories on Adonis did equally terrible things. Once there was open fighting on the barricades, the violence started spiralling out of control on both sides. My point is that this punishment is brutal, but at least it doesn't do any lasting physical damage. It also has the huge advantage that it has to be done outside in public, rather than in some private division area. That means I can have one of my officers keeping an eye on things."

Phoenix frowned as if she was considering Donnell's words. I saw Major had moved to stand by the glass wall now, and was looking out at Rogue with a gloating smile on his florid face that reminded me of Cage. I automatically turned to look at the

Manhattan division area, and was shocked to see Cage standing there with his eyes fixed on Major.

I remembered the conversation I'd overheard between the two of them that morning. I hadn't understood what it was about then, but it seemed blindingly obvious now.

Phoenix was still talking to Donnell. "Even if you don't have other options, wouldn't one falling star be enough of a punishment?"

Donnell shrugged. "At the trial, the Manhattan alliance representatives called for a harsh punishment of three falling stars because of their feud with Queens Island. According to the alliance rules, Rogue's division leader had the chance to speak in his defence and argue for a lower penalty, but he just accepted it."

"Major didn't defend Rogue because he was angry with him and wanted him to suffer," I said.

"I know," said Donnell. "Natsumi warned me that there'd been some sort of leadership challenge in Queens Island. The division members are keeping the details secret as usual, but it looks like Rogue made a bid for the leadership and failed. That's probably a good thing. Major has a lot of flaws as a division leader, but at least he's never stolen food."

"Don't you think it was an interesting coincidence that Rogue was accused of stealing food so soon after annoying Major?" I asked, in a meaningful voice.

Donnell beckoned me to move aside with him. He glanced back at the off-worlders before speaking in a low voice.

"What are you suggesting? It wasn't one of the Queens Island members who accused Rogue of stealing food, but Shark of Manhattan division."

"And everyone knows that Shark is Cage's most loyal and obedient servant."

"You think Cage is involved in this?" asked Donnell sharply.

"This morning, I was in one of the Sanctuary storerooms when Cage arrived. I hid to avoid him, and I overheard a secret meeting between Cage and Major. Cage said that he'd done what Major wanted, and in exchange there'd be a time when he'd expect Major to use his division leader vote as he wished."

I paused. "I think Cage and Major set up Rogue for this punishment. Only a few people were well enough to go hunting or fishing before the last blizzard. All the men, including Major and Rogue, were in one hunting group. It would have been easy for Major to take something from Rogue's bag and put the duck in its place. When the hunting group got back, Rogue didn't hand the duck in because he didn't know it was there. Then Cage got his friend, Shark, to accuse Rogue of stealing food, and demand that his bag was searched."

"Chaos," muttered Donnell. "Major has won a double victory here. Destroying Rogue's character and chances of taking Queens Island's leadership, and having the pleasure of watching him suffer at the punishment post as well."

"Cage wins too. I didn't understand how he expected to get two division leaders to support him becoming an officer. Now it's clear that he plans to talk Wall into giving him the first vote, and blackmail Major into giving him the second."

Donnell groaned. "We don't have enough evidence to stop Rogue's punishment or throw accusations at Major and Cage. If you publicly repeat what you heard, it would put you in danger and achieve nothing. They'd claim you misunderstood something perfectly innocent."

"They never actually mentioned Rogue's name," I admitted, "but I'm sure that's what they were talking about. I think at least one of the Queens Island members has worked out what really happened too. Did you notice the way Raeni called out to Rogue when he was dragged through Reception?"

"Raeni is Rogue's girlfriend. She'd take his side even if she thought he was guilty."

I shook my head. "No, she wouldn't. After I broke my arm in the summer, I spent two months helping with the crèche and the school. Raeni was helping there too, because she'd injured her ankle, and we ended up getting quite friendly. Raeni's a hard-working girl, with a sort of steely integrity to her. I don't believe she'd stay loyal to a man who stole food when children were going hungry."

"Let's hope Raeni can convince some of the other Queens

Island members that Rogue is innocent." Donnell turned to frown at the scene outside. "I hate watching a man being punished for a crime he didn't commit."

Donnell had listened to me about Rogue, so I felt this was a good time to talk to him about Hannah's troubles too. "I need to talk to you about something else. My going fishing with Tad is making things very difficult for Hannah."

"Hannah survived two months of going fishing with other people when you broke your arm," said Donnell. "I don't see why it's a problem now."

"People have this silly idea you sent me fishing with Tad to stop me being friends with Hannah. Can you please show everyone that isn't true? Perhaps by making Hannah a full member of the Resistance at last?"

Donnell hesitated before answering. "I didn't send you fishing with Tad to get you away from Hannah, but it's true that I don't think she's a good friend for you."

I'd dismissed Hannah's fear that Donnell disliked her as ridiculous, but she'd been right after all. "Yes, she is! Hannah's the best of friends to me."

"Blaze, you've been blindly loyal to Hannah for years now. You see her as a devoted friend, but there's a point where devoted friendship crosses the line into unhealthy possessiveness. Hannah keeps chasing away any Resistance member who tries to make friends with you."

I was shocked. No, I wasn't shocked, but angry. I fought to keep the bitterness out of my voice. "When did any Resistance member ever try to make friends with me? Since my brother left, they've barely been willing to talk to me."

Donnell flushed. "I'm afraid the older Resistance members can be unreasonably partisan. When the cities were abandoned, I sent most of my people to join the citizens' settlements. Those who stayed were the most deeply committed to our cause, and to me as a person. They were bound to react badly to Seamus's actions, and Hannah's stealing didn't help the situation."

"Hannah never stole anything. She made a simple mistake."

"It wasn't a mistake," said Donnell.

"Yes, it was," I said hotly. "When we arrived in New York, Hannah had to have stitches in a gashed arm and was given medicine for pain. A couple of months later, she fell and hurt her wrist. She was in her room on the sixth floor when the accident happened, only two corridors away from the medicine supply room. She was in a lot of pain, and she knew what tablet to take, so rather than go all the way downstairs to the hospital area she went to get a tablet herself. I know she should have asked permission from an officer or a nurse, but..."

Donnell shook his head. "If Hannah had only taken one tablet, I'd have let her off with a quiet warning, but she was caught with two boxes of them. I couldn't possibly overlook that. The other divisions trust the Resistance to store all the most rare and vital supplies, and make sure they're rationed out to everyone in the alliance with total fairness. We have to honour that trust."

Two boxes? All my passionate certainty in Hannah's cause changed to doubt. Hannah had always told me she'd only taken one tablet.

"Hannah had just had her twelfth birthday and started doing adult work," said Donnell. "I should have treated her as an adult, and handed her over to stand trial and be punished under the general justice rules. Instead, I chose to treat her offence as if she was still a child, and did nothing more than take away her sixth floor access and give her rooms on the lowest floor of the Resistance wing."

He paused. "In retrospect, it would have been kinder to let Hannah stand trial back then. The alliance representatives from the other divisions would have called for a harsh punishment for stealing something as valuable as medicine, but I could have used Hannah's age to bargain them down to something more reasonable. Treating her so leniently just made everyone determined to make her suffer for it in other ways. That's why Marsha painted the thief's hand on Hannah's knife belt."

I barely heard his words. My head was still focused on the huge difference between two boxes and one tablet. Hannah found it hard to cope with pain or illness, so I'd understood her rushing to take a painkiller if her wrist was hurting her, but why would she want two boxes?

Medicine stocks had already been running low back then. Had Hannah planned to hide away those two boxes of painkillers? Had her idea been that whoever was left in pain in future, it wouldn't be her?

Donnell seemed to be studying my face closely as he spoke again. "Six months after that, Natsumi and Machico's two daughters tried to make friends with you. Hannah made it clear they weren't welcome, and then there was an argument where you took Hannah's side."

I dimly remembered that argument. "Hannah told me they'd called her a thief and a liar."

"I suppose it's possible they did call her some names. All I know for sure is that a lot of people were upset by what happened, especially Natsumi. She's protective of her daughters."

Donnell shrugged. "As for making Hannah a full member of the Resistance... On the rare occasions we take someone new into the Resistance, my policy is that they remain a trial member until the rest of my people fully accept them. After over six years, they still haven't accepted Hannah."

When my brother and I came to New York, we'd joined the Resistance as full members from the start. I wondered if I dared to ask Donnell about that. If I did, what would he say? That there were different rules for the children of Resistance members? That there were different rules for *his* children?

I wanted to hear Donnell say that, but I daren't risk asking him the question in case he said something else instead, and then it was too late to ask anything because he abruptly walked off.

I turned to see where Donnell had gone, and saw he was standing by the glass front wall of Reception, gazing out at where another falling star had attacked Rogue. I hastily turned my back on what was happening outside, and called to the off-worlders.

"I'll take you upstairs until dinner."

CHAPTER THIRTEEN

Four days later, Tad and I were fishing on the pier. I went into the building to fetch some extra fishing lines. When I came out of the door again, something leathery engulfed my head and most of my body.

Falling star! I took a deep breath, threw myself to the ground, and rolled sideways trying to dislodge the thing. If a falling star hadn't managed a clean attack, you could sometimes shake it free in the first few seconds, but this one had a good hold on me so I failed to achieve anything but hurting my left arm. I was already totally blind, and now the falling star tightened its grip, clamping over my mouth to suffocate me.

I'd been attacked by falling stars enough times in the past to know there was no chance of freeing myself now. I was totally dependent on my fishing partner to save me. I forced myself to lie still, cursing the fact my current fishing partner wasn't Hannah but an inexperienced off-worlder.

The downside of lying still was that once its prey stopped fighting back, a falling star began the eating phase. I felt its stinging digestive juices flood over me. I had to keep my eyes and mouth tight shut, and not breathe through my nose, or the stench and taste of the filthy stuff would have me retching and choking on my own vomit.

Why wasn't Tad doing anything? Didn't he realize that I was running out of air? Was the off-worlder standing frozen in shock, gaping at what was happening rather than...

I felt the body of the falling star convulse round me, once, twice, three times. That meant Tad was stabbing it. A moment later, the leathery grip on me loosened. One frantic effort and I was free, rolling clear with my eyes still tightly closed. Don't breathe, don't breathe, don't breathe. I repeated the words in my head over and over again, as I snatched at the fastenings of my coat, ripping it and my wet hat off, and then discarded my gloves as well.

I couldn't hold my breath long enough to clean my face. I had to take a gulp of air to fill my greedy lungs, and was nearly sick from the smell of it. I fought off the nausea, and found some dry coat lining to scrub the remaining falling star saliva from my face. Something touched me on the shoulder, and I flinched away in panic, but then I heard Tad's voice.

"Are you all right, Blaze?"

I opened my eyes and looked up at his anxious face. "Is it dead?"

"Not yet," he said. "I was worried you..."

A falling star tentacle lashed into my side like a whip, and another swept Tad's legs from under him so he fell on top of me.

"Chaos weeping!" I struggled out from under Tad, and snatched the knife from my belt. I had to dodge more flailing tentacles to reach the main body of the falling star, kneel down, and start stabbing it. A couple of seconds later, Tad was kneeling at my side, frantically stabbing too.

"You have to keep fighting it!" I screamed at him. "You don't stop in the middle and go wandering off to have a conversation."

"Sorry," he shouted back.

A few more stabs and the falling star was dead. I stayed kneeling there for a moment to get my breath back and calm down.

Tad got to his feet. "Sorry," he repeated. "I was worried about you."

I felt guilty now. "I shouldn't have yelled at you. You did well for a novice. Thank you for saving me."

I moved to stand up, and Tad casually reached down a hand to help me. He was standing by my left side, so it was my left arm

113

that he caught and pulled upwards. I felt a sharp pain, and gave a yelp of alarm.

Tad instantly let go of me, his face appalled. "What's wrong? Did I stab you earlier by mistake?"

"No. I broke my left arm last August, and it's still complaining a little." The pain was easing now. I tried making some cautious movements with my left arm, and relaxed. "It's fine."

"You should have warned me you had an injured arm. You've been doing far too much work."

"The break itself doesn't seem to be a problem now," I said, "but I had a muscle injury that's slower to heal."

"You should ask a doctor to..." Tad broke off his sentence and buried his head in his hands. "No, you can't ask a doctor for help, because there isn't one here. Back on Adonis, you'd have been treated with regrowth fluid, and your broken arm would have healed perfectly within a couple of days, but you can't even take a tablet to ease your pain. Chaos take this primitive place!"

"There's nothing to worry about," I said. "My arm just aches a little sometimes. I think having it immobilized in plaster for weeks made the muscle injury worse, but I've nearly got the full range of movement back now. Only the odd thing, like reaching up high above my head, is uncomfortable."

"Or when a fool like me tries to pull you up by your injured arm." Tad lifted his head again. "What do we do now? You'll freeze dressed like that."

He started taking off his coat, but I stopped him. "There are spare clothes in the building."

I went to wash my face and hands in a nearby puddle, then headed inside the building. I found an old coat, hat, and gloves. The gloves were a size too big, and everything smelled strongly of fish, but that was still a big improvement on the falling star saliva. When I went back to Tad, I found him already cutting up the falling star. I tried to help, but he raised a hand to stop me.

"No, Blaze! Let me do this and carry the pieces over the building. I can see you're still in shock, and your hands are shaking from cold."

I reluctantly accepted he was right, sat down and watched him working, feeling embarrassed and useless. Eventually, Tad had the pieces of falling star loaded into fish bags. He tossed them up on to the roof, then frowned as I salvaged the stinking clothes I'd tossed aside.

"Do you really want to keep those?" he asked.

"I'm not throwing out my best winter clothing," I said. "They just need soaking in water for a while to get rid of the smell."

He sighed, took the clothes from me, climbed up to the roof, and then carried the clothes and fish bags over to drop them on the other side of the building. It was late in the day, so we'd barely time to load the bags into a cart before we heard Natsumi whistling the signal to pack up the fishing gear.

Phoenix joined us on the way back to the Americas Parliament House, and I found Braden waiting just inside the doorway. We handed our knife belts over to Marsha, and then I grabbed the smelly clothes from the cart and bundled them under my right arm.

"I see a falling star attacked you," said Donnell, from behind me. "How did that happen? Falling stars don't usually attack near water, so I thought your pier was a safe spot."

I turned to face him. "The pier is normally safe, but the falling star grabbed its chance to attack me when I went to get extra fishing lines from the building. That's never happened before. I think the falling star must have been desperately hungry to risk an attack so close to the water."

"The falling stars are growing bigger and more numerous each year, so I expect they're running out of prey." Donnell paused and studied me. "You don't look well. Was Tad slow helping you?"

I hastily straightened up. "No. Tad did a good job."

"Tindra and Meria arrived a few minutes ago. Meria had been attacked by a falling star too. Tindra said it was a very large and stubborn one that took a long time to let go. Meria was running out of air, panicked, rolled around at the wrong moment, and got a nasty cut on her arm from Tindra's knife. They're over in the hospital area now getting the wound treated. You're sure that you haven't been hurt?"

"I'm just a bit sick from the stench. I'll feel better when I've had a proper wash."

Donnell waved an arm and Luther came hurrying over. "Luther, take charge of the off-worlders for a few minutes. Blaze, I need a quick conference with you. There's no need to go upstairs for this, we can borrow Marsha's storeroom."

Donnell unlocked the door near the knife and bow tables, led the way inside, and turned on a lamp. The walls of this large, windowless room were lined with neatly numbered shelves. Security staff had once used them to store the bags of people going on guided tours of this building. Now Marsha used them to store bows and knife belts.

The only other furnishings in the room were a narrow bed, a table that held an array of brushes and paints, and a couple of crates where Marsha kept her clothes and personal belongings. Other people filled their rooms with clutter scavenged from abandoned apartments, but Marsha focused her life on her paintings.

Donnell perched on one of Marsha's crates and gestured that I should sit on the other. "Cage was in my hunting group today and grabbed his chance to have a private word with me. We have a bit of a problem."

"Cage doesn't believe I'm really considering his offer?"

"Oh, he believes that," said Donnell. "The problem is that he's demanding definite promises, and not just about marrying you and getting the vacant officer position. He's pushing for me to make him my deputy too."

I blinked. "Seriously? Cage thinks he can join the Resistance and instantly become your deputy? What about the alliance rules? They're stricter on you appointing a new alliance deputy than just an officer, because your deputy may succeed you as leader one day. At least three of the other division leaders have to vote in favour to confirm the appointment. Cage might be able to talk Wall into voting for him, and blackmail Major into supporting him too, but how the chaos would he get the extra third vote?"

Donnell hesitated a moment before speaking. "Cage's

attitude has completely changed in the last few days. He seems far more confident now. We thought he was blackmailing Major into being the second division leader to support him, but I'm afraid we misjudged the situation."

His voice gained a grim edge. "Cage has had six years to prepare for this bid for power. I think he'd already arranged to get the two division leader votes needed to make him an officer long before your eighteenth birthday. Blackmailing Major has given him the extra third vote needed for the deputy position."

"What?" I shook my head. "That can't be right. Why would Ice or Ghost vote for Cage as deputy alliance leader?"

"I realized that if Cage was blackmailing Major, then he was probably blackmailing others as well. I've spent the last few days chatting to division men, mentioning Cage's name and watching how they reacted. The results were worrying. A lot of people seem to be scared of Cage. My impression is that some have a specific reason to fear him, while others are just worried about becoming his next target."

I had a sudden image of Cage as a gloating spider, with dozens of victims trapped in his web. "I can believe that Cage has found out the disreputable secrets of a lot of division members, but not that he's able to blackmail Ghost or Ice. Both of them are popular with their people. What secret could Cage have discovered that could threaten their leadership positions?"

"I admit it's hard to accept Ghost has ever done anything terrible – the man seems positively angelic compared to the other division leaders – while it would be easier to put pressure on a lump of granite than on Ice. It's possible that Cage isn't blackmailing Ghost or Ice themselves, but some of their division members, and his plan is to put a new leader in power."

"And that new leader would have to vote for Cage. Yes, that's possible, but if you're right that Cage has a way to control three division leader votes he can do anything he wants." My voice rose louder in alarm. "He could get them to change the alliance rules, or even mount a leadership challenge against you."

"Calm down, Blaze," said Donnell. "If Cage could get three division leaders to vote for him as alliance leader, he wouldn't still be pushing to marry you. I think the situation is that Cage can control two division leader votes, but he has to coax the third vote out of Wall. It would obviously be a lot easier for Cage to persuade Wall to vote for my son-in-law and chosen candidate for the deputy position, than it would be to get him to support a bid to depose me as leader."

"I suppose so," I muttered, "but how do we deal with this situation?"

"Cage is even more dangerous than we thought. We have to delay a confrontation with him while I do some quiet investigating, find out who is being blackmailed by him, and see if I can offer them an escape route from his power."

"But how can we delay a confrontation if Cage is getting impatient?"

Donnell gave me a nervous look. "The easiest way, perhaps the only way, is for me to tell Cage what he wants to hear. Tell him that I'll keep the officer and deputy positions open for him, get you to marry him, arrange for him to join the Resistance, and do my best to make him deputy leader. My only conditions are that the marriage can't happen until April, and he has to keep everything secret until then. I'll say that's because his appointment will be controversial, and I've got more than enough problems to deal with at the moment."

I stared at him in disbelief. "But what happens in April?"

"That's when I tell Cage that I've changed my mind," said Donnell.

I was frozen, exhausted, and starving hungry. My left arm was throbbing painfully. The stench of the falling star was still lingering in my hair and my clothes. I was in no state to cope with this conversation. "I'm not sure this is a good idea."

"I hate the plan too," said Donnell. "I'm not in the habit of making agreements I've no intention of honouring, but we can't risk Cage making a bid for the alliance leadership now. The situation is too unstable. Whether Cage won or lost, tempers would be fraying on both sides, and it could easily end in open fighting between the divisions."

I stared at him in shock. I'd always thought of Donnell as

superhuman, but now I could see a grey weariness in his face. He'd had Kasim helping him in the past, but now he had to manage alone. I had a vision of a nightmare future where Donnell was killed, and Cage took over as ruler of the alliance.

That future mustn't happen. I moistened my lips and tried to sound calm as I spoke. "In that case, we have to do this."

CHAPTER FOURTEEN

Breakfast next morning was a silent meal. Braden never talked very much anyway. Phoenix had taken one look at my face and realized I was upset. Even Tad had clearly worked out something was wrong, because he wasn't saying a word, but kept staring anxiously at me.

I'd just finished eating when I heard a gasp from Phoenix. I turned my head to see what had frightened her, and saw Major had climbed onto one of the Queens Island tables and was staring aggressively round the room. I tensed, instinctively looked for Donnell, saw him standing nearby, and relaxed again.

Major waited until everyone in the room had fallen silent and was watching him. "Queens Island has an announcement to make," he shouted. "We're formally discarding Raeni. She's brought discredit on us and is outside our protection from this moment."

He turned to glare at Raeni. I saw her stand up, her face shocked, her hands gripping the table in front of her for support. I felt my own hands clench in sympathy. Chaos, being a member of Queens Island division was bad enough, but the perilous existence of an outcast on the fringes of the scavenger alliance would be even worse.

"Take your personal rubbish and go!" Major turned towards where a stunned and silent Rogue was standing, gave him a triumphant smile, and then clapped his hands. A couple of men appeared, and threw two bulging sacks on the floor beyond the Queens Island tables.

Raeni slowly let go of the table in front of her, and walked across to stand by the sacks. She reached down to pick one up, then dropped it again, and seemed to make an effort to stand tall and straight.

"I'm in search of a new division," she called out, turning to look hopefully round Reception.

I saw all three of the other division leaders were busily conferring with their key men. Everyone must be thinking exactly the same thing as me. Raeni had only been discarded by Queens Island because she'd got caught in the conflict between Major and Rogue. Ice valued strict obedience to your leader above everything, so I doubted that he'd take Raeni into London division. It was possible Ghost would be generous enough to give her a trial in Brooklyn though, while Wall might take her into Manhattan just to annoy Queens Island.

"The Resistance offers Raeni a trial membership," shouted Donnell.

I turned to stare at him. Everyone else was staring at him too, and I heard a loud burst of distinctive laughter that had to be coming from Wall.

I couldn't believe this was happening. The Resistance had gained a few members in the past through marriage, there'd been the special cases of my brother, myself and Hannah, and a couple of orphaned children had been adopted by Resistance members. This was the first time the Resistance had ever offered membership to a discarded division member.

Raeni looked like she couldn't believe this was happening either, but she hastily grabbed at her chance for safety. "I accept trial membership of the Resistance."

Donnell nodded. "Raeni, you'll have a room on the lowest level of the Resistance wing. You aren't to go upstairs unless ordered to do so by myself or one of my officers. If you cause any trouble, you'll be told to leave. If you successfully settle in with us, I'll review your membership status in six months' time. Do you understand?"

"Yes, sir," said Raeni. "Thank you, sir."

"I appreciate you may be ignorant of some of our Resistance

ways. I expect all my people to be helpful, offering advice and answering your questions. You can go fishing with Tindra for the next few days because her regular fishing partner has been injured. If you have any difficulties, you should discuss them with either Natsumi or Blaze."

Donnell gestured at Vijay and Weston, and the two of them went over to help Raeni carry her sacks of belongings through to the Resistance wing. There was a buzz of conversation now, and people were getting ready to go outside, so I stood up, and pulled on my coat and hat. Donnell took Braden off with him, and Natsumi beckoned Phoenix over to join her, then I headed outside with Tad, my head so dazed that I nearly forgot to collect my knife belt.

"What's going on?" Hannah's voice came from beside me. "Why has Donnell invited Raeni to join the Resistance?"

I turned to face her. "I've no idea. I'm just glad she'll be safe now."

Hannah grimaced. "But it isn't fair."

"What isn't fair?"

"Donnell said he'd review Raeni's trial membership in six months' time," said Hannah. "I've been a trial member of the Resistance for six years, but he's never reviewed my membership."

She paused to give me a reproachful look. "You said you'd talk to Donnell and get him to help me, but nothing's changed. Everyone's still ignoring me. Even when we're fishing, Himeko only speaks to me to give orders."

I hesitated before replying. I'd been stunned by Donnell's statement that Hannah hadn't taken a single tablet but two boxes of them. I'd spent the last four days thinking that over, but still hadn't decided what I should do about it.

No, to be honest I'd made my decision days ago. I had to tell Hannah what Donnell had said and ask her if it was true. The problem was that I already knew the answer. Of course it was true.

I'd never understood why everyone had been so unfairly harsh to Hannah back then. Fiercely loyal, I'd believed the story

Hannah told me, and refused to listen to anyone else. If I accepted that Hannah had lied to me, that she'd only admitted taking one tablet when she'd actually taken two boxes, then everything made far more sense.

I had to talk to Hannah, but I knew it would be a long and unpleasant conversation. I'd been shamelessly delaying it for days, and I was going to delay it yet again. Within the next few hours, Donnell would be talking to Cage about my fake engagement. I was feeling sick from nervous tension, and couldn't cope with having a huge argument with Hannah.

"It turned out to be a bit more complicated than I expected," I said. "There isn't time to talk about it now."

"Can we talk this evening then?"

"I'm not sure. As soon as I get back from fishing, I've got to go to a meeting with Donnell."

"That's good. You'll be able to talk to Donnell about me, and then come downstairs and tell me what you've arranged."

"Hannah!" Himeko's voice called.

Hannah groaned. "We'll talk after your meeting then, Blaze."

"It's not a good time to..."

Hannah was already running off to join Himeko, so I abandoned my sentence. I went to join the line of fishing pairs too, scarcely aware of Tad trailing after me. The line started moving and I followed it. A nasty thought occurred to me. What if Cage wouldn't wait until April? What if he insisted on marrying me in March, in February, or next week? What if the lie became reality?

I drifted off into hideous thoughts of life with Cage. Even if my life was at stake, even if the lives of everyone in the alliance were at stake, I didn't think I could...

"Blaze." Tad tapped me cautiously on the shoulder.

I stopped walking and gave him a bewildered look. "What?"

"We're here," he said.

I realized I'd just walked straight past our fishing spot, and flushed with embarrassment. "I'm a bit distracted at the moment."

We'd climbed over the roof and set out the fishing lines

before Tad spoke again. "Phoenix, Braden, and I all realize you're desperately worried about something. We're sorry if our presence has been causing trouble for you. If there's anything we can do, or avoid doing, that will help make things easier, then please tell us."

The concerned note in his voice somehow churned up my emotions. I wondered what he'd think if he knew I'd agreed to a secret engagement with Cage. "This isn't really because of your arrival."

"I hope that..." Tad broke off his sentence. "What's all that whistling about?"

I stood still for a moment and listened, but the sounds were too distant for me to distinguish the short and long whistle blasts.

"Some of the other fishing pairs must be chatting to each other. Probably talking about what happened with Raeni." I shrugged. "You take charge of the fishing lines. I'll try using the cast net."

I concentrated on the fishing after that, counting the times I threw the cast net into the water, counting the fish, even counting the holes in the net, in an attempt to block out any thoughts of Cage.

The day seemed endless, but finally the sun started dropping towards the horizon, and I heard Natsumi whistling the order to head home.

Time had been passing horribly slowly during the day, but now it started racing by. It seemed barely a couple of minutes before I was back at Parliament House with all three of the off-worlders clustered round me.

"I need to take you upstairs right away. I've an important meeting with Donnell."

I hustled the off-worlders across Reception and upstairs to their rooms, then hurried to Donnell's apartment. Once outside his door, I stopped, torn between reluctance to start this talk and eagerness for it to be over.

The door looked exactly like genuine wood, except where one deep scratch showed the natural grey of flexiplas under the surface. Beside it was a golden metal plate. Six years ago, putting your hand on that plate had made it play a glorious medley of soaring notes. Since then, all the high notes had gradually faded out, so now it just made a deep grunting noise. Donnell said it sounded like a falling star with chronic indigestion.

I took a deep breath and put my hand on the plate. I heard the grunting noise, and the sound of Donnell calling out in response. "Come in."

I opened the door and went inside. Donnell had been standing looking out of the window, but he turned towards me and gestured at a chair.

I went and sat down. It was the same chair again, the one I always sat in during a crisis. I had a ridiculous urge to ask to sit somewhere else, in case there really was a curse on the thing.

Donnell came to sit opposite me. "I talked to Cage as planned. He agreed to everything, but was stubborn about waiting until April for the wedding. We settled on a compromise of the middle of March if there was an early spring, and early April if there wasn't."

I stared down at my hands. The middle of March was less than two months away.

"We can't let this situation drag on until March anyway," said Donnell. "We have to be ready to take action against Cage by the end of February at the latest. Don't you agree?"

"Definitely."

Donnell leaned back in his chair and sighed. "Now I've made an actual agreement with Cage, I think I have to tell Machico the full story. Apart from anything else, I'll need his help approaching possible blackmail victims and talking them into working against Cage. The question is whether I should tell the rest of my officers as well."

I pulled a face. I could see Donnell's point about needing Machico's help, but I hated the idea of all the rest of Donnell's officers knowing about my fake engagement to Cage as well. I trusted Aaron, Vijay and Weston to be totally discreet, but I was less confident about Julien and Luther. Tad already knew I had a serious problem, and was trying to work out what it was. One unwary comment in front of him could give him the clue he needed.

I wasn't sure why I was so eager to keep the secret of my engagement from Tad. Perhaps it was because of the days I'd have to spend fishing with him, wondering what he thought about it, whether he understood it was a desperate response to a desperate situation, or despised me as a liar.

"I agree you have to tell Machico," I said, "but it would be less embarrassing for me if the rest of them didn't know."

"It would be less embarrassing for me too. Chaos knows, I'm not eager to admit to my officers that I've been driven to lying to Cage because I'm struggling to hold the alliance together, but your safety comes first."

Donnell leaned forward in his chair. "If you find this situation getting too difficult for you, then you must tell me at once. If necessary, there's another option I can use."

I guessed the other option was shooting Cage, and that would create as much havoc in the alliance as a leadership challenge. "I can cope with being engaged to Cage, so long as I don't have to spend time alone with him. I couldn't cope with being married to him though."

"You're absolutely not going to marry Cage." Donnell stood up. "I'll get Machico to join us now so we can discuss what you've found out about the off-worlders, but I'll leave explaining the Cage situation to him until after you've gone."

"I've been too worried about Cage to think about why the off-worlders came to New York," I admitted. "It doesn't seem very important at the moment."

"Any potential source of trouble is important at the moment. If the off-worlders do anything damaging, then Cage will blame me for trusting them, and try to seize control of the alliance."

Donnell went over to the door, opened it, stuck his head out into the corridor, and shouted. "Mac!"

He came to sit down again, and a minute or two later Machico strolled in through the door. "You screamed, oh beloved leader?"

Donnell pointed at a spare chair. "We're having a conference about the off-worlder situation."

Machico picked up the squashed remains of a paper cup from the chair, threw it in the waste bin, and sat down.

"Have people fallen for my act of being interested in that girl with the ridiculous bird name? I keep forgetting whether she's called Griffin, Roc, or..." Donnell snapped his fingers. "Phoenix, that's it!"

Machico laughed. "You're not just interested in her, Sean, you're so jealous that you don't even trust your own officers near her without either your daughter or my wife on guard."

Donnell made a choking noise. "Don't spare my feelings here, Mac. Am I obsessed with the girl?"

"You are totally and utterly besotted," said Machico, in a solemn voice. "It's because of your age, Sean. You're making a desperate bid to reclaim your lost youth. You're..."

Donnell held up a hand to stop him. "I get the idea. Chaos weeping, all I did was play with the girl's hair for a few minutes."

"You haven't looked at a woman since you split up with Keira," said Machico. "If you'd stopped to think about it, you'd have realized people were bound to over react, but you rushed into things as usual. Acting rapidly and decisively is a vital quality for a leader, but you always take things to extremes, and the rest of us have to pick up the pieces afterwards. I've no idea why I've put up with it all these years."

"Enough preaching about my faults," said Donnell. "Is this causing trouble?"

"Not exactly trouble," said Machico. "Some of the Resistance women feel that if you're finally going to marry again, then it should be to one of them rather than an off-worlder. You may get a few advances. I just hope Natsumi doesn't start throwing herself at you again."

I gave him a shocked look.

Donnell groaned. "There's no need to drag up ancient history, Mac. Nothing ever happened between me and Natsumi. Anyway, what about the way you behaved on Year Day 2378?"

"I was young, foolish, and I'd drunk four glasses of Kasim's lethal fruit punch," said Machico, in a dignified voice. "Getting back to more recent events, there's a huge amount of gossip about Raeni joining the Resistance."

"How do our Resistance people feel about her?" asked Donnell.

Machico shrugged his shoulders. "If you want Raeni to join us, people are willing to make the girl welcome, but they're expecting some problems."

Donnell turned to look at me. "Blaze, you mentioned you were friends with Raeni. Perhaps you can help her settle into life in the Resistance."

There was something far too artificially casual about the way he said that. I frowned at him. "Did you invite Raeni to join the Resistance because you want her to replace Hannah as my friend?"

Donnell looked evasive. "You told me that Raeni was hard working and had great integrity. Major was clearly discarding her from Queens Island as part of his feud with Rogue, so I invited her to join the Resistance to make sure she was safe. I admit the fact you liked the girl was an added incentive."

He firmly changed the subject. "I'd like your report on the off-worlders now, Blaze. I've tried talking to Braden, but I can hardly get a word out of the man. Natsumi doesn't seem to be getting anywhere with Phoenix either. Have you found out anything useful from Tad?"

I tried to thrust aside my worries about Cage, and focus on Tad. "Most of it seems more odd than useful, but you were right about Tad being someone very important on Adonis, because he mentioned having powerful friends. The off-worlders don't all work together. It's possible that Tad works with Phoenix, but Braden is just someone Tad met at a gym."

"At a gym," Donnell repeated. "Why the chaos would someone very important on Adonis come to Earth with someone he met at a gym?"

"Tad needed a pilot to fly the aircraft," said Machico.

"If Tad's so important, he shouldn't need to hire a random pilot at a gym," said Donnell. "Anything else?"

"Tad knows too much, and about things that don't make any sense." I tried to remember the mental list I'd been making. "He knows the districts of New York, can identify Canada geese, and understands Morse code messages. There was the strange way he reacted to the falling stars as well. He seemed to have no idea what they were to start with, but then he suddenly said they were starbirds from Danae, and started talking about them living on cliffs and hunting mice-like creatures."

"And he's right," said Donnell. "They *are* starbirds from..."

He broke off and turned to Machico. "Are you thinking what I'm thinking? I know it's impossible, but that boy's acting exactly as if he's webbed and his mind is pulling information from the Earth data net."

"It's completely impossible," said Machico. "Nobody has been webbed for over half a century. My older brother's year group were the last of them; webbed when they were seven years old. The next year group had their webbing postponed for two years because of component shortages, and then there was the shock announcement. We couldn't manufacture the web implants any longer. It was the first technology to be lost because of experts leaving for other worlds, and the first warning sign that Earth's infrastructure was falling apart."

He gave a strange laugh. "I hated my brother for having what I would never have. He could access the Earth data net with a single thought, search through the accumulated knowledge of humanity, and view thousands of images directly with his brain. I had to work with a clumsy wall vid. I felt like a stupid tortoise chasing a brilliant hare."

He grimaced. "Then I found out I was the lucky one after all. Implanted webs needed retuning every year or so to compensate for changes in the brain. Earth didn't have enough experts to make webs any longer, and it didn't have the equipment or specialists to tune them either. I watched my parents and my brother go through torment as their links to the Earth data net grew erratic, and eventually broke down entirely. My brilliant brother wasn't brilliant any longer, and I heard him crying at night for the visions he couldn't see, and the voices he couldn't hear."

"I'm the key few years younger than you," said Donnell. "I don't remember the last people being webbed, just the suicide decade when the webs were breaking down. It was a total nightmare as a child, never knowing which adult would crack next. My uncle seemed to have readjusted to life without a web perfectly well, but then..."

He shook his head. "Never mind the past. The point is that if any world still has the technology to web someone, it would be Adonis."

"Yes, but even if Tad was webbed, he couldn't be accessing the Earth data net from here," said Machico. "None of the wall vids or other technology in New York can link to it any longer and..."

He broke off and frowned. "Actually, I may be wrong about that. Webbed people would have a direct link to the main Earth data net, while the wall vids get their operating software from an entirely separate technical area. Not that it matters, because it's impossible for Tad to be webbed. Perhaps he's one of the rare people with an eidetic memory, who can remember everything they've ever read."

Donnell pulled a face of disbelief. "I could believe Tad had read a lot of information about New York before coming here, but why would he read about Morse code and the starbirds of Danae?"

Machico waved his hands. "Those are just some things he read about years ago by pure chance."

"Pure chance." Donnell stood up and headed for the door. "Let's see just how many things Tad has read about by pure chance."

Machico and I stood up and hurried after him. When we arrived in corridor B6, Donnell thumped on Tad's door, and all three off-worlders appeared from their rooms.

"Have you been enjoying learning about hunting and fishing?" Donnell asked.

Tad nodded, while Phoenix gave a depressed grunt.

"I've always loved fishing," said Donnell. "I lived in Ireland until I was eight years old. My parents had a house in a place called Durrow. It was right by the beach, we had our own boat, and once a week my father would take me sea fishing."

"But Durrow isn't on the coast of Ireland," said Tad. "It's inland."

Donnell smiled at him. "I know it is. I just wondered if you'd know it too, and of course you did because you're webbed. The moment you thought about Durrow, the information about it appeared in your mind. Now tell me who the chaos you are, and how you have fifty-year-old technology imbedded in your skull."

Tad glanced at Phoenix, then faced Donnell again and took a deep breath before answering. "I'm Thaddeus Wallam-Crane."

CHAPTER FIFTEEN

I was aware of Donnell laughing, great booms of laughter that somehow weren't funny but frightening. My eyes were fixed on Tad's apprehensive face. My head was replaying memories of children weaving in and out of portals while chanting their ritual song.

"Dial it! Dial it! Portal, dial it! We're ordering you by Newton. We're commanding you by Einstein. We're conjuring you by Thaddeus Wallam-Crane!"

Donnell's laughter suddenly stopped, and he spoke in a voice that had the brittle edge of ice cracking under a heavy boot. "Thaddeus Wallam-Crane invented the portal in 2206 when he was sixty-four years old. If he was alive now in 2408, he'd be..."

He hesitated, and Machico supplied the number for him. "Two hundred and sixty-six years old."

"I'm obviously not the Thaddeus Wallam-Crane who invented portal technology," said Tad. "I'm his heir, Thaddeus Wallam-Crane the Eighth."

Donnell took a deep breath. "There are something like two hundred colony worlds in the star systems of Alpha sector, two hundred more in Beta sector, and a hundred in Gamma sector. Five hundred worlds to choose from, Thaddeus Wallam-Crane the Eighth. Every single one of them would welcome the heir of the fabulously rich and powerful Wallam-Crane family, but you chose to come to *my* world, to the world that your ancestor's portals destroyed, to Earth!"

Donnell's voice was growing louder with every word. I saw a movement out of the corner of my eye, and turned to see Luther and Julien watching us from the end of the corridor. They must have come to find out what all the noise was about.

"And of all the cities on Earth, you chose to come to New York. *My* city!" Donnell was shouting now, his voice echoing down the corridor. "And of all the buildings in this city, you chose to come to this one!"

"I had to come to Earth, and to New York in particular, because I needed a component from my ancestor's original prototype portal." Tad's voice seemed like a whisper after Donnell's shouting. "That prototype was stored in the Wallam-Crane Science Museum in Manhattan. I retrieved the component successfully, but then we found our aircraft was damaged, so there was no choice but to..."

Donnell cut into his sentence. "Enough!" He stabbed a finger at Phoenix and then at Braden, the red targeting light of his gun flashing on each of them in turn. "Bird woman and Braden, into your rooms. Now!"

Phoenix and Braden gave last anxious looks at Tad before obeying. Donnell slammed the doors shut on them, glanced round, and saw Luther and Julien. "You two, find the keys to those rooms and lock the off-worlders in!"

He didn't wait for a response, just grabbed Tad's arm and towed him along the corridor. Machico and I chased after them, and Luther and Julien hastily jumped aside to let us past.

My stunned brain finally started thinking. As the heir of the inventor of portal technology, bearing the same name as his famous ancestor, Tad wouldn't just be an immensely wealthy and privileged person on Adonis, but practically worshipped. If an ordinary off-worlder was *an* enemy of the Earth Resistance, then Tad was *the* enemy!

Donnell took a left turn and then a right, dragging Tad along with him. I scurried after them, with Machico at my shoulder. I could hear running footsteps, but I didn't bother to look over my shoulder to see who was following us. I was too worried about where we were going. If Donnell took Tad down to Reception, and told the division members who he was, then the boy would be ripped apart.

Donnell took another right turn, and I let out a gasp of relief. We weren't going downstairs then. Of course we weren't. What had I been thinking, imagining Donnell throwing Tad to the division wolves to be torn apart?

Donnell suddenly stopped, and opened a very familiar door. I was instantly tense again. I'd been both right and wrong earlier. Donnell was taking Tad to the stairs, but not the ones leading down to Reception. We were going up to the roof!

Donnell still had Tad by one arm, yanking him up the flight of narrow stairs. Machico thrust his way ahead of me, his figure blocking my view until we went through the doorway to the roof. It was dark up here, the only light coming from the last red ribbons of the sunset fading in the west. I couldn't see either Donnell or Tad for a second, then I spotted two dark figures by the edge of the roof.

I took a few steps towards them, but was scared to go too close. If Donnell was considering throwing Tad off the roof, then my intervening might just...

"Look at it!" Donnell released Tad and waved both his arms in an expansive gesture aimed at Manhattan. "Look what your family have done to New York, Thaddeus Wallam-Crane the Eighth. For centuries, this city was a magnificent place, packed with millions of people, illuminated by dazzling lights that could be seen from orbit."

He let his arms drop to his sides. "Then, in 2206, your ancestor used a portal to transport himself from one end of his laboratory to the other. Within ten years, there were portals on every street corner. People could take one step through a portal and travel between streets, between cities, or deep into the heart of the countryside. Vehicles vanished from the streets, and a lot of people moved away from the cities."

I'd been aware of sounds behind me, the door opening and shutting several times. Now I heard Julien's voice. "We've left the other two locked in their rooms."

I glanced round, and saw that both Luther and Julien were

standing with Machico. The three shadowy shapes beyond them looked like Aaron, Vijay and Weston, so all six of Donnell's officers were here.

Donnell ignored the interruption and kept talking. "New York adapted to the new way of life, streets were turned into gardens, several apartments were knocked together to become one, but then came the intercontinental portal. You couldn't just portal from one end of the Americas to another now. You could portal to one of a dozen Transits, and then join the queue for an intercontinental portal to anywhere in the world."

Donnell stabbed an accusing finger at Tad's chest. "Less than forty years later, countries had become irrelevant because your family owned the world."

Tad was standing on the edge of a roof with a furiously angry man targeting him with an Armed Agent weapon. If he had any sense, he'd keep quiet rather than arguing and making things worse, but Tad had no sense at all. I cringed as he opened his mouth for what would probably be the very last time.

"It wasn't really like that. My family was..."

"Your family owned the Wallam-Crane Portal Company, and had direct control over every portal on the planet, able to order them to self-destruct at any moment." Donnell yelled the words at him. "Any countries that tried to stand against the Company were defeated by sheer logistical reality. They couldn't trade, because they had to ship goods by road, rail, air or ocean, while their competition could deliver within minutes at a fraction of the transport cost. They couldn't fight, because their armed forces had no chance against enemies who could instantaneously portal troops anywhere."

He shook his head. "One by one, the countries surrendered to the might of the Company. We had the era of the United Earth, with its five great Regional Parliaments, free to vote for whatever they wanted so long as your family approved. We had the officially imposed global culture and common Language, which was a deliberate attempt to obliterate all the glorious diversity of Earth."

"It was a deliberate attempt to break the cycle of warfare that was ravaging Earth and wasting countless human lives," said Tad.

Donnell ranted on, ignoring him. "But your family weren't satisfied with ruling the Earth. They had to invent interstellar portals and destroy it!"

"Humanity desperately needed new worlds," said Tad. "There were far too many people for Earth's resources back then. Competition for food and power was generating conflict. Pollution was causing huge damage to the environment. The air was so bad that it was poisoning people. Using portal transportation helped a little, but it wasn't enough."

He paused. "Humanity needed new colony worlds, but my family never intended there to be hundreds of them. The original plan was sensibly unambitious. First colonize Adonis, then expand to twenty or thirty more colony worlds, gradually relieving the population pressure on Earth."

"But things didn't go according to that plan, did they?" demanded Donnell. "The colonists of Adonis were proud and independent people, selected from every region of Earth. In 2340, they formed their own government, declared themselves a free world, and the first of their laws was that no Earth company could own property on Adonis. Everyone expected your family to react to the rebellion by sending self-destruct commands to every interstellar portal on Adonis, but they didn't."

"My family couldn't order those portals to self-destruct," said Tad. "The other colony worlds were already joining Adonis in declaring independence. Cutting off supplies to all of those worlds would have caused the deaths of tens of thousands of people, destroyed decades of work, and endangered the future survival of humanity."

"What you mean is that your family had decided to relocate to Adonis, and didn't want to destroy their new home. Just when Earth most needed the Company to keep control of the colonization process, your family made a deal with Adonis, and handed the new worlds their freedom. Those new worlds formed the Parliament of Planets, started making their own decisions on how many colonists to admit, and the floodgates opened."

Donnell gave another of those terrifying laughs. "New worlds with clean air, pure water, and uncontaminated land were only one step away through an interstellar portal. There were far more people eager to take that step to a better life than the existing fledging worlds could cope with, so there had to be more colony worlds, until Earth was crumbling under the strain of settling two hundred of them."

Donnell's voice changed from bellowing fury to quiet mourning. "And that was when the Earth Loyalist Party recruited me to sing their songs and try to save our world. We won the vote in 2365, but failed to achieve our pledge to restore law and order in the cities. Five years later, the Expansionist party defeated us, and the relentless colonization of new worlds resumed."

He paused. "I was nineteen years old, and my war and my world were both lost, but I couldn't accept it. I organized protests, I formed the Earth Resistance, and in 2375 I led the occupation of this building and raised that flag."

Donnell turned to point at the flag of the Earth Resistance, a vague shadow at the top of the flagpole. "That flag kept flying here while the number of new worlds increased from two hundred to five hundred, and New York went through its death throes."

"'Earth in chaos, weeping tears of blood,'" murmured Tad.

Donnell whirled round to face Tad again. "Don't you dare quote the words of Okoro's *Requiem For Earth* to me! You've no idea what they mean to someone who loves this world, because you're no son of Earth. You were born on your bright, new, prosperous Adonis."

"But Adonis isn't prosperous." Tad's voice was urgent, gabbling out words so fast I could barely understand him. "The newer colony worlds were always struggling from lack of resources, but even Adonis is in crisis now. That's why I had to come to New York. You said you lost access to the Earth data net in 2389. You don't know about the problems the colony worlds have suffered since then. They never had time to establish a proper industrial and technological foundation of their own. They depended on Earth to supply key electrical components.

Now Earth can't do that, all the old equipment is breaking down."

Donnell shrugged. "Do you expect me to be broken hearted that Adonis may have to cope without new wall vids?"

"I'm not worried about the wall vids, but the interstellar portals," said Tad. "They're breaking down and can't be replaced. The colony worlds are being cut off from each other and that's disastrous."

"I don't care about your interstellar portals," said Donnell. "All that matters to me is that the lights in New York have gone out forever, and I'm standing under the last flag of the Earth Resistance and facing my enemy. You talk a lot, Thaddeus Wallam-Crane the Eighth. Talk to me now. Look at the ruin your family have made of my city and my world, and tell me one good reason why I shouldn't throw you off this roof."

I held my breath. Tad had a habit of saying the wrong thing and he was bound to do it now. I shouldn't care about that. I should be stepping forward to push him off the roof myself. Only days ago, I'd stood on this roof, seen the aircraft arriving, and been eager to go to Manhattan and fight the faceless enemy. Now the enemy had a face, and somehow that made a difference.

"You said the reason yourself," said Tad. "Earth was lost when the Expansionist party won the vote in 2370. Am I responsible for something that happened long before I was born?"

"Your ancestors are responsible. Your family were drunk on power."

"If I could go back in time, I'd tell my ancestors to do some things differently, but I can't. Imagine how you'd feel if someone made your daughter suffer because of your choices."

Donnell's voice held an even more bitter note as he replied to that. "You think I need to imagine that, Thaddeus Wallam-Crane? Every day of my life, I see my daughter suffer for my decisions. I see the children of everyone who was fool enough to follow me suffering too. This winter I watched thirty-two people die of winter fever, seven of them my own Resistance members, and knew it was my fault. My people are paying the price for my actions and my choices, and I know the future won't get better but worse. No wonder my son chose to betray me."

There'd been odd background noises until now. A whisper or two. The occasional muffled cough. The crunching of frost when someone moved their feet. Now there was utter silence for at least a minute before Donnell groaned.

"I need a drink." He walked swiftly towards the door to the stairs, pausing as he opened it to say a single sentence. "Someone deal with that boy for me."

A second later, Donnell was gone. There was another brief silence before Julien spoke.

"Did Donnell mean we should kill this leech?"

I waited for Machico to say something, but he didn't. Nobody else was saying anything either.

"Perhaps we should kill all three of them," added Julien.

There were times when I couldn't help myself speaking instinctively. This was one of them. "No!"

CHAPTER SIXTEEN

In the darkness of the rooftop, the shadowy figures of six men turned to look at me. I could back down, say I hadn't meant it, let them do whatever they wanted to Tad, but...

If I did that, how would I live with the memory afterwards? Only yesterday, Tad had saved me from a falling star. However annoying he was, whatever the crimes of his ancestors, Tad didn't deserve to be murdered, and after he was dead then Phoenix and Braden would be next.

I could imagine Braden holding fast to his pacifist principles, and standing stoically still while he was murdered. That was admirable in its way, but Phoenix... Oh, Phoenix would fight a hopeless battle for her life until the last breath was beaten out of her body, and that was something that struck an answering chord deep inside me.

"No," I repeated. "Donnell just meant someone should take Tad away and lock him up."

"It didn't sound like that to me," said Julien.

I was still waiting for Machico to intervene in this, for Luther to speak up, for anyone else to do something, but they were all just standing and watching me and Julien.

"Donnell said to deal with the boy," continued Julien, "so I'll deal with him. After we've disposed of him, we can decide what to do about the others."

He made a movement towards where Tad was standing at

the edge of the roof. Julien could brush me aside like an ant, but I stepped forward to block his way anyway.

"I said no!"

Julien loomed over me, twice my size. "I should have guessed you'd defend the off-worlders. You're as big a traitor as your brother."

"I'm not like Seamus," I said. "I'm loyal to Earth and to the Resistance."

He laughed. "Really? If you're loyal to the Earth Resistance, why are you protecting our enemy?"

"Because I won't let you bring dishonour on the name of the Earth Resistance. I won't let you shame us by murdering prisoners of war."

Julien hesitated, frowning, and someone else finally spoke. Not Machico, or Luther, but Aaron. "Blaze is right. The Earth Resistance doesn't murder prisoners of war."

I had someone on my side. I had to take advantage of that before anyone started supporting Julien. "I'll take the prisoner and lock him up. Give me the keys to the off-worlders' rooms."

Julien stood motionless for a nerve-wracking, endless second, then silently took three keys from his pocket and put them into my outstretched palm.

I clenched my gloved fingers tightly round them, and turned towards Tad. I still had to get him off this roof without the situation exploding. I daren't call him Thaddeus Wallam-Crane, or even Tad, and I didn't trust him not to open his big mouth and get us both killed.

"Leech, don't say a single word, just come with me."

I held my breath as Tad walked across to stand next to me, and Aaron grabbed his arm. It was only then, when the battle was already won, that Machico finally spoke.

"Donnell's daughter is right. Donnell was lost in emotion when he said those words. I doubt if even he knew precisely what he meant by them, but I'm very sure how he'd feel if he woke up tomorrow to find that we'd made him a murderer."

There was an instant of pure relief, before my mind started

frantically worrying about the next problem. Donnell had gone off to his room for a drink, and we all knew what that meant. Every month or two, Donnell would be hit by depression and try drowning his mood in alcohol. Everyone was used to him doing that, and to Kasim keeping order during his absence, but we didn't have Kasim any longer.

"Donnell won't appear again this evening, and we can't count on him being around tomorrow either," I said. "This is the first time he's been... absent since Kasim's death. Things will be tense without him, so we can't afford to have any rumours flying round about Tad."

"I hope everyone here knows better than to gossip about Resistance secrets," said Machico.

"There's no need to hide the fact that Donnell lost his temper with the off-world boy," I said. "In fact, it's best if everyone hears they had an argument. Nobody will find it at all surprising, and it will explain why Donnell has gone off to get drunk. The only thing we must keep secret is Tad's full name."

Machico nodded, and went over to hold the door to the stairs open. I went through first, with Tad and Aaron following me, and Machico bringing up the rear. As the door was closing behind us, there was an angry comment from Julien.

"So we're expected to take orders from a girl now?"

It was best to pretend I hadn't heard him, rather than go back on the roof for a second argument that I might lose. I headed to corridor B6, unlocked Tad's door, and opened it. Aaron thrust him inside, and I locked the door again.

There was a muffled sound from my right, which had to be Phoenix calling out from inside her room, but I didn't reply. The top floor rooms had been designed to hold confidential meetings, so they were solidly built and sound proofed. If I tried shouting a conversation to Phoenix through her door, I could attract unwanted attention.

Machico turned to Aaron. "Get back to the others and tell them to go downstairs now. The bell for dinner will be sounding soon. With Donnell missing, the rest of us need to be conspic-uously present."

I watched Aaron head off down the corridor, then leant my back against the wall opposite Tad's door. I felt terribly tired, so I let myself slide gradually down the wall until I was sitting on the floor. It was a moment before I realized Machico was still standing there watching me.

"Shouldn't you be going to check on Donnell?" I asked.

"And do what exactly?" asked Machico. "Tell him that getting drunk won't change history? Stand there while he yells insults and throws things at me?"

I frowned. "Does he get that bad? I know people keep out of his way when he's drinking, but..."

"Oh, Donnell throws things to vent his temper, but he's always careful to miss his target."

There were a couple of minutes of silence. I finally gave in and asked the question that was bothering me. "Why didn't you say something when Julien suggested killing Tad?"

Machico laughed. "Partly because I've a few grudges myself, and enjoyed watching the heir of Thaddeus Wallam-Crane sweat in fear for a few minutes. Mostly because it was a golden opportunity to see how our younger officers reacted in a real crisis."

"Oh." I thought that over.

"Donnell chose Aaron, Julien, and Luther to be officers because they're all the sons of people who played key roles in the early days of the Resistance. He had especially high hopes of Luther because he's Kasim's son."

Machico sighed. "You'd think that Donnell would have learned by now that there's no guarantee a son will be like his father."

I bit my lip. "Because of what happened with my brother?"

"Yes. The way those three behaved on the roof was deeply revealing. Julien let his temper rule him, and demonstrated he'd picked up far too many ideas from his friends in the other divisions. Aaron was reliable following your lead, but made no attempt to take the lead himself. Luther, chaos take the boy, just stood watching events in total silence."

Machico shrugged. "I'll have to discuss that with Donnell

when he sobers up. Are you planning to sit there on guard duty all night, Blaze?"

"No," I said. "I'm sitting here until ten minutes after the dinner bell rings to give everyone time to go downstairs. After that, I'm taking the off-worlders to my apartment and barricading us in there until the morning."

Machico smiled. "A good plan. I'd better get downstairs now. I'm sorry I can't bring any food up for you, but..."

I shook my head. "We can't risk causing trouble while Donnell is unavailable."

Machico walked off, and I sat there trying to think through the situation. My immediate priority was keeping the off-worlders alive until Donnell was sober and back in charge. I hoped that would be some time tomorrow. If Donnell reappeared and announced he wanted the off-worlders dead after all, then there was nothing I could do to save them, but I didn't believe Donnell would murder someone, even Thaddeus Wallam-Crane's heir, in cold blood. More importantly, Machico didn't believe he would, and Machico knew my father far better than I did.

The dinner bell sounded, and I got to my feet, looking warily first one way and then the other. Nobody should need to go along this corridor to reach the stairs. If anyone did appear, it probably meant they'd been following the same logic as me, but with the opposite motives. I was waiting for everyone to go downstairs so I could safely move the off-worlders. Someone else might be waiting for everyone to go downstairs so they could safely commit murder.

I heard distant voices and tensed, then saw Vijay and Weston hurry straight past the end of the corridor. Seemingly fully occupied bickering with each other, they didn't even turn their heads to look at me. Minutes ticked by without anyone else appearing, and I slowly relaxed. I told myself that I shouldn't have been so ridiculously nervous. Machico was bound to be keeping a close eye on Julien.

I fumbled in my pocket for the keys, went to Phoenix's door, unlocked it and shoved it open. I saw her standing at the far end of the room, her back to the wall, palms pressed against it as if she was trying to push her way through it.

"Blaze!" She hurried towards me. "What's happening? I heard Tad being locked in again earlier. Are we safe now?"

"No, you aren't," I said. "I have to move you somewhere else quickly. Grab your bedding and bring it with you."

I let Braden out next, repeating my instructions and getting a tense nod in response. Finally, I unlocked Tad's door, opened it, and instantly lifted my hand in a stop signal.

"Shut up! No talking, no questions, no arguments. We're moving. Bring your bedding."

Tad turned, grabbed everything from the bed, and came out into the corridor. I locked the three doors again to make it less obvious their inmates had gone, and led the heavily burdened off-worlders down the corridor.

We reached my apartment without meeting anyone. I unlocked the door, stepped inside, grabbed the smooth metal hilt of the sword that leant against the wall, and then waved the off-worlders in after me. They watched me shut the door behind them, lock it, and start methodically bolting it from top to bottom, slightly hampered by the sword in my right hand.

"Why are you brandishing a sword?" asked Phoenix, in a faint thread of a voice.

I slid the third bolt into place. "I keep a sword by my apartment door in case I open it and the wrong people are outside. I'm holding the sword now because the wrong people are inside with me."

"But I thought weapons weren't allowed here," said Phoenix.

I worked my way through the rest of the bolts before straightening up and answering her. "Weapons aren't allowed on common ground, but we're in Resistance territory here. Donnell doesn't like his people carrying weapons in the corridors, but I can have as many of them as I want in my own apartment."

Braden pulled a face at the door. "And as many bolts as you like too."

"I spent the first eleven years of my life living with London division," I said. "My mother had two bolts on the door to our rooms. One night when I was three years old, a drunken man kicked his way through our door. My mother stabbed him, and then Ice showed up and beat him to a pulp. After that, we had eight bolts on our door, and the next man to try breaking it down gave up in disgust."

I paused. "In theory, it's safe up here on the sixth floor, but one day the security system will break down like everything else round here. I sleep better with bolts on my door."

"What's been happening, Blaze?" asked Phoenix. "Why have you brought us to your own rooms?"

"Only Donnell, Machico, and I know that Tad is webbed, but all of Donnell's officers have heard that he's Thaddeus Wallam-Crane's heir. At least one of them wants to kill Tad, and preferably all three of you, so you have to stay in here tonight."

I gestured round the room. "You can sleep on the chairs or the floor in here. There are bottles of drinking water in the cupboard. The bathroom is through there." I pointed. "The other door is to my bedroom. If any of you try to set foot in there, I'll stick this sword through you."

"This is all my fault," said Tad. "You kept warning me, Phoenix, but I was too stupidly sure of myself to listen. I kept talking too much, I kept asking too many questions, and I gave myself away. I messed up and I'm really, really sorry."

"It's a bit late to be sorry." Phoenix turned back to me. "Where's Donnell and what's he doing about this? He won't let them kill us, will he?"

"Donnell's in his room getting drunk," I said.

Phoenix gave an urgent shake of her head. "Donnell can't do that. He mustn't do that. Without him this place will explode into open warfare. The things Natsumi told me when we were fishing..."

I wondered what Natsumi had told Phoenix. Stories about the battles at the barricades? Warning tales about the divisions? Blunt truths about just how much people here hated off-worlders? Whatever it was, Phoenix was terrified.

"Donnell will be sober again tomorrow, or the day after at the latest," I said. "Until then we..."

I was interrupted by a burst of hammering on the door.

CHAPTER SEVENTEEN

Everyone turned to look apprehensively at the door. I put my finger to my lips to warn the off-worlders to keep quiet.

"Blaze!" called a muffled voice from outside. "It's me, Luther."

I frowned. I wasn't sure if that was good news or bad. When we were up on the roof, Luther hadn't argued in favour of killing Tad, but he hadn't done a thing to prevent it either.

"You were quite impressive on the roof," Luther continued. "I suppose I could have done a bit more to help."

What did he mean by saying he could have done a bit more to help? He hadn't done anything at all!

"I was taken by surprise though," he added, "and wasn't sure what to do."

I could understand Luther being shocked to discover Tad was Thaddeus Wallam-Crane the Eighth. I'd been just as shocked myself, but I hadn't stood motionless while Julien tried to throw Tad off the roof, I'd stepped forward to stop him. Perhaps I was being unfair about this; I wasn't in a good mood at the moment, but...

"I hadn't understood why the deputy position was being kept vacant for so long," said Luther, "but given the way Donnell's been acting towards you these last few days, and the fact he called you his daughter... Well, now it's obvious that Donnell's planning to appoint your husband as the new deputy leader of the alliance."

I blinked.

Luther was still talking. "I've always liked you more than any of the other girls, Blaze. I know you're attracted to me too, so I can't see any reason why we shouldn't announce our engagement right away."

I'd had a colossal crush on Luther back when I was fifteen, and he'd totally ignored me. Now, at the very moment he'd proved he was handsome but completely useless in a crisis, he'd announced he wanted to marry me. Just to be extra annoying, he was making it clear that his change of heart was solely because he wanted to be deputy alliance leader. I felt like banging my head against the nearest wall.

"Blaze?" Luther called. "You can hear me, can't you?"

Oh yes, I could hear him, and so could an audience of three off-worlders. I had to shut Luther up and get rid of him.

"We can't discuss this now, Luther," I shouted through the door.

"I expect you're frightened after what happened on the roof."

I raised my eyes to the ceiling in despair. "Yes, I'm terrified. I daren't open my door tonight. I'll talk to you in the morning."

"I could come in and protect you. We should get a bit more... intimate now that we're getting married."

I cringed at the suggestion, and glanced at the off-worlders. Tad and Phoenix were looking embarrassed. Braden was giving a brilliant impersonation of someone who was so fascinated by the pattern of the carpet that he hadn't heard anything at all.

"I don't think that's a good idea," I said, in what I thought was an impressively calm voice. "Donnell might not like it."

"It's true that Donnell is fiercely opposed to underage marriages." Luther's voice sounded as if he was doing some hard thinking. "He's never seemed worried about casual relationships, at least not unless there was a big age gap involved, but he might have stricter views where his own daughter is concerned."

He paused for a moment. "We should probably wait until we're actually married before getting too friendly. Do you think Donnell will expect me to ask him for your hand in marriage?"

"We'd better discuss this in the morning," I said.

"All right," said Luther. "I'll see you in the morning then."

Everyone stayed warily silent for the next two minutes. Once I was convinced Luther had gone, I spoke myself. "Ask for my hand in marriage? What does that mean? Doesn't Luther want to marry the rest of me as well?"

"It's an archaic phrase that dates from long before Language became the common tongue of humanity," said Tad. "It originated in a time when a girl needed her father's permission to marry."

"Really? I suppose Luther must have learnt it from his father. Kasim picked up a lot of strange information on his undercover assignments, and I'm sure he mentioned pretending to be a history professor once. Mind you, Kasim also claimed he'd gone undercover as a horse, so..."

Tad interrupted me. "You mustn't marry Luther, Blaze. He doesn't care about you as a person. He's only interested in becoming deputy leader of the alliance."

"I'm fully aware of that," I said bitterly. "I'm a human being, not a stepping stone, and Luther can..."

I was interrupted by another burst of hammering on the door, more aggressive than last time. "Blaze! I know you've got those leeches in there. Open the door!"

"That's Julien," whispered Tad.

The door shook from what had to be a kick on the other side. "I told you to open the door!"

"From the way he's slurring his words," said Braden, "I think he's been drinking."

"The bolts must hold," muttered Phoenix, "but what about the hinges?"

"They're very solid hinges," I said.

There were several more kicks on the other side of the door. Silence obviously wasn't going to get rid of Julien, so I clenched my right hand tightly on the hilt of my sword and tried some yelling myself. "I'm not letting you in here, Julien. Go away!"

"If you don't open this door, Blaze, I'll set fire to it! You hear me? I'll pour this whiskey on it and set fire to it!"

Sick panic hit me. The whiskey from our stills had a high enough alcohol content to catch fire easily. The door was flexiplas reinforced with metal. I'd seen doors exactly like this burn in London. I knew how the smoke would drift under the door, the way the flexiplas would start to bubble, and then the flames...

"Blaze." Tad's voice was startlingly close to my ear. "What's wrong, Blaze?"

I realized I was sitting on the floor, hugging my knees close to me like a frightened child. I'd no recollection of getting there, of dropping the sword that was lying beside me, or of Tad kneeling beside me and putting his arms round me.

I made a whimpering noise. I felt too terrified to move, but if I stayed huddled here in the comforting warmth of Tad's arms, then all four of us could end up burning to death. I forced my hands to let go of my knees, picked up the sword from the floor, and lurched to my feet again.

There was the sound of smashing glass from outside. That had to be Julien breaking his whiskey bottle against the door.

"What happened to you just then?" asked Tad.

"I'm afraid of fire." I took a deep breath, and shouted through the door at the top of my voice. "Your threats don't scare me, Julien. If you start a fire, you'll set off the alarm and bring the whole Resistance up here."

"Most of them would agree that..."

Julien broke off his sentence. There was a thump against the door, followed by a yell of pain.

"Sorry about that," called Machico's voice. "I wanted to see what Julien would do, but I didn't expect him to go that far. Aaron and I will lock him up now."

I screamed back at him. "You mean you and Aaron were skulking nearby all the time, eavesdropping while Julien... Chaos take it, Machico!"

"Have a good night, Blaze," he said cheerfully.

"You can go pollute yourself!" I closed my eyes and slumped against the door.

There was a mere five seconds of peace before Tad spoke in a puzzled voice. "Was what you just said supposed to be rude?"

I opened my eyes again. "If I'd let Julien throw you off the roof, you'd still have been asking questions while plummeting towards the ground, wouldn't you? This world suffered centuries of people dumping every type of poison from toxic chemicals to radioactive waste, Tad, so yes, what I said was very rude."

"Machico said he'd lock up Julien," said Phoenix. "Does that mean we're safe now?"

I shrugged. "It means we're slightly safer."

"Why did Donnell have to go and get drunk?" she wailed.

"He's being totally irresponsible," said Braden.

I felt I should say something in Donnell's defence, but at this particular moment I agreed with both of them.

"Donnell isn't being irresponsible," said Tad.

I turned to stare at him in disbelief.

"He's just being human," continued Tad. "Imagine what Donnell's life has been like. The Earth data net is full of pictures, news reports, recordings of him singing. I can see tens of thousands of them whirling round me right now like a hurricane. The Loyalists found a boy of fourteen with an incredible voice that could break hearts, and they made him famous. Sean Donnelly sang the Loyalist songs for years, became the face and the voice of their cause, and when their politicians failed to save Earth, he took up the fight himself and started the Earth Resistance."

Tad's eyes moved oddly, seeming to focus on things that weren't there. I tried to imagine what he was seeing right now, a tornado of data snatched by his thoughts from the Earth data net.

"Donnell tried to save the Earth he loved from destruction," said Tad, "but he had no chance at all of success. It was already too late when he started the Earth Resistance. It was probably too late before he even sang his first song."

Tad shook his head in a mourning gesture. "So Donnell lost his battle, and he's been living in the ruins of the world he loved for decades. He's only human, so he cracks under the pressure sometimes, when things remind him of his lost cause, when insensitive off-worlders rub his nose in his failure."

His voice was shaking now. "I can't blame Donnell for that. He's handling his failure far better than I'll do in ten years' time, in twenty years' time..."

Tad's eyes stopped looking at invisible images and he turned to Phoenix. "When I was up on the roof arguing with Donnell, and he talked about watching people suffer for his actions and his choices and his failure, I suddenly realized something. Donnell's me, isn't he?"

He paused to tug at his hair with both hands. "Donnell was fourteen years old when the Loyalists recruited him to their cause. I was fourteen years old when my grandfather put me in charge of the interstellar portal research. Donnell had to save one world and failed. I have to save five hundred of them, and I'm going to fail too."

I'd no idea what Tad was talking about or... Yes, I did. On the roof, Tad had said something about problems on the new colony worlds, and the interstellar portals breaking down.

"You won't fail!" Phoenix grabbed Tad by the shoulders and shook him. "What happened to your insufferable ego? You're Thaddeus Wallam-Crane the Eighth. You're the last man in humanity to be webbed. You'll re-invent interstellar portal technology and stop civilization from falling!"

"My ego has been crumbling for years," said Tad. "My grandfather told everyone I was a genius, promised them I could build new interstellar portals, and then I couldn't. I was too young, too unprepared, and no genius at all, just a bright boy with the advantage of being webbed. The problem of the Rosetta component made my limitations painfully clear to everyone. I spent over a year working on that, but couldn't find a solution. No wonder the government of Adonis lost faith in me."

"You *have* found a solution to the problem of the Rosetta component," said Phoenix fiercely. "You came to Earth in search of answers, and you succeeded in finding them."

"I succeeded in getting all three of us stuck in New York," said Tad. "You saw the children dancing round the portals and singing rhymes to try to make the old magic work? That's what the future will be like after I've failed. Life here is what life on the other worlds will be like after I've failed. Donnell is the man I'll be after I've failed."

Phoenix shook him again. "You won't fail. The Adonis

politicians may not understand how much time it takes to recreate interstellar portal technology, but there's still Beta sector and the Fidelis Project."

I opened my mouth to ask what the Fidelis Project was, but closed it again without speaking. I had too much to cope with right here and now in New York. I couldn't worry about what was happening on colony worlds in distant star systems as well.

"I'm going to bed," I said instead. "Call me if there's any trouble."

I opened my bedroom door, and then paused in the doorway to frown at Phoenix. Tad and Braden seemed to be civilized, but I still felt guilty about leaving her to sleep in here with the two of them. Not guilty enough to risk letting an off-worlder into my bedroom, or hand her a sword, but...

"Phoenix, you may want to lock yourself in the bathroom."

I closed my bedroom door, and started sliding its array of eight bolts into place.

CHAPTER EIGHTEEN

My idea was to have an early night, and be up well before dawn next morning, but it was hard to get to sleep. I was tensely aware of the off-worlders in the next room, alert for any sound that might mean danger, and desperately hungry.

When I did finally get to sleep, I dreamt of London burning. I was eleven years old again, terrified by the blistering heat of the flames, the acrid stench of smoke, and the piercing sound of people screaming. My brother was tugging at my arm, shouting at me to run, but my legs wouldn't move.

I woke up covered in sweat despite the cold, and had a moment of confusion wondering why I was fully dressed, but then the memories of yesterday flooded back. Of course I was still fully dressed. With off-worlders in the next room, and Julien threatening to set fire to my door, I'd been reluctant to take off my boots let alone risk changing into night clothes.

I regularly had nightmares about the London firestorm, but the one last night had been far worse than usual. I blamed Julien for that. I glanced at the dawn sky outside my window, realized I'd woken up late rather than early, groaned, and rolled out of bed. I should be making plans, but my sluggish brain didn't want to think. I collected oddments of clean clothing, unbolted my bedroom door, and found all three off-worlders were on their feet and looking expectantly at me.

My apartment had been my safe refuge for six years. No one but myself had set foot in here since Hannah had been banned from the top floor of the Resistance wing. Now my head was full of horrendous dream images, and three invaders had taken possession of my living room.

I fought the urge to retreat back into my bedroom, picked my way between the heaps of cushions and bedding strewn across the floor, locked myself in the bathroom, and reluctantly stripped off my warm clothing to wash. The icy water shocked me fully awake, banishing the last aftermath of my dream.

I took my time getting dressed again, went out of the bathroom, and headed back through the bedding obstacle course to toss my spare clothing into my bedroom. I locked my bedroom door, then went over to the door to the corridor and listened for a moment. Everything seemed quiet outside.

I turned to speak to the waiting off-worlders. "I'm going downstairs to find out what's happening. You stay here. I'll lock the door when I'm outside, then you bolt it from this side, and you don't open it again for anyone other than me. Understand?"

Tad and Braden looked at Phoenix. The frustrated look on Tad's face gave me the impression that Phoenix had given him a forceful lecture about keeping quiet.

"We understand," said Phoenix.

I turned back to the door, but froze as I noticed something was missing from the shelf by the door. No, not missing, but moved, as if someone had picked it up to look at it and then put it back in the wrong place. It was a small picture of my father, dating from when he was nineteen. I'd had it since I was a child in London. Back then, I'd looked at it and been reassured by how much my famous father looked like Seamus. Now that resemblance was an uncomfortable reminder of my renegade brother, so I kept the picture here rather than in my bedroom, but I still didn't like the idea of other people touching it.

I carefully restored the picture to its rightful place at the centre of the shelf. "For chaos sake, tidy up in here," I snapped.

"We will," said Phoenix hastily.

I unbolted the door, opened it just wide enough to slip through the gap, closed it behind me, and locked it before looking round. There was a broken bottle on the corridor floor, a souvenir of Julien's visit last night, but nobody was in sight.

I kicked the pieces of bottle to the side of the corridor to be dealt with later, and headed to the roof for my morning routine of saluting the flag. The minute I opened the door to the outside world, I was hit by a torrent of freezing cold raindrops.

"Chaos!" I'd already decided it was too dangerous for the off-worlders to go hunting or fishing today, and I'd have to stay here and guard them myself since I didn't trust anyone else to do it, but I didn't want everyone else in the alliance stuck indoors because of the weather as well.

I spent a few minutes standing out in the rain, saluting the flag and studying the sky, then went back indoors and headed down to Reception. At first glance, everything seemed normal. Most people were sitting at tables and eating, but a few were still queuing up for their breakfast. I was looking round the room for Machico, when Hannah's voice came from beside me.

"Blaze! You promised to talk to me yesterday evening, but you went upstairs for your meeting with Donnell and never came back down again."

Hannah had obviously been lurking near the Resistance staircase, waiting for me to appear. I reluctantly turned to face her. "I'm sorry, but you must have heard there was trouble yesterday evening. I couldn't come downstairs even for five minutes to eat." I looked wistfully in the direction of the cooking fire.

Hannah completely ignored my heavy hint. "People are saying Donnell had an argument with the off-worlders and then went off and got drunk. Did you manage to talk to him about me before that?"

I couldn't keep dodging this issue any longer. "Yes, I've talked to Donnell about you."

"Is he going to make me a full member of the Resistance?" she asked eagerly. "Are we going fishing together again?"

"I'm sorry but the answer to both questions is no."

"But why?" demanded Hannah. "If you could get Donnell to invite Raeni into the Resistance, then you must be able to get him to confirm me as a full Resistance member as well."

I stared at her. "What makes you think I got Donnell to invite Raeni into the Resistance?"

"Everyone knows you arranged it. The women were all gossiping about it while we were fishing yesterday. Natsumi said that you'd told Donnell about Raeni's good character, and that was why he invited her to join the Resistance." Hannah shook her head. "Forget Raeni. What matters is that you can persuade Donnell to make me a full member of the Resistance at last."

"No, I can't," I said. "Donnell's memory of what happened six years ago is rather different to yours."

Hannah's expression changed to one of alarm. I'd already guessed she'd lied to me, but it was still depressing to see her guilt confirmed in her face. I could imagine how the lies had started. Hannah would have been trying to justify what she'd done, and bent the truth to make me sympathize with her. Once she'd started lying, she had to stick with her story, and after six years of repeating it, she probably half believed it herself.

"We need to have a long discussion about what really happened back then," I said, "but we can't do that in a rushed few minutes in a public place."

Hannah gave me a calculating look. "We could discuss it if we went fishing together."

"I won't be going fishing today. Donnell isn't available, and there are problems with the off-worlders, so I'll have to stay here to guard them."

"Chaos take the off-worlders." Hannah spat the words out in pure exasperation. "If you, Tad, and Phoenix aren't fishing today, then what happens to me?"

"I don't understand."

She gave an impatient sigh. "Natsumi and Himeko will go fishing together again, which leaves me without a partner. I could have gone fishing with Tindra, but Donnell's partnered her with your precious Raeni."

"Perhaps you could join up with one of the other fishing pairs?"

"If they won't even speak to me, they certainly won't let me join them as an unwanted and useless third person for a whole day."

I had to admit Hannah was right about that. "If someone in

the other divisions is short of a partner, then you could fish with them."

"Going fishing with someone from another division will make the Resistance even more unfriendly to me."

Hannah was right about that too. "Well, you'll have to help out in the vegetable garden today."

"Seriously? You want me to spend the day picking wintereat leaves like an infant?"

I was losing patience with Hannah. She knew I'd just found out she'd been lying to me for years, she must realize I'd be upset about that, but she was still making demands on me. "I'm sorry, but there's nothing I can do about this. I can't be in two places at once."

"And you'd rather be with the off-worlders than with me!"

Hannah turned and stalked off. I started moving after her, but stopped. There was no point in me chasing after Hannah. The only thing that would calm her down now was if I agreed to go fishing with her, and I couldn't do that. Hannah was only in danger of suffering an unpleasant day, while the off-worlders were in danger of suffering an unpleasant death.

"Blaze!" Luther came hurrying up.

I held back a groan. I'd been desperate to get rid of Luther as fast as possible last night, so I'd agreed we'd talk this morning, but I'd just had one difficult conversation and didn't need another.

"I just wanted to let you know that I'll be discussing our wedding plans with Donnell as soon as he's... back."

I opened my mouth to say that Luther should ask if I wanted to marry him before discussing our wedding plans, but he kept talking over the top of me.

"Machico says he needs to speak to you right away." He pointed at where Machico and the four division leaders were standing by the front glass wall looking out at the rain.

I saw Machico start walking towards me, and hurried to meet him halfway.

"Have you talked to Donnell?" I asked urgently.

"I called in on Donnell half an hour ago, and gave him a quick update on events," said Machico. "He's a little unwell at the moment, but he should be around this evening."

"What about Julien?"

"You don't have to worry about Julien causing you trouble today. I'm keeping him locked up until Donnell is able to talk to him."

I nodded. "I thought it would be a bad idea for Tad to go fishing today, but if Julien is locked up..."

Machico shook his head. "I don't think Luther, Aaron, Vijay or Weston are likely to try murdering anyone, but it's safest if you keep all three off-worlders here today. Once everyone else has gone hunting and fishing, you can bring them down to eat and help out with some jobs. I arranged for your evening meals from yesterday to be saved for you."

He paused before speaking in a louder voice. "The question is whether anyone goes hunting at all. We're just deciding that. Come and join us."

He headed back towards the group of division leaders. I hesitated, but Machico paused and beckoned to me, so I reluctantly went to join him.

"We were discussing whether the weather is good enough for us to hunt," said Machico. "What do you think, Blaze?"

Why the chaos was Machico dragging me into this? I didn't know what to say, and all my instincts were telling me I shouldn't be saying anything anyway, but then Major's voice called out.

"We've five men here. Why are we asking a woman's opinion?"

The words stung me into speech. "I've just been up on the roof. You can only see clouds from this side of the building, but there is clear sky moving towards us. The rain should be stopping any minute, and it will stay dry for at least two or three hours after that."

When I finished speaking, I looked at Machico, but he didn't say anything. I'd started to realize he used silence as a tactic, pushing other people to speak and tell him what they were thinking, but why would...?

"We should definitely go hunting then," said the youngest of the division leaders, Ghost of Brooklyn.

"I don't think it will stop raining at all," said the Manhattan leader, Wall.

There was a weirdly tense few seconds before Major spoke for Queens Island division. "I expect it will rain all day."

Everyone turned now and looked towards Ice, leader of London division. Again there was that strange tension in the air, and I noticed Marsha had moved away from her knife tables to watch what was happening here.

"The rain seems to be stopping," said Ice.

"We'll go hunting then," said Machico, in a brisk voice. "We're short of leaders today, so we'll be running with four larger than usual hunting groups."

There was the soft sigh of held breaths being released, and the group of men split up to rejoin their divisions. I had the feeling something important had just happened, but I'd no idea what the chaos it was.

Luther had been standing nearby, watching us with a confused frown on his face. Now he came hurrying up to Machico. "You can't do that!"

"What can't I do?" asked Machico.

"Send out only four hunting groups."

"We usually have six people leading hunting groups," said Machico. "Donnell is unavailable. Julien is locked up. If you subtract two from six, then you get four."

"Donnell delaying sending me out as a hunting group leader was just frustrating when we could send out six hunting parties anyway, but now..." Luther shook his head. "If you send out less than the usual number of hunting parties, and still don't let me lead, it will make everyone think I'm totally incompetent."

Machico looked at him doubtfully. "The division men are still mocking you."

"One of the reasons they're mocking me is because I'm not leading hunting groups," said Luther fiercely. "They won't stop until I prove myself."

"Chaos knows, I'm on your side over this," said Machico. "Donnell won't like it, but he'll have plenty of other things to worry about when he stops making love to his whiskey bottle, so I'll send you out if you want. You'll have to lead a bigger than usual group, but I'll make sure it doesn't include any of the main troublemakers. You're sure you want to do this?"

Luther nodded his head eagerly.

"Then you can take a group to that flooded recreation area," said Machico. "It attracts a lot of geese at this time of year, and we haven't hunted there since before the winter fever hit us. Your group will have every chance to bring home a lot of geese, and establish your credibility as a hunting group leader."

Luther threw a triumphant look in my direction before heading off, while Machico went over to the knife tables and spoke to Marsha. She picked up a belt from the Resistance table, and started dabbing paint on it with a small brush.

Did that belt belong to Julien? Was Marsha removing the white circle that marked him as an officer? For years, Donnell had had a deputy and six officers to help him. Losing his deputy had weakened his position, and if he'd lost another officer as well...

I waited until Marsha finished work and put the knife belt back on the table with the others, then hurried over to take a look. I spotted Julien's belt, with the bottle that was his personal tag and the white circle still next to it. He was still an officer then.

I was trying to work out if I was glad or sorry, when I saw my own belt. The leaping flames didn't have a blue planet next to them any longer, but a white circle.

My belt had the mark of an officer on it! Chaos weeping, what was happening here?

"Congratulations," said Machico's voice from behind me.

I whirled round to face him. "What have you done?"

"Not very much. There were some interesting developments last night. I just encouraged them a little."

"What developments?"

"After the scene on the roof, Julien went downstairs and drank an incredible amount of whiskey amazingly quickly. He then started shouting his head off about having to obey orders from a girl."

Machico smiled. "As you can imagine, everyone instantly realized Julien was talking about you. Donnell has been treating you like an officer lately, putting you in charge of the off-worlders.

People originally thought that was because he was too jealous to let another man near Phoenix, but there've been a host of rumours circulating about what happened with Raeni, and the outburst from Julien started everyone rethinking the whole situation."

"Was this just before Julien tried to set fire to my door?"

"That's right. All four division leaders cornered me, asking if Donnell was planning to give you the vacant officer position. I said that he'd been testing out the public reaction to you, and there'd be a formal vote on whether to confirm your appointment within the next day or two."

He laughed. "There was a sudden mass exodus as the division leaders took their members off to hold urgent conferences in their own areas. This morning, a random conversation about the weather somehow turned into a pre-emptive vote on accepting you as an officer."

"There was nothing random about that conversation," I said. "You set it up very carefully."

"Random or not, the important thing is you needed the support of two division leaders to confirm you as an officer. I knew Brooklyn division would vote in your favour. They've several extremely able women in their ranks, and they're eager for the alliance to set the precedent of female officers so they can have female alliance representatives. Manhattan and Queens Island were equally certain to vote against a woman. Everything depended on Ice's vote."

Machico gave me a jubilant look. "I hoped he'd count the fact you used to belong to London division in your favour, and judge you on your own actions rather than those of your brother, and he did. Donnell has been trying to get the divisions to accept a female officer for years, and we've finally made the breakthrough."

He obviously noticed my expression at this point, because his smile changed to a frown. "Is something wrong, Blaze?"

I looked at where Cage was standing among the Manhattan tables. Yesterday, Donnell had promised to save the vacant officer position for him. Now Cage had watched me take it for myself. It was hardly surprising that he was staring at me with implacable hatred.

CHAPTER NINETEEN

"Chaos weeping, Mac," said Donnell. "I turn my back for five minutes..."

"Eighteen hours," interjected Machico.

"Five minutes," repeated Donnell, "and you create havoc."

The three of us were in Donnell's rooms. Machico and Donnell were standing up facing each other, their voices hovering on the edge of outright shouting at each other. I was huddled in my usual chair again. There'd been a crisis every time I sat in this chair before, but today's crisis looked like being bigger than any of them.

"If you'd warned me about your agreement with Cage, I'd never have done it. Not that I did much anyway. I just..."

"No!" Donnell held up a hand to stop him. "Don't pretend this just happened naturally. We've worked together for decades. I know all your tactics, and exactly how good you are at manipulating people."

Machico sighed. "I didn't set up what happened on the roof, or Julien shouting his head off about Blaze giving him orders, but I admit I arranged for the vote this morning. I knew this was our best ever chance of getting a female officer. The divisions would see your daughter as being a special case, they'd already accepted her being in charge of the off-worlders, but there'd still be a huge risk in you proposing her as an officer. If the division leaders voted against it, you'd suffer an embarrassing public defeat."

He shrugged. "The big advantage of me doing this while you

were... indisposed, was that a failure wouldn't damage your position. You could genuinely claim complete ignorance of the whole thing. Say that you'd never intended Blaze to be a proper officer in the first place, and blame me for making a stupid mistake."

Machico paused for a second. "I suppose we could still try that. It would annoy the divisions who've voted in favour, but..."

"Cage wouldn't be satisfied with me saying it was a mistake," said Donnell. "He'd demand to marry Blaze and become my deputy right away."

A wave of panic hit me. Machico had sent everyone else off hunting and fishing, and then spent the whole morning getting Donnell in a fit state for conversation. While he was doing that, I'd taken the off-worlders downstairs so they could eat breakfast. I was used to just having soup for breakfast, but instead we'd had the meals saved from last night and kept hot in a stasis box. I'd forced myself to eat despite my stomach being in turmoil from stress, but now I wished I hadn't. I was in danger of being sick on Donnell's carpet.

"You can't make Cage deputy alliance leader," said Machico. "If you do, then Cage just has to find a discreet way to murder you, and he automatically inherits your position."

"I'm well aware of that," snapped Donnell, "but nothing less will placate him now. Cage is bound to think I planned this whole sequence of events. Deliberately lied to him to make him think he'd got what he wanted, hid in my room so it looked as if nothing could possibly happen, then caught him off guard by getting you to push the division leaders into a vote on Blaze becoming an officer. With all the divisions having private conferences in their own areas, he had no opportunity to talk to his puppets and tell them how to vote."

Donnell groaned. "I wanted to delay a confrontation with Cage until the spring, but there's no hope of that now. He'll be furious, and his logical next move is an alliance leadership challenge. Chaos knows, the strain of leading the alliance is wearing me out, I'd love to hand over the burden to any reasonable leader candidate, but can you imagine the sort of things Cage would do if he took power?"

I could imagine exactly the sort of things Cage would do if he took power. One of them would be to roast me on a spit over the cooking fire.

Donnell wandered over to kick the waste bin. "Cage winning a leadership challenge would be a nightmare, and him losing could be even worse. He's not the type of man to accept defeat quietly. He'd try to get his two division leader puppets fighting on his side, and once two of the divisions are fighting the other three, then we're all doomed. Whichever side wins the battle is just going to starve to death."

He turned to face us again. "I'll have to go for the simple, direct solution. Wait for the hunting groups to get back, and shoot Cage."

I gave him a shocked look.

"You can't do that, Sean," said Machico, in the pitying voice of someone addressing a particularly stupid child. "You know you haven't held the leadership of this alliance all these years because you wear a gun on your arm, but because people trust you to treat them fairly. The second you shoot Cage, all that trust would be destroyed."

"I've shot people before," said Donnell. "I know the last time was years ago, but..."

"That wasn't just years ago," interrupted Machico, "it was in a hostage situation where the lives of children were in danger. Everyone agreed your action was perfectly justified. Shooting Cage in cold blood, without a trial or obvious reason, would be completely different. People wouldn't know which of them you'd decide to shoot next. Even the Resistance's faith in you would be shaken. You'd instantly change from being a trusted leader to a feared dictator."

"I'd have to step down as alliance leader afterwards," said Donnell, "but it would be worth it."

Machico shook his head. "Even by your standards, that's a ridiculous plan."

Donnell glared at him. "It's not ridiculous."

"It's totally ridiculous," said Machico. "If Kasim was still here to take over as leader, then your idea might be worth considering as a last desperate resort, but Kasim's dead and you haven't got another established successor in place. The alliance would fall apart without you, and the fighting would start anyway."

"What else can I do?" demanded Donnell. "I can't call general justice against Cage without any evidence."

"You can talk to Major," said Machico. "We know Cage is blackmailing him. Whatever Cage is planning, he'll be counting on Major supporting him. You use your skill with words, and your famous charm, to talk Major into turning against his master."

"That's easier said than done," said Donnell. "Cage is holding a huge threat over Major's head."

"True, but remember that Major got his nickname because he likes barking orders at other people," said Machico. "He won't like having to obey orders from Cage. You promise Major you'll help keep his secret, flatter his ego, tell him how much you admire him."

"You want me to tell Major that I admire him?" Donnell repeated, in tones of revulsion.

"You say whatever it takes to make him change sides," said Machico.

"You'll be telling me to kiss him next!" Donnell's voice had got quieter during the discussion, but now he was shouting again. "I had this situation under control until you wrecked everything."

"That wasn't my fault," said Machico. "You should have told me you'd made that agreement with Cage."

"I was going to tell you everything last night, but then we found out about Tad being webbed and..." Donnell waved his arm in a despairing gesture. "You should have asked me before leaping into making Blaze an officer, but we both know why you didn't. You already knew I'd say no."

I suddenly swapped from panicking to being as angry as they were. I found myself on my feet, with furious words spilling out of my mouth. "Of course you'd say no. Sean Donnelly wouldn't want a mere useless girl as an officer!"

Donnell gave me a startled look. "I didn't mean it that way, Blaze."

"Didn't you?" I demanded. "When my brother arrived in New York, he was only sixteen. You were still happy to make him an officer straight away, trust him with all the Resistance secrets, even teach him how to hardwire portals."

There was a moment of sick silence before I plunged on, finally saying all the things I'd never said in six long years. "The minute he knew how to do that, Seamus portalled to America Off-world and made a deal with the off-worlders. He came back to plant a bomb in the main New York portal relay centre, and then portalled off again before it exploded and took out every portal in the city."

I had to pause an instant to breathe. "And after Seamus had gone, you ignored me! Chaos weeping, I did all I could to please you, but you ignored me for six years! I thought things were finally different now, that you actually had a genuine shred of feeling for me after all, but I was wrong. I've done everything you asked of me, even agreed to a fake engagement with a loathsome man who terrifies me, but it's still unthinkable that you'd make me an officer."

I glared at Donnell. "Why is that exactly? Because I'm a girl, because you think I'll turn traitor like my brother, or because you believe Ice is my real father, not you?"

I stopped talking, horrified. Oh chaos, oh chaos, oh chaos. What had I done? What had I said? This was just like the argument I'd had with Donnell after my brother left. I'd screamed words in anger then and never been able to take them back. Now I'd done it for the second time. I buried my face in my hands, trying to blot out the whole universe.

CHAPTER TWENTY

I stood there, my hands still covering my eyes, feeling the warm wetness of tears against my palms. I could hear Donnell speaking, his voice seeming oddly distant.

"Machico, did you set this up to happen? Because if you did then I swear I'll kill you."

"I didn't," said Machico. "I'd no idea that Blaze thought…"

"Get out of this room, Machico," said Donnell. "Get out right now!"

A ludicrous thought hit me. It was the chair that had made me say those things. It really was cursed.

I heard the door open and shut. Machico had gone, and I was alone with Donnell. There was a long silence before I took my hands away from my face and opened my eyes to look at him. I'd expected him to be angry, but instead he looked pale and uncertain.

I was suddenly, weirdly calm. Cage was going to try to take the alliance leadership. I'd just screamed in fury at Donnell and said the unsayable. I had nothing to lose now because things couldn't get any worse. "Please answer my questions."

Donnell ran his fingers through his hair and took a deep breath. "Seamus left me a note when he left. He hated me for abandoning him as a child. He blamed me for your mother dying in London. He said that it made sense not to risk her going through a hardwired portal when she was expecting a baby, but I could have brought all three of you to New York a few months later, and then she'd still be alive."

He sighed. "I understood why Seamus blamed me for your mother's death, because I felt the same way. Then I tried talking to you, and you screamed that you hated me even more than Seamus did, and I understood that as well. Ever since then, I've been so scared to talk to you about London, or your mother, or your brother, that I've hardly dared to speak to you at all."

Those words startled me. For six years, I'd been afraid to speak to Donnell. I'd never considered that he might be afraid to speak to me as well.

"I hoped you'd approach me," said Donnell. "Give me the chance to patch things up between us. When that didn't happen, I decided I'd have to do something myself, but kept losing my nerve and delaying things, making the same mistake with you as I did with your mother. Weeks turned into months and years, and the wall between us seemed to keep getting higher."

He paused. "Can we please sit down and try to talk calmly about this?"

I nodded, and we both sat down. I was struggling to absorb his words and deal with the whirlpool of emotions that came with them.

"Do you still hate me?" asked Donnell.

"No." I rubbed my moist eyes with the back of my hand. "I didn't hate you back then either. I know I shouted that during the argument after my brother left. I shouted lots of things, but I didn't mean any of them. I was so hurt and angry at everything that had happened. The firestorm had taken my mother and my home. My brother had gone off to a new world, and left me behind in an alien place full of strangers. I was overwhelmed by the situation, and I was hitting out blindly."

I made a sound that was a mixture of a groan and a sob. "I did exactly the same thing just now, didn't I? I was overwhelmed by worries about Cage, so I started hitting out at you."

"So what did you really feel about me when you arrived in New York?" asked Donnell. "What had your mother told you about me? My relationship with Keira was always explosive, especially the ending, so I expect it was bad."

"She never told me anything about you at all," I said. "She

told me stories about her childhood, and I think she discussed you with Seamus sometimes, but she never mentioned your name to me. Other people told me my father was the living legend the London Resistance talked about, the man who wrote *Anthem to Earth*. One of them gave me an old picture of you, so I knew you looked very like Seamus, but you seemed more like a myth than a real person."

"Ouch. That totally damns me as a father." Donnell shook his head. "There's one thing I've never understood. Why didn't Seamus take you with him? It was clear the two of you were devoted to each other. Seamus made a deal with the off-worlders who hated us for delaying the colonization of their worlds. He told them we were still able to use portals by hardwiring them, and agreed to plant a bomb in the New York portal relay centre in exchange for a place for himself on one of the new worlds. Why didn't he insist on a place for you as well?"

"He did insist on a place for me," I said, "but I refused to go with him."

Donnell gave me a startled look. "You knew what Seamus was going to do?"

"I didn't know anything about the bomb. After Seamus made his deal with the off-worlders, he came back to see me. He said that he hated New York, and he'd arranged for us to go to a new and better world called Pyrrhus. I should have realized the off-worlders wouldn't give us places on a new world without getting something in exchange, but I was too stupid to think of that. All I cared about was the fact that Seamus was leaving and I'd never see him again."

"But if Seamus asked you to go with him, why did you refuse?"

I stared at Donnell in disbelief. "Isn't it obvious? I'd have gone with Seamus to anywhere on this planet, but I'd never leave Earth."

There was a long pause before Donnell started talking again. "As for me thinking you're Ice's daughter, not mine... I don't know who suggested that to you, but they clearly never knew what things were like between me and Keira. Our relationship was a disaster, but a magnificent disaster, and there could never be anyone else for either of us. I've never doubted you were my daughter. Not for a second."

I sat in silence for a moment, letting the reassuringly fierce sincerity in his voice sink into my brain and chase away the doubts.

"Years ago, I settled on your eighteenth birthday as the time when I'd have to gamble everything and talk to you," continued Donnell. "I'd made every possible mistake with your brother. Trying to impose my dreams on him the second he arrived here. I never stopped to think that Seamus was only sixteen and devastated by grief for his mother."

He waved his hands. "I knew I mustn't repeat my mistakes with you, Blaze. I had to let you make your own free choice about your future, rather than force my own wishes on you. My plan was to talk to you on your eighteenth birthday, and offer you all the possible options for your future. If you wanted to become an officer, and possibly succeed me as alliance leader one day, then I'd support you. If you wanted to stay in the background as an ordinary member of the Resistance, I'd support that too. I discussed it with Machico and Kasim, and they agreed it was as close to sensible as any of my ideas ever were."

I gave a bewildered shake of my head. "We talked on my birthday, but you didn't say a word about me becoming an officer."

"I got as far as discussing having to find a new deputy leader, tried asking you what you thought about my newer officers, but you didn't give me a hint of whether you were interested in becoming one yourself or not."

I blinked. "You discussed your officers with me to see if I'd suggest becoming an officer myself?"

"Yes, but you said nothing. I decided not to push the issue further because the off-worlders' arrival had complicated the situation. I had a conversation with Machico the next morning, and told him that I was going to delay raising the officer issue with you until the spring."

He waved his hands. "When I said to Machico that he knew I'd say no to him trying to make you an officer, I was referring to that conversation. Machico knew that Kasim's death had weakened my position, the alliance was in a discontented mood, and appointing our first female officer was bound to stir up trouble. I still can't believe that Machico went ahead with it behind my back."

"You're right. It makes no sense at all. Can we get Machico back in here now, please? I'd like to ask him some questions."

Donnell gave me a puzzled look. "If that's what you want. I'll be back in a few minutes."

He stood up and headed out of the door. I was alone in Donnell's rooms for the first time ever. I stood up, looked down at my cursed chair, and across at the one Machico had been sitting in. This was totally childish, but...

The chairs were too heavy for me to lift, but I could drag them across the floor. It only took a minute to swap them over. I was innocently sitting in my new chair again well before Donnell and Machico came back into the room. When they arrived, I noticed Machico had a red swelling round his right eye, but that didn't stop him giving a confused look at his chair. I spoke before he had time to ask how it had magically changed colour.

"Why?"

"What?" Machico instantly responded.

"You carefully set things up for me to be Donnell's first female officer. I can understand you wanting me to lead the way for your wife and daughters to become officers, but why do it at a time like this instead of waiting until the spring? You must realize that getting me confirmed as an officer is only the first battle in what will be a long war. Those division men opposed to having female officers will grab every chance to stir up trouble and refuse to accept my orders, and there'll be huge arguments over whether I can use a bow or lead hunting groups."

Machico smiled. "You're much more intelligent than your father."

"Thank you," muttered Donnell.

Machico ignored him, keeping his eyes focused on me. "I've been watching you closely for years, Blaze. I thought you'd make a good officer, because you were intelligent, loyal, and caring, but

I didn't know if you had the extra qualities a future alliance leader would need."

He paused. "What happened on the roof was fascinating. Julien went rogue, Luther stood there in total indecision, while Aaron waited for someone else to take the lead. You were the one who took charge of the situation, Blaze, and you used exactly the right words. 'I won't let you shame us by murdering prisoners of war.'"

He shook his head. "I shouldn't have been so surprised by that. Donnell fought with his songs for years before he formed the Earth Resistance and started fighting with weapons instead. It makes sense that his daughter would know how to fight with words as well."

He shrugged. "That moment on the roof convinced me you'd make a far better leader than any one of Julien, Luther and Aaron, but you're right that this is a bad time to start arguments over having a female officer. I wouldn't have risked it if there wasn't another factor involved. We need you as an officer right now, Blaze, because you were in London when it burned."

His words scared me. "London burned six years ago. Why does that matter now?"

"London was abandoned in 2382," said Machico. "Nineteen years later, firestorms swept across it. New York was abandoned in 2389. The firestorms are due to hit here next summer."

I was on the edge of panic now. "What are you talking about?"

"Machico got unreasonably worried about the number of fires last summer," said Donnell. "I kept telling him it was natural to have more fires in such hot, dry weather, but he wouldn't listen."

"Those fires didn't happen just because of the hot summer," said Machico. "I've talked to the people who came from London. The number of small fires kept increasing for several years, and then there were a whole rash of them in the summer of 2400. Things went quiet again in the winter, but then the massive firestorm hit in the summer of 2401. The same pattern is happening here."

My head blurred, and images from six years ago mixed with

the present. Smoke and flames were all around me, but the burning buildings were those of New York not London.

"We must leave New York this spring," said Machico. "I've been warning Donnell about this for months now. He hasn't been taking the firestorm threat seriously, but I know you will, Blaze. We need you as an officer because you'll believe in the danger of the coming firestorm, and you'll find the words to convince Donnell and the others."

"I'm already convinced we have to leave New York," said Donnell. "With every year that passes, more of the old supplies go rotten from damp, or are gnawed by rats, and the falling stars become a bigger threat. I accept we have to start planning a move to a new location, probably somewhere upriver, but it won't be easy to find suitable buildings that are still in good repair and have solar power."

"It's not enough to start planning a move upriver that will happen in two or three or five years' time," said Machico. "We must move this spring, and we have to leave the New York area entirely. Ideally, we should head south for milder winters. Find somewhere deep in the countryside, with a lake or river so we can still hunt wildfowl and go fishing, but with fields where we can grow proper crops as well. Think how good it would be to have bread again."

He leaned forward eagerly. "The problem with trying to head south has always been that the fortifications round the citizens' settlements block off a whole swathe of countryside in that direction, and seven hundred people can't sneak alongside Fence without being noticed and attacked. Thaddeus Wallam-Crane the Eighth and his friends are the answer to that problem, because we can trade them in exchange for safe passage."

"Trading the off-worlders would be an advantage," said Donnell. "Getting safely round the edge of Fence would open up a lot of new options for us, but it doesn't outweigh the dangers of a hurried move. We should spend at least one year, and preferably two, preparing for this."

Machico thought New York was going to burn like London. Donnell didn't believe him. I had a gut feeling that Machico was right, but Donnell would think that was just because I was scared of fire. We needed hard evidence rather than opinions here, and we didn't have... Yes, we did!

"Other cities have been abandoned as long as London," I said. "Tad has access to all the information on the Earth data net. He can tell us if those other cities went up in flames."

Donnell and Machico exchanged glances. "Get Tad," said Donnell. "Don't tell him what it's about though. I don't want him making up lies about fires to encourage us to rush him over to Fence."

I hurried off to fetch Tad. I'd left the off-worlders locked in my rooms, and they'd bolted the door, so I had to wait for them to open it. I'd been too distracted to pay attention to the room when I took them down to breakfast, but now I noticed they'd folded up their bedding, and stacked it in obsessively neat piles in a corner of the room.

Phoenix saw me looking at the bedding. "We tidied up," she said nervously.

"Thank you," I said. "I'm sorry I snapped at you about that earlier. I'm not used to sharing my rooms with other people."

"Tad has told us all about what happened on the roof," said Braden. "We understand you were taking a huge risk sheltering us in your own rooms. We're very grateful to you."

"Donnell's back in charge now," I said. "He wants to talk to Tad."

The three off-worlders exchanged panicky looks. "Is he going to throw me off the roof?" asked Tad.

"No, nothing like that," I said. "He just wants you to give him some information on what's been happening over the last few years."

"Just answer his questions, Tad," said Phoenix. "Don't say anything that gets us into more trouble."

"I'll try not to," said Tad.

Two minutes later we were in Donnell's rooms. Donnell dragged another chair into the circle. Tad sat down, but frowned at Machico.

"What happened to your face?" he asked.

"You mean the eye?" Machico pointed at it. "Donnell punched me."

Tad looked stunned. "But... Why?"

"I was making the point that he should consult me before taking drastic actions," said Donnell, "especially when those actions put my daughter in danger."

"Please don't look so shocked, Tad," said Machico, in a cheerful voice. "You know the Earth Resistance was a group of freedom fighters prepared to use violence to promote their cause. The first thing you saw when you arrived was Donnell punching someone in one of the other divisions. You shouldn't be surprised that we throw the odd punch at each other as well."

"We've more urgent things to discuss than my leadership style," said Donnell. "Tad, I want to know what's been happening in the other cities."

Tad's eyes started focusing on invisible objects. "They've all been abandoned except for Eden in Earth Africa. There are some off-world working parties there, maintaining the Earth data net and the..."

"Eden was the last city built on Earth," interrupted Donnell. "One of your family's pet projects before the invention of interstellar portals. I'm not interested in Eden. I'm interested in what happened to the older cities after the last of the citizens left."

"There's not much information," said Tad. "I'm seeing a couple of reports of gangs of criminals leaving cities and trying to take over citizens' settlements. There've been a few museum retrieval missions. One to Paris Coeur last year, trying to track down some missing paintings."

Donnell gave Machico a pointed look. "Paris Coeur was abandoned about the same time as London, wasn't it?"

"Yes," said Tad. "You already know London burned in 2401. There are reports from nearby settlements about the fire. The images look utterly terrifying. There's one of the night sky lit up with... No, sorry, that's not London. The image came up because of a link about fires. It's actually an image of a massive fire in Lagos, Earth Africa, in 2400."

"We had to pull our people out of Lagos because of flooding

in 2380," said Machico. "There were still some citizens there then. When was it finally abandoned?"

"2381," said Tad.

"The year before London was abandoned," said Machico, in a pointed voice.

Donnell ignored him. "Anything about Dublin?"

"There's a settlement very close to Dublin. They don't report any problems with criminals. They send parties into the city for supplies sometimes."

Donnell laughed. "So the respectable citizens go scavenging too these days."

"What about New Tokyo?" asked Machico.

"Lots of fire images again. There are lots of reports of minor fires in abandoned cities, but only four with the really huge ones. London, New Tokyo, Lagos, Sydney."

Donnell stood up. "Those names... In 2375, the Earth Resistance attempted to occupy all five of the United Earth Regional Parliament complexes. Five buildings in five cities on five continents. London, New Tokyo, Lagos, Sydney, New York. You're telling me that all four of the other cities have gone up in firestorms? No other cities, just those four?"

"Yes," said Tad. "Let me..."

Machico was on his feet now too. "Is it always the same gap in time? Nineteen years after the city was abandoned?"

"Minimum elapsed time between city being abandoned and firestorm is seventeen years eleven months. Maximum is twenty years two months." Tad snapped out the words. "Please let me try to work out why it's just those cities."

There was grim silence for the next few minutes. New York was abandoned the summer before I was born. We were already in the danger period.

"It has to be the power grid," said Tad at last. "The United Earth Regional Parliament complexes included a lot of power and water conservation features, and the grid networks of their cities were upgraded to use a new, more efficient design as well. It had a power reservoir system to average out demand. That stored excess power in buffers to..."

He tugged at his hair. "I don't know how to explain this simply."

"Power reservoir," I repeated. "We have a water tank on the roof. When we use water, the level goes down. When it rains, the level goes up again."

"Yes," said Tad. "It's not quite the same thing, but your parallel works. When people abandoned the city, the authorities shut down the water supply and the power grid. Nobody was using power any longer, but it was still arriving in the power reservoir system."

Machico frowned. "How? Where was this power coming from? Nobody would send power into an empty city."

"There'd be no power coming in from outside the city," said Tad, "but there'd be solar power from a lot of the buildings like this one."

"If we don't use any water," I said, "and it keeps raining, our water tank doesn't just overflow, the spare water starts going down a pipe to the drains."

Tad's eyes did their rapid focusing thing again. "The power reservoir system had an overflow safety system too. I think what happened in those four cities was that the overflow system failed. The equivalent thing with your water tank would be the overflow pipe getting blocked so there's a flood."

"There were warning signs in London," said Machico. "The number of random fires increased."

"That would make sense," said Tad. "The power overflow system has lots of sections. If one of those breaks down, there's likely to be a power surge that starts a minor fire. Failed sections will automatically be cut out of the system, the power will be sent elsewhere, but that puts the remaining sections under more pressure. That pressure gradually builds as more sections fail until you hit catastrophic failure point. All the remaining sections break at once and..."

"And you get a firestorm," said Donnell harshly. "How long have we got until it happens here?"

"The amount of solar power being fed into the power reservoir peaks in the summer months," said Tad. "That's the main danger period. The firestorms in the other four cities all started during the summer weather on their continent."

Donnell glanced at Machico. "You're right, Mac. The fires last summer were a warning sign that the power overflow system was nearing the point of catastrophic failure. We have to leave New York this spring."

I didn't hear Machico's reply. I was lost in my memories of the London firestorm. That nightmare was going to happen again. New York was going to burn!

CHAPTER TWENTY-ONE

Ten minutes later, Donnell was pacing round the room, while the rest of us sat watching him. "It's taken Mac six months to convince me the firestorm threat is real. How the chaos can I persuade everyone else to take it seriously enough to abandon their homes and possessions and leave New York this spring? I daren't even tell them Tad is webbed. If I do, then someone is bound to try digging the web out of his head in the vain hope of using it themselves."

A gory image of that appeared in my mind and I felt sick. Tad looked understandably nauseous too.

"The Resistance won't need convincing to follow you out of New York. They'd follow you anywhere," said Machico.

"I know that," said Donnell. "Chaos knows why the Resistance members are still so loyal to me given the way I've failed them in the past, but they are. The other divisions are an entirely different matter though."

Machico gave a dismissive shrug of his shoulders. "It's not your fault if the other divisions choose to stay in New York."

Donnell glared at him. "I'm not just the leader of the Resistance, Mac, but the leader of the whole alliance as well. Do you expect me to light-heartedly walk away in the spring and leave all the division men, women and children to burn to death?"

I felt as angry as Donnell. I knew many of the division people, especially the children, as well as I knew the Resistance members. I'd taught school classes, helped with the crèche, and done some nursing. It was horrific to think of leaving the babies and children I'd taught, cuddled, and nursed through the winter fever to die in a firestorm.

Machico lifted his hands in surrender. "I'm sorry if I seem callous about what happens to the other divisions, but try to understand my viewpoint, Sean. I've spent six months picturing a nightmare future. Even if I could persuade Natsumi and my daughters to leave New York with me, what chance would we have of surviving on our own? Right now I can't think of anything other than the fact my family and the rest of the Resistance people may survive this."

"Yes, from your viewpoint things have improved," said Donnell, in a calmer voice, "but I'm the one having nightmares now. Think about the fact there can't be any last minute escapes from a New York firestorm like there were in London, because we have no working portals here. Then remember that it's my fault that those portals aren't working."

"It was Seamus who killed the portals, not you," said Machico. "You misjudged the boy, but so did the rest of us. You have to focus your mind on planning for the future rather than brooding on past mistakes, Sean, or we're all doomed."

"You're right," said Donnell. "We'll have to keep the firestorm threat secret until we've got a proper plan worked out. I can't just tell people we have to leave New York. I need to offer them the prospect of a new and better home."

He flopped down into his chair. "I think we should tentatively plan on leaving at the start of April. We'll head for the southern tip of Fence, and hopefully trade in Tad, Phoenix and Braden in exchange for safe passage between their defences and the coast. We might even manage to beg some vegetable seeds and livestock as well."

He turned to look at Tad. "Do you think the fabulously wealthy and influential Thaddeus Wallam-Crane the Eighth is worth a few chickens?"

"I'm sure my grandfather would be happy to pay for some chickens to get me back," said Tad.

"Once Fence is safely behind us, we'll keep heading south

until we find somewhere that looks like it could make a good new home," said Donnell. "Travelling will be painfully slow. All the old land routes have been abandoned for nearly two centuries, so chaos knows what obstacles we'll hit on our way."

"Fence blocks off Pennsylvania," muttered Tad, "and Virginia would be too far on foot."

"Those are the old state names, aren't they?" said Donnell. "I've heard of them, but I don't know where they are. I'm proud to think of myself as Irish, the Irish have a grand tradition of rebellion, but the truth is I've spent most of my life in London and New York. You'd think I'd know lots of details about the area around this city, but I don't. When I was a boy, everywhere was just one step away through a portal. It never occurred to me to wonder how far away places were, or in what direction. I wouldn't even have been aware of what continent I was on, if it wasn't for the different time zones and having to go to a Transit area to portal between continents."

He sighed. "Now the portals are all dead, and we'll have to do our travelling the hard way, dragging carts loaded with supplies and babies."

"I really don't want to ask difficult or annoying questions," said Tad, "but have you considered that the portals here only stopped working because the New York portal relay centre broke down?"

"The New York portal relay centre didn't break down, Tad," said Donnell. "It was blown up with a bomb."

"It was?" Tad seemed startled. "You mentioned an explosion, but I thought that was an accident. Something like a power storage unit overloading. I can see plenty of records about the New York portal relay centre breaking down, but no mention of a bombing."

He shook his head. "Well, whatever happened to it, my point is that there are still plenty of working portals outside the New York area."

"If you're talking about the ones in the citizens' settlements behind Fence, then they might as well be on the moon," said Donnell. "We may be able to trade you for the privilege of walking peacefully along the outside of Fence, but there's no way in chaos that the citizens will let us go inside and use their portals. They won't have forgotten the citizens who died defending the New York barricades, or that some of our division members were the ones who killed them."

"I'm sure that's perfectly true," said Tad, in a cautious voice, "but I'm actually thinking of the portals in Philadelphia. There's another portal relay centre there, and it's definitely still working because the portals in the settlements behind Fence are linked into it."

"You mean we could go to Philadelphia and hardwire a portal there to travel wherever we wanted?" asked Donnell.

Tad nodded. "You wouldn't have to risk hardwiring the portals though. I've cancelled the security block that was stopping you from using them."

I stared at him. Donnell stared at him. Even Machico looked stunned.

"How did you cancel the security block?" asked Machico.

"I used the old Wallam-Crane family security codes to access the global portal control systems," said Tad.

Donnell seemed to be struggling to speak. "Can you get the wall vids working again as well?"

"I've already tried and failed," said Tad. "A major solar storm in 2389 caused a failure of the technical area of the Earth data net across most of Earth Europe and Earth America. The repair work afterwards was patchy and there are still big areas without coverage, particularly abandoned city areas like this."

"Fixing them could be a bad idea anyway," said Donnell. "We need people working, not sitting staring at wall vids all day. The important thing is that we may not have to walk all the way to our new home, just to Philadelphia."

He paused for a moment, before asking in an embarrassed voice. "Where is Philadelphia anyway?"

"It's south-west of here," said Tad. "I'm looking at old maps now. I wish I could show them to you."

Donnell stood up, went over to a cupboard, came back again, and tossed some paper and a couple of pencils onto the table. "Draw us a map."

Tad picked up a pencil and studied the pointed end. "Pencils. How... historic. I see you've got genuine paper too."

"This was a United Earth government building," said Machico. "Certain things needed to be physically written or printed on paper for legal reasons, so we have huge amounts of the stuff. We also have a fair number of pencils, and about a million pens that no longer work because the ink dried up years ago."

Tad started making a clumsy drawing. "This line is the coast. New York is this big blob here, and Philadelphia is this smaller blob inland to the south-west of us."

He added a series of small crosses. "When the citizens abandoned New York, they moved southwest and settled in a string of smaller places running from Old Bridge Township all the way to Washington Township. The defences around that area are what you call Fence."

He paused and frowned at his piece of paper. "Once you're past the southern tip of Fence, you'll need to find the remains of a road leading to the old New Jersey Turnpike. That should take you close enough to Philadelphia to find working portals."

"There aren't any major rivers blocking that route, are there?" I asked anxiously. "Given how long the roads have been abandoned, we can't depend on the bridges still being usable."

"You'd be staying south of the big Delaware river, but you might have to cross smaller creeks," said Tad.

"Is there anywhere closer than Philadelphia that might have working portals?" asked Donnell.

"I'll check." Tad was silent for two minutes before speaking again. "Saratoga Springs is a lot further away than Philadelphia, but it might be possible to reach it by taking boats up the Hudson River."

Donnell shook his head. "The Hudson River is blocked at Bear Mountain."

"In that case, Philadelphia is your best option. The portal relay centre in New York covered a huge area to the north and east. When it stopped working, the settlements behind Fence had huge problems, because it took months to link their portals to the Philadelphia portal relay centre."

He paused before continuing in a puzzled voice. "I still can't find any mention of the New York portal relay centre being bombed."

Donnell and Machico exchanged glances. "We knew it was off-worlders, not Earth citizens, who gave Seamus the bomb," said Machico, "but I thought the citizens would at least know about it."

"I suppose we should be grateful my son chose to plant that bomb in the New York portal relay centre instead of in this building." Donnell's voice had a harsh note to it. "I expect that was because of Blaze. I'm sure Seamus would have loved to kill me, he blamed me for his mother dying when London burned, but he wouldn't harm his little sister."

Tad's eyes widened, and he glanced at me. I gave him a warning look, and was relieved when he didn't say a word.

"The off-worlders promised my son a place on a new world in exchange for betraying us," said Donnell. "Do you know if they kept their side of the deal? Is there any record of a Seamus Donnelly leaving Earth in 2401?"

There was what seemed like a long silence before Tad answered. "No record of any deal with Seamus Donnelly. No Seamus Donnelly on the America Off-world departures listing for 2401 or 2402."

I clenched my hands together. The off-worlders had lied to Seamus. He'd betrayed us for nothing. What had happened to him after that? Was he still alive in some civilian settlement somewhere, or was he dead? I shouldn't care. I didn't care. I...

"I've found him now," said Tad. "A Seamus Blaze leaving for Pyrrhus in Beta sector. Half the standard departure records for him are missing. It looks like someone sneaked him through illegally."

Seamus Blaze! My brother had taken my name. Chaos, I could see he wouldn't want to keep using the name Donnelly, but why did he have to drag me into his treachery?

"So Seamus is living on Pyrrhus in Beta sector now," muttered Donnell.

There was a long silence. I disentangled my clenched hands,

and examined the little dents left by my own nails pressing into the skin.

Donnell finally spoke again. "Let's forget the past and concentrate on the present. If we can reach working portals, then we can pick a new home anywhere in the Americas. Tad, will you be able to find out the portal codes for places, and check there aren't people already living there? It would be a very bad idea for us to portal into the middle of an existing citizen settlement."

"That's easy," said Tad. "I can use the portal network diagnostic systems to check when a portal was last used. I can also remotely activate a portal to check it's still working. I'm currently checking a random sample of portals in Philadelphia. So far none of them have been activated for over a decade, but about half of them are still functioning."

Donnell gave a slight shake of his head, as if he couldn't believe that. I felt the same way. Tad was standing here in this room with us, but he was remotely activating portals in another city. However impossible that seemed, it had to be true. Tad had no reason to lie about it. In fact, if he'd had any sense at all he'd never have mentioned it. I could understand why Phoenix had been so worried about what Tad might say to us.

The ritual chant from the children's portal game ran through my mind. "Dial it! Dial it! Portal, dial it! We're ordering you by Newton. We're commanding you by Einstein. We're conjuring you by Thaddeus Wallam-Crane!"

I had a mad urge to say it aloud. If Tad could control portals with his thoughts, the children's idea that the name Thaddeus Wallam-Crane had magic powers over portals wasn't totally silly after all.

"Right," said Donnell, in a bemused voice. "Well, we have a rough plan now, but we need to work out a lot more details before I announce the threat of a firestorm to the alliance. Until then, nobody says a word about it to anyone outside this room." He turned to look pointedly at Tad. "That includes you, Thaddeus Wallam-Crane!"

"Can't I even tell Phoenix and Braden about it?" asked Tad. "They're totally trustworthy."

"They're also totally terrified already," I said. "I don't think it would help them to learn that New York is likely to burst into flames at any moment."

Tad sighed. "You're probably right."

Donnell turned to me. "Blaze, I'm sending you and Tad away on a supply run for the next few days."

"What?" I stared at him. "I can't go on a supply run when Cage is on the brink of starting a war."

"A war?" Tad gave me a shocked look. "What do you mean?"

"Quiet!" Donnell snapped the word at him before turning his attention back to me. "Yes, Cage is on the brink of starting a war, and that's exactly why you have to go on a supply run, Blaze. Cage has a calculating nature, and has always prepared his bids for power very carefully. I'm hoping he'll take at least a few days to prepare his challenge for the alliance leadership, so I have time to talk Major into joining our side, but everything depends on Cage keeping his temper under control."

Donnell pulled a face. "If you stay here, then the mere sight of you will bring Cage to fury point. Brooklyn will be celebrating having a female officer at last, and they just have to make one badly timed, gloating remark about it, to trigger Cage into taking instant violent action. Even if that didn't happen, Major is fervently opposed to having female officers, so he'll be nearly as angry about your appointment as Cage. I'll stand a much better chance of getting Major to join our side if you're away on a supply run."

I frowned as I thought that over. I didn't want to run away like a coward, but Donnell was right. My presence here would just add to his problems.

"You can't go alone," said Donnell, "and taking Tad with you will give the rest of my officers time to get over any lingering urges to throw him off the roof."

I reluctantly nodded. "All right, we'll go."

"I'm not sending you off on foot in midwinter," said Donnell, "so you'll have to take a boat somewhere. I'm not sure what supplies to send you after, but..."

"Medicine," interrupted Tad, in an eager voice. "You said that you ran out of medicine years ago."

"We'd dearly love to have more medicine," said Donnell, "but the citizens took almost all the medical supplies with them when they left New York. We visited all the hospitals long ago, scavenging every oddment they'd left behind."

"Let me check the Earth data net." Tad was silent for several minutes. "The citizens might not have known about Military storage facilities. There's one on the riverbank between Yonkers and the Kerr Monument at Tarrytown. That includes a big medical area, and if the stock records are accurate, then there was still a lot of medicine there when it was abandoned. Everything was stored in stasis cabinets so should still be in good condition."

"It sounds worth a look," said Donnell. "If you're lucky enough to find any medicines, remember we'll need full instructions on how to use them."

"If they don't have detailed labels, I can look up the information on the Earth data net," said Tad.

"You can also use the Earth data net to do some research on possible new homes for us." Donnell turned to me. "Blaze, I think you've been upriver as far as Tarrytown twice already."

"Three times," I said.

"Then you know what to do," said Donnell. "In other circumstances, I'd ask you to send up a green flare at sunset and sunrise each day, so we know you're all right, but it might be better not to advertise your location to Cage. If you have any problems, send up a distress flare at once."

"Yes."

"You, Tad, Phoenix and Braden can have an early dinner before Cage gets back from hunting. After that, you have to come back up to the sixth floor and stay here. Machico and I will fetch everything you need for your trip and store it by the back door of the Resistance wing."

He paused. "You and Tad can get up before dawn tomorrow, take your supplies, and sneak away at first light. You should be far upriver before Cage finds out that you're gone. When you come back, make sure you arrive while the hunting parties are out."

Donnell paused for a second. "Tad, can you please wait outside while I have a quick word with Blaze?"

Tad obediently headed out into the corridor. Donnell waited for him to close the door behind him before speaking.

"Do you have any worries about going off alone with that boy, Blaze?"

I gave a startled laugh. "Tad's not dangerous."

"Personally, I think someone who can remotely activate any portal on Earth isn't just dangerous but absolutely terrifying," said Machico.

"Yes, that was a stunning revelation," said Donnell. "I don't think it changes anything though. We know Tad can't do any magic tricks with the dead portals in New York. If he could, he'd have portalled out of New York after damaging his aircraft instead of coming to ask us for help. Whether he's here or upriver with Blaze, Tad's effectively still our prisoner."

"There's the one extra detail that Blaze would make a perfect hostage," said Machico drily. "I know Tad's being almost embarrassingly helpful, but that could be an act to fool us into trusting him."

"Perhaps I should send Luther or Aaron with them," said Donnell.

"You need Luther and Aaron here," I said. "Besides, we don't want anyone else discovering Tad is webbed. Anyone who comes with us would be bound to work that out, because Tad will be constantly looking up information about medicines and new homes on the Earth data net."

"That's true," said Donnell.

"I don't think Tad's acting a part," I said. "I think he's genuinely eager to help us. It's not as if he's capable of taking me hostage anyway. A five-year-old child could beat him in a fight."

Donnell nodded acceptance, and I went out of the room to collect Tad.

CHAPTER TWENTY-TWO

My sleep that night was haunted by firestorm nightmares again, but this time it was New York burning rather than London, and I kept waking up, gasping in terror. I got into a routine after a while. I'd wake in panic, peer out of my window to check New York was still peacefully dark rather than glowing red with flames, and then go back to sleep for another half an hour.

My interrupted night meant I was awake in plenty of time to help move the off-worlders' belongings back to their own rooms before we left. Phoenix and Braden seemed deeply relieved by the news that I was taking Tad away on a supply run for a few days. They obviously thought he'd be a lot safer at a distance from Donnell, so he couldn't say anything to annoy him. Quite possibly, they thought they'd be safer too.

When Tad and I headed downstairs, we found Machico waiting by the back door to the Resistance wing. He gestured at the two carts by his side.

"We've got you all the standard items like thermal mattresses, sleeping bags, and flashlights. The small flexiplas box holds a list of the most common injuries and illnesses we have to deal with, as well as plenty of spare paper and pencils for Tad to write notes about any medicines you find. The active stasis boxes at the bottom hold your meals and the signal flares."

"I see." I'd only expected us to be taking one cart to the boathouse, but there was a whole pile of inactive stasis boxes as well as the other supplies. Of course we'd need those if we were lucky enough to find medicines.

"I've given you a lot of useful information," said Tad. "Can I ask one question in return?"

"That rather depends what it is," said Machico.

"When Donnell went to London to negotiate an alliance, he ended up marrying one of the London division members. Was that marriage part of the alliance negotiations? A marriage of convenience?"

"Believe me," said Machico, "there was nothing convenient about Donnell and Keira falling for each other. Most of the Resistance had been trying to catch Donnell's attention for years without the slightest success. We'd all decided he was only attracted to planets, preferably blue and white ones, when Donnell portalled into London, took one look at Keira, threw himself on his knees and started kissing her feet."

Machico laughed. "I'm not exaggerating what happened back then. I portalled to London with Donnell, and that's literally what he did. For the next few days, I was convinced that something had gone wrong with our portal transmission, and Donnell's brain had been scrambled in transit."

"So it wasn't arranged, Donnell and Keira just got together." Tad frowned, as if he was trying to work something out.

"Those two didn't just get together. They collided, and everyone around them was caught in the explosion. It added a host of extra problems to the alliance negotiations. Keira had been about to marry someone else, so the man was naturally furious. Ice thought Donnell was just playing games with Keira, planning to have a few days' casual entertainment before dumping her and going back to New York. The Resistance were all in shock, and..."

Machico broke off because the back door had opened and Donnell was coming in. He stopped when he saw us, swung a bag off his shoulder, opened it, and handed Tad and me our knife belts.

"Marsha wishes you a successful trip." He hesitated, and then stepped forward to give me a nervous, split-second embrace.

"Be careful," he said, as he released me.

"I will."

Donnell held the door open while Tad and I pushed the carts through it. I shivered as the bitter cold dawn air hit us, but kept moving along the path. Once we'd gone round the corner of the Parliament House, I spoke in a frosty voice.

"If you insist on asking nosy questions about my parents, I'd rather you asked me than other people."

"I would have asked you," said Tad, "but you obviously weren't there when they first met. Is it hurting your arm to push that cart?"

His concern placated me. "No. Your cart has all the heavier items like water bottles. Mine is mostly loaded with empty stasis boxes, and they're very light."

"Please tell me if you need help."

"I will, but the path to the boathouse is in better condition than most, so I should be able to manage. We'll need to stop in a minute to collect something from the small concraz building ahead of us."

"What is that place?" asked Tad.

"It used to be a security checkpoint, but we keep power storage units in it. They have to be kept somewhere well away from the main buildings in case one of them fails from old age and explodes."

"That's nice," said Tad, in a strained voice. "Why do we want an exploding power storage unit?"

"So we can recharge our boat's power when the built in battery goes flat."

We reached the building, and I left my cart and went inside. There were a dozen or so power storage units on the bare concraz floor. I used a flashlight to examine my chosen power unit closely before lugging it outside.

"If there are dark spots on the grey flexiplas casing, then the power unit is going bad," I said. "This one looks safe."

"I'd better put it on my cart." Tad shoved the sleeping bags and mattresses aside to make space.

"Wedge it between the mattresses to stop it from being jolted around."

Tad frowned. "I thought you said it was safe."

"I said it looked safe, but it's still a good idea to be careful."

Tad packed the power unit in his cart, and we started moving again. "Machico said your mother's name was Keira."

"Yes."

"So your mother used her real name. I've noticed the Resistance use real names, but a lot of the other division members use nicknames."

"When my mother first joined the London division, people called her Blaze because she'd been convicted of arson, but Ice kept using her real name. Eventually, everyone was calling her Keira again."

"So you were named Blaze after your mother." Tad laughed. "I wasn't sure if it was your real name or a nickname, but actually it's both."

I nodded.

"How did your mother end up in London division?"

I wasn't sure that I wanted to share my mother's story with Tad. It would involve explaining a lot of things that I found upsetting.

"I remember you said something about her being in the wrong place at the wrong time," Tad added.

The sympathetic tone of his voice made me start talking. "My mother was born in 2360. Her parents were a perfectly respectable couple living in Dublin. They'd already been on the waiting list to go to new colony worlds for several years before my mother was born, but they didn't have any off-world relatives so they were low priority. By the time my mother was five years old, the Alpha sector planets had all closed their doors to new colonists, and the Loyalist party had blocked the opening of new worlds in Beta sector."

Tad pulled a pained face. "So the family lost their chance to go off world."

"The United Earth Government kept promising to restore order in the cities, but they still grew more dangerous every year. Large areas of Dublin had been abandoned to the looters. The remaining residents put up barricades to defend their neighbourhoods, but they faced a host of other difficulties too. The weather was causing major problems, and buildings damaged in storms were never repaired. Deliveries of food and other supplies were erratic."

I sighed. "The richer people left for smaller, safer communities, but my grandparents couldn't afford to move to the countryside. They were too deeply in debt on a Dublin house that was impossible to sell."

"Was there no way to escape the house and debt?" asked Tad.

"So many people were trying to walk away from debts back then, that the United Earth Government brought in a new law. You could evade your debt if you wanted, but doing it gave you a criminal record for fraud, so you'd never be allowed entry by any colony world."

Tad frowned but didn't say anything.

"My grandparents chose to stay in Dublin, and had two more children there. When my mother was ten, the Expansionists won the key vote to continue opening up Beta sector. My grandfather joined the queue to register for the Beta sector waiting list at dawn the next day, but half of the population of Dublin did the same thing. He spent three nights camped out in the queue before he even got into the building."

I shrugged. "There must have been queues like that in every city, and the new worlds didn't open up overnight. It was five years before my grandparents were offered a chance to go off-world. My mother was fifteen years old when the family went to Europe Off-world to start their journey to their new home."

"Clearly something went wrong and stopped them from leaving. An administrative error?"

I was silent for a moment, remembering the distress in my mother's face whenever she talked about this. One in a thousand people had an immune system problem that meant they'd die on any world other than Earth. My mother had been one of them. She'd stepped out of the portal on Danae, the Alpha sector world that was the first step on their journey, collapsed, and the people there dialled a portal to send her back to Earth.

My mother had been vaguely aware of voices. A man asking her parents if they wanted to portal back to Earth with their daughter. Her father saying they'd never get another chance to go off world. Her mother agreeing they should take their two younger children on to Beta sector.

I daren't tell that part of the story to Tad in case I burst into tears. "Yes, something went wrong. My mother's parents and her brothers went off to their new world – I think it was one of the worlds in Beta sector – but my mother was left behind. She was only fifteen years old and totally alone. She went back to Dublin, but it was too dangerous for her to stay there. She packed a couple of bags with her things, and set fire to the house before leaving."

Tad blinked. "She set fire to the house? Why?"

My mother had told me she wanted to destroy the last link with the parents who had abandoned her, but I didn't want to explain that to Tad. "She knew she'd never be coming back, but burning the house was a bad mistake. The police caught her leaving, arrested her, and she had her five minutes in court the next day. Literally five minutes. You didn't get much of a trial under the riot control emergency powers."

"But if the house belonged to her family, your mother hadn't committed any crime."

"The court said she had. She'd set fire to a house, so she was guilty of arson. She'd taken goods from the house before burning it, so she was guilty of looting."

"But that's completely unfair," said Tad. "Why didn't her defence lawyer do something about it?"

"Under the riot control emergency powers she didn't have a defence lawyer," I said. "It was her first offence, no one had been hurt, and the prisons were all overflowing, so they just registered her genetic code as a criminal, stamped her, and released her."

"Stamped her?" asked Tad.

"Tattooed the back of her right hand with her conviction number, so anyone looking at it could see she was a criminal. If you look at the right hands of most of the older division members, you'll see conviction numbers on them. Anyway, after that no law-abiding citizen would give my mother food, shelter, or work. Her only option was to go to London and try to find a cousin who'd been running with the London gangs. Chaos knows how she tracked down Ice, but she did."

There was silence for the next couple of minutes. We were approaching the boathouse now. Tad gave it an appraising look.

"You use this as a boathouse? What was it used for originally?"

"It's always been a boathouse," I said. "We're still using the same boats the security staff used to patrol the river."

The boathouse door had fallen to pieces years ago, so Tad and I could push our carts in through the open doorway. I was positioning mine next to the steps that led down to the boats, when a figure appeared from the shadows.

"Hello, Blaze," said Cage.

CHAPTER TWENTY-THREE

I stared at Cage in sheer disbelief. How could he be here lying in wait for me? How had he found out Tad and I were leaving on a trip? I instinctively glanced back at the doorway.

Cage laughed. "Thinking of running, Blaze? You wouldn't make it."

I knew I wouldn't. Cage was much closer to the doorway than I was, but Tad might stand a chance of reaching it. I wondered whether to scream at him to run, but if he tried to get away and failed, then Cage would probably kill him. I just had to hope that Tad had learned enough sense by now to stay perfectly quiet.

"I was promised that you'd marry me," said Cage. "I was promised I'd have the vacant officer position and become Donnell's deputy, but then you stole the officer position yourself, Blaze. You stole *my* officer position."

"That was a mistake," I said hastily.

"It was a huge mistake," said Cage. "One that you're going to correct. When you come back from this trip, you'll tell Donnell that you've decided you want to marry me right away, that you want me to have your officer position, that you want me to become his deputy as well. You're going to make sure that I get everything I was promised, because if you don't then I'll rip the alliance apart."

He paused for a second as if savouring the moment. "I'll begin by calling general justice on you for hiding the fact you still can't use your left arm properly."

"There's nothing wrong with my arm," I said. "It aches a little sometimes, that's all."

"Really? Only a few days ago, Hannah was having to help you carry things."

I shook my head. "Hannah was just being overprotective. Fussing over nothing."

"There was rather more to it than Hannah being overprotective. You were a troublesome child six years ago, humiliating me when you bit my arm. I thought you might be troublesome again, and refuse to marry me, so I made some preparations." Cage made a beckoning gesture with his right hand. "Come and join us, Hannah!"

I gave a frantic look round, and saw a movement in the darkest corner of the boathouse. Hannah walked slowly out of her hiding place and turned to face me. Now I knew how Cage had magically appeared here. Hannah was working for him. She must have seen Machico collecting the equipment we needed for our trip, and told Cage about it.

"Don't give me that wounded look, Blaze," said Hannah. "The Resistance were making it clear that they didn't want me any longer. You wouldn't get Donnell to help me, so I had to help myself. This is your fault, not mine."

My brain seemed too numb to think properly. "I don't understand. How does working for Cage help you get more popular with the Resistance?"

"Hannah doesn't have to worry about her popularity with the Resistance any longer," said Cage. "She belongs to Manhattan division now."

My best friend had betrayed me. Hannah had been working for Cage, spying on me and the Resistance, to buy herself a new future with Manhattan division.

I was still absorbing that, still deep in shock, when Cage took a sudden step forward. He grabbed hold of my left arm with both hands, yanked it up into the air, and gave it a brutal twist. There was a snapping sound, and agonizing pain shot through my arm and shoulder. I gave a piercing scream, and Tad's voice shouted from behind me.

"Let her go!"

He was trying to help me, I thought through the haze of pain, but he'd just get himself killed. "No, Tad," I yelled. "Stay out of this!"

"Let her go," he shouted again.

Cage dropped me. I landed on my feet, but toppled backwards, and ended up sitting on the ground holding my left arm with my right hand. Oh chaos, oh chaos, oh chaos it hurt!

Cage swung round to face Tad. "Don't interfere in my business, leech."

I managed to scuffle round on the floor so I could see them. The bulky figure of Cage facing the slimmer one of Tad. Beyond them, Hannah was standing with her hands over her mouth. She wasn't looking at Cage or Tad, but at me.

"This is my business too," said Tad.

Cage stepped forward and swung his right fist towards Tad. My mind was already picturing it smashing into Tad's jaw, the way Tad would fall to the ground, and what Cage would do to him then. Kicking Tad's stomach, ribs and face until he was just a bloodied, lifeless heap on the floor.

Somehow that didn't happen. Tad moved sideways and forwards. His hands were a blur of motion, so I couldn't work out exactly what he did with them, but one foot definitely kicked Cage on the leg. The next second, Cage was lying on the ground and clutching his right knee.

I stared at them, thinking for a moment that I'd broken under stress, and abandoned an unbearable reality for some comforting fantasy. I tried blinking, but the scene didn't change. Cage was still lying on the ground, staring up at Tad in stunned disbelief. Tad looked oddly startled too, as if he couldn't believe what had happened either.

Cage rolled over onto his stomach, and got up on his hands and left knee, before finally making it to his feet and glaring at Tad. "I'll tell people how you attacked me, leech, call for general justice against you, and you'll be executed!"

"Are you really planning to tell everyone that you couldn't last three seconds in a fight with the weedy leech boy?" asked

Tad, in a mocking voice. "Just think how they'll laugh at you. It will be even more humiliating than when Blaze bit you."

Cage's face flushed and he took a step towards Tad.

"If you try to hit me again," said Tad, "I'll break one of your bones. Your left arm would seem an appropriate choice."

There was a faint squeaking sound from Hannah. Cage gave her a sharp glance, as if he'd forgotten she was here. "The fight didn't happen," he said. "You didn't see anything."

"It didn't happen," repeated Hannah, in a shaky voice. "I didn't see anything."

Cage swung round to glare down at me. "If you don't give me what I want, Blaze, then I'll bring down Donnell and take it for myself. Donnell has held his position as alliance leader for eighteen years because of three things. His popularity, the gun on his arm, and the fact everyone trusts him to follow the alliance rules with scrupulous fairness. The winter fever has damaged his popularity."

"The fever wasn't Donnell's fault," I said. "It was just random bad luck."

"Leaders always get blamed for random bad luck. It's been easy to spread whispers that Donnell should have managed the medicine supplies better, kept a stock in reserve for a disaster like that, and then point out that we wouldn't have needed food rationing if the winter fever hadn't hit us so hard."

Cage made a sound like a warped, angry laugh. "People don't adore Donnell quite as much as usual, and his gun is far less of a factor now he doesn't have Kasim watching his back. Donnell's biggest strength now is the trust people have in him, and I can use you to attack that. As I said, I'll begin by calling general justice on you."

He was smiling now. "I've had Hannah preparing the ground to make you as vulnerable as possible. Encouraging you to doubt your relationship with Donnell, and hinting to the other women that you had problems with your arm. Yesterday, I got her to step up the campaign. She's been telling the division women that your broken arm is still terribly painful, and she's worried sick how you're coping fishing without her. By now, half the women in the alliance must believe you can barely use your left arm."

He paused. "And that's perfectly true now, isn't it? I'll call general justice against you for lying about your arm for months, and accuse Hannah of helping you deceive everyone. She'll make a show of reluctance before admitting it's true, and the whole alliance will believe her."

Cage was right, I thought, feeling a wave of nausea as pain mixed with despair. Everyone knew Hannah was my best friend. Everyone would believe her when she said my arm had been useless for months.

"You're the weak point in Donnell's armour," Cage continued. "Years ago at the cooking fire, he rushed to defend you with his fists. Now he'll rush to defend you with his position as alliance leader. Once Donnell's protecting you from punishment, I'll accuse him of knowing about your arm problems all along, and ordering Hannah to help you hide them."

Only days ago, I hadn't been sure Donnell would help me at all if I was in trouble. Now I thought about that confrontation with him yesterday, and the desperation in his face as he tried to convince me he believed I was his daughter. I couldn't doubt his feelings for me any longer. Cage was right. Donnell would rush to defend me. Even if I warned him it was a trap, even if he knew it would end in catastrophe, he'd still do it.

Cage's smile widened. "Hannah will back up my story again, and that's the key point where my allies will join me in calling general justice. Not just against you, but against Donnell himself, for abusing his position by making a girl with a useless arm into an officer. Wall and Major are already annoyed about having a female officer foisted on them. They'll be utterly furious when they hear about you and Donnell lying to them, and how do you think Ice will react to the news that Donnell tricked him into voting for you?"

I knew exactly how Ice would react to that. He'd be coldly, implacably angry about being made to look a fool.

"Even Ghost's faith in Donnell will be shaken, so only the Resistance will be left defending their precious leader. They'll never hand Donnell over for punishment without a fight, but what chance will they have when the other divisions outnumber them by four to one? My side will win the battle, and I'll take Donnell's place as alliance leader."

I was dizzy from pain, and beset by nightmare images, but I forced myself to speak. "If it came to open fighting, then it wouldn't be four to one against the Resistance. Even if you got all four division leaders to fight for you, there are plenty of people in the alliance who hate you enough to defy orders and either stay out of the fight or take Donnell's side."

"Enough will fight for me to win the battle," said Cage, "and that's all that matters."

"What about the people who'll be injured or killed in the fighting?"

"I spent four years preparing to take the leadership of Manhattan from Wall, and you wrecked all my efforts by making me look a fool in front of the whole alliance. I spent another six years preparing my bid to become an alliance officer, and you're trying to wreck my efforts for a second time. Do you think I'll burst into tears and abandon my plans because a few insignificant people may die?"

"But we're still short of food. If we start fighting amongst ourselves instead of hunting, then everyone will starve."

Cage's smile didn't falter. "The people who prove themselves useful to me won't starve, and the rest don't matter. Your arguments won't work on me, Blaze, but you should listen to them yourself. Picture your Resistance friends dying to defend Donnell. Imagine their children starving after the battle."

He paused. "You can prevent all those deaths, Blaze. You can stop that pointless waste of lives. All you have to do is make Donnell give me the deputy position I was promised. Think about it while you're on your supply trip. I'll want your answer as soon as you return."

Cage limped off out of the door, and then Hannah stepped towards me. "Blaze, I..."

I struggled to my feet, swaying with dizziness and pain, my right hand still cradling my left arm against my chest. "No, Hannah! Don't try telling me again how this is all my fault."

"But it *is* your fault. When we talked on our last fishing trip together, you lied to me. You told me Donnell was going to throw us both out of the Resistance, and Ice wouldn't take us back into London division. The best option for both of us seemed to be for me to agree to work for Cage. If you'd told me the truth, said that Donnell was going to make you an officer, none of this would have happened."

"On our last fishing trip together, I told you the precise truth, which was that Donnell had said he wanted to discuss my future with me. You're the one that's been lying to me. You're still lying to me even now. You weren't trying to decide whether to work for Cage that day. You'd already been working for him for years. You stole two boxes of painkillers. Not one tablet, but two boxes!"

Hannah's expression changed to something furtive. "I don't know what you mean."

"Yes, you do. Donnell told me the true facts about you getting caught stealing the painkillers. I knew you were scared of pain, so I thought you wanted to keep all those painkillers for yourself, but you'd actually stolen them for Cage. You'd probably stolen a lot of other medicines before that too. You've been working for Cage ever since we came to New York, haven't you?"

Hannah put a hand to her mouth, and chewed on her glove in the familiar mannerism that meant she was considering what to say.

"Answer me!" I snapped.

"I didn't have any choice. After your brother turned traitor and left, you were out of favour with Donnell, and I was scared I'd be thrown out of the Resistance. I knew what it would be like struggling to survive alone. My mother and I had lived like that for two nightmare years in London, and I couldn't face going through it again. When Cage said he could arrange the option of a place in Manhattan division in exchange for a couple of boxes of fever medicine…"

She waved her hands. "It didn't stop at that though. Cage kept asking for more things. When I refused, he threatened to send an anonymous message to Donnell telling him what I'd done, so I had to keep stealing. After I got caught, and didn't have access to the stores on the top floor of the Resistance wing any longer, Cage started giving me orders about you. He wanted me to..."

"Enough!" I interrupted her. "I don't want to know how much medicine you stole for Cage before you got caught and moved downstairs. I don't want to know how many of my secrets you've whispered to Cage. I don't want to know how many lies you've told me to poison my relationship with Donnell. I just want you to get out of here. You belong with Cage and Manhattan now."

Hannah scuttled off through the door. I closed my eyes for a moment, fighting off the dual physical and emotional pain of my arm and her betrayal, and then turned to Tad. Only yesterday, I'd told Donnell that Tad couldn't beat a five-year-old child in a fight, but he'd ripped Cage apart in seconds.

"How the chaos did you do that to Cage?" I asked.

"It's mostly to do with balance," said Tad. "You destroy your opponent's balance while keeping your own. I'm a bit surprised it worked though. I've never been in a real fight before, just fought in training."

"You've been trained to fight?" I shook my head in bewilderment, and instantly regretted it as my left shoulder hit a new peak of agony that made me dizzy. "Why? I thought Adonis was civilized."

"Every world has its shady areas and its unscrupulous people, even Adonis. My family is very rich and that can be a mixed blessing. When I was six years old, my father was kidnapped. My grandfather paid the ransom, but all we got back was a dead body."

I was shocked. "So that was how your father died."

"After that, my grandfather doubled the guards, and hired experts to teach me to fight. I always suspected the instructors were letting me win to please me, but maybe they weren't." Tad shrugged. "Forget that. We have to go back and tell everyone how Cage attacked you and injured your arm. He's planning to call general justice against you, but we can call general justice against him first."

I tried to ignore the agony in my shoulder and think what to do. "That won't work. Cage will say that he never touched me, my arm has been like this all along, and Hannah will support his story."

"I'll tell people what really happened."

"People won't listen to evidence from an off-worlder, Tad. Even if they were prepared to give you a hearing, Cage could just point out that your life depends on Donnell protecting you, so you'll obviously tell any story that he wants."

I curbed the urge to shake my head again. "After that, everything would happen exactly the way Cage described. Everyone will believe Hannah because she is... she *was* my best friend, Donnell gets drawn into defending me, and Cage uses that to start his leadership battle."

"So what do we do?" asked Tad.

It was pure folly to carry on with the trip upriver when I was injured and helpless with pain, but if I went back then Cage would start his war right away. Donnell needed time to talk Major into changing sides, and I needed time to think. The foundations of my world had just been shattered. My best friend had been betraying me for years, and my enemy had fought Cage in my defence. Where did that leave me now?

"We're going upriver," I said.

CHAPTER TWENTY-FOUR

I expected Tad to argue with me, try to insist on us going back to get medical treatment for my arm and shoulder, but he just accepted my decision. There were four boats of varying sizes in the boathouse. I chose the largest one since we had so many stasis boxes, and Tad spread out the thermal mattresses in the bottom of the boat and said I should rest while he loaded the supplies. I told him I was perfectly fine, which was a lie. He told me I looked like I was about to pass out, which was probably true.

I gave in, and Tad helped me down the steps and into the boat. I lay down, and he covered me with our sleeping bags. It felt strange having an off-worlder taking care of me.

Now I was lying down, the pain in my left arm and shoulder eased a little, but I was panicking that Cage would come back before we left. I watched impatiently as Tad piled the supplies and stasis boxes at the back of the boat, and finally went to the controls.

I explained to Tad how the controls worked, and he manoeuvred the boat out of the boathouse and turned upriver. I'd have been happier if I was the one driving the boat, but that wasn't physically possible.

"Make sure you stay in the centre of the river," I called out. "There's a fallen crane near the bank just ahead of us, and any number of sunken boats."

"I'll..." Tad's head suddenly swung round to look at something. "What the chaos is that?"

I tensed, hastily lifted my head to look over the side of the boat, and then relaxed again as I realized Tad was looking at the elegant white shape by the nearest riverbank. "That's the Spirit of New York. She's far too big to fit in any boathouse, so we keep her moored to a pier."

"I've never seen a boat on that scale," said Tad. "Why does she have huge wheels on each side?"

"The Spirit of New York is a reproduction paddle steamer," I said. "She was built as a novelty pleasure boat to take people on river cruises from New York up to Albany and back. The reproduction engines are far easier to maintain than modern ones, so we use her to bring wood and other supplies from upriver, though we can't go as far as Albany."

Tad nodded. "Donnell mentioned the Hudson River was blocked by wreckage at Bear Mountain."

We were passing the Spirit of New York, leaving Cage behind us at the Americas Parliament House. We should be perfectly safe now. There was no reason for Cage to chase us upriver, when he just had to wait a few days for us to return.

I sank back onto the thin thermal mattresses, and focused on my conversation with Tad to try to distract myself from the shooting pains in my left arm and shoulder.

"The river isn't blocked by wreckage, but by guards on the Bear Mountain Bridge. There's a settlement just past there. The citizens keep guards stationed on the bridge, and shoot at us with laser weapons if we get too near."

"It's totally irresponsible of them to shoot at people like that," said Tad.

"They wouldn't think we counted as people."

There was a brief pause before Tad spoke again. "When you leave in the spring, could you take the Spirit of New York down-river, out to sea, and round to the Delaware River to reach Philadelphia? That would be much easier than making the journey on foot."

I was hit by a dizzy spell, and had to wait for it to end before speaking. "The Spirit of New York might not survive that sort of voyage. She was never designed to go to sea, and she's an elderly ship. We wouldn't be able to fit everyone in the alliance aboard her anyway, let alone the basic supplies we'd need."

We were heading under the Unity Bridge now. I stared up at its ridiculously ornate design of linked hands. The bridge was built back in the twenty-third century, to mark the opening of the United Earth Americas Parliament complex, the renaming of the Union City area to be Unity City, and its formal recognition as a new borough of New York. The Unity Bridge was supposed to be an everlasting monument to a united city in a united world. It was already falling apart.

As we came out from under the bridge, I saw a movement in the sky to my right. A falling star had launched itself from one of the Manhattan skyscrapers and was gliding across the river. Tad noticed it too, turning his head to look at it.

"Falling stars won't bother us on this boat, will they?"

"We're perfectly safe out here in mid-river. The adult falling star population is all concentrated around Lower Manhattan and the old Midtown area, and even the baby ones haven't spread upriver as far as the Presidents' Bridge. The boat batteries are suffering from age, so they don't hold their charge well, but they should last until we're past that."

"I'm looking at some old images of the river," said Tad. "Is the Presidents' Bridge the massive thing with lots of faces on the side?"

"That's right." I closed my eyes again and shifted cautiously on the mattresses, trying to find a position where my left arm and shoulder were comfortable. I couldn't. Cage had nearly ripped my arm out of its socket. I remembered the snapping sound that I'd heard. I wasn't sure if it was the bone in my upper arm that had broken again, or something in my shoulder.

Tad had gone quiet now, so I lay listening to the steady humming sound of the boat's engines as we headed slowly upriver. Even the pain in my arm couldn't distract me from brooding on Cage's threat.

He was going to use me to attack Donnell's leadership of the alliance. That would be bad at any time, but for it to happen now, at the very moment when Donnell had to convince everyone that

New York was going to burn and they should follow him to a new home, would be disastrous.

I groaned. I was going to cause Donnell more trouble than my traitor brother had ever done. I couldn't give in to Cage's demands. It wasn't just that I'd rather be eaten by a falling star than marry him. Giving Cage the deputy position would mean he'd automatically succeed Donnell as leader. As Machico had pointed out, Cage would probably murder Donnell to speed up his rise to power.

I had to find another way out of this, but how? I was still trying to find a way to solve the unsolvable problem, when I noticed the sound of the boat engine had changed to include a faint hiccupping.

"The boat battery needs recharging, Tad. You'd better take us in towards the bank. Remember to watch out for underwater obstacles."

A few minutes later, I felt the jolt of the boat bumping gently against the bank. I opened my eyes, looked round, and saw we'd stopped by an area of grass and trees just past the Presidents' Bridge.

Tad cut the engine, and tied the boat up to an old signpost. "How do I recharge the battery?"

"You don't." I struggled up into a sitting position, holding my injured left arm with my right hand to stop it moving. "I have to do this myself. Tie the aft mooring rope as well to make sure the boat keeps perfectly still while I connect the cables. I don't want the power storage unit exploding and..."

I broke off and pulled a face. "Or perhaps I do. Getting blown up would solve all my problems. Cage couldn't use me to destroy Donnell if I was dead."

"I feel there has to be a better way to deal with Cage's threats than blowing ourselves up," said Tad. "I've strong objections to dying."

He tied the aft mooring rope to a jagged spike of metal. "Will that keep the boat still enough?"

"I think so."

"You aren't seriously considering drastic measures, are you?"

"No. Donnell says that dying is a bad tactical move, because being dead severely limits your future actions."

Tad laughed. "He's right."

"Donnell is usually right, except about his drinking. Help me make my scarf into a sling for my arm."

Tad carefully wrapped my scarf round my left arm, and knotted it at the back of my neck to form a sling.

"Now fetch the power storage unit and put it next to the boat controls."

He obeyed my instructions and grinned. "If we're going to use this to blow someone up, I suggest we blow up Cage."

I shuffled closer to the boat controls. "I'll give that idea serious consideration. Quiet now. I need to listen to the power storage unit talking to me."

Tad gave me a bewildered look, but shut up.

I opened the flap that covered the boat's built in battery, and took out the charging lead and several short lengths of cable. It took me two attempts to plug the charging lead into the socket in the top of the power storage unit, because it was awkward working one-handed.

"Safety system auto block engaged," said the power storage unit sternly. "You have connected an incompatible device to this unit."

I plugged both ends of a cable into sockets on one side of the power storage unit. It started beeping. "Warning," said the voice. "Safety system has been overridden."

I concentrated on counting the beeps.

"Danger. Power instability."

As the power unit beeped for the twentieth time, I braced myself ready to bring my left hand into use. There was a moment of agony as I simultaneously plugged both ends of another cable into the other side of the power storage unit. The bleeping instantly speeded up.

"Danger. Critical power instability."

I yanked out all the cables with my right hand. "I'm afraid this can get rather boring. You have to make the final connection at precisely the right instant for this to work, so it usually takes a few attempts."

"If you're doing what I think you're doing to that power unit, there's nothing remotely boring about it." Tad sounded close to panic.

"Don't worry. You get one more message before anything bad happens. Something about explosion imminent. I've never heard it myself, but..."

"Let's try not to hear it today," said Tad. "How the chaos did you people work out how to do this?"

"Kasim discovered it by accident years ago. He was rigging a power unit to explode, but it didn't. Quiet now while I try again."

I went through the routine of connecting cables again. I must have made the final connection at the right time because the beeping stopped.

"That's done it." I nodded at the flashing green light on the boat controls. "The boat battery is charging."

I slowly settled back on my mattresses again, careful not to jar my shoulder. "We haven't had any food yet today. My arm hurts too much for me to eat anything, but you must be hungry."

"I'm starving," admitted Tad.

He got a plate of food out of one of the stasis boxes, and wolfed it down before moving to sit beside me. "Blaze, I want to ask you something."

I was feeling sick from pain, but I still laughed. "You've been asking me things ever since you arrived in New York."

He frowned down at me. "I know, but... You said the Spirit of New York could go upriver as far as the Bear Mountain Bridge. Would this boat be able to make it there as well?"

"Yes, but I told you it's far too dangerous. The citizens have some fancy, long-range, laser rifles, and shoot at any boat they see coming from New York."

"They wouldn't shoot if I sent them a message to tell them who I was."

I stared at him. "How are you planning to do that? Whistle some Morse code at them, or use smoke signals?"

"I can use my link to the Earth data net to message people," said Tad. "Once Donnell and Machico found out I was webbed, I thought they'd realize that. They haven't said a word about it though. Perhaps they thought I could only message other people who were webbed, and of course there aren't any others now."

I stared at him, too stunned and angry to speak.

"Phoenix said I mustn't mention it," Tad continued, "because we'd no idea how you'd react, but I need to explain how I've been messaging the..."

My anger finally broke through into words. "You've been secretly messaging people? Who have you been contacting? What have you said? Have you been talking to the citizens behind Fence about us?"

Tad gave an urgent shake of his head. "No. I've only sent messages to the people running the interstellar portals at Earth America Off-world. Remember that Phoenix, Braden, and I had flown off in the aircraft and not come back. I had to tell people we were alive and well, or they'd have assumed we'd crashed and sent word to Adonis that we were dead."

He paused for a second. "Think how our families would have felt. My relationship with my grandfather is problematic at best, but the man's nearing his hundredth. When my father died, it wasn't just a devastating personal blow, but it wrecked all the plans to recreate portal technology as well. My grandfather rebuilt everything centring on me. If he heard I was dead too, then the shock would kill him."

I tried to force my voice back under control. "What have you told the people at America Off-world?"

"That we were being cared for by a group of people still living in New York. That you were struggling to survive yourselves, but you were sharing what you had with us. That we should be able to reach a nearby settlement in the spring."

"You didn't mention the Earth Resistance, or the divisions, or...?"

"No, I didn't," said Tad. "I knew anything I said would be passed on to Adonis. I didn't want to frighten my grandfather or cause trouble for you. I tried to give the impression we were staying with a group of especially stubborn citizens who'd never left New York."

He waved both hands. "Earth America Off-world is entirely

run by teams of off-worlders. They accepted what I said without asking any questions. I'm sure they don't even know the Earth Resistance are still in New York."

I abandoned any attempt to stay calm. Thaddeus Wallam-Crane the Eighth was an utter fool. "They do know we're in New York, Tad! My brother told them all about us, and they bombed the New York portal relay centre to stop us using portals!"

"Yes, but that was six years ago."

I groaned. "You think six years is long enough for people to forget about us?"

"No. I told you before that there was no mention of the bombing, or the deal with your brother, on the Earth data net. That means it was done without official approval, by a few individuals who hated the Earth Resistance. Everyone involved must have gone back to their own worlds years ago."

"You can't be sure of that."

"Yes, I can," said Tad. "Off-worlders hate coming to work on Earth, because their only contact with friends and family is by recorded messages sent through portals on data chips. Assignments are only for one year."

"Oh." I thought that over for a minute.

"Nobody has mentioned the Earth Resistance to me," added Tad. "They just keep talking about the angry messages they're getting from Adonis about the aircraft I stole."

I blinked. "You came to New York in a stolen aircraft?"

Tad sighed. "Yes. I hoped that no one would ever find out it was missing. I'd faked some documentation about it going off for six weeks for essential maintenance work. I thought that would be long enough for us to do what we needed and return the aircraft before anyone started asking questions, but our quarantine period was extended because of..."

I lifted my right hand to stop him. "I'm not interested in how people on Adonis found out you'd stolen their aircraft. You haven't sent messages to anyone other than the people at America Off-world?"

"No."

"But you could do?"

He nodded. "I could send a message to the citizens at Bear Mountain. Tell them that I'm coming so they wouldn't shoot at the boat."

I had a horrible sinking feeling in my stomach. Hannah had been my best friend for the whole of my life. It had been a huge blow to realize that she'd betrayed me to Cage. I'd only known Tad for a few days, and he wasn't my friend but my enemy, but for some reason his betrayal hurt me even more than Hannah's had done.

"Yes, you can take the boat upriver, Tad," I said, in a cold voice. "You can send the citizens a message. You can go to Bear Mountain, use their portal to travel to America Off-world, and then go back to Adonis. I'm injured and helpless, so I can't do anything to stop you."

I gave him a bitter look. "When you steal the boat, are you planning to kill me, or just abandon me here? Don't pretend to yourself that abandoning me wouldn't be murder too. Even if I was uninjured, the odds are that I'd starve, freeze to death, or get eaten by a falling star long before I made it back to the Americas Parliament House."

"Do you really believe I'd do anything to hurt you?" Tad demanded. "Do you think I'd leave Phoenix and Braden behind in New York while I go back to Adonis alone? Do you consider me so inhumanly selfish?"

I looked at his wounded expression, and realized I'd been a fool. Tad had just fought off Cage to help me. Of course I could trust him.

"No. Sorry. It was stupid of me to accuse you like that, but I'm in shock after what happened with Hannah. I told her all my secrets, I believed everything she told me, and now I find she's been working for Cage for the last six years."

Tad seemed to calm down. "I can see that would hit you hard."

"Yes. My head is still reeling from it. I keep thinking about our last day fishing together, remembering how I told her about Cage wanting to marry me and become an officer. Hannah pretended to be shocked at the news, but I'm sure Cage had warned her about it in advance. Everything I said to her that day must have been reported back to him."

I paused. "I don't trust my own judgement any longer. When Hannah said painful things that hurt me, I thought it was because she was my friend and she felt she had to warn me about unpleasant truths. Looking back now though, it's obvious that Cage had ordered her to undermine my confidence, and isolate me from my father and the rest of the Resistance."

I pulled a face. "Hannah did a great job of both those things. She's still doing a great job at undermining my confidence even now. She's got me so shaken that I accused you of planning to murder me only hours after you'd rescued me from Cage. I don't think I've thanked you properly for that yet."

"I don't think I've thanked you properly for rescuing me from being thrown off the roof either," said Tad. "That doesn't matter. Nobody does that sort of thing because they want to be thanked. They do it because it's not possible to do anything else. I didn't think I could win a fight against Cage, but I couldn't stand there watching him torture you when..."

His voice suddenly changed and he started talking in weirdly rushed sentences. "Blaze, I've been telling myself I have to be sensible. Phoenix has been telling me I have to be sensible. Chaos, even Braden has been telling me I have to be sensible! I've been trying to do that because I thought I was the only one feeling this way, but the way you screamed at me when I tried fighting Cage..."

He broke off and looked at me expectantly. I'd been feeling tense ever since I walked into the boathouse and saw Cage waiting for me. I felt even more tense now, but it was a very different sort of tension.

"Admit it, Blaze," said Tad. "It isn't just me caring about you, is it? There's some emotion on your side as well."

I'd been trying to ignore what was happening between myself and Tad, but there are times when you can't hide from your own feelings. The moment in the boathouse, when I thought Cage was going to beat Tad to death, had been one of them. Tad could be incredibly annoying, with his unconscious arrogance and unending questions, but beneath that was a core of deeply sensitive humanity.

"I may not be totally uninterested in you," I said, "but nothing can happen between us. We literally belong to different worlds. In the spring, we'll go to Fence and say goodbye. You'll be on one side of its barricades and I'll be on the other. After that, you'll go back to Adonis and I'll stay on Earth."

"Something has already happened between us," said Tad. "We've stopped pretending our feelings aren't real, and we're talking about them. We can't put the genie back in the bottle."

"What?" I asked, utterly bewildered.

"Sorry, that's a centuries old phrase that my grandfather uses. I meant that now we've started this conversation, we really have to finish it. My idea wasn't to go to Bear Mountain alone, but to take you, Phoenix and Braden with me. All four of us would go to America Off-world together. The doctors there could give you proper advanced medical treatment for your injured arm, so it would only take a couple of days for it to heal, and then we could all go off world together."

"We've had this conversation before, Tad. No colony world would accept Sean Donnelly's daughter."

"Last time we had this conversation, I couldn't say some things. Now I can. I'm Thaddeus Wallam-Crane the Eighth. I'm rather unpopular on Adonis right now, but I still have a lot of influence on other worlds."

I frowned. "Why are you unpopular on Adonis? Because you stole the aircraft?"

Tad shrugged. "It's more because of the funding issue. My grandfather promised the Adonis Government unrealistically fast results if they funded my research and gave me all the resources I needed."

He waved a hand dismissively. "Forget about that. My point is that I'll be going to Zeus, capital planet of Beta sector, to continue my work with their Fidelis Project. I can take you there with me. They may argue about you being Sean Donnelly's daughter, but I can talk them into accepting you. Once we're safely on Zeus, you can take all the time you need to decide whether you want us to try having a relationship or not. My goal is to give you the chance of a new life on a new world. Whether you choose to spend that new life with me, someone else, or on your own, is entirely your choice."

I sighed. "Tad, that's an incredibly generous offer, but I can't go with you. It's not just that we belong to different worlds. We have nothing in common. You're fabulously important and wealthy, while I'm a scavenger from the New York ruins."

"I think I have more in common with you than anyone I've ever met," said Tad. "My future was decided for me before I was born. So was yours. I'm the heir of the inventor of the portal. You're the daughter of the leader of the Earth Resistance. We're both living our lives in the shadow of legends."

"We're enemies," I said.

"We're enemies with feelings for each other. We aren't the first to be in that situation. It happened to your parents. When Donnell arrived in London, he was on the opposite side to your mother, but they made it work. We can make this work too."

I shook my head. "My parents made it work while they were together, but their relationship fell apart when Donnell left for New York."

"Which is exactly why we mustn't split up," said Tad. "I can't stay on Earth, because I have to re-invent portal technology to save civilization. That isn't possible here, because Earth doesn't have enough people, experts, or manufacturing capability any longer."

"You can't stay," I said, "and I can't go. Earth is my world."

"It doesn't have to be," said Tad. "I can't break free from my duty, I've got five hundred worlds to save, but you could come to Zeus with me. There's no point in you sacrificing your life for a cause that was lost before you were born. Donnell would tell you that himself."

Tad leaned eagerly towards me. "If we go back to the Parliament House now, we'll arrive when everyone's out hunting. We could sneak back up to the top floor of the Resistance wing, wait until Donnell's back, tell him how I can send messages and explain my plan. I'm sure he'd agree to let the four of us go to

Bear Mountain. He loves you and wants you to have the best possible life."

"Yes, you're right," I said. "Donnell would agree to your plan whatever the consequences for him and the alliance, but I can't let him do that. It's not just that Earth is my world and I don't want to leave it. It's that if you, Phoenix and Braden go off world now, then a lot of people will die."

Tad frowned. "But Cage is planning to attack you as a way of harming Donnell. Surely taking you off world with us would help the situation."

"It would help the situation now," I said, "but remember there's a firestorm coming. Everyone has to leave New York in the spring or burn to death. They'll need to go alongside Fence to reach Philadelphia, and Donnell's counting on using you three off-worlders to negotiate safe passage. Without you, he'd either have to try fighting a way through, or take a huge detour to avoid Fence entirely."

I paused. "Either way, a lot of people would die, Tad. Fighting laser weapons with bows would mean quick deaths. Detouring round Fence would mean the deaths came slower but just as inevitably. The longer the journey, the more food needed, the more danger of hitting impassable terrain, places where radioactive or chemical waste have been dumped, or just stumbling across another armed settlement. Once the alliance had sick or injured people to carry, travelling would become even slower."

"You're right," muttered Tad. "The longer the journey, the more danger and deaths on the way, and the less time they'd have in their new home to prepare to survive the next winter."

"I'm sorry," I said. "I wish we could let you, Phoenix and Braden take a boat and go home, but we can't. I know that must seem harsh."

Tad shook his head. "No, it doesn't. I don't want anyone dying because of me, and obviously the small children would be the most vulnerable."

He paused for a second. "Phoenix, Braden and I would be dead by now if your people hadn't helped us, and the least we can do in return is stay and help them get past Fence. You won't have to make a final decision about whether you go off world with us until then."

"I've already made my decision, Tad. Accept it. We'll go to Fence, we'll say goodbye, and you'll go to Zeus while I stay on Earth."

He sighed. "So we aren't doing the relationship thing?"

"We aren't doing the relationship thing."

CHAPTER TWENTY-FIVE

Once the boat battery was fully charged again, we continued upriver. Now my arm was in the sling, I could manage to sit up next to Tad rather than lie down on the mattresses, but it was an awkwardly silent journey until we were past Yonkers, when Tad started talking again.

"The storage facility is supposed to be on our right, very close to the riverbank. It should be impossible to miss."

We carried on up the river for about fifteen minutes.

"On the other hand, it's clearly possible to miss it," said Tad. "The big building on our left has to be the sports centre, and that's further upriver than the storage facility. I'll turn the boat round and we'll go back."

He turned the boat round and we went back. Fifteen minutes later he was turning the boat round again. "I don't understand why we can't find it. I expected there to be huge signs."

"A lot of the signs have fallen off buildings," I said. "You need to look for distinctive landmarks."

"Perhaps I can find a picture of it. Ah yes, it's a huge single-storey warehouse complex like... like that one!" Tad pointed triumphantly at the riverbank.

I stared at the sprawling building. "The roof looks intact, and the doors on this side are closed. That's a good sign."

Tad brought the boat into the bank, and tied it to a post conveniently near a door. "Let's go and explore," he said eagerly. "See if the medicine is still here."

220

"The first priority on supply trips is staying alive," I said, "especially in midwinter. If you look at the sky, you'll see there's either rain or snow coming soon, and there's no point in us collecting medicine if we freeze to death before we can take it back downriver. We need to check this building is in a good enough state to give us shelter tonight, and get our bedding and food inside. After that, we can search for medicines."

Tad helped me out of the boat and we went to the door. That was locked, so Tad had to use a metal lever to force it open. An alarm shrilled, Tad jumped nervously, and I laughed at the look on his face.

"What are you panicking about? Do you think the police will hear the alarm and come and arrest you?"

"Sorry. This is my first burglary. Well, we did break into the Wallam-Crane Science Museum, but that didn't really count since my grandfather owns it." Tad paused. "That alarm's painfully loud. If we go inside, we'll be deafened."

"It will stop in a minute. The alarm systems all had power cells to keep them functioning if the power supply was cut, but they've gone flat over the years."

A few seconds later, the shrilling faltered, hiccupped a few times, and then finally stopped. I led the way into a vast room. There were windows running the whole length of the outside wall, their dirt-encrusted glass still letting in enough light to show regimented rows of stasis cabinets. Most of them were surrounded by the fuzzy black of stasis fields, but I could see a scattering of grey cabinets, where either the battery powering the stasis field had failed or the stasis field had never been turned on.

Tad hurried to the nearest cabinet, deactivated the field, and peered inside. "The storage records on the Earth data net are right," he said in triumph. "This cabinet is half full of medicine."

"That's very good news, but survival first, medicines later."

"Sorry." He closed the cabinet and activated the field again. "I'm looking at the building plans now. We're currently in hall 3, which is part of the main medical supply area."

I studied the room carefully. "The roof is leaking in a couple of places, there are three broken windows down the far end, and cockroaches have been nesting under the cabinets. Are there any smaller rooms in this place where we could store our supplies and sleep?"

"There's a whole row of offices."

Tad led the way across the room, through a door, and into a corridor. Windows ran along the wall to our left, while there were a series of doors to our right. I opened the nearest one and saw a small room with a grimy desk and half a dozen flexiplas chairs. The vital thing was the ceiling was unblemished by damp, and the windows were all intact. I did a circuit of the room, carefully inspecting where the walls met the floor.

"What are you doing?" asked Tad.

"Checking the rats haven't gnawed a way in. Everything looks fine. I can't even see any cockroaches."

"That's good," said Tad. "I don't want rats and cockroaches running over me when I'm asleep."

"The problem isn't rats running over you, but them stopping to bite you," I said grimly. "Rat bites can get infected or give you fever."

There was a two second pause before Tad made a noise of revulsion. I guessed he'd just looked up rat bite fever on the Earth data net.

"You can pile the empty stasis boxes in hall 3 for now," I said, "but you'd better bring the bedding and stasis boxes of food in here. Be careful to keep the door closed after that. If rats get in, they won't be able to chew their way into an active stasis box, but they'll destroy the sleeping bags."

Once Tad had unloaded the boat, he finally got his chance to explore the building. The place was far bigger than I'd realized, with corridors linking multiple warehouses together. Tad strode purposefully through the vast halls, while I trailed uselessly after him, trying to ignore the painful throbbing in my left arm and shoulder. Occasionally, he'd stop to open one of the stasis cabinets and peer inside, before closing it again, re-activating the stasis field, and moving on.

I assumed Tad was checking what medicines were available so he could choose the best ones to take back with us, but then he stopped in an area where there was a whole row of glass-fronted cupboards filled with gruesome surgical instruments, and the stasis cabinets contained syringes, tubes of liquid, and other things that I didn't recognize at all.

After ten minutes of watching him open and close the stasis cabinets, I got restless. "We've used a few medicines in the past that have to be injected into people, but tablets and ointments are much simpler and easier."

"I realize that," said Tad. "I'm planning to take back tablets and ointments, but while we're here..."

He turned to face me. "I didn't argue about us carrying on with this trip, because I knew this place held a whole range of medical supplies. I thought I could use them to treat your arm."

Treat my arm? I glanced at a fearsome array of surgical instruments in a nearby cupboard, and took a nervous step backwards.

"It's entirely your decision whether you allow me to treat your arm or not," added Tad hastily.

"You're an expert on portals, not a doctor," I said. "What are you planning to do? Rewire me?"

"For the last hour I've been using my web to discuss your case with a qualified doctor at Earth America Off-world," said Tad. "I've told her I can set things up to send the sounds I'm hearing, and the images of the view through my eyes, to a wall vid for her. She thinks that should be enough for her to talk me through the treatment procedure."

Tad wanted me to let one of the leeches at America Off-world talk him through messing with my arm! "Is this doctor watching us now?"

"Of course not," said Tad. "I wouldn't let her watch us without warning you what was happening."

"You're sure she doesn't know what I am?"

"Perfectly sure."

"Because if she finds out I belong to the Earth Resistance, or that my mother was on the wrong side of the barricades in London, she might try to make my arm worse rather than better."

"She's a doctor, Blaze," said Tad. "All she cares about is that you're a patient who needs help."

I closed my eyes, struggling to think. My left arm and my shoulder were throbbing painfully even when I kept them perfectly still. Was there any chance of this injury healing naturally, or was this my only hope of ever using my arm again?

"I realize this comes as a big shock to you," said Tad. "I couldn't warn you about my plan, because it would have been horrible to raise your hopes and then find the vital regrowth fluid was gone, or the stasis field preserving it had failed. I'd like to give you time to consider the decision, but we don't have it. If we're going to do this while we're here, we must start work now, because the healing process will take a couple of days."

Did I trust an unknown off-world doctor to give Tad the right instructions? Did I trust Tad to follow those instructions correctly?

"We could take everything back to the Parliament House and try to fix your arm there," Tad continued, "but it would be difficult to explain the situation to your father, and Cage might do something to complicate things."

I pictured Tad trying to explain this to my father. I wasn't sure if Donnell would throw him off the roof or just go and get drunk again, but there was absolutely no doubt that Cage would do something to complicate things. If I didn't agree to his demands the second I arrived back at the Parliament House, then he'd launch his attack on me and Donnell.

The pain from my arm must have been stopping me thinking properly, because it was only now that I realized the obvious point. Cage would start his attack by calling general justice against me for hiding an injury to my arm. If there was any chance that Tad could heal my arm before then, I had to take it.

"Let's do this," I said.

Tad took a bag of ominously red fluid from the nearest stasis cabinet, then moved to another to get two tubes. "Local anaesthetic and hibernation trigger," he muttered. "Now I need..."

I watched him get a couple of syringes, one small and one

terrifyingly large. When I was a small child in London, I'd seen someone have an injection. He'd screamed a lot, but he'd been screaming a lot before that as well.

Tad walked towards the aisle with the cabinets of fearsome medical instruments. I was relieved to see him walk straight past them to collect some cotton wool swabs and a bottle of antiseptic lotion.

"Let's go back to the office," he said. "That's just as filthy as the rest of this place, and there's no way we can clean it to hospital standards, but there shouldn't be a danger of infection if we can avoid using an open wound procedure."

I didn't know what an open wound procedure was, but it sounded like a very good thing to avoid. The only time precious old medicines had been used on me was when I first arrived in New York. Donnell had simply spread ointment on my burned hands back then. I'd been stunned by the way my pain had instantly vanished, and the skin had healed perfectly in twenty-four hours, but fixing my arm was bound to be far more complex than that.

I followed Tad back to the small office where we'd left the mattresses and sleeping bags. He shoved the dusty desk and chairs out of the way, and laid out one mattress and sleeping bag in the centre of the room.

"I told the doctor you broke your arm last summer," he said. "She wants to know if your new injury is in the same place."

"It seems to be higher up this time," I said. "It may be the shoulder itself that's injured, but I've got a lot of pain in the arm too."

"The doctor says we'll need to examine your arm to locate the injury." Tad looked embarrassed. "We'll need you to take off some clothes for that. I've never seen anything other than a woman's face and hands uncovered here, so you obviously have very strict rules on clothing, but I'm afraid it's unavoidable."

"Strict rules on clothing?" I laughed. "Tad, everyone's been bundled up in coats, even indoors, because it's midwinter and we've little heating."

"Oh," said Tad. "Many of the Alpha sector worlds were

settled from specific parts of Earth, and some have strong cultural traditions about clothing, so I thought..."

"There are a few people in the alliance who have strong cultural rules about clothing," I said, "but I'm not one of them. Donnell and my mother both identified as Irish, I suppose I do too, though I was born in London and my ancestors aren't all from Ireland or even Europe."

I started unbuttoning my coat, but it was a struggle one-handed. "Chaos take it! Tad, can you help me with this?"

Tad helped me take off my coat and the thick top beneath it. I was wearing a clinging top with long sleeves underneath that, because several layers kept you warmer during cold winter days. It was perfectly respectable, but Tad looked at me with an odd expression on his face.

"What's the matter? Haven't you seen a girl before?" The words slipped out before I realized I might have made the wrong assumption myself. "Sorry, I hadn't thought... Do people on Adonis have strict rules about clothing?"

"No," said Tad. "It's just that I'd only seen you wrapped up in coats. I hadn't realized you were such a delicate thing."

I nearly said something extremely rude, but realized at the last moment that Tad's tone of voice meant he thought the word delicate was a compliment rather than an insult. Possibly people on Adonis admired a totally different type of figure in a girl than people in our alliance.

"I've seen plenty of girls before," continued Tad. "Far too many of them, in fact. For the last couple of years, I've had to attend a succession of parties where every aristocratic family on Adonis has paraded their daughters in front of me. Most of them wearing the minimal possible clothing."

The set of buttons on my long-sleeved top were much smaller and easier to undo, so I could handle them myself without any problems, but I paused and frowned at Tad's words. It had been a shock to discover Tad could flatten Cage. Hearing that Tad had been pursued by hordes of girls was even more disconcerting.

Tad sighed. "Of course they're parading the girls in front of my name and my fortune, not me as a person. I hate the insincerity of it, but my grandfather insists I attend the parties. He wants me to marry and have children as soon as possible because of what happened to my father."

I slipped off the long-sleeved top, so now I was just wearing a sleeveless vest with tiny straps.

"Well, there's a good side to me being caught stealing that aircraft," said Tad, in a more cheerful voice. "Even if I return to Adonis instead of going to Zeus, I'll be in disgrace. No more parties. No more functions. No more having to be polite to endless identical girls decked out in the latest fashion of glittering wigs. They all look the same. They all ask the same boring questions. They're all grovellingly polite to me. That's one of the things that attracted me to you. You're so different."

"I certainly wasn't grovellingly polite to you," I said.

Tad laughed. "No, your reactions to me were gloriously genuine. You weren't impressed by me and you showed it. That stung my pride to start with, but then I realized this was the first time in my life I'd ever had an honest interaction with a girl."

I lay down on the sleeping bag. "Surely you'd had honest interactions with Phoenix? She doesn't wear a glittering wig either."

"Phoenix is a hard-working research assistant, not an aristocratic party girl, but she was as dreadfully polite to me as everyone else when we were on Adonis. She only started telling me what she really thought of me after we arrived in New York."

Tad knelt down beside me. "I'm setting up contact with the doctor now. As I said, I'll be showing her the images I'm seeing on a wall vid. She'll be hearing our voices too, and I'll be hearing what she says to me and relaying it on to you. Understand?"

"I think so. That means we have to be careful what we say now."

"That's right. I'll let you know when I break contact and we can talk freely again."

There was a short pause. "I'm talking to the doctor now," said Tad. "I have to check your arm bones to locate the injury. Tell me if there's any pain, how much, and exactly where it hurts."

I had the urge to look round the room, as if the doctor was hiding in the corner watching us. "It already hurts everywhere. Shooting pains running up and down my arm and shoulder."

"Then tell me when the pain changes." He held my arm steady with one hand and ran the other up and down it. "Anything?"

"No, just the same pain as before."

"I'll be squeezing your arm in different places now," said Tad.

He squeezed my wrist with one hand, lightly at first then harder, repeated that half a dozen times as he worked his way up my arm, and then sat back. "No especially painful area in the arm at all?"

"No."

"The doctor thinks the main problem is in your shoulder. She's working out what to do next. I've cut the sound and vision stream while she does that, because I wanted to check... Does this situation, me examining your arm, feel as awkward to you as it does to me?"

"Yes." I pulled a face. "The invisible doctor watching us isn't helping either."

"I hope it's not creepy."

"It's not creepy."

"Good," said Tad. "I admit I've pictured the possibility of... touching you, but this isn't how I imagined it happening. I'm doing my best to be as distantly polite as the circumstances allow."

I laughed. "You're being icily impersonal."

"Ah, the doctor's sent me a lot of instructions." Tad frowned. "I'm opening the sound and vision stream again. I'm afraid this is going to hurt."

CHAPTER TWENTY-SIX

"Are you awake?" Tad's voice asked. "It's time for me to check your pulse and temperature again."

I opened my eyes, glanced across at the windows, and saw the red light of dawn in the sky. "Chaos, I hadn't realized it was morning already."

"Oh, you're back to just politely saying chaos now. You really surprised me yesterday. I'd no idea you had such an extensive vocabulary of rude words." Tad seemed to be struggling not to laugh.

I blushed. "I spent the first eleven years of my life as a member of London division. Of course I know plenty of rude words. I don't normally use them myself, but I was in a lot of pain."

"I'm really sorry about that," said Tad. "We didn't have a body scanner to show what was wrong inside your shoulder, so we had to see what movements were physically possible and how painful they were."

"I understand it was necessary, and I apologize for calling you names."

"The one that really confused me was when you called me a skunk. How do you know about Cassandrian skunks?"

"I don't," I said. "When I said skunk, I meant an Earth skunk, some of which live in New York. If you ever meet something with black and white stripes, then I strongly recommend you leave it alone. One of the Manhattan division children teased one once, and even throwing the boy in the river didn't get rid of the smell afterwards."

Tad had the characteristic, distant expression that meant he was checking something on the Earth data net. "Ah, yes. Humans can smell the skunk spray in concentrations as low as ten parts per billion. Anyway, I didn't mind you calling me names when I was hurting you. I was just as relieved as you were when I could inject you with the local anaesthetic."

I was too embarrassed to admit it to Tad, but I hadn't gone quiet then out of relief, but out of pure terror. I'd been totally panic-stricken when I couldn't feel or move my arm, worrying that it had died. If I'd had any sense, I'd have asked Tad if that was what was supposed to happen with an anaesthetic, but I'd been much too afraid to put my fear into words.

"That injection will be wearing off now, but I can give you another, slightly smaller dose," he added.

"I don't think I need any more local anaesthetic," I said hastily.

"You still can't feel your shoulder and arm?"

"Only a bit," I lied. "They feel warm."

The truth was that my shoulder and arm felt hot, like I was outside in the sun on a very warm day instead of huddled in a sleeping bag in a freezing cold room. There was also a strange, throbbing sensation that felt as if it was deep inside the bones. The feeling hovered somewhere on the edge of pain, but it reassured me that my arm was still alive and part of me.

"Well, all right," said Tad, in a doubtful voice. "Anaesthetics do last longer on some people than others, but let me know if it starts hurting you."

"I will," I said, though I was determined that I wouldn't.

"Just remember that you must stay perfectly still until the full thirty-six hours of healing is complete. The bones knitting together is a relatively simple process, but any disruption to the muscle regeneration phase could leave you with a paralyzed arm."

Tad had been checking my pulse and temperature every hour during the night. Every time, he'd given me the same lecture about the need to keep perfectly still. The constant repetition was unnecessary. I could hardly forget the need to keep still when

Tad had borrowed both our knife belts to buckle round me, holding my left arm rigidly immobile against a piece of wood at my side.

The repetition was unnecessary, but I understood why Tad was acting this way. He'd appeared perfectly confident when he was working on my shoulder and arm, perhaps he'd truly been perfectly confident back then, but now he was suffering the strain of waiting thirty-six hours to find out if the treatment had worked. His mind was coming up with a host of things that could have gone wrong.

I knew that because my mind was thinking of those things as well. The doctor hadn't been able to examine me herself, so she could have misdiagnosed my injury. Tad could have made the injections into the wrong points in my shoulder. The stasis cabinet holding the vital regrowth fluid could have had a fault in the stasis field so the fluid had gone bad. I could have wrecked everything by making one incautious movement when Tad was wrapping me inside my sleeping bag.

"I won't move," I said.

Tad went to one of the stasis boxes that held our food supply, and shut down the field. "I'll have my breakfast now. Would you like something to eat?"

"I know I didn't eat anything yesterday, but I still don't seem hungry."

"Some of the medication I gave you slows your general metabolism so your body can focus its efforts on healing your injury," said Tad. "You'll need to catch up on eating the meals you missed when it wears off."

He took a plate of steaming hot food from the stasis box, activated the field again, sat on his mattress, and started eating. "This is wintereat again?"

"Yes, there's wintereat in almost every meal we eat."

"And the white stuff?"

I grinned. "That's chopped falling star meat."

"Oh." He tried a mouthful of it dubiously. "It's not that bad. There's a faint taste of cinnamon."

I'd never heard of cinnamon, so I didn't say anything.

"There were more meals in the stasis boxes than I expected," continued Tad. "I thought we were only spending three or four days here."

"On trips like this you have to take spare food. If there's a blizzard or something we could be stuck here for a while. If not, then we take back the extra meals."

Tad concentrated on his food for the next few minutes, then helped me drink a few sips of water. "I'll be making a list of medicines today, noting down the instructions for them from the Earth data net, and packing them into boxes. I'll only need to keep checking your pulse and temperature every two hours from now on, so you should try to get some sleep."

I hated leaving Tad to do all the work, it was a matter of pride to always contribute as much as I could, but I didn't argue. After all the effort trying to heal my arm, it would be stupid to mess things up now.

"Thank you for waking up every hour to check on me. How did you manage to do that?"

"I set something up on the Earth data net to wake me." He laughed. "Imagine a bell going off inside your head."

"What's it like being able to do all these amazing things?"

"All the girls on Adonis kept asking me that," said Tad. "They gushed at me about it being wonderful, so I had to say it was, but I can be honest with you. It feels horribly lonely."

He shook his head. "It must have been incredible in the days when everyone was webbed. Talking to other people with just your thoughts would have been almost like telepathy, but I'm the only one now, so…"

"Your grandfather isn't webbed then?"

"He was webbed as a child, just like everyone else was back then. And just like everyone else, his implanted web was designed to last a lifetime, but it needed retuning every year or so to compensate for changes in his brain."

Tad made a pained noise. "My grandfather told me how dreadful it was when his connection to the local data net became erratic and finally died. He said it was like losing part of his own mind."

I remembered Machico talking about his brother crying at

night as he went through that. "So how did you get webbed, and why is your web still working?"

"My grandfather realized civilization was heading off a cliff edge. The colony worlds traded some goods and raw materials with each other, but they all depended on Earth for vital equipment parts, medicines, and other items they couldn't make themselves because they didn't have the experts or the technology or the resources. Once Earth didn't have the experts or technology to make those items either, everything that depended on them was going to fail. It might take months, years, decades, or even centuries, but they'd all fail in the end."

I nodded. I'd helped to scavenge replacement parts to keep the equipment in the Parliament House working, so I knew all about technology failing.

"Most of those things weren't vital to civilization," said Tad. "The big exception was the interstellar portals. People could manage without ordinary portals, because they could use vehicles or walk, but once the interstellar portals were gone, there'd be no way to travel or trade supplies between worlds."

He waved his hands. "Colony worlds wouldn't just have to cope without the supplies from Earth, but without all the things from other worlds as well. Adonis is the most advanced of the colony worlds, the best equipped to cope alone, but would still be in trouble without the rare metals and the medicines it imports from dozens of other worlds."

Tad frowned at his empty plate. "My grandfather decided it was the duty of the family of Thaddeus Wallam-Crane to save interstellar portal technology. He knew that Adonis didn't have the technology to make replacement parts for the old portals, so his idea was to invent new interstellar portals that used much simpler components. He believed he might be able to do that, but only if he was webbed again."

"Does it really make that big a difference?" I asked.

"I honestly don't know. I'm so used to having all the information just a thought away, that... What matters is that my grandfather believed it did. He felt he was only half the man he'd been when he was webbed. He shamelessly used his position to corner web experts and resources. They managed to modify a couple of old webs to make them much easier to tune, but they couldn't change or replace the one in my grandfather's head without causing brain damage."

Tad pulled a face. "My grandfather had to make a new plan. He couldn't be webbed and re-invent interstellar portal technology himself, so his son would have to take his place. My father was webbed, studied portal technology, and started work on the problem, but he was kidnapped and killed. After that, it was my turn, and I had to learn everything faster than my father, start work younger than my father, because we were running out of time to save civilization."

He sighed. "I was webbed at seven years old. From what I've heard my grandfather say, I don't think the web in my head has ever been perfectly tuned. It's probably only working at 90 per cent efficiency, but the point is that I can retune it myself with simple tools and keep it at that 90 per cent."

"It's lucky your grandfather could find those experts and some spare webs," I said.

Tad hesitated before answering. "There weren't any spare webs left. My father's web, and my own, were both second-hand."

"What? You mean they'd been implanted into someone else's head before...?"

"Yes. All the webs had identification numbers, and I looked up the information for mine. I knew it was a stupid mistake, but I couldn't stop myself. It only took a single thought to get the data, and it's hard to stop thinking."

He paused. "The... previous owner was a girl. Her name was Ellie. She had dark hair like you, loved animals, and was smiling in all the images of her. She was only twelve years old when she was killed in an accident. Of course it made sense to use the newest webs possible, which meant taking ones from children, but..."

Tad got up, and stood with his back to me, looking out of the window. "That's why I can't stay on Earth. I have to go to Zeus and find a way to re-invent interstellar portals. It's not just for my grandfather, or to save civilization. It's because I promised Ellie that I'd make the best possible use of her legacy."

There was silence for a moment.

"That must sound strange to you," said Tad.

"No, I understand. At least, I understand a bit. Everything I have was owned by other people before me. When I play my flute, I often wonder who else played it before me, and what happened to them. It makes sense to me that you'd feel like that about Ellie."

"You're the only person I've ever told about her." Tad's voice was shaking. "I knew that my grandfather would think me a sentimental fool for caring about the previous owner of my web. He's a fiercely practical man without much time for emotions."

I pictured Tad's grandfather. A cold, harsh man driven by his obsession with interstellar portals.

"I'd better start packing those medicines." Tad hurried out of the room, still keeping his face turned away from me.

I lay staring up at the cracked ceiling above me. I imagined the childhood Tad had had on Adonis, and compared it to mine. He'd never been hungry, never fled from a firestorm, or had to worry about falling stars attacking him, but I'd never had something taken from a dead girl's brain and implanted into mine.

Tad had only been seven years old when that happened, and I was sure he had no choice about it. His grandfather wouldn't have asked his opinion, or listened to a refusal. Tad's father was already dead then, but hadn't the boy had anyone else to care for him? Tad had never mentioned his mother. Was she dead too?

It was two hours before Tad reappeared. He checked my temperature and pulse, and chatted for a couple of minutes about different parts of the Americas that might be a suitable new home for the alliance. He didn't mention Ellie again, so neither did I.

I spent the rest of the day lying still, bored and frustrated, with Tad appearing every two hours to have brief discussions about places called Virginia, Ohio, and Dakota. Eventually, the light from the windows started fading. I wondered if Tad would be able to sleep properly tonight, or if he'd still have to keep checking on me.

It was then that I smelt the smoke.

CHAPTER TWENTY-SEVEN

"Tad!" I shrieked. "Tad, I can smell something burning!" There was no response, so I tried yelling again. "Tad!"

Still no response. Tad could be in an entirely different area of the storage facility, well out of earshot. I was supposed to keep perfectly still for a full thirty-six hours, and it couldn't have been more than twenty-four so far. If I tried to get out of my sleeping bag, then I could do something dreadful to my healing shoulder, but I couldn't keep lying here when the building was on fire.

I tried one last desperate scream. "Tad!"

"I'm here." He appeared in the doorway, breathing heavily as if he'd run to reach me. "What's wrong? Is it your shoulder?"

"I can smell smoke. Something's on fire."

He sniffed. "I can't smell anything. Are you sure?"

"Of course I'm sure! I was in London when it burned, and I know the smell of smoke!"

He lifted his hands in surrender. "Calm down, Blaze. I believe you. I'll have a look round. Don't move."

He hurried off, and I lay there fighting against my panic. "We must have a clear escape route. We're on the ground floor of the building. I can't see any flames outside, so we just have to smash the window, climb out, and get to the river."

I realized I was talking to myself, and put my right hand over my mouth to shut myself up. I didn't want Tad to hear me babbling hysterically. Where the chaos was Tad anyway? How long did it take someone to...?

"You're right." Tad hurried back into the room. "An apartment block is burning. There seems to be more smoke than fire, and there's another building between it and us, but the wind is blowing this way. We need to keep an eye on the situation."

"We need to leave," I said. "Right now. We grab the boxes of medicine you've packed, put them in the boat, and head downriver."

"That's a really bad idea," said Tad. "If we move you to the boat now, then we'll wreck your shoulder. It'll be pitch dark outside soon as well. There's thick cloud cover, so no moonlight to help us get the boat downriver."

"It's a wide river, Tad. It flows towards the sea. We can't possibly get lost."

"No, but we could hit something and sink the boat. On the way here, we passed..."

"I know that," I interrupted. "Moving me to the boat could wreck my shoulder, and taking the boat downriver in the dark is risky, but it's better than staying here to be burnt alive."

"If the fire gets dangerously close to us, I promise we'll leave, but it really isn't necessary yet. Please try to calm down, Blaze." He tugged a chair over to the desk by the far end of the windows. "If I sit here, then I can keep an eye on the burning building. There's no need for you to worry."

Telling me not to worry about a burning building was like telling gravity to make things go up instead of down. I couldn't see the fire from where I was lying. Why the chaos had we put my mattress in the middle of this room, instead of where Tad was sitting? "Do you think the firestorm is starting?"

He sighed. "It's not the firestorm, Blaze. This is just a single random fire. Let's relax and eat our evening meal."

"I'm still not hungry."

"Well, I am. It's best if I eat now just in case the fire does turn out to be dangerous. If we have to head downriver at night, the most sensible thing would be to stop once we're well clear of the fire, tie up the boat, and wait until morning before we make the rest of the journey. If I'm going to spend the night freezing in a boat on the river, I'd rather do it with a full stomach."

I grudgingly felt Tad had a point there. He seemed to take my silence as agreement, because he fetched a plate of food, took it over to the desk, and sat there eating while watching the fire. At least, I hoped he was watching the fire.

I opened my mouth to ask if he was watching the fire, but managed to stop myself before I actually said the words. Chaos, Tad had told me he'd keep an eye on the burning building, and he was sitting facing it. It was perfectly irrational to keep nagging him every few seconds.

When Tad had swallowed his last mouthful of food, he sat frowning out of the window for a while before finally speaking. "The fire has spread to the second apartment block. That's the one next to us."

"We have to leave then. If you unzip the sleeping bag, and steady me as I get up, then..."

"No, you lie still! There has to be a better solution than wrecking your shoulder by running away. This storage facility must have fire defences. Everything built after 2150 had to... Yes, I've found the original fire defence specifications."

We should be leaving, but Tad was happily studying things on the Earth data net. I considered which insult I should yell at him. None of them were bad enough.

"We do have fire defences," said Tad, "so I just have to get them working. The master building controls are only two rooms away. I'll be back in less than a minute, so don't you dare move!"

He hurried off, and I lay there biting my lip. The fire defences for the Americas Parliament House still worked. At least, they'd worked the last time someone got drunk and accidentally started a fire, because the internal sprinkler system had drenched everyone in the Brooklyn division area. A different division leader would have beaten up the guilty party, but Ghost had ordered him to do sewer cleaning duty for the next six months which was probably worse.

Of course the fact the Parliament House fire defences worked didn't mean the ones here would. Machico did maintenance checks on our defences, but this building had been abandoned for decades.

Tad reappeared. "The fire defences are on, so there's no need to worry."

No need to worry? The smell of smoke was getting stronger, but I tried to argue rationally instead of just screaming. "Presumably the other buildings have fire defences too, and those don't seem to be doing anything to stop the fire."

"Yes, but those are ordinary apartment blocks," said Tad. "Their power was cut off when the New York power supply was shut down. This building is part of a Military complex, with a backup emergency power storage system that should keep the fire defences running for weeks."

"You don't just need power for fire defences to work, you need water too. Our building uses the rain water collected in the roof tank, but this building doesn't have a roof tank."

"This building is right next to the river," said Tad. "The fire defences take their water directly from that."

I groaned. "The pumps could have failed, the pipes could have clogged, the..."

"I realize all that," said Tad. "The heat levels on the side of this building closest to the fire should be high enough to trigger the external water jets soon. If they don't start up in the next five minutes, we'll leave. I'll get you into the boat, then I'll grab the boxes of medicine. I've piled them up by the door to the riverbank, so it will only take a couple of minutes to get them aboard the boat."

Five minutes. Tad had promised that we'd leave in five minutes. I stared at the windows. It was dark outside, but there was a faint glow to the right that must be coming from the fire. I started counting seconds, and had just got past two hundred when there was a slight pattering sound on the ceiling like light rain.

"That's one of the external water jets coming on," said Tad.

The rain on the roof suddenly got a lot heavier.

"That's the rest of the water jets starting up," he added. "We can stop worrying now."

I was much less joyful about it. The external water jets were on, but I'd still feel much safer on a boat in the middle of the Hudson River.

Tad peered out of the window. "We'd better stay awake until those two apartment blocks burn themselves out."

"I wasn't planning to go to sleep while the building next door is on fire!"

"I understand you've got a phobia of fires after what happened in London, but you really don't..." Tad broke off, because the pattering sound of the water jets had stopped. "What's gone wrong?"

I stared at him in disbelief. "What's gone wrong is the fire defences have broken down, just like everything else in this city breaks down."

"They all cut out at once," said Tad. "The emergency power system must have failed, or perhaps just run out of stored power. It would only take a light accidentally left on for a few decades to..."

"Tad, it doesn't matter why the fire defences stopped working. The fact is they've stopped, so we need to leave."

"This building hasn't even been singed yet, and it has just been drenched with water. Just give me two more minutes to work on this. If we move you now, we'll seriously damage your shoulder."

"It's already had twenty-four hours to heal, so it'll probably be fine."

"It won't be fine, Blaze. There's an intricate group of tendons and muscles in your shoulder. The slightest interruption in the muscle regeneration process can make those tendons and muscles attach to the wrong places or even fuse together."

I chewed at my lower lip. If we messed this up, then we wouldn't have another chance to heal my arm, at least not before I had to face Cage. My head was a battleground of conflicting fears. I was afraid of Cage. I was scared of being left with a useless arm. I was terrified of fire.

"All right," I said. "But only two minutes."

"We need power." Tad paced round the room, muttering rapidly to himself. "Power has been building up in the New York power reservoir for the last eighteen years. There's plenty of power if I can just reach it. This building is part of power grid reference TT617/388. The power grid control system is... Chaos, I need security codes to access it. Well, naturally I'd need security codes, because... Yes, it's accepted the old Wallam-Crane family security codes! I'm into the power grid control system!"

He was jabbering so fast now that I could hardly follow what he was saying. "Everything is set to off because they shut down the whole New York area power grid. I just need to turn on grid reference TT617/388 and... Chaos, it won't let me do that. Why won't it let me do that? Maybe I need to turn on the... No, it won't let me do that either. What fool designed this system? Well, if..."

There was rain on the roof again. I gazed at Tad in awe. "The fire defences are working again. You did it!"

"I think I did rather more than I intended," said Tad. "I was desperate, and couldn't think what else to do."

I didn't understand the anxious look on his face. "What's wrong?"

"It's not wrong exactly," said Tad. "It's just that I couldn't work out how to turn on the power for this specific building, so I turned on the whole New York area power grid. Look!"

He pointed at the windows. The view through them wasn't dark any longer. There were lights out there. Hundreds of lights, thousands of lights, tens of thousands of lights. Mostly white, but some in reds, and blues, and greens, and one massive flashing sign on the side of an apartment block showing an image of a girl dancing.

The heir of Thaddeus Wallam-Crane was standing beside me. He'd just had to think an order and New York had obeyed him. The magic of the past was alive again.

CHAPTER TWENTY-EIGHT

"Blaze, wake up!"

I opened my eyes, and saw the shadowy figure of Tad kneeling next to me. It was still dark in the room, I could still see the blazing lights of New York through the windows, but something had changed. It took me a moment to pin down what it was. The sound of rain on the roof had gone.

"The fire defences have stopped working again! Why? What's wrong this time?"

Tad laughed. "Nothing's wrong. They turned themselves off hours ago when the fire in the building next door went out."

"Oh." I felt a fool.

"I woke you up because it's been thirty-six hours since your first injection of regrowth fluid. Your shoulder should have finished healing."

I expected Tad to unseal my sleeping bag, but instead he stood up and went across to the door. I wondered where the chaos he was going, but he stopped by the door, flicked a switch, and the room was flooded with light. Of course it made perfect sense to turn the lights on now that we had power. I was just so used to wandering round abandoned buildings waving a flashlight that the thought of turning the lights on hadn't occurred to me.

Tad came to kneel next to me again, and this time he did open my sleeping bag. I started shivering as he undid the belts holding my left arm to my body. Partly from cold, but mostly from fear. If the treatment hadn't worked...

"Go ahead and try moving your arm." Tad sat back on his own mattress and watched me anxiously. "The doctor says it should respond perfectly normally now."

I tentatively lifted my arm up from the mattress. "It moves and there's no pain!"

Tad gave a long sigh of relief. "The doctor said this should work, I knew it should work, but I couldn't help imagining all the things that could go wrong."

"Me too," I said. "I've been scared to death. Can I sit up now?"

"You can do any normal movements. It's not a good idea to lift anything really heavy with your left arm until you've been moving it for two or three hours. After that, you don't need to worry at all."

I sat up, tried lifting my left arm up to shoulder height, and then pointed high above my head. I looked up at my own left hand in awe. "It's better. It's really better. Cage can't use me to destroy Donnell any longer. Thank you."

Tad's smile widened as he watched my face. "I'm truly glad I could help."

I lowered my arm and then reached out to take Tad's right hand. His fingers squeezed mine, and he looked down at our linked hands.

"We're still not doing the relationship thing?"

I shook my head. "No, we're still on opposite sides. We're enemies, but we're good enemies."

"The very best sort of enemies," said Tad.

We held hands for a moment longer, and then I gave a sudden, bigger shiver that was nothing to do with fear, just pure cold.

"You'd better get properly dressed again," said Tad.

"Yes." I let go of his hand. "Thank you again. Please thank the doctor as well."

I hunted among the heap of bedding for the rest of my clothes, and put them on, glorying in the simple fact I could thrust my left arm into a sleeve without pain.

"I'm sorry it's so cold in here," said Tad. "I tried turning the heating on in this row of offices, but there was a nasty buzzing sound and the heaters went dead. When I had a closer look, I found some of the corridor wiring had been nibbled by rats."

I pulled my jacket on. "I'm used to cold buildings."

"I'm getting used to the cold too. I'm not so sure about rats though."

I stood up, went over to the window, and looked out at a New York that was resplendent with light and colour. "I suppose you have lots of brightly lit cities on Adonis."

Tad came to stand beside me. "We don't have any cities at all. People didn't want a repeat of the ecological and pollution issues that happened on Earth, so it was decided that only one continent would be inhabited on each world, and incoming colonists would be strictly limited in number. Humanity scattered across five hundred new worlds. Adonis has the largest population of any of them, but it still isn't that high, and people live in thousands of small settlements."

He paused to pull a face. "That will probably change now the portals are failing. People are already abandoning the more isolated settlements to cluster closer together. Perhaps when all the portals are gone, there'll be cities on Adonis. It's one of the few worlds with enough people, experts, and technology to keep some sort of civilization going. Most of the others don't have a chance."

"They do have a chance," I said. "Thaddeus Wallam-Crane the Eighth will build new interstellar portals and stop civilization from falling."

Tad laughed. "Do you really believe that?"

"Actually, I do. I've grown up hearing tales of a past that sounded magical, but I thought all the magicians were gone forever. Looking out of this window, seeing the buildings look as dazzling as in all the old stories, I believe there's one last magician walking among us and he'll succeed in his goal."

Tad frowned at me. "This isn't about magic. I can't wave a hand and work miracles. This is about science, technology, and the difficulty of manufacturing tiny components to precise standards."

"But the difference between science and magic is getting paper thin from my point of view," I said. "My grandparents were webbed. They lived in a world full of scientific wonders. If they wanted to know how any of those wonders worked, they could get the information from the Earth data net with a single thought."

I turned to face Tad. "Those days were already fading when my parents were children. They were never webbed. They knew things like portals were scientific wonders, but they didn't know how the science worked. Now there's my generation."

I shook my head. "I'm hovering between seeing things as science and magic. I've travelled by portal once in my life, escaping the London firestorm to come to New York. I've seen you fix an injury that should have taken months to heal, if it healed at all, within a few hours. I'm looking at a girl of light dancing on the side of a building. My head knows that these things are achieved by advanced technology, and there are scientific rules behind how they work, but I can't stop my emotions reacting to them as if they're magic. I know that my children, if I ever have children, will just see them as pure magic."

"I understand," said Tad. "When I saw the children here dancing round the portals, trying to make them work with their chants, I realized I was seeing the future of all the other worlds. Once the ability to make something is lost, then it only takes a generation or two for it to change from science to magic."

"Yes," I said, "and that's why I agree you have to leave Earth. This is the last chance to save interstellar portal technology. There won't be another magician in the next generation, or enough experts and technology left to help him. I don't want the other worlds to end up in the same mess as Earth."

"I thought you hated off-worlders," said Tad.

I grinned. "Phoenix and Braden are quite likeable."

Tad laughed.

"So you'll go to Zeus to build your new interstellar portals?" I asked.

"I may go to Adonis first to see my grandfather, but then I'll be going to Zeus. Adonis has lost faith in me, and the other planets in Alpha sector take the view that if Adonis can't do this, then they can't either, but Beta sector is taking a different approach. They've been organizing their society based on a clan and craft system, grouping the families of similar experts together, with the idea of handing knowledge down through the generations."

He shrugged. "Each Betan world already has clans specializing in different areas like medicine or electronics. Now one of the leading political clans is organizing the Fidelis Project. This aims to take the approach a step further, by getting every Betan world to send its best portal experts and other scientists to Zeus in a final attempt to save interstellar portal technology. The organizers sent a deputation to Adonis a few months ago, inviting me to lead the project."

"But you didn't go to Zeus," I said. "You came to Earth instead. You mentioned that was because you needed to find something called the Rosetta component."

Tad nodded. "I'd been trying to invent an interstellar portal that we can build with current technology, but my work had hit a concraz wall. There's a component in every portal that's tuned to its own position in space, and is key to successfully locating and connecting to destination portals. That component is totally impossible to manufacture now, and I couldn't come up with a simpler version to replace it."

He waved his hands. "I had one last hope. I knew Thaddeus Wallam-Crane's original prototype portal had used a different version of the Rosetta component, so I needed to get my hands on that component before I went to Zeus. The Adonis authorities wouldn't agree to send a retrieval mission to New York, so I decided to come myself. Phoenix and Braden agreed to help me because they desperately wanted to go to Zeus. Given the limited availability of interstellar portal travel now, their only chance of getting there was if I took them with me."

"Why would Braden and Phoenix want to leave Adonis for Zeus?"

Tad smiled. "When the deputation from Zeus came to

negotiate with me, Phoenix got into a relationship with one of the women. Livia tried to stay on Adonis with Phoenix, but the Adonis authorities insisted on her going back to Zeus."

"So Phoenix wants to go to Zeus to be with her partner, Livia. What about Braden?"

"I met Braden when I was weight lifting at the gym," said Tad. "One day, I noticed he looked upset. When I asked what was wrong, he told me that his parents split up when he was a small child. Braden went to Adonis with his mother, but his older brother went to Zeus with their father. Interstellar mail is very limited, but Braden had had a handful of messages from his brother over the years. Now a message had arrived telling him his brother and his sister-in-law had been killed in an accident."

Tad pulled a pained face. "Braden was worried about his orphaned nephews and nieces on Zeus. He tried to get to Zeus to help care for them, but his application for an interstellar portal trip on compassionate grounds was rejected."

I made a sympathetic noise intended for the absent Braden rather than Tad.

"When I found I needed a pilot to fly a plane for me, I naturally went to Braden." Tad sighed. "This trip was supposed to be so simple. Everything went perfectly to start with. We flew to Manhattan, broke into the museum, and found what we needed packed away in a stasis box. I was nearly dancing with delight when we came out of the museum, but then we saw the aircraft was smashed."

"So you found your Rosetta component," I murmured.

"Yes." Tad dug into a pocket and held something out in the palm of his hand. "I know it doesn't look much, just a tiny thing of glass and metal, but combined with a lot of information only available on the Earth data net it's given me the answers I needed. My ancestor really was a genius. I hadn't thought of this. I could have kept working until my hundredth and died without thinking of this. It's utterly brilliant in its simplicity, but I understand why he changed to the later, more sophisticated version. It's all in your children's chant."

"What?"

"Dial it! Dial it! Portal, dial it!" Tad chanted the words. "If you use this simple component, you have to turn a dial to do manual tuning before the portal establishes. That wasn't ideal, so my ancestor developed the later version of the Rosetta component, which could locate destination portals more accurately."

Tad paused. "It should be possible to manufacture the prototype version of the Rosetta component on Zeus. It doesn't matter if we build new interstellar portals where you have to turn a dial manually to make the final connection, so long as they work."

I looked back out of the window. Tad would go back to Adonis, and then travel on to the even more distant star system of Zeus in Beta sector. The lights of New York were beautiful, but now I studied them in more detail I could see the ones that were missing. The signs that were lit up but missing some letters. The buildings that had lights in some windows but not others.

"It's nearly dawn," I said. "We should eat and get on with some work."

"There's not much left to do now. I've filled all the stasis boxes with medicines, and made notes on how to use them. I'll get us some breakfast."

"No, let me do it. I've felt so frustrated and useless lying still while you did all the work."

I fetched us two meals. They weren't quite as hot as they'd been when we arrived. Stasis boxes preserved their contents perfectly, but every time we opened and shut them the meals inside lost some of their heat.

Tad looked at his meal and groaned. "Wintereat and chopped falling star again."

We pulled up chairs and sat at the desk to eat. After two days of not wanting to eat, I was ravenously hungry, gulping down every morsel of my food. I didn't notice that Tad was barely eating until he spoke in a discontented voice.

"They've put far too much cinnamon on this."

"I don't know what cinnamon is, but I do know we don't have any. That's just the way falling stars taste."

"The last meal wasn't nearly as..." Tad broke off and made an odd hiccupping noise. He stood up, looked round urgently, grabbed a waste bin from under the desk, and was sick in it.

For about one second I was just shocked, but then my brain started working. I'd seen this happen to other people, and I'd suffered it myself. "Tad, I think you have..."

"I think I have your winter fever." Tad dropped the waste bin onto the floor, and slumped down on his chair.

"How could this happen?" I asked. "You said you'd been vaccinated against Earth diseases when you arrived here."

"Those vaccinations wouldn't cover new diseases," said Tad. "From what I'd heard about the incubation period of your winter fever, there was every chance I'd get ill sometime in the next three days. That's why I was working so hard to get the medicines packed."

"Why didn't you warn us you were likely to get ill?"

"What I'd learned about your winter fever terrified me. Donnell said you'd had over thirty deaths from it. That was an appallingly high mortality rate, and it wasn't just the especially vulnerable who'd died, like babies and the elderly, but healthy young adults as well. When Donnell mentioned supply runs, I grabbed the chance to suggest we could get medicines. If I'd warned him I might get ill, he wouldn't have sent me upriver with you, and I had to come myself because there'd be little chance of you getting the right medicines for winter fever without me."

He pulled a face. "I knew I was taking a chance doing this, but I've already messed up Phoenix and Braden's lives by dragging them here with me. I couldn't risk them dying of this fever, so I had to get you the medicines to treat us."

He dug a hand into his pocket, and put some boxes of tablets on the table. "I've discussed the winter fever symptoms with the doctor. She thinks it's a mutated version of a fever that hit the settlements a few years ago. There was a theory it was spread by birds, and your people hunt ducks and geese for food, so..."

"Never mind how we caught it," I interrupted. "What tablets do you need to take?"

"One of these large white ones, and two of the small blue

ones. Four times a day, with at least four hours between each dose, until the fever breaks. I'll take my first dose now."

I watched him struggling to open the boxes, and took them out of his hands. "Let me help you. You've been taking care of me, and now it's my turn to take care of you."

I handed Tad his tablets, and watched him gulp them down with a drink from a water bottle. "Have you packed plenty of these medicines?"

"A whole stasis box full," he said. "We have to load the boat and head back downriver now."

"We can't," I said. "I know how fast this illness hits people. You may not even make it as far as the boat before passing out."

"I'm fine."

Tad stood up, wavered, and started falling. I managed to catch him on the way down and steer him across to land on his mattress.

"My legs wouldn't hold me," he said, in a disbelieving voice.

"I told you it comes on fast. I can't take you downriver like this."

"But we must go," said Tad. "If I'm sick, then Braden and Phoenix must be sick too. We have to get the medicine to them."

"Don't worry. I can send up a distress flare and Donnell will send help. There'll be a boat here by…"

I broke off my sentence because there was the distant wailing sound of a familiar siren.

"What the chaos is that?" asked Tad. "Some sort of alarm?"

I stood up and looked out of the window. There she was, white and graceful, powering her way through the water. We didn't have to call for help, because it had already arrived.

"That's a ship's siren," I said. "The Spirit of New York is here."

CHAPTER TWENTY-NINE

I ran to the riverside door, opened it, and waited impatiently for the Spirit of New York to make her way to the bank. What looked like Aaron and Julien jumped down to tie mooring ropes and put the gangplank in place, then the unmistakable figure of Donnell came down it.

I hurried to meet him. "Why did you risk bringing the Spirit of New York upriver in the dark?"

"Phoenix and Braden started showing winter fever symptoms yesterday evening. I knew that if they were sick, then Tad was probably ill too. I was going to bring the Spirit of New York upriver at dawn to fetch you home, but then all the lights in New York came on. I wasn't sure what was happening, and the steadily strengthening wind made it obvious a storm was on its way, so I decided to head upriver right away to get you home before the storm hit. With all the lights blazing in Manhattan and Yonkers, it was nearly as bright as day on the river anyway."

Donnell glanced over his shoulder and lowered his voice. "What the chaos was Tad thinking of, turning on the New York power supply without warning me?"

"We had a bit of a crisis," I said.

"I don't see why turning on the power would help Tad with the winter fever."

"Tad turned on the power because the building next door was on fire. We needed the fire defences working."

"Ah." Donnell turned to look at the burned out apartment

blocks. "I noticed there'd been a recent fire. That happened last night, and Tad was already too sick to head downriver?"

It was far too complicated to explain that it had been me who couldn't run away, not Tad. It would be a bad idea to explain anyway. If Donnell found out about everything that had happened, then he'd try to protect me from Cage, and that could lead to disaster. We'd have a much better chance of winning the coming battle if I fought it alone.

"Yes," I said.

"I suppose that's a reasonable excuse."

"We've found a lot of medicine," I added hastily.

"That's very good news. The arrival of more medicine will boost the mood of the alliance, and strengthen our position against Cage. I wish I had equally good news to report, but sadly I don't. I've had a couple of chats with Major, but I'm making no progress with him at all. My impression is that Major has inside knowledge of Cage's plans, and he seems worryingly confident those plans will succeed. I just hope we get back to the Parliament House before Cage does anything drastic."

I didn't say anything. I knew that Cage wouldn't do anything drastic before we got back. His attack would start when I arrived.

"Where's Tad?" asked Donnell.

"In here." I led the way into the building, and through to the office where Tad was lying on his mattress. I thought for a moment that he was unconscious, but his eyes flickered open as Donnell went to stand over him.

"Oh, it's you," he said.

"Yes, it's me," said Donnell. "I appreciate you had a fire heading towards you, but did you have to turn on all the power in New York?"

"I only meant to turn on the power to this building," said Tad.

"Well, most of the lights in the city seem to be on now," said Donnell, "which makes no sense to me. The street lighting should be on, and possibly the lights in offices, but why are there so many lights in private apartments? Surely most people heading off to other worlds would turn off their power and water before they left?"

"That's true. Control system made no sense either." Tad rubbed his hand across his forehead. "Maybe because power reservoir nearing critical point. Safety systems breaking down. Can't seem to think."

Donnell sighed. "Well, turning everything on may be a good thing. All those lights, and chaos knows what other things as well, are all using power. That surely must be helping the problem with the power reservoir and delaying the firestorm."

He shrugged. "Forget that now and listen carefully to me. Everyone got very excited when the lights came on. Machico and I did some fast thinking, and claimed that Machico had turned the New York power supply on."

He paused. "Are you hearing this, Tad?"

Tad's eyes had closed, but they opened again. "Yes."

"When people asked, as they naturally did, why Machico hadn't managed to do that for the past eighteen years, we said that Braden had given him some extra information that helped."

"Braden," repeated Tad, in a dazed voice.

"We wanted to divert attention away from you, and thought that Braden was a pilot so he'd know a bit about electronics and engines," said Donnell. "Most people seem to have accepted that explanation, but my officers know who you are, so I'm sure they suspect you're more deeply involved than we're admitting."

"I saw Julien outside," I said anxiously. "Is he still an officer?"

"Julien's situation is a bit debatable at the moment," said Donnell. "I didn't know what I'd find when I got here, so I daren't include anyone in my party who didn't know who Tad was. I chose to bring Aaron and Luther along as reasonably trustworthy, and Julien because it seemed safer than leaving him behind."

Donnell looked down at Tad. "Please try not to do anything else dramatic for a while, because there's a limit to how much we can explain away. If people guess you're webbed, then your life expectancy is going to be measured in hours, if not minutes."

"Understood." Tad's eyes closed again.

"Chaos," said Donnell. "I could never shut the boy up before, but now I can barely drag a word out of him. He must be desperately ill. Is all the medicine we need in the piles of active stasis boxes by the door?"

"Yes. Instructions too." I waved the packs of tablets. "I've got some of the medicine for Tad's fever right here."

"Then we'll get Tad on board the ship first, and load up the boxes afterwards." Donnell stuck his head out of the door and shouted. "Aaron!"

Aaron appeared in response. "Yes?"

"Give me a hand carrying Tad," said Donnell. "You take his legs, while I carry the mouth end."

The two of them lifted Tad. I gathered up his mattress and sleeping bag, and followed them out to the riverbank. As I went outside, a gust of wind snatched at the hood of my coat and blew it down. Donnell was right. There was definitely a storm on the way.

I sprinted ahead and up the gangplank to where Luther was holding the door to the huge main cabin open. I went inside, and managed to get the mattress spread out in time for Donnell and Aaron to dump Tad down on it.

Donnell turned to Luther and Aaron. "We'll load up the stasis boxes and other supplies now. We can tow the small boat downriver behind us."

They hurried off. I wrapped Tad up in his sleeping bag, and stared down at him anxiously. He was already unconscious, which was an ominous sign. I wondered if Phoenix and Braden had got the winter fever this badly as well. I hoped the medicine would start helping Tad soon. We needed to get back to the Parliament House as soon as possible, so I could give the medicine to Phoenix and Braden too.

It seemed like a long time before I heard the engines cough their way into life, and the Spirit of New York started moving. There was a slight lurch as we left the riverbank, some swaying as the ship turned round, and then things steadied again. I glanced out of the window to the east, and saw the rising sun was competing with the lights of New York, and adding a flush of red to the sky.

The door opened. I turned to look at it, expecting Donnell to walk in, but it was Julien. I hastily moved to stand between him and the unconscious, helpless Tad, and my hand hovered over the knife on my belt.

"What do you want?" I demanded.

"I want to apologize," said Julien. "The way I reacted on the roof was wrong, but understandable. We've all got good reason to hate the name Thaddeus Wallam-Crane. There was no excuse for my behaviour later on though. I've had silly moments before when I was drunk, but I went much too far that time."

I'd no idea whether he was genuinely sorry, or was just saying this because he thought it might help him keep his position as an officer. I knew Hannah's betrayal had made me suspicious of everyone's motives, so I tried to keep my tone of voice perfectly neutral as I replied.

"Thank you for the apology. If drinking alcohol affects you so badly that you..."

"I know!" Julien interrupted me, lifting his hands in surrender. "You don't need to tell me because I've spent the last few days telling myself. Marsha changed the personal tag on my knife belt to be a bottle nearly a year ago."

He pulled a face. "I knew that tag meant people thought I wasn't in control of my drinking, my drinking was controlling me. I made excuses to myself and pretended the tag was unfair. I can't make those excuses any longer. I'm going to have to..."

The door opened again, and this time it was Luther. He glared at Julien. "What are you doing in here? Donnell told you to stay away from Blaze and the off-worlders."

Julien muttered something rude and headed off, closing the door behind him. Luther gave an irritated look after him, before taking a step closer to me. "I've been worried sick about you, Blaze. Chaos knows what Donnell was thinking of, sending you upriver alone with that leech."

I'd used the leech word myself often enough, but I hated Luther using it now. We called the off-worlders leeches because they took things without giving anything in return. We might have helped Tad with food and shelter, but he'd done plenty of things to help us too.

"Anyway, I'm here now," said Luther. "I sorted out the hunting group leadership problem while you were away. My group has been very successful, so now everyone knows I'm a great leader."

I'd forgotten all about the issue of Luther leading hunting groups. It sounded as if Machico's tactic of giving Luther's group the best hunting area had worked, or maybe I was just being uncharitable and Luther really was a brilliant hunting group leader.

"I'm pleased to hear that," I said politely.

"We can carry on and get married now. On the way upriver, I tried talking to Donnell about our wedding plans, but he said that anything about your marriage had to be discussed with you not him."

Wedding plans? Chaos, with everything else that had been happening, I'd totally forgotten about Luther's high-handed decision to marry me.

"I think the day after tomorrow would be best for the wedding," Luther continued. "The sooner we get this settled, the better."

I was annoyed about Luther calling Tad a leech, and I resented his assumption that he just had to say the word and I'd eagerly marry him. "Haven't you forgotten something important?"

Luther looked puzzled. "I don't know of anything else happening the day after tomorrow."

I sighed. "You've told me you're going to marry me, but you haven't asked my opinion about it. If you had, then I'd have told you that I don't want to marry you."

He seemed totally bewildered. "What are you talking about? I know you love me, Blaze. When you were fifteen, you kept looking at me and..."

I hurriedly interrupted him. "I know I used to have a silly crush on you, but I've fully recovered from it, and I don't want to marry you."

Luther frowned. "You don't mean that. You have to marry me. You need someone to take care of you, and I want to take my father's place as deputy alliance leader."

"I didn't notice you doing anything to take care of me on the roof," I said.

Luther's frown deepened into a glower. "That's completely unfair. If Julien had tried to harm you, then of course I'd have done something about it. I threw him out of here just now, didn't I?"

"I suppose so," I grudgingly admitted, "but the point is I'm not marrying anyone just to get them to take care of me. I intend to take care of myself."

Luther gave me a look of offended dignity. "We'll talk about this later, when you're in a more reasonable mood."

"No, we won't," I said. "There's nothing to talk about. I'm saying this for the third and final time now, Luther. I don't want to marry you. I'm not going to marry you. I wouldn't marry you if you were the last man in New York. Are you going to accept that now, or do I have to paint it in large letters on the wall of Reception for everyone to read?"

Luther abruptly turned and stalked out of the cabin, leaving the door flapping open in the wind. I hurried to close it, and then knelt down by Tad's side. His forehead was hot to the touch, his eyes were closed, and he was moving restlessly. I held a bottle of water to his lips, and he sucked at it greedily.

I looked out of the window at the lights of New York, and saw a few snowflakes were appearing, swirling wildly in the wind. We were racing the storm downriver. When we arrived at Parliament House, it would be time for me to face Cage.

CHAPTER THIRTY

By the time the Spirit of New York arrived at her regular spot on the riverbank, it was snowing hard. Aaron and Luther found an old door to use as a stretcher to carry Tad, while Donnell, Julien and I carried some of the stasis boxes. Donnell and Julien led the way along the path, while I trailed behind the stretcher, fretting every step of the way about Tad being out in the snow and the bitter cold wind. He was running a high temperature and was still unconscious.

I'd expected the tablets Tad had taken to have more effect than this. Before we ran out of medicine, I'd seen sick people given tablets, and there was usually an instant improvement. There was the worrying possibility that the tablets were actually helping a lot, but Tad had a particularly severe case of winter fever.

As we finally neared the building, Donnell beckoned me to join him. I hurried past the stretcher, casting one last anxious glance at Tad.

"I'm afraid I've got some bad news for you," said Donnell, in a wary voice. "Hannah's decided to move to Manhattan division. I hope you understand why I didn't try to stop her. The other divisions only allow people to leave in special circumstances, but I've never forced anyone to stay in the Earth Resistance against their will."

"Don't worry," I said. "I already knew Hannah was moving to Manhattan division. She told me about it before Tad and I went upriver."

"I didn't realize that," said Donnell. "Hannah's decision must have been terribly upsetting for you."

"I found it extremely disappointing," I said, in what I hoped was a coolly neutral voice.

I was relieved that Donnell didn't ask any more questions, just hurried on to the Parliament House door and elbowed it open. I followed him inside, and was startled by warm air hitting my face. Donnell dumped his stasis boxes on the floor against the wall, and I automatically put mine next to them, before looking round in wonder.

There might be snow outside, but it was summer in Reception. All the lights were on, blazing brighter than I'd seen them in years. The air wasn't just warm, it was almost hot. It looked like the whole of the alliance was sitting at the tables, but instead of being huddled in thick coats they were wearing short-sleeved summer clothes. Weirdest of all, there was no scent of smoke in the air. The cooking fire, which burned day and night all year round, was out. The metal grating over it was bare of the usual cooking pots and kettles. Those were standing on some alien flexiplas and metal objects instead.

Donnell gave a faint groan and leaned to mutter in my right ear. "Oh, wonderful. Heat. Lights. Electric cooking. Everyone's getting really comfortable for the first time in decades, just as I have to persuade them to leave New York."

I had no chance to reply because the others had arrived at the door. I held it open for them, and watched Tad's stretcher being carried inside and put on the floor. We'd covered him with a sleeping bag, which had a thin layer of snow on it. I hastily grabbed the sleeping bag, shook away the white flakes before they could melt, and then peeled off my own frozen gloves and coat so I could feel the warm air. Rapture!

Marsha came hurrying up to collect our knife belts. I unbuckled mine, my fingers slow and clumsy from cold. Tad was still wearing his belt, so I undid that as well, and tugged it out from under him, before handing both belts to Marsha.

Donnell handed his own belt over to Marsha as well. "Where's Machico?" he asked.

"Rigging an engine to pump river water up to the roof tank," said Marsha. "Now we have proper hot water, everyone's having showers and catching up on washing clothes, so we're getting through the water fast."

I looked round for Cage, and tensed as I saw he was walking across Reception towards us. Donnell took a couple of steps forward to meet him, but Cage ignored his approach, coming to stand facing me instead.

"Are you going to do what I want, Blaze?" he asked. "Yes or no?"

"No," I said.

He laughed as if he was pleased at my refusal. Perhaps he was. I could imagine that Cage was so angry by now that he'd prefer to take the alliance leadership by force rather than have his enemies meekly surrender.

Cage turned to face the room and raised both arms above his head. "Everyone, pay attention!" he shouted. "I have important news for you."

There was no need for Cage to yell like that. Everyone had already been nosily watching us come in with the stretcher. They'd obviously seen Cage coming over to me, and were wondering what was going on. Cage was just shouting to maximize the drama.

Donnell took a step towards me. "What's happening, Blaze?"

I gave an urgent shake of my head. "Please trust me to handle this myself. It's vital you don't get involved."

He frowned.

"Trust me," I repeated. "I've got this under control."

Donnell nodded in acknowledgement, but shrugged off his coat and dumped it on the floor, clearly braced for a fight. Everyone else in Reception was sitting or standing perfectly still, so the single movement over by the entrance to Sanctuary caught my eye. Machico had just walked in and was watching this too.

"Blaze has been lying to us." Cage's voice boomed out across Reception. "Months and months of lies. She's made fools of us all very successfully, but that wasn't enough for her. She had to push her luck too far, and mock us by becoming an officer."

Over at the Brooklyn division tables, Ghost stood up. "Is there any point to this speech, Cage, or are you just indulging your usual desire to be the centre of attention?"

Cage turned towards him. "My point is this. Blaze has problems with her arm. We've had her forced on us as an officer, when she isn't just a girl, but a burden on the rest of us."

There was a sudden burst of whispering round Reception. I'd spent the journey back downriver planning how to handle this. I couldn't fight Cage physically, but I didn't need to. This battle would be fought with words, and the more noise Cage made at the beginning, the deeper he committed himself to the attack, the better. He was aiming to use me to destroy Donnell and the alliance, but I could turn the full force of that destruction back against him.

The biggest danger was that nobody would listen to what I said, or even hear it. I was an insignificant figure standing next to the bulk of Cage, and I couldn't shout as loudly as him. I marched straight past Cage to reach the Resistance tables, and used a chair as a stepping stone to stand on one of them.

"I'm no burden," I shouted. "I bring home as many fish as anyone."

"Fish!" A male voice jeered from somewhere behind me. "Fish don't count for anything."

"If anyone would rather not eat on fish days, then just let me know and I'll give bigger helpings to everyone else," yelled a woman's voice from my left.

There was a ripple of female laughter, and Ghost's wife, Ludmilla, called out from over in the Brooklyn division area. "Everyone knows Blaze broke her arm last summer. She's still having a few minor aches and pains, but it hasn't stopped her doing her share of the work, so why make a big drama about it? Do you think that having a female officer will bring the world to an end?"

I hadn't expected other women to join in on my side against Cage. Why the chaos were they risking his anger? I glanced round, and the mixture of apprehension and defeat on a dozen female faces gave me my answer. Hannah had done her work well, making them believe I had serious problems with my arm. They were afraid that I'd lose my new officer position, and no other woman would ever have a chance at power again.

"The point is that your precious female officer doesn't have a few aches and pains, but a totally useless arm," shouted Cage. "Hannah will confirm what I've been saying. She's been helping Blaze hide the truth for months."

Everyone turned to look at where Hannah was sitting at one of the Manhattan tables. She seemed to shrink down into her chair for a moment, before forcing herself to stand.

"Cage is right," she called out. "I've spent months carrying things for Blaze and doing most of her work for her. We've been pretending she just had a few aches and pains in her left arm, but the truth was that she could hardly use it. Blaze said that I had to help keep her secret or I'd be thrown out of the Resistance."

She shook her head. "I gave in and did what Blaze wanted. I thought that as long as I could struggle on with the double workload, nobody else was being hurt, but then Blaze became an officer. I realized we wouldn't just be lying to a few of the other fisherwomen now, but deceiving the whole alliance. I couldn't bear the situation any longer, so I moved to Manhattan."

She sat down again, and people looked back at me. I had to admit that Hannah had told her story well. The hint of wounded righteousness in her voice when she mentioned the double workload was very convincing. But of course Hannah was a convincing liar. She'd had a lot of practice lying to me over the years.

I couldn't tell the truth and accuse Cage of attacking me, because explaining that Tad had defended and healed me would lead to questions that put him in danger. It was time for me to tell a few lies myself.

"There's nothing wrong with my arm," I said. "It healed perfectly weeks ago, but I suspected Hannah was spying on the Resistance for Cage. I told her I still had problems with my arm, swore her to secrecy, and waited to see if she'd go running to Cage with her story. Of course she did."

Cage laughed. "There's no point in denying things, Blaze. We've all been watching your arm while you've been standing there. You haven't moved it because you can't move it. I'm an alliance representative of Manhattan division, and I call general justice on Blaze of the Resistance for hiding a useless arm for months and making Hannah do all her work for her. Who supports my call?"

"There's nothing wrong with my arm," I shouted, before anyone had time to answer. "Look!"

I stooped and grabbed a full jug of water with my right hand, then stood up again holding it over my head.

Cage strode towards me, making a spitting sound of impatience. "Your other arm, Blaze."

Standing on the table meant that for the first time in my life I had the advantage of height over Cage. I smiled down at him, lowered the jug, swapped it from my right hand to my left, and raised it high overhead again. "You mean this arm, or are we talking about a third one?"

There was laughter from all sides, and Ghost called out from the Brooklyn corner. "There doesn't seem to be anything wrong with either of Blaze's arms, but I notice you still have a scar on yours, Cage. Teeth marks from a little girl!"

Everyone's eyes went to the scar on Cage's bare right arm, and there was a wild roar of laughter. Cage looked up at me in fury. I noticed a movement over in the Manhattan area. Hannah had stood up again. She was staring at me, her right hand covering her mouth, and her face pale with shock.

I forced my eyes back to Cage. "Hannah has been your spy in the Resistance for a long time, hasn't she, Cage? You've been threatening her. Forcing her to do everything you wanted. It wasn't just spying either. Six years ago, she was caught stealing medicine. She'd been taking it for some time. Giving it all to you."

There were gasps from round the room.

"Did you share any of that medicine with the rest of Manhattan division?" I asked, "or did you hoard it all for your own private use?"

Wall had been silently watching this from the Manhattan division area. Now he got to his feet in a sudden, decisive movement. "Manhattan division has no knowledge of any stolen medicine!"

I saw a movement in the Queens Island division area. Their rebel, Rogue, was climbing onto a table, an eye-catching figure in a short-sleeved shirt with yellow, green, and black stripes.

"Cage has been boasting about how fast he recovered from the winter fever," he called out. "Now we know the reason for that fast recovery. When other people were dying of winter fever, Cage was treating himself with his hoard of stolen medicine."

I was stunned at Rogue joining in my attack on Cage. I stared across at him, and he gave me a fierce smile in return. His skin a fraction darker than Luther's, Rogue didn't have Luther's classic good looks, but there was something arresting about the sheer energy in his face.

It was clear Major disapproved of this. He was glaring up at Rogue as if he'd cheerfully strangle him, but Rogue was totally ignoring his division leader, turning to look round the room. He obviously knew that Cage had helped Major set him up for a brutal punishment. Now Rogue was grabbing his chance to hit back.

Cage glared at Rogue. "Lies!" he snapped. "Nothing but empty lies. I don't have any spies working for me, or any hoard of stolen medicine. Blaze tricked Hannah into believing there was a problem with her arm and drove her into leaving the Resistance. Hannah told me her story, and I was fooled into believing it too."

There was a moment of tense silence. Wall had pointedly spoken in defence of Manhattan rather than Cage himself. Rogue had joined me in accusing Cage. Now everyone else was looking round, waiting for others to speak rather than risking it themselves. Ghost, leader of Brooklyn division, had the calculating expression of a hunter considering whether this was the right moment to shoot an arrow at his prey.

Donnell had been standing perfectly still, watching events with a frown, but now he started moving towards me. I caught his eye, and gave an urgent shake of my head. Donnell mustn't get involved in this.

There were words that needed to be said now. I waited

hopefully for Ghost to say them, but he leaned back in his chair instead.

I bit my lip. Only Rogue had joined me in standing up to Cage. The rebel of Queens Island, in constant disfavour with their leader, wasn't one of their alliance representatives. He couldn't say these words, so I'd have to say them myself.

I shouted at the top of my voice. "I call general justice against Cage of Manhattan. He is guilty of hoarding stolen medicine, and using threats to force a Resistance member to work for him."

Cage laughed. "You can't call general justice against me, little girl."

"Blaze is an officer of the Resistance, and as entitled to call general justice as any other alliance representative." Rogue's voice rang round the room. "Does any other representative here have the courage to speak in support, or is every last one of you a craven coward?"

There was a few seconds of silence, and then I heard a rhythmic sound to my right. I turned my head and saw Raeni was using her fists to pound on the table in front of her. After a moment, the sound got louder as Natsumi and Himeko joined in, then it suddenly spread round the room and grew to a deafening volume. The women of the Resistance and all four of the other divisions were hammering on the tables, some using their hands, and others a boot or water jug.

The hammering abruptly stopped. I saw Ice was climbing onto a table, his face flushed a deep red. "I call general justice against Cage!"

I'd believed it impossible for Cage to be blackmailing Ice, and I'd still no idea what threat Cage could have used to pierce Ice's armour, but I had to accept he'd managed it somehow. I'd been born into London division, and lived under Ice's rule for eleven years without ever seeing a hint of emotion in him, but now his face and voice were filled with a mixture of anger and shame.

"Two representatives from two divisions," screamed Rogue. He waved his arms like someone conducting music, and the hammering started again, only to stop as Hannah moved clear of the Manhattan tables.

"What Blaze said is true," she said, in a shaky voice. "Cage forced me to steal medicines for him. It wasn't my fault. I was..."

Her voice was drowned out by Aaron shouting. "I call general justice against Cage."

I was startled by the pure fury in Aaron's voice, then realized I was a fool. Cage's stolen medicine had helped him make a fast recovery from the winter fever, while Aaron's wife had died.

"Three representatives from two divisions call general justice against Cage!" Rogue looked expectantly round the room.

Ghost stood up. "I call general justice against Cage."

"Four representatives from three divisions!" Rogue called. "Which of you wants the honour of casting the final vote to bring Cage to justice?"

Several voices answered him. Rogue turned to give a triumphant look at Raeni, and she smiled joyously back at him. Cage had helped Major set Rogue up to face a general justice trial. Now Cage would stand trial himself.

I felt the table under me shake as Donnell climbed up to stand next to me. "The necessary five alliance representatives, including representatives from three different divisions, have called for general justice against Cage," he said. "Under the rules of this alliance he will stand formal trial in seven days' time."

He paused. "Anyone wishing to speak in accusation or defence should notify me at least one hour before that trial starts. Due to the nature of the charges, I wish to make it clear that anyone accusing Cage of threatening them will not be asked to give specific details of the threat."

Hannah hurried over to stand looking up at Donnell. "I told the truth, Donnell. Supported Blaze's story to help bring Cage to justice. You have to ask Wall to let me rejoin the Resistance now."

Donnell shrugged. "I felt that was a very last minute change of heart when you saw the tide of opinion had already turned against Cage, but I'll accept Blaze's decision on this."

I remembered how Hannah had helped Cage ambush me. I

remembered Hannah standing by watching him attack me. I remembered the whining self-justification in Hannah's voice as she told me it was my fault not hers. I wasn't sure if it was vindictiveness or simple common sense on my part, but I wasn't inviting her back into the Resistance.

"You chose Manhattan over the Resistance, Hannah. You made that choice in the full knowledge that the other divisions demand allegiance for life. You belong to Manhattan now."

"But..."

I interrupted her, shouting to drown her out. "The Resistance will not take you back, Hannah. You belong to Manhattan now."

"You heard the decision, Hannah," said Donnell. "Go back to your chosen division." He turned to look at Cage. "You too, Cage. You're trespassing on Resistance ground. Leave it now before I shoot you!"

Cage glanced down at his feet. Maybe he'd been so intent on our argument, that he hadn't been aware he'd walked the last crucial couple of steps that took him among the Resistance tables. For a second, I thought he might be furious enough to refuse to move, but he backed away, turned, and headed for the Manhattan corner. Hannah threw a last pleading look at me, before turning to trail after him. I saw Wall striding to meet the two of them.

"Why didn't you defend me?" Cage demanded.

"Defend you?" Wall laughed. "I'll be keeping you locked up until your trial, and I won't be speaking a single word in your defence. If the alliance rules allowed a division leader to call general justice against his own division member, I'd have done it years ago."

Wall punched Cage after that. I didn't stay to watch the rest of the fight, because I was more interested in getting Tad off his stretcher and into a proper bed in Sanctuary. There was no need to watch the fight anyway, because I knew exactly how it would end. Wall had got his nickname from the fact that hitting him had as little effect as hitting a concrete wall, so Cage wouldn't stand a chance.

CHAPTER THIRTY-ONE

During the height of the winter fever, we'd had a couple of hundred sick people on mattresses in Reception, but now things were back to normal. The hospital area of Sanctuary consisted of three large rooms, each with eight beds, and Phoenix and Braden were the only patients in one of them.

When I entered the room, Nadira, our most experienced nurse, was standing by Phoenix. She glanced at me, then watched Luther and Aaron carrying Tad into the room on his makeshift stretcher.

"Put him over there." Nadira pointed at the bed next to Phoenix.

Luther and Aaron obediently lifted Tad onto the bed.

"How are the other two off-worlders?" I asked.

Nadira's hair was covered with a red and gold silk headscarf, but one long, greying strand had escaped. She brushed it back into place and sighed. "They both have the winter fever extremely badly. Perhaps off-worlders have less resistance to it. The man may survive, but the woman is definitely going to die."

I hurried across to where Phoenix was lying, face flushed and eyes closed. I touched her forehead with the back of my hand and felt the burning heat of her, then leaned so my right ear was close to her mouth. There was a faint whistling sound as she breathed in and out.

Chaos weeping, Nadira was right. I'd heard that whistling sound too often to mistake it. People who breathed like that on the first day they got ill, never made it through the critical third day of the winter fever.

As I straightened up, Phoenix opened her eyes, and her hand shot out to grab mine. "Wait for me, Livia! I'm coming to Zeus to be with you. Wait for me!"

There was a dazed look in her eyes, and I knew that she wasn't seeing me but the woman she loved. "I'll wait for you," I said.

Phoenix smiled, her eyes closed, and her hand relaxed its grip on mine and fell back to her side.

I turned to Nadira. "I'll need you to help me give her the fever medicine."

She stared at me. "You've got medicine? Where from?"

"From a place between Yonkers and Tarrytown," I said. "We've brought boxes and boxes of it. I've got some of the tablets to treat the winter fever here with me."

Nadira helped me lift Phoenix into a sitting position. There was a bottle of water and paper cups on a bedside table. I filled a cup with water, and coaxed Phoenix into swallowing her tablets. The two small blue ones went down easily, but the one large white one was a struggle.

We kept Phoenix sitting up for a couple of minutes, until we were sure she wouldn't be sick, then laid her down again. I could tell from the conversation going on behind me that Luther and Aaron were stripping Tad's clothes off and putting him to bed, so I was careful to keep my back to them as I moved from Phoenix to check on Braden. Tad had done his best to respect my privacy when he was working on my arm, so I should do the same for him now.

Braden's breathing was still quite normal, and his eyes were open. He turned his head to look at me.

"Braden," I said. "You have to take some tablets now to make you well."

"Tablets," he repeated, in a confused voice.

Nadira and I went through the routine of lifting him up to swallow the tablets. He gulped them down quite easily, but the effort seemed to exhaust him. When we laid him down again, he lost consciousness.

I heard the door open, and turned to see Donnell and Julien coming in carrying stasis boxes. They stacked them neatly against the wall. I turned cautiously, saw Tad was in bed and covered by a sheet, and went past him to get the small flexiplas box that held his notes on the medicines.

I handed it to Nadira. "This is the full list of medicines. Some of them are in these boxes, but the rest are still on board the Spirit of New York."

Nadira opened the box and started rapidly scanning the pieces of paper. "We've got a very sick baby in Room 1, so I'll need the other medicines here as soon as possible."

Donnell nodded and turned to his officers. "Go and fetch the rest of the boxes. Once Nadira has sorted out what she wants for immediate use, you can take the rest up to the top floor of the Resistance wing."

"Back out into the cold before we've even had a chance to get warm," said Julien. "I don't know why people think being an officer is a privilege."

"I don't know why you think you're still an officer," Donnell snapped the words at him in an icy voice.

Julien hastily headed for the door, while Luther and Aaron exchanged graphic glances.

"And you two can stop pulling faces at each other and do as you're told," added Donnell.

Luther and Aaron sprinted after Julien. Donnell watched them go, and then went across to study each of the off-worlders in turn before facing me.

"Blaze, we need to talk," he said. "Upstairs. Now."

I glanced at Tad. "I'd prefer to stay..."

Donnell cut into my sentence, his voice even harsher than when he'd spoken to Julien. "When I say I want to talk to you now, I mean it!"

He turned and stalked out of the room. I chased after him, my stomach churning. I'd only heard Donnell use that tone of voice to men just before he punched them. Why was he using it on me? What had I done wrong?

We went straight through Reception, with people taking one

look at Donnell's face and rapidly getting out of his way, and then headed up the Resistance staircase. Donnell didn't say a word until after we'd reached his apartment on the sixth floor and he'd slammed the door shut behind us.

"Chaos weeping, Blaze, why didn't you tell me you'd got a problem with your arm? Why didn't you warn me that Cage was going to call general justice on you? I thought we were finally talking to each other, and building a proper relationship at last. I was obviously fooling myself."

I moistened my lips. "My arm is perfectly fine. I lied to Hannah about having a..."

"Don't do it!" Donnell pointed an accusing finger at me. "Don't you dare look me in the eyes and lie to me! You may have fooled people down there in Reception with your story, but I know things that they don't. I know you were pleading Hannah's cause to me only days ago. I know Tad is Thaddeus Wallam-Crane the Eighth, the last man in humanity to be webbed. I know the pair of you spent the last few days in a storage facility packed with medical supplies."

I sighed. "All right. I still had some aches and pains after breaking my arm. Nothing significant, but Cage got Hannah to make a big fuss about it in front of the other women so they'd think there was a serious problem. Then Cage ambushed me and Tad as we set off for the trip upriver. Cage attacked me and injured my shoulder, but Tad treated it at the medical facility."

"Why didn't you tell me that Cage had attacked you?" demanded Donnell. "I admit that carrying on to the medical facility made sense if Tad could treat your injury there, but you could have told me the whole story as we were coming back downriver on the Spirit of New York."

"Cage told me he'd call general justice on me for hiding an injured arm for months, and get Hannah to confirm his story so everyone would believe it. His plan was to drag you into defending me, claim you'd been lying about my arm as well, and then challenge your leadership of the alliance. It was much safer for me to deal with him myself. Once Tad had treated my arm, I was in the perfect position to turn Cage's plan against him."

"It was my job to deal with a leadership challenge, not yours," said Donnell.

"Yes. No." I shook my head. "The whole situation was my fault. My mess. My responsibility. I was the one who insisted on you accepting Hannah into the Resistance. I thought she was my best friend, and was fool enough to believe everything she told me. The lies about what happened when she was caught stealing. The hints about how I couldn't trust you, that you were ignoring me because you didn't think you were my father, that..."

"Hannah!" Donnell turned and hammered his fist against the wall.

"I'm sorry." I eyed him nervously. "I only found out Hannah had been working for Cage when I was leaving for the medical supply run. But you see that this mess was all my fault for trusting Hannah, so I had to be the one to deal with Cage."

"Not your fault," said Donnell. "Mine. I should have stopped you being friends with that girl years ago. I should have thrown her out of the Resistance the moment I caught her stealing. I should never have let her join the Resistance in the first place."

He faced me again, and spoke in a quiet voice that had lost the edge of anger. "Hannah could only convince you of her lies because I was too scared to talk to you myself. I wasted six years of our lives because I was afraid of making a bad situation even worse. Your brother hated me enough to risk his life making a deal with the off-worlders and planting a bomb for them. I thought you hated me just as much. I was terrified that if I tried to force you into a father and daughter relationship, you'd do something equally desperate."

His face twisted in pain. "There was no way for you to portal out of New York the way your brother did. I had a recurring nightmare where you sneaked away, tried to make it to America Off-world alone on foot, and got yourself killed. I took the cowardly option of leaving you in peace, not realizing Hannah was dripping poison in your ear."

"I was a fool to believe the things she said."

Donnell stood there in silence for a moment, before speaking again in a more normal voice. "We have to forget the mistakes of the past and concentrate on the present situation. You asked me to let you deal with Cage, so I did. By the time I realized you were planning to make this a full scale confrontation with him, it was too late for me to stop you. Do you have the faintest idea how much danger you're in now?"

I shook my head. "I knew I was taking a risk, but it worked. We've won. People were too scared to speak out against Cage before, but they're doing it now."

"Oh yes," said Donnell. "You led the way, you defied Cage, and broke his rule of fear. His victims are queuing up to say they want to accuse him at his trial. I had to leave Machico making the list of witness names, or I'd have been stuck in Reception for hours."

His bitter tone of voice was worrying me. "But that's good, isn't it?"

"No, it's horrendously bad! Cage is going to stand trial. He knows a host of his victims are eager to be witnesses against him, he knows the only way to stop them is to re-establish his rule of fear, and he knows he has exactly seven days to do it."

Donnell paused to give a heavy groan. "It's my fault that Cage has those seven days to save himself. In the early days of the alliance, we held trials immediately, and in some cases the true facts only became known after punishment had been carried out. I finally got the alliance to agree that there should always be a seven day delay between an accusation and a trial."

He paused. "Well, Cage has seven days to re-establish his rule of fear, and the only way he can do that is to kill you, Blaze."

I blinked. "You really think he'll try to murder me?"

"I'm certain he will," said Donnell. "If you die in the next few days, all the witnesses queuing up to give evidence against Cage will realize they could be next to die. They'll hastily change their minds about accusing him. Cage will walk free from his trial, and be more powerful than before."

"But how could Cage murder me? Wall said that he'd keep him locked up until his trial."

"Cage will still have some friends in Manhattan," said Donnell, "or at least some allies who'll be scared of being implicated in his crimes. They just have to let him out for a few hours so he can kill you. Once you're dead, Cage can happily go back to his prison cell, and use his imprisonment to claim total innocence of being involved in your death."

I stared down at my hands in silence.

"Cage has got away with murder before," added Donnell. "The first time we talked about him, I warned you that I'd seen his enemies die suspiciously convenient deaths. It's happened at least three times now. A man publicly clashing with Cage, humiliating him, and dying a few days later in what was allegedly an accident."

Donnell waved his hands in a despairing gesture. "If you were just going to be in danger for the next seven days, I could stand guard over you myself for every minute of them, but the danger won't end with Cage's trial. Unless we can prove one of his murders, Cage is unlikely to get a death sentence. After his victims have spoken out at his trial, he'll have lost his power base forever, but he'll endure whatever punishment he's given and be even more eager to kill you out of revenge."

I took a deep breath. "I don't regret what I did. Someone had to challenge Cage."

"That someone should have been me," said Donnell.

"It couldn't be you," I said. "When I called general justice against Cage, the only risk was that I'd be ignored or laughed at. If you'd called general justice against him, and nobody supported you, then you'd have lost control of the alliance."

Donnell sighed. "Well, we can't change what has already happened. We have a decision to make for the future. Let's sit down."

I sank into a chair, remembering at the last minute to check it wasn't the cursed one.

Donnell sat in the chair opposite me. "I told you that I'd planned to discuss your future with you on your eighteenth birthday, but I decided to delay part of that discussion, including the bit about you becoming an officer."

He hesitated. "I wasn't entirely honest with you about my reasons for delaying things. It was nothing to do with the unstable situation in the alliance. It was because I'd seen the way Tad was looking at you during the meeting and had a whole new idea about your future. If that boy took you to Adonis with him, you could have a far better life than any I could give you."

"What?" I squeaked the word in shock.

"So I decided to delay my original plan for a while, ask you to make friends with Tad, and see what happened between you."

I waved my hands in bewilderment. "You didn't want me to make friends with Tad to get information out of him? You were really hoping he'd offer to take me to Adonis with him?"

Donnell nodded.

I was struggling to make sense of this. "You took one look at Tad and decided to marry me off to him?"

"I wasn't necessarily thinking of marriage. Lover, friend, any relationship that got him to take you with him to Adonis would be enough. It wouldn't have to be a long-lasting relationship either. You'd just have to stay with him long enough for you to reach Adonis, and you'd have a secure, bright future ahead of you."

Donnell shrugged. "Unfortunately, Tad's interest in you didn't go as far as offering to take you to Adonis."

"Actually, Tad offered to take me off-world on the first day we went fishing together. Not to Adonis, but to Zeus. He's expecting to go there to continue his research."

Donnell let his head fall forward into his hands and made a low moaning noise. "Why the chaos didn't you tell me that right away? I'd have taken you and the off-worlders to Fence myself despite the snow. You could have been safely on Zeus by now."

It didn't seem the best moment to tell him that Tad could use the Earth data net to send messages to people, so we wouldn't even have needed to go to Fence but could have just taken a boat up to Bear Mountain. "I didn't tell you because I didn't want to go with Tad. You should know that I'd never leave Earth."

Donnell lifted his head. "Was loyalty to Earth your only problem, or was it Tad himself? I'm still bitterly angry about the people who plundered Earth to found their new worlds, but I accept that Tad, Phoenix and Braden were too young to be guilty of any crime other than being born on those new worlds. When I found out Tad was the heir of Thaddeus Wallam-Crane..."

Donnell waved both hands. "Well that was a bit much to cope with, so I didn't react well at the time, but now I've had time to calm down again. Tad has caused me a lot of trouble, and he talks far too much, but he's helped us as well. I've a reluctant liking for the boy, and I had the impression you did too."

"Whether I care about Tad or not doesn't matter. I've only known him for days. I'm not going to literally give up my whole world and run off with him."

"Take a moment to think about the life you could have on Zeus, Blaze," said Donnell. "It would be safe and luxurious, with plentiful food and medicine."

I thought about it. I remembered what Tad had said about Braden only getting a handful of messages from his brother over the years. If I went off-world, there'd be no hope of getting any messages from Donnell at all. I'd be living my luxurious life, aware that I'd left everyone in the alliance struggling to survive. I'd be eating generous meals every day, and picturing them starving to death back on Earth. Every time I saw a flame or even a light, I'd wonder if they'd made it out of New York or died in the coming firestorm. I'd never know if Donnell was alive or dead.

"It would be utterly unbearable," I said.

Donnell shook his head. "You had one chance to go off world with your brother when you were eleven years old, and you refused. Tad is your second chance. If you refuse that too, then you'll never get a third one."

"I'm not going," I said flatly.

"If the boy wasn't so sick with winter fever, I'd order you to go off world with him. Drag you to Fence by force if necessary."

"You want me to leave?"

"Of course not. After all these years, the wall between us has finally gone. I'd hate to see you go, but not nearly as much as I'd hate to bury you. When I was eighteen, I thought I was immortal. You probably feel immortal too, but eighteen-year-olds can die, especially in a time and a place like this one. You could have died when London burned, from the winter fever, from a falling star attack, or in that accident where you broke your arm. You've been lucky so far, but next time your luck may run out."

"I know all that," I said. "I'm still not leaving Earth."

Donnell let out a heavy sigh. "If you're definitely staying on Earth, then we need to have the conversation I'd planned for your eighteenth birthday."

I was getting a bit confused by now. "The conversation about me becoming an officer? Isn't it a bit late to discuss that?"

"When I told you about my plans for your eighteenth birthday, everything I said to you was perfectly true, but there was an extra factor I didn't mention. Something that only Kasim, Machico, and I knew existed."

I frowned. "What are you talking about?"

Donnell stood up, went across to his wall safe, opened it, and took out something wrapped in cloth. He came back and put it on the table in front of me, then sat down again. "Open it."

I unfolded the heavy cloth, and looked down at an intricately segmented, grey metal object. It was a gun, exactly like the one clinging to Donnell's arm, but the strands trailing from it were dark and lifeless.

I gave Donnell a puzzled look. "Why have you kept Kasim's gun? I thought it self-destructed when he died and was buried with him."

"That isn't Kasim's gun."

I looked from the gun on the table, to the one glowing on Donnell's right arm, and back again. "Kasim was a Military Security Armed Agent. He already had his own gun, and he stole another one for you before he defected to the Earth Resistance, so where...?"

"That's the story we always told people," said Donnell. "The truth is that Kasim stole two guns. The second one was intended to be for Machico, but Mac wouldn't accept it."

I rubbed my forehead in bewilderment. "He wouldn't? Why?"

"Because he'd seen what happened to people who were webbed when their brain gradually changed over the years and their link to the Earth data net broke down. He knew these guns formed connections to their owner's brain in a similar way, and he didn't want to risk experiencing that connection failing. I didn't trust anyone else enough to hand them a gun, so I kept its existence secret and locked it away in case Mac changed his mind."

I was staring at Donnell's gun now, studying the glowing tendrils that ran into his arm. "Your gun is connected to your brain?"

"Yes. An Armed Agent weapon can do far more than shoot people. It has its own artificial intelligence, which handles jobs like tracking potential enemies and transmitting information to its owner. The brain connection turned out not to be the problem Machico feared, perhaps because the gun's artificial intelligence is fully self contained with no link to the Earth data net."

I frowned. "I didn't know your gun had artificial intelligence."

"Kasim and I carefully kept the full details of our guns' abilities secret. Being able to track the movements of people we considered dangerous gave us a huge advantage. The gun tracking range is limited, but it crucially extends well beyond bow range, so we couldn't be taken by surprise and shot in the back."

"Oh." That explained several odd incidents that I'd witnessed over the years, where Donnell seemed to be expecting trouble before it happened.

"Getting back to the history of this gun." Donnell tapped the table next to it. "After Kasim and I had been Armed for a few years, it was clear the brain connection wasn't changing, but Mac still didn't want a gun himself. He said that the way he messed things up in Asia had proved he was a good technical expert but a terrible soldier. For a long time, I planned to give the gun to your brother one day."

"But you didn't. Why?" I hoped I wasn't sounding too resentful. "When we arrived in New York, you made Seamus an officer, you trusted him with everything else, so why not give him the gun as well?"

"Because the guns were specifically designed to be used by people who were at least eighteen. Seamus was only sixteen, so I was worried the brain connections might not form properly." Donnell sighed. "Well, Seamus didn't stay around long enough for me to give him the gun, and only weeks later there was that clash between you and Cage. When he told me his plan to marry you, I decided to encourage him. My idea was to use his ambition to keep you safe until your eighteenth birthday, and then give you the gun."

I stared at him. "If the off-worlders hadn't arrived, you'd have given me this gun on my birthday?"

"Yes. It seemed possible that you'd decide to shoot me with it, but if you did then I felt I deserved it. The important thing was that once you had the gun, you'd be able to protect yourself from Cage."

I was rethinking the events of the last couple of weeks. "You've just been complaining about me not telling you things, but all the time I was going frantic with worry about Cage, you never mentioned that you had this gun in your safe."

"When we discussed arranging your engagement to Cage, I said that you had to tell me if the situation got too difficult for you, and mentioned there was another option I could use."

I groaned. "How could I possibly guess that option was a secret gun? Machico knew it existed. Is that an extra reason he made me an officer?"

"Yes. Ever since your birthday, Machico's been nagging me to give you the gun so you could watch my back the way Kasim did. Mac said he was convinced you were too loyal to go off world, so delaying things would achieve nothing except making a dangerous situation worse. He made you an officer to try to force me into action, and that was why I punched him."

I waved my arms in disbelief. "And even when we were facing Cage starting a war, you still didn't tell me about the gun. Why?"

"Because I knew that giving you the gun would put you in the centre of that war." Donnell gave me a rueful smile. "I've told you about the gun now, Blaze. I was going to offer it to you as your birthday present. I'm offering it to you today instead, but please take a minute to think carefully before accepting it."

I dutifully thought about it for a minute. I thought about all the problems the alliance had suffered this winter. I thought about Kasim's death. I thought how Donnell had been struggling to control the alliance alone.

"Once you're Armed, there'll be no going back," said Donnell. "Tad looks deathly ill to me, but if he does manage to survive to go off world, then you won't be going with him. However much influence Tad has, the authorities of Zeus will never admit someone with your background once you've got that gun on your arm, and you can't remove a gun that's connected to your brain without killing yourself. You'll be committing yourself to spending the rest of your life on Earth."

Once I was Armed, there'd be no going back, and no chance of leaving Earth, but I'd no intention of leaving Earth anyway. I might not be the best choice of person to help Donnell keep order in the alliance, but he'd been saving this gun for me for six years, and I knew he wouldn't give it to anyone else. I could stay a burden to Donnell, someone he had to protect, or I could help protect him.

I picked up the gun. "How do we do this?"

"You put the gun on the back of your bare wrist, and it does the rest."

I tugged up my right sleeve, put the metal centre section of the gun on my wrist, and waited tensely. For a few seconds nothing happened, but then there was a tingling in my arm and the lights of the gun flickered.

"The gun charges itself by a combination of taking power from nearby electrical sources, and using excess heat from your own body," said Donnell. "You'll notice a significant drain as it starts to function. You may feel cold, a little breathless, and giddy."

He was right. The effect of the gun charging, or possibly the nervous strain, was making me feel dizzy. The gun startled me by adjusting its position, and then the grey tendrils started to glow with life.

"If you ever notice those symptoms again in future," said Donnell, "then it means you've fired the gun too many times and exhausted its power. You must stop firing the gun immediately, or the energy drain on your body could become life threatening."

One of the tendrils slithered creepily over my skin. It was tempting to rip the gun off, but I held still.

"Last chance to change your mind," said Donnell. "Once those tendrils enter your arm..."

All the tendrils were moving now, some slithering down to my right hand, some wrapping round my arm, while others explored upwards towards my shoulder.

"Very last chance," said Donnell.

I watched the point of one of the tendrils pressing down against the back of my right hand. It seemed to be forcing its way through the skin, but it didn't hurt me. In fact, I couldn't feel anything at all.

The gun lights flickered again, there was a single stab of pain in the back of my neck that made me gasp, and then a calm female voice spoke inside my head. "Connection established. Initialization sequence entering phase two. Please state owner name."

I took a deep breath. "Blaze."

"Owner name acknowledged," said the voice. "Thank you, Blaze."

The lights of the gun started flashing. I was Armed!

CHAPTER THIRTY-TWO

"Perimeter breach zone one." The voice of my gun spoke in my head, and a mass of black lines and glowing white dots appeared to float in front of my eyes, superimposed on my view of the room around me.

It was almost midnight, and I was in the off-worlders' hospital room in Sanctuary. I was bathing Phoenix's face with tepid water, and trying to persuade myself there was still some hope of her surviving the winter fever, while knowing there wasn't. The medicine had eased her symptoms for a while, but now she was struggling for every breath.

Tomorrow would be the critical third day of the off-worlders' illness. Phoenix had tried so hard to adapt to life in hostile New York, but she was going to die tomorrow. She might not even live until dawn.

I put down my cloth and bowl to concentrate on the tracking display that my gun was sending directly to the visual centre of my brain. The confusing mass of lines showed the layout of the ground floor of Sanctuary, and the glowing dots were people. I'd ordered my gun to warn me whenever someone new entered the hospital area, which happened a lot during the day but was strange this late at night.

The tracking display responded to me studying the hospital area by magnifying it. There were clusters of stationary white dots in each of the three hospital rooms, which were the patients and the people on nursing duty. Another white dot was moving along a corridor. I frowned. The day nurses wouldn't be arriving until dawn, and no one would be bringing supplies or visiting patients in the middle of the night.

The dot had reached the junction at the end of the corridor. It would now turn left or right for one of the other two hospital rooms, or go through the double doors straight ahead to carry on towards us.

"Perimeter breach zone two," said my gun.

The white dot was now moving down the corridor that only led to this room. Nobody but Donnell should be coming here. He'd announced that Nadira and I would be nursing the off-worlders, he'd bring food and drinking water to us himself, and this area was strictly off limits to everyone else. That arrangement wasn't just to keep the off-worlders safe, but to give me time to adjust to the gun before the rest of the alliance knew I had it.

Whoever this was, it couldn't be Donnell. My gun had automatically registered that Donnell was the owner of an Armed Agent weapon, and designated him as my ally, marking him with a green dot.

The white dot couldn't be Donnell, but it couldn't be Cage either. Years ago, Donnell had ordered his gun to designate Cage as an enemy. That information had been shared with my gun, so Cage would be shown as a red dot not white.

I glanced round the room. Nadira was fast asleep on the bed nearest the window. After spending years caring for our sickest patients, she was an expert in grabbing sleep whenever she could. Braden was asleep too. Tad and Phoenix were both unconscious. Tad had been breathing with the distinctive whistling sounds of winter fever for the last day, which was a very bad sign. He might not be quite as sick as Phoenix, but...

I forced my thoughts away from whether Tad was going to live or die tomorrow. I had to focus my mind on keeping us all alive tonight. The intruder coming towards us could be dangerous, but it was possible that someone had a perfectly innocent reason for coming here. Perhaps Machico was bringing me a message from Donnell. If the visitor turned out to be someone else unthreatening, I'd have to make sure they didn't see my gun. Donnell had only trusted Machico and Nadira with the secret of me having the weapon.

I picked up a blanket from the top of a nearby cupboard, draped it carefully over my right arm, and then moved to the door. I was about to open it and challenge whoever was out there, when I saw the white dot had stopped halfway down the corridor. It stayed still for about a minute, before retreating back through the double doors, and continuing out of the hospital area.

"Intruder has cleared perimeter," said my gun, and the display of lines and dots vanished.

I sighed in relief, and went to dump my blanket back on the cupboard. There were some storage rooms in the corridor leading here. The intruder must have been fetching something from one of them, probably something they'd no right to take since they'd come for it at night. I didn't try to work out who might be stealing oddments from Sanctuary, because my mind was back to worrying about Tad again. I could hear his breathing from where I was standing. There were obvious hesitations in the whistling now, soon he'd be struggling for every gulp of air like Phoenix, and then...

No! Tad couldn't die. Tad mustn't die. I knew we could never have a life together, but our relationship had to end with him going off to the bright new world of Zeus, not dying a pointless death here in abandoned New York. It wasn't just that Tad's death would be as big a personal blow as losing my mother in the London firestorm. He was the last of the magicians, and the last hope of saving the interstellar portals that were the fragile links between worlds scattered across space.

"Perimeter breach zone one," said my gun.

The tracking display reappeared, and this time the dot entering the hospital area was far more conspicuous because it wasn't white but red.

Cage was coming! Now I understood why the first intruder had come to this corridor and then gone away again. Cage had sent someone to check whether Donnell had left guards outside this room. His accomplice had reported back that there was no one here, so now Cage was coming to kill me.

I fought back against my instinctive fear. I should be triumphant, not afraid. Cage was coming to kill me, which was exactly what I'd planned to happen.

There were no guards here to help me, because that was part of my plan. I'd insisted Donnell and his officers should stay in the Resistance wing at the other side of the sprawling Americas Parliament House. I was apparently defenceless in an isolated area of Sanctuary, my only companions a single elderly nurse and three desperately ill patients.

How could Cage resist such an ideal chance to kill me? There was even the added incentive that he could kill the off-world boy as well, getting his revenge for that humiliating defeat at the boathouse. Cage didn't know that he was walking into a trap, and his supposedly defenceless target had an Armed Agent weapon on her arm.

After the scene between us in Reception, the fact Cage had escaped from his imprisonment in the Manhattan division area and come here was enough to convince everyone he intended murder. Not just any murder either, but one in the hospital area of Sanctuary, which the whole alliance considered the most dishonourable of crimes and carried an automatic death sentence.

I could do anything I wished to defend myself, and no one would question my actions. Donnell hadn't given me any specific orders about Cage, so I was free to kill him myself, or just capture him and hand him over to stand trial.

A civilized person would probably be reluctant to kill Cage, but I wasn't feeling very civilized. Someone had released Cage from his prison cell so he could come here to kill me. If I captured him now, we could insist on him being held prisoner by the Resistance instead of Manhattan division, but he might have found a way to blackmail other Resistance members as well as Hannah and escape a second time. I felt that death was the only truly secure prison for someone like Cage.

I picked up my blanket again, went out from the dimly lit room into the even darker corridor, and shut the door carefully behind me. The lights in the ceiling here were on the lowest possible setting, and half of them were broken or missing. I walked down the corridor to the furthest storage room, opened the door, went into the room, and then pushed the door almost closed again behind me.

"Gun command designate approaching enemy as primary target." I murmured the words aloud. In theory, I just had to think them and the gun would obey, but I wasn't confident enough to trust in that yet.

The red dot that was Cage started flashing. It had reached the double doors now.

"Primary target has breached perimeter zone two," said my gun.

I heard the faint creak that must be one of the double doors opening, and covered the betraying flashing lights of my gun with the blanket. My plan was to let Cage walk past my hiding place, wait until he reached the door to the hospital room, then step out into the corridor and call his name.

I would make a single token gesture of being civilized. I'd let Cage see my gun and order him to surrender. If he didn't do that immediately, and I was sure he wouldn't, then I'd shoot him. The targeting system of my gun would have automatically locked on to him as my primary target, so it would be virtually impossible for me to miss.

"Perimeter breach zone one," said the gun. "Second intruder."

I frowned and studied the gun's display. The red dot that was Cage was still slowly approaching me. A white dot, moving much faster, had just entered the hospital area. Cage's accomplice was back!

I hesitated. If I stepped out into the corridor now, Cage would turn and run. If he got away, then he could deny ever being here. I had to wait for him to move on past me, so I was blocking his retreat. Ideally, I should wait until his accomplice was past me too, so I could either kill or capture them both. The danger was that Cage would try to enter the hospital room where the off-worlders and Nadira were helpless in bed, forcing me into showing myself while his accomplice was coming up behind me.

The shadowy figure of Cage walked past my partially open door, near enough that I could have reached out and touched him. He was moving so slowly and furtively that I couldn't hear him at all.

"Perimeter breach zone two," said the gun. "Second intruder."

That meant Cage's accomplice was through the double doors. If I stepped into the corridor now, then I'd have one of them on each side of me.

I hadn't expected to be in this situation. I'd been certain that Cage would come here alone. Who was his accomplice? If it was Hannah, then she wouldn't be a physical threat.

No, on reflection it couldn't possibly be Hannah. I was surprised that Cage was trusting anyone to help him commit a murder that could earn him a death sentence. He surely wouldn't be fool enough to put himself into the power of someone with Hannah's history of betraying people for her own advantage.

"Cage," said Wall's voice.

I blinked. Wall was helping Cage! I hadn't expected the leader of Manhattan division to...

"What are you doing here?" Cage sounded startled.

"I thought you'd get someone to let you out of your prison cell," said Wall, in a coldly furious voice, "so I made a spy hole in the ceiling of the corridor outside it. I've been sleeping in the room above that, with a couple of my own nephews taking turns to watch through the spy hole. A few minutes ago, they woke me to tell me that no one had gone near your prison cell, but you'd somehow escaped anyway."

Cage laughed. "I didn't need anyone to come and let me out of my prison. Not when I'd got one of my supporters to hide a spare key inside the room before I was locked in there."

Wall made a spluttering noise of exasperation. "Given your obsession with Donnell's daughter, it was obvious you'd be getting weapons and heading here to murder her. I sent one of my nephews to run ahead and warn Donnell's guards you were coming, because they wouldn't mistake an eight-year-old boy for a threat. I expected Donnell to have left two or three men outside the hospital room door to guard his daughter, or even be guarding her himself, but my nephew came back and told me there was no one there."

I realized I'd got things entirely wrong. The first intruder hadn't been Cage's accomplice, but Wall's nephew bringing a warning message. Cage was working alone as I'd expected, and Wall was on my side.

From the sound of Wall's voice, a fight was going to break out at any moment. I wasn't going to step out into the corridor into the middle of that, but I risked opening the door a fraction further to see what was happening. The two heavily muscled men were facing each other, each holding a sword. I was stupidly shocked to see the glistening blades openly brandished in the sacrosanct hospital area of Sanctuary.

"So you came to stop me yourself," said Cage. "How long have you been Donnell's devoted slave?"

"Eighteen years ago, a Manhattan man murdered a Queens Island man when he was unconscious in his hospital bed," said Wall. "The murderer was executed, and Manhattan division narrowly escaped being expelled from the alliance. Queens Island has taken every opportunity to make sure no one ever forgot what happened."

Wall groaned. "Manhattan has spent eighteen years trying to put one murder in hospital behind us, and you've come here to commit another, with Donnell's own daughter as your chosen victim. No, not just one murder, but five, since I suppose you're planning to wipe out Nadira and her off-worlder patients as well. Don't you realize how the whole alliance would react to that, especially so soon after the winter fever, when the memory of lying utterly helpless on a sick bed is fresh in all their minds?"

He shook his head. "Your execution wouldn't be enough to appease them, Cage. The whole of Manhattan division would be sent out into the snow to starve to death."

"I'm not stupid," said Cage. "I'll make sure the deaths look like an accident, and be back locked in prison before the bodies are discovered."

"Yet another accidental death?" Wall gave a totally humourless laugh. "You've played that game too often already. If

Donnell's daughter so much as stubs her toe in the next few months, then people will be blaming you."

"So you're going to kill me now?"

"No," said Wall. "I'd much rather we both quietly walk back to the Manhattan wing. There'll be less trouble for Manhattan if we deal with your behaviour in private."

"I'm not going to play the leading role in a discreet hanging." Cage smiled. "I have a much better idea. You're right about people being suspicious of an accident, so I'll make it an obvious murder. The girl and all the witnesses will be dead, but I'll pose your body in there as well. You'll be the murderer killed by the desperate, dying attack of Donnell's daughter."

"You've never beaten me in a fight before, Cage, and you won't beat me now."

"I'd never beat you in a fair fight, but..."

Cage threw his sword at Wall, and there was the clanging sound of metal on metal as Wall used his own sword to sweep the incoming missile aside. That distracted me, so I didn't see whether Cage reached into his pocket or he'd already had the tiny grenade concealed in his left hand. All I saw was it hitting the corridor floor.

I instinctively threw myself behind the storage room door. I was expecting an explosion, but instead there was a hiss of gas. I'd been well trained by falling star attacks over the years, so I held my breath the instant the musty, metallic smell hit my nose.

When I rolled across to look out through the door again, I saw the corridor was filling with a misty white gas. Wall had thrown himself to the floor like me, and Cage had got past him and was running for the double doors.

I couldn't get a clear shot at Cage from here. I scrambled on my hands and knees through the doorway, but was too late. Cage was already opening the double doors, and Wall was on his feet chasing after him, his bulky figure blocking my line of fire. The doors closed behind Cage, and when Wall reached them, he hammered on them but they didn't open.

Wall was kicking the doors now, but they still weren't moving. Cage must have rigged something so he could quickly jam them. That meant Wall and I were stuck in here with what I guessed was anaesthetic gas.

This must be how Cage had arranged his previous accidents, by using gas to knock out his victims. Once Wall and I were unconscious, Cage would come back to set up his murder scene. He probably wouldn't bother to use another gas grenade on the off-worlders and Nadira, just stab them while they were asleep or unconscious.

I wasn't going to let that happen. Wall was making no impression on the double doors, because they were fire doors made of solid metal. The glass panes in the centre of each door were reinforced glass, virtually unbreakable, but...

I grabbed Wall's arm and tugged at it, using the last air in my lungs to yell at him. "Out of my way!"

He gave me a look of sheer disbelief, his eyes widening even further as he saw the lights of the gun flashing on my arm, then he moved rapidly back down the corridor. I took a few steps backwards myself, targeted the left-hand window, and fired.

I was expecting to make a hole in the glass, but instead the whole pane blew apart into thousands of tiny pieces. I shot out the window in the other door as well, before running up to gulp in the good air coming from outside. A moment later, Wall was beside me, reaching through the gap in one of the doors where the window had been, and wrenching at something on the other side.

"Primary target has cleared perimeter," said the voice of the gun in my head.

The doors opened. Wall and I tumbled through them, and Wall glanced down each of the three other corridors in turn.

"No sign of Cage," he said. "He would have started running the instant he heard your first gunshot, so he's probably already back in the main Sanctuary area."

"I think you're right." In fact, I knew Wall was right. Since I'd designated Cage as my primary target, the area covered by my gun's tracking display had expanded to follow him.

"That area is a maze of corridors and store rooms," said Wall, "and Cage could be in any of them."

Right now, the flashing red dot of Cage was in one of the main storage rooms. I couldn't go after him myself, because I had to stay and guard the off-worlders. I couldn't send Wall after him without giving away the secret of my gun's tracking system.

"We'll call for help to search for him," I said.

There was a fire alarm box on the wall next to us. The cover glass had been broken long ago, so I just had to hit the red alarm button, let it ring for a couple of seconds, then hit the green button to stop it. All over the Parliament House, people would be cursing a false alarm and trying to get back to sleep, but Donnell would know what that prearranged signal meant.

I frowned at where the white gas from the grenade was still coming through the holes in the fire doors. "We'd better get clear of that gas."

We moved a little further down the corridor, and Wall turned to face me. "Once I saw your gun, I realized you and Donnell had carefully planned this situation. I'd like to know how that gun suddenly appeared, but far more importantly I need to know how this will affect Manhattan division."

His voice took on a grim edge. "Cage has attempted murder in the hospital area of Sanctuary. Queens Island will grab their chance to take revenge on us. They'll demand Cage's head, and they're welcome to have it. I was caught here in Cage's company, and carrying a sword myself, so they'll want my head too. They could have it if that would satisfy them, but it won't. They'll demand retribution against all of my people, even the children."

"Manhattan division won't try to shelter Cage in future?"

"Manhattan division declares Cage renegade from this moment. We'll kill him on sight and hand over his body for inspection."

"Then I'll speak in defence of both you and Manhattan division," I said. "I was the intended murder victim, so people will surely listen when I say you only came here to protect me."

Wall gave an oddly formal nod of his head, and said words that bewildered me. "In that case, you have Manhattan's allegiance, Blaze."

CHAPTER THIRTY-THREE

When Donnell arrived to join us at the hospital entrance, he had all of his other officers with him except Julien. Machico laughed at the sight of me with the gun on my arm, while the other four looked totally stunned.

I ignored Machico, concentrating on the revealing expressions of Donnell's other officers as they adjusted to the situation. Vijay and Weston exchanged startled glances before joining Machico in laughing, while Luther's face slowly changed from shocked to deeply resentful. He opened his mouth, looking like a toddler about to throw a tantrum, but closed it again without saying a word. I noticed Aaron's face changing too, but he just looked deeply thoughtful rather than aggrieved.

Donnell gave a single bemused look at Wall, who was standing at my side with his sword still openly in his hand, and then turned to me. "Anyone hurt?"

I shook my head. "Wall came here to try to stop Cage murdering me. We had Cage cornered, but he threw an anaesthetic gas grenade at us, and then jammed the fire doors at the end of the corridor to trap us inside with the gas. He planned to come back and murder us when we were unconscious."

"I see you shot your way through the fire doors," said Donnell. "What happened to Cage?"

"He ran off towards the main area of Sanctuary. He's armed with gas grenades, and probably other weapons too."

With an audience listening to every word I said, I couldn't

tell Donnell that I'd watched the red flashing dot that was Cage move through Sanctuary into Reception, and then out of the range of my gun tracking system. That didn't matter though. Donnell would have his own gun tracking Cage, so he'd already know he'd left the Sanctuary wing.

Wall joined in the conversation. "Manhattan division has declared Cage renegade. I'd like to help you search for him."

Donnell nodded. "My guess is that Cage has already left the Sanctuary wing, and most likely left Parliament House too. Hunting him down won't be easy when he has the whole of New York to hide in."

"Cage can't survive long on his own in the middle of winter," said Weston. "It's snowing outside right now."

"I wouldn't bet on Cage conveniently dying," said Donnell. "He had weapons with him, and it would have only taken him a couple of minutes to collect outdoor clothing, a sleeping bag, and some fishing lines from the store rooms on his way out."

"The power is back on everywhere," said Machico, "so Cage just has to find somewhere with working heating and he won't freeze. His biggest problem will be the falling stars. He won't be able to hunt for food in daylight unless the temperature is below freezing, but it should be possible to do a lot at night now all the New York lights are on."

"I expect Cage has already gone," said Donnell, "but we need to search the building to make sure. I want to stay here and get a full report on the situation from Blaze. I left guards on the entrances to the Resistance wing, so Cage can't have got in there."

"I left guards in the Manhattan wing too," said Wall, in a grim voice. "I gave them orders to kill Cage on sight if he returned alone, and they'll obey them. I carefully chose men who lost family members to the winter fever while Cage was smugly taking his hoarded medicine."

"Vijay and Weston, go and wake up the Resistance messenger boys," said Donnell. "Send them to alert the other three divisions to search their territories for Cage."

Vijay and Weston hurried off.

"The rest of you can start searching Sanctuary in pairs.

Aaron and Luther together." Donnell gave a pointed look at the sword in Wall's hand. "Wall, you can go and search Sanctuary with Machico, but you'd better leave that sword with me. I appreciate you brought it here for good reasons, but only my officers should be carrying weapons here from now on. We don't want any unfortunate misunderstandings."

"Of course." Wall gave him the sword.

Now I'd handed the responsibility for dealing with Cage back to Donnell, I was worrying about the off-worlders. They should have been safe from the gas with their room door closed, but the winter fever would still be killing Tad and Phoenix.

I'd hoped the medicine we'd brought would save Phoenix, I'd been certain it would save Tad, but only Braden seemed to have really improved after being given the tablets. I was scared of what I'd find when I went back to their hospital room.

Tad's treatment had fixed my arm, so why wasn't the medicine helping him and Phoenix? I'd been carefully following Tad's instructions, and I had my gun to tell me the precise time, so I was definitely giving the off-worlders their tablets on schedule.

Nadira didn't understand why the medicine wasn't helping them either. She said that medicines had always worked in the past, except when they'd run out of the right one and had to use a substitute.

It made sense that taking the wrong medicine wouldn't help anyone, but Tad couldn't have made a mistake about the tablets. He had access to all the information on the Earth data net, and he'd discussed the winter fever treatment with a doctor as well. They couldn't both have made a mistake.

No, I realized that both Tad and the doctor could have made a mistake after all. They might know everything about the medicines, but they had limited knowledge of the winter fever. Tad had said he'd told the doctor about the symptoms, but how had Tad found out about them? I was sure he hadn't asked me any details of the winter fever.

The searchers were already heading off down the corridor, but I called after them. "Wait! Did Tad ask any of you about the winter fever?"

Luther turned to glare at me. "The leech asked me what it had been like having winter fever. Why?"

Luther had been one of the lucky ones like me, having a mild version of the winter fever. He hadn't been involved with nursing patients the way I had, so his only experience with a patient struggling to breathe would have been when his father died.

"Did you say anything to Tad about the breathing problems?" I asked.

"I don't think so," said Luther. "Since you've let Cage get away despite your fancy weapon, the rest of us have to go and hunt him down. Can we go and do that now, or do you have some more pointless questions to ask us?"

I felt a surge of blind fury, and the lights of my gun started flashing rapidly as it responded to my anger by moving to alert status. I had an urge to point my right forefinger at Luther, see if he was brave enough to keep using that sarcastic tone of voice to me when I had the red targeting light of my gun focused on his chest, but I mustn't do that. Everyone else had stopped to watch our exchange. Targeting Luther would make them think I was dangerously uncontrolled, likely to start shooting people on a whim.

I clenched my right hand rapidly twice to take the gun off alert status, and its lights returned to normal operating levels. Machico obviously noticed that, because he gave me an approving look before speaking.

"Luther, do you really believe you'd have done better against Cage? Having watched you conspicuously failing to do anything at all in a crisis, I strongly doubt it."

Luther opened his mouth to reply, but I interrupted before he could say anything. I didn't have time to get involved in arguments. I understood what had gone wrong with the medicines now. The doctor and Tad hadn't known about the breathing problems, so naturally the medicines they'd chosen did nothing to treat them.

"Luther's right," I said. "You'd better go and hunt for Cage now."

Donnell watched them go before turning to face me. "Why is Wall suddenly acting like you're his favourite niece?"

"I'm not entirely sure," I said. "I'm sorry I let Cage get away."

"You mustn't let Luther upset you," said Donnell. "The first time you shoot someone, you're hit by the knowledge that you're ending a human life. That's a dreadful idea, breaking one of the basic tenets of civilized behaviour, so it's perfectly understandable that you hesitated a little too long before firing at Cage."

"I'm afraid I'm not that civilized," I said. "I didn't hesitate to fire at Cage. When he threw a grenade, I thought it was a bomb, so I took cover behind a door. By the time I realized it was actually a gas grenade, Wall was chasing Cage, and blocking my line of fire."

I glanced at the last few wisps of white gas still coming from the double fire doors. Was it safe to try to get back to the off-worlders yet? Tad and I had brought a lot of new medicines back from the supply facility. Ideally, Tad should contact the doctor again, and ask her which of those medicines was best for the breathing problems of winter fever, but Tad had been unconscious for hours.

If Tad couldn't tell us the best medicine to use, then Nadira and I would have to pick one ourselves, but we'd only have one chance to get this right before Phoenix died.

"If I'd realized Cage would be attacking you with anything more than a sword," said Donnell, "I'd never have left you to deal with him alone, but I'd no idea Manhattan had gas grenades in their armoury."

"I don't think they do," I said vaguely. "Wall threw himself to the ground too, which meant he didn't recognize what type of grenade it was either."

"That's interesting. Cage must have found a cache of gas grenades somewhere and..." Donnell's voice trailed off and he frowned at me. "You aren't listening to me, are you?"

"I'm worried about the off-worlders," I said. "Can we check on them now?"

"What about the gas in the corridor?"

"Most of it was at this end, and it seems to have cleared now. I can hold my breath going through, and take a gulp of air when

I'm at the far end to make sure it's safe. If it's all right, then you can come and join me."

He nodded. "And if you have problems, I can run in and carry you out."

Donnell waited outside the fire doors while I sprinted along the corridor and stopped outside the door of the off-worlders' room. I took several cautious breaths before beckoning to Donnell to join me.

As soon as Donnell was at my side, I opened the door and we both went in. As I closed the door behind me, there was a soft sigh by my left ear. I turned and saw Nadira dropping a heavy metal bar onto the empty bed next to her.

"The sound of gunshots woke me up, Blaze," she said. "What's been happening out there, and why have you been gone so long?"

"Sorry," I said. "Cage came to attack us. He's gone now, but there was gas in the corridor so I had to wait for it to clear."

I hurried across to Tad, and groaned as I saw his flushed face. His breathing had already worsened in the short time I'd been away. A quick look at Phoenix, still valiantly fighting for her life but losing the battle, decided me. Tad was solidly unconscious, but I had to find a way to get through to him. Nadira didn't know who Tad was, or that he was webbed, and she might try to stop me doing this, so...

"Nadira, where did you put the new medicine list?" I asked.

"The original is in the hospital office," she said, "but we've made ten copies and one of them is here in the..."

"I need the original for this," I interrupted. "Can you get it for me please? It's perfectly safe outside now, though you'd better hold your breath until you're through the fire doors."

Nadira gave a last anxious look at Phoenix before going out of the door. I instantly leant over Tad.

"Tad! Wake up! I have to talk to you."

There was no response at all.

"He looks too far gone to talk, Blaze," said Donnell, in a gentle, sympathetic voice. "I'm afraid we won't be trading either him or Phoenix for safe passage past Fence. I don't know how the citizens will react to us just returning Braden, but..."

His sentence trailed off into nothing, because I'd just grabbed both of Tad's shoulders and was shaking him. "Tad, wake up!" I yelled.

"I haven't done any nursing myself," said Donnell, "but I don't think that's going to help the boy."

I ignored him. "Tad, if you don't wake up right now then you and Phoenix are both going to die."

There was a faint movement of Tad's lips, but it stopped again. I dropped him back on the pillows and slapped his face. Donnell started saying something, but stopped when I slapped Tad for the second time. Tad's eyes finally opened, and he looked at me with a bewildered, reproachful face.

"Wha...?" he gasped.

"Tad, you and Phoenix are dying," I said urgently. "You have to contact the doctor at America Off-world again. Tell her some people have breathing complications with winter fever. It begins with a whistling sound when they breathe, then they start struggling for air and finally die. Send her the list of medicines we brought back from the storage facility. Ask her what we should use."

I waited. Tad wasn't saying anything. His eyes were still open but had a vacant look to them.

"Tad, have you contacted the doctor?" I demanded.

"Ye..."

"Tell her that Phoenix will be dead within the next four hours," I said. "You'll die within eight hours."

There was a long wait. I reminded myself that the doctor had to read the message and decide what to do before replying. Tad's eyelids drooped closed, but I shook his shoulders and they opened again.

More waiting. Had the doctor read the message? Was she still asleep or did an incoming urgent message have a way of waking her up? Had Tad actually managed to send a message at all in his current state?

"Mir..." Tad gasped.

"What?" I asked.

"Mir... ror."

A mirror? Why would he want a mirror? I looked round, saw a small mirror hanging on the wall, went to grab it and held it in front of Tad. "This?"

Tad managed a faint nod. "Doctor see patient."

Now I understood. Tad was looking in the mirror, seeing his own face, and sending that image to the doctor. Was he sending sound too, so she could hear his breathing?

Tad started talking again, but I couldn't make any sense of the mangled syllables. He must be trying to say the name of a medicine. I dropped the mirror, snatched a pencil and paper from the top of the cupboard, and thrust them into his hands.

"Write it down."

He was trying to sit up. I put my arm round him to help, and watched anxiously as he wrote an unintelligibly technical word, followed by something I did understand. I frowned. "Why does Phoenix get more tablets than you?"

"Kill or cure." Tad let go of the pencil and paper, then flopped back onto his pillow. "My fault."

The door opened, and Nadira brought a sheaf of papers across to me. I searched through them, looking for the medicine name that Tad had written down. I was panicking, thinking it wasn't there and Tad had been lost in winter fever dreams when he wrote it, then I found it on the last page. The notes against it said it was for breathing problems. The dose there was lower than Tad had written, but he'd already explained why the doctor had suggested higher doses. This was kill or cure for both him and Phoenix.

"We need this one." I stabbed a finger at the name on the list. "Is it on the top floor of the Resistance wing?"

"We've kept one box of each medicine locked up here in Sanctuary," said Nadira. "I'll get it."

She hurried off again, and there was a moment of silence before Donnell spoke. "I realize this isn't a good time for questions, but... Tad just exchanged messages with a doctor at America Off-world?"

"Yes," I said, "but don't worry. Tad hasn't said anything to the people at America Off-world about the Resistance or the divisions. He's been letting them think he's with a group of stubborn citizens who stayed in New York."

"That's nice of him," said Donnell, in a strained voice.

I rubbed my forehead. "I only found out he could send messages when we were going to the storage facility. Tad was exchanging messages with the doctor then, getting her to help fix my arm. I meant to tell you about it earlier, but I completely forgot. I know that sounds ridiculous, but what with Cage, and the gun, and the off-worlders being so sick..."

Donnell nodded. "I know you've been frantic with worry about the boy."

We sat in silence until Nadira came back, and then I had to shake Tad awake again to give him the new tablets. Getting the medicine into Phoenix was harder. She was much too far gone to swallow tablets, so we had to grind them into a powder and mix them with water for her to drink.

After that was done, I went back to the routine of bathing hot flushed faces and listening to struggling breaths. There was nothing else I could do to help Tad or Phoenix now.

As I moved between the beds, I was aware of the sun rising outside the window, its brightness lifting above the skyline of abandoned New York. This treatment would either kill or cure Tad and Phoenix. I would find out which by the time the sun set again tonight.

CHAPTER THIRTY-FOUR

Four hours later, I was alone in the hospital room with the three off-worlders. Nadira had been called away to help with an emergency, which was a good thing in the circumstances. Tad had just gasped out the doctor's instructions to me, and I'd written them down so I couldn't make a mistake. I had the scalpel and the piece of tubing lying ready on the cupboard next to Phoenix's bed. Now I stared into the mirror, and tried to ignore the sound of agonized breathing coming from beside me as I studied my own neck.

I prodded my windpipe cautiously. I could feel the indentation between two bulges that had to be the right spot. I just had to find exactly the same spot on Phoenix's neck, make a small horizontal cut, and insert the tube so she could keep breathing until the medicine had time to help her.

This is perfectly simple, I told myself, but my hand was still shaking as I picked up the scalpel. Phoenix was dying anyway, and the doctor said this was the last hope of saving her life, but I was still terrified of making a mistake and killing her.

"You're sure I have to do this, Tad?" I asked.

There was no reply. I turned to look at him and saw his eyes were closed. "Tad?" I called in a louder voice.

"Key component," he muttered. "She's the key component, but I can't get her to Zeus."

I stared at him in bewilderment, trying to make sense of that, before realizing he was lost in the delirium of winter fever. That meant he couldn't relay messages from the doctor any longer. I'd have to do this alone.

A horrible thought occurred to me. Tad was definitely delirious now. Had he been delirious fifteen minutes ago too? Were the instructions he'd gasped out, and I'd painstakingly written down, really coming from a doctor at America Off-world, or were they just fever inspired ramblings?

I went over to where Braden was tossing and turning in his sleep, knelt beside him, and called into his ear. "Braden! Wake up."

His eyes flickered open.

"Tad says I have to give Phoenix an emergency trache... something. Cut into her neck to help her breathe. Do you know how to do this operation?"

Braden looked appalled and shook his head. "I'm a pilot, not a doctor."

I sighed and stood up. I'd nothing but instinct to help me decide what to do here. I'd happily gamble my own life on Tad being right, but this was Phoenix's life not mine. On the other hand, my bitter experience of the winter fever told me that Phoenix's life probably only had minutes to run.

I was doing the same thing as Luther had done on the roof. Standing in helpless indecision while a life was being taken away. I took a tighter grip on the scalpel with my right hand, marched up to Phoenix's bedside, and used the fingers of my left hand to search for the right spot on her windpipe.

Then I realized I couldn't hear her breathing any longer. For a dreadful moment, I thought I'd left things too late, and Phoenix was already dead, then I saw her chest was still rising and falling. She was getting air without the desperate struggle now.

The medicine had started to work! I watched Phoenix closely, counting each breath she took. One. Two. Ten. Twenty. When I reached a hundred, I put the scalpel back on the cupboard, sat on the chair next to it, and let my head fall into my hands. This time my shaking wasn't from panic, but relief at my last minute reprieve.

I might have sat there for as long as an hour, watching Phoenix breathe, listening to the occasional meaningless fragments of sentences from Tad, and noting the way Braden's restless turning in his sleep grew gradually quieter. Finally, Donnell and Nadira came into the room. Nadira hurried to look at Phoenix and gave a nod of satisfaction, while Donnell just glanced at the off-worlders before beckoning to me.

"I need you for a moment, Blaze."

I frowned, stood up, and followed him out of the door. "What's wrong?"

He closed the door behind us before speaking. "Cage killed someone on his way out of the building. I thought I'd wait and see if Nadira could save her life before telling you, but the wound was too deep and too close to the heart."

It was a woman that had died, but Donnell hadn't said her name yet. I forced out a single word question. "Hannah?"

"No. Hannah was safe in the Manhattan wing, but Marsha was asleep in the bow and knife storage room off Reception. Cage must have gone in there to get a bow and some arrows, and stabbed Marsha when she tried to stop him. The door wasn't forced, and I can't believe Marsha let Cage in, so he must have somehow got hold of a key."

Marsha was dead. I felt the same shocked disbelief as when Kasim had died. I'd admired Marsha more than liked her, but she'd been one of the central figures in the alliance, and now she was gone. "Can I see her?"

Donnell led the way down the corridor and along to another hospital room. It was empty apart from the body lying on the bed. In death, Marsha seemed somehow much smaller, her face unfamiliar without its habitual smile.

I looked down at her in mournful silence. The door to her room had been reinforced. Marsha had trusted in its strength to keep her safe, and it had. It was the lock that had failed to protect her. If she'd had eight bolts on that door as well as the lock, she'd be alive now.

I was so focused on Marsha that it was a minute or two before I saw the knife lying on the nearby cupboard. I noticed the grim red stains on the blade first – Marsha's blood – and then the tag painted on the knife hilt.

Cage hadn't gone into that room just to get a bow and arrows, but to take revenge on Marsha as well. He must have got a key to her room long ago. He'd probably been carrying it round with him for years, trying to work out a way to kill her without bringing suspicion down on himself.

He'd never managed to do that, never come up with a convincing accident that could happen to her locked up alone in her room, but today he'd been fleeing the building with nothing left to lose except his life. He'd stopped to kill Marsha, and he'd savoured his vengeance to the full. He could have used a random knife to kill Marsha in her sleep, but he'd spent valuable extra seconds finding his own knife belt on her shelves so he could stab her with this specific knife.

"Cage did this because of the tag Marsha painted on his knife belt," I said. "The tag that showed the scar my teeth left on his arm."

"I expect that's true," said Donnell. "People have been laughing at Cage for years because of that tag. He likes laughing at other people, but he doesn't like being targeted himself."

While I'd been hesitating to help Phoenix, panicking that I might cause her death, another person had been dying because of me. For six years, I'd been agonizingly careful not to say this word to Donnell, but now it slipped out. "This is my fault, Father."

"This was Marsha's fault," said Donnell. "She liked the power the knife tags gave her, and chose to humiliate some dangerous people. Someone was bound to hit back in the end."

"It's my fault," I repeated. "If I'd shot Cage the second he was in range, if I'd got through that fire door faster, or followed him myself instead of calling for help, then Marsha could still be alive."

"If you'd done things differently, Blaze, then Marsha might have lived but other people could have died instead. You, me, Wall, Tad, Hannah."

Donnell hugged me close to him. "I know this is hard, because I've been through it a dozen times myself, but you can't let yourself obsess over what happened to Marsha. As my deputy and the future leader of this alliance, you have to do the best you can for your people, while accepting that your decisions won't be perfect because no human being is infallible."

I took a step backwards and stared at him. "You can't make me your deputy. There's a big difference between getting two division leaders to accept your daughter as a token female officer, and getting three division leaders to agree to her being the future alliance leader."

"I've been planning to give you that gun for over six years," said Donnell. "I'd no idea what would happen after that. I certainly never expected us to be in the situation where you were already an officer when I gave it to you."

He paused. "For eighteen years, only myself and my deputy have had Armed Agent weapons. Now you're an officer and the deputy position is vacant. The minute my officers saw you with that gun on your arm, they assumed I'd chosen you as my deputy. As soon as the rest of the alliance find out you're Armed, they'll be thinking the same thing."

"Then you have to reassure them by making one of your other officers your deputy, at least for a while."

"Who should I choose? Machico refuses the job. Everyone has watched Weston and Vijay doing their comedy routines for nearly two decades now, so they won't take either of them seriously as my deputy. Julien claims to be a reformed character, but I won't be able to trust him with anything important until he proves he's overcome his problems with alcohol. As for Luther, I just had to physically drag the boy out of Reception because he was throwing a tantrum in front of half the alliance."

"You choose Aaron, of course."

Donnell smiled. "Aaron wants you to be my deputy and future leader, not him. He talked to me about this when we were heading upriver on the Spirit of New York. He's worried about what sort of future his daughter will have, and eager to get the leadership succession settled. He thinks he could make you a reliable deputy at some time in the future, but he wouldn't be a good leader himself."

"You can't afford to stir up trouble now. You need to focus all your efforts on persuading people to leave New York."

Donnell shrugged. "I don't think suggesting you as deputy leader will cause as much trouble as you think. Aaron, Julien and Luther all suffered a testing period of ritual ridicule from the division men when they became officers, but you've barely had an out of place comment."

"The division men haven't had the chance to say anything to me since I became an officer."

"They didn't have a chance to say anything before you went upriver, but you've walked through Reception a dozen times in the last two days. There've been no insults, not even a joking question about why you're continually carrying a blanket or coat over your arm. Haven't you noticed that and worked out why?"

I shook my head.

"Your first action as an officer was to challenge and defeat Cage in full view of the whole alliance. The division men have no need to test you, because they've already seen you do something that none of them dared to do themselves."

Donnell paused. "Defeating Cage has made you popular with most of the alliance, and bringing fresh supplies of vital medicine from upriver has helped as well. If we don't get the necessary three division leaders to vote in favour of making you deputy, then we'll wait a month to let them get used to the idea and try again."

"What if I tell you I don't want to be deputy leader?"

Donnell smiled. "You spent years hiding in the shadows, but you came out of them, Blaze. You took command when I went off to my room and got drunk. You stood on a table in Reception and challenged Cage. You picked up the gun and acted as bait to trap him. I don't believe the person who did those things wants to run away and hide in the shadows again. Even if you did, I don't think it's possible any longer. The situation has changed too much. People's opinion of you has changed too much. *You've* changed too much."

I turned to look at Marsha's body lying on the bed. Donnell was right. I couldn't change what my decisions had done to Marsha. I couldn't change what they'd done to me either. I couldn't take the gun from my arm and give it to someone else. I was Armed and there was no going back.

CHAPTER THIRTY-FIVE

"How could you do something so stupid?" Tad couldn't quite manage a full blown yell yet, but he was getting remarkably close to it for someone who'd been dying only yesterday. "I can't possibly get you to Zeus now you've got that gun on your arm, and there's no way to remove it without killing you."

"I was never going to leave Earth anyway," I said, in my best soothing voice. "You knew that."

"I thought there was still a chance you might change your mind. Now you can't. To make matters even worse, you're looking deliriously happy about it."

"I'm not exactly happy right now," I said. "I keep thinking that Marsha would be alive if I'd handled the situation better. I'm aware things could be far worse though."

I leaned back in my chair, and looked round the hospital room. All three of the off-worlders were lying in bed. Tad had his eyes open and was glaring at me. Braden had his eyes shut, but judging from his pained expression was still awake. Phoenix was deep in healing sleep, and genuinely oblivious to everything around her. After her long battle for her life, her body was finally getting the rest it needed to recover.

"You're going to live to go to Zeus and save civilization," I said. "Phoenix's breathing started improving before I had to cut her throat. Things could be far, far worse."

"For the tenth time, an emergency tracheotomy is very different from cutting someone's throat," croaked Tad, "and you may be pleased about the fact I'll have to go to Zeus and leave you behind on Earth, but I'm not!"

During the ordeal of waiting to see if the new medicine would save Tad and Phoenix, I'd desperately bargained with fate, pleading that Tad would live and promising I'd say farewell to him with a smile when he left to go off world. I smiled now.

"Things were always going to end that way for us. You should be grateful that I've got the gun. Without it, Cage would have murdered both of us by now."

"Well, I'm not grateful," said Tad. "In fact, I'm distinctly ungrateful. If I was strong enough to stand up, I'd be tempted to murder you myself and..."

The door opened and Donnell came in. "I see the mouth is talking again. I suppose that's good news. I'm hoping to trade him for at least a dozen chickens when we get to Fence, but we'll have to leave fast before they find out how much he talks or they'll want us to pay them to take him."

Tad frowned. "I don't talk that much, and I wish you'd stop estimating my value in chickens."

"You never talk for more than twenty-four hours in a single day," said Donnell cheerfully. "Blaze, we have to go to the alliance leadership meeting now."

I gave him a startled look. "I wasn't expecting you to call a meeting so quickly."

"Wall knows about your gun, so it's vital we tell the other division leaders you have it before the news leaks out by accident."

I felt we could trust Wall to keep the secret of my gun, but Luther might start shouting about it in a public fit of anger, so Donnell was right to call a meeting right away.

"There's no need to worry about leaving the mouth and his friends," added Donnell. "Nadira will be here in a minute to take care of them, and I've got four men outside to stand guard while you're away. We're only going up to the third floor of Sanctuary, so we can get back here fast if there are any problems."

What he meant was that we'd still be in the tracking range of our guns, so we could keep an eye on the situation while we were upstairs.

A moment later, Nadira arrived. I stood up and smiled at Tad.

"Try to keep quiet while I'm away. Your throat needs the rest, and I expect Braden would like to get some sleep."

"I would," said Braden, in a weary voice.

Tad gave a depressed grunt, and I followed Donnell out of the room. We met his other officers, including a subdued-looking Julien, over by the main Sanctuary staircase, and climbed it to reach the third floor. We went into the largest of the conference rooms there, and I saw five long tables arranged to form a ring, with a row of eight chairs at each of them.

Donnell went across to the table marked with the blue planet, sat in one of the two central chairs, and gestured for me to sit at his right side. Machico took the chair on Donnell's left, and everyone else sat down as well. I checked my gun tracking display, saw the four dots that were Nadira and the off-worlders in their hospital room, and the four dots of the guards outside. Everything looked peaceful down there, and I'd get an alert from my gun if anyone else approached them.

"I don't think a dramatic unveiling of your gun will help matters, Blaze," said Donnell. "It's best if everyone sees it as they arrive, so you'd better stop clutching that blanket now."

"Oh." I looked down at the blanket I'd been carrying over my arm, and hastily shoved it under my chair. Sitting with my hands resting on my lap would mean the lights of the gun were half hidden by the table. I tried resting my hands on the table instead, but felt horribly self-conscious.

I was experimenting with linking my fingers together, trying to work out if that would make me look more relaxed or not, when the door opened. Ice entered with a group of men I knew well from my days with London division. Ice casually nodded at Donnell, then froze as he saw the black tendrils of the gun hugging my bare right arm, its lights flashing peacefully in standby mode.

Ice stood there staring at me for a few seconds longer, then moved to the London table, but didn't sit down. His men gathered round him in an urgent murmured conference. I couldn't tell much from their shocked faces, and barely a minute later the scene was being repeated as Brooklyn division arrived, and then Queens Island.

Manhattan division came in a few minutes after everyone else. Wall led his party to their table, and they all instantly sat down. I guessed that Wall had warned his men about my gun before bringing them to this meeting. That way Manhattan division could look calm and controlled while everyone else was in confusion.

I hoped Donnell would start the meeting now, but instead he let everyone continue their discussions. I had to endure another ten minutes of furtive stares before the deputation from London division sat down, followed a minute later by Brooklyn and Queens Island.

Donnell stood up. "You've all seen Blaze is wearing a gun. I've been keeping this gun in my safe for decades. I intended to give it to my son when he was eighteen. You know why that didn't happen. Now my daughter is eighteen, and I've given it to her instead. Any questions?"

Over at the Brooklyn division table, Ghost stood up. "There aren't any more guns hidden away in your safe?"

"No," said Donnell. "This was the last one."

Ghost sat down and Major stood up. "Queens Island calls for closed session. Do I have a second?"

"London seconds," Ice called out.

"We have a vote for closed session," said Donnell. "All in favour?" He lifted his hand and so did all four division leaders. "Carried."

Donnell and the division leaders stood up and went out of the room. I looked after them in bewilderment. "What's going on?"

Machico grinned at me. "Donnell needs to bring his deputy and officers to the alliance leadership meetings to make sure they're kept fully informed of events. That means each division leader insists on bringing all their seven alliance representatives as well to maintain their status, but they're never entirely sure they can trust them. Whenever there's anything controversial to discuss, the leaders insist on going off to have a private huddle with Donnell. That way they don't have to worry about their own men misquoting something to other members of their division."

I shook my head. "That's ridiculous."

"That's politics and power play." Machico yawned and closed his eyes. "We could have a long wait."

Over at the other tables, people were standing up and moving into groups to start animated whispered conversations. At our table, Vijay and Weston started discussing a new comedy routine. Aaron leaned back in his chair, and gazed peacefully up at the ceiling. Julien and Luther were talking in such low voices that I couldn't hear a word they were saying.

I stared out of the window at the falling snow. Despite the dangerous weather conditions, Manhattan division had had search parties out looking for Cage for several hours today. They'd probably still be out there if Donnell hadn't called this meeting.

Luther's voice suddenly got a lot louder. "Don't start preaching to me, Julien!"

"Behave yourselves, children." Machico didn't even open his eyes, let alone turn his head to look at them. "You know the rules. No arguing in front of the division members."

Luther shut up, and pointedly turned his back on Julien. Thirty seconds later, the door opened, Donnell and the four division leaders came in and went to their seats, and everyone else hurriedly sat down as well. Once everyone was settled, Donnell stood up again and started talking.

"I've been asked whether my giving a gun to Blaze has implications for the vacant deputy post. The answer is that it does. I'm now formally proposing Blaze as my new deputy." Donnell paused for a moment. "The alliance rules state that my choice of deputy must be confirmed by at least three other division leaders. We'll now break for group consultations before returning to vote."

The four division groups promptly stood up and headed out of the room, presumably heading for smaller meeting rooms where they could talk freely in private. I prepared to suffer another long period of boredom mixed with a particularly strange kind of suspense. I was nervous about the vote, but still unsure whether I wanted to win or lose it.

As the door closed behind the other divisions, Luther jumped to his feet and turned to glare at Donnell. "You should be giving the deputy position to me, not Blaze. My father was your deputy for three decades!"

I winced. Apparently I wasn't going to suffer from boredom after all.

Donnell leaned back lazily in his chair and smiled at Luther. "That doesn't mean you automatically inherit his position."

"You mean I can't inherit my father's position, but your daughter can inherit yours!" said Luther. "This is Seamus all over again, isn't it? You made your son an officer, started talking about him succeeding you as alliance leader, and we all know what happened next. Now you're repeating your mistake with Blaze."

Donnell didn't seem annoyed by Luther's words, but I was furious. I reminded myself that shooting Luther would give people a bad impression of me.

"It wasn't just Donnell who made the mistake about Seamus," said Aaron.

"Yes, it was!" said Luther.

"No, it wasn't!" Aaron stood up and turned to face him. "*You* were a child back then, Luther. *I* was already an officer, and in the alliance leadership meeting where it all happened. Yes, it was clear Donnell was thinking of Seamus succeeding him as leader one day, but it was the division leaders that pushed him into making Seamus an officer when he was only sixteen."

"I don't believe that," said Luther.

"Whether your lordship believes it or not," said Vijay, "it's perfectly true."

I saw Donnell glance at Machico, who gave an almost imperceptible nod in return. I realized they were deliberately letting this situation develop.

"People were already worried about the future leadership," said Weston. "The arrival of London division had meant hasty adjustments that annoyed a lot of people. The Resistance itself was in disorder, trying to merge the London and New York members. It was blatantly obvious to everyone that the only thing holding the alliance together was the sheer force of Donnell's personality. One of his original officers had just died, so everyone was disturbingly well aware that Donnell wasn't immortal either."

"Then Seamus and Blaze walked into that alliance leadership meeting," said Vijay. "They were there for less than two minutes, only appearing as part of the discussion about them moving from London division to the Resistance, but after they walked out of the door everyone started talking at once. Seamus *looked* exactly like Donnell, so we all leapt at the idea that he *was* exactly like Donnell. The boy was the answer to our problems, a walking symbol of our future security, and had to be made an officer straight away as preparation for him taking Donnell's place one day."

I frowned. Seamus and I had never appeared at an alliance leadership meeting. Or had we? My memories of my first few days in New York were a confused blur. I vaguely remembered something about a room full of people staring at me.

Vijay turned to look at Aaron. "You were only a few years older than Seamus back then, and got to know him better than the rest of us. Did you have any suspicions that the boy would betray us?"

"Chaos, no," said Aaron. "I was just like everyone else, falling at Seamus's feet and worshipping him."

Luther shrugged. "So you were all fooled by Seamus. Doesn't that make it even more obvious it's a mistake to appoint Blaze as deputy alliance leader?"

"Oh, stop whining, Luther," said Julien. "Donnell needs a new deputy. We all know that deputy has to be one of you, me, Aaron, and Blaze, because Vijay, Weston and Machico are too old."

"Ouch," said Weston. "I'm hurt. Are you hurt by that, Vijay?"

"Stabbed to the heart." Vijay wiped away imaginary tears from his eyes. "I may never recover."

Julien ignored them. "Blaze hasn't been getting any special treatment for being Donnell's daughter. Quite the opposite, in fact. After the way we were fooled by her brother, everyone was suspicious of Blaze."

He stabbed his right forefinger in Luther's direction. "It's you that's had everything handed to you on a golden plate. Your mother adored you, your father adored you, and Donnell thought the world of Kasim so he adored you too, but look how you behaved on the roof."

"I didn't do anything wrong on the roof," said Luther.

"You didn't do anything wrong because you didn't do anything at all," said Julien.

"You can't criticize me when you were the one causing all the trouble!" Luther loomed over him, clenching his fists.

"Oh yes." Julien stood up so rapidly that he knocked his chair over. "I was the one who caused all the trouble. I proved I was a clueless hothead who couldn't control his temper, while you showed yourself totally useless in a crisis. It was Blaze who took charge of everything. The only one who has any right to complain at Blaze being made deputy is Aaron."

"I've no right to complain," said Aaron, in a strangely bitter voice. "We all watched as Blaze brought down Cage. We all saw her do what any one of us could have done months ago if we'd had the courage."

Aaron suddenly swung round so his next words were aimed directly at me. "Manhattan division invited us to search their wing of the building to prove that Cage wasn't hiding there. We found his hoard of medicine. When I think that I could have accused him myself months ago, I hate myself."

He gave a despairing shake of his head. "I'd heard some of the things Cage had done, but I didn't say a word to anyone. I was scared what might happen to my wife and daughter if I talked. I kept quiet to protect them, and it was the worst decision of my life. If I'd done something back then, if those medicines had been found back then, my wife could be alive right now!"

"I still think Manhattan division knew all about those medicines," said Luther. "They've only admitted their existence now, because we've got that huge supply of medicine from upriver, so there's plenty for everyone."

"If you think Manhattan division knew Cage had those medicines hidden away, then it proves your total lack of judgement," said Julien. "They lost children to the winter fever, including one of Wall's own nephews. If they catch Cage, then I don't think there's going to be a hanging. Wall will just rip his heart out with his bare hands."

"And I'll cheer while he does it," said Aaron.

Donnell and Machico had been silently sitting and watching this. I'd stayed quiet too, because it seemed a bad idea to get involved in an angry argument about my own fitness for being Donnell's deputy. Now Machico finally spoke.

"Entertaining though it is watching you children bicker, I suggest you all sit down now. The divisions will be coming back soon."

Julien and Aaron came back to their seats. Luther didn't.

Donnell sighed. "You can criticize me as much as you like in private, Luther, but it's essential we appear united in public. Sit down."

Luther didn't move.

"Luther, sit down!" snapped Donnell. "You threw a tantrum at breakfast time that embarrassed me in front of all four division leaders. If you embarrass me in front of them for a second time today, you won't be an officer any longer."

"Good!" Luther stalked to the door, opened it, walked out, and slammed it shut behind him.

Donnell turned to Machico. "Do I stick to that threat, Mac, or give Luther another chance?"

"Luther doesn't believe your threats," said Machico. "He thinks he can do anything he likes, and you'll let him get away with it because he's Kasim's son. It's not surprising he thinks that, because it's what you've done every time so far."

Donnell drummed his fingers on the table. "You're saying it's time I called a halt to Luther's antics?"

"I'm saying you should have called a halt to them days ago, Sean," said Machico. "Luther's been creating minor scenes ever since he became an officer, but they've reached a whole new height of childish drama since Blaze got back from upriver."

"I was a little unkind to Luther on the trip back," I said guiltily.

Machico groaned. "It's bad enough with Donnell constantly making excuses for the boy. Please don't start doing it as well, Blaze."

"I felt there was some excuse for Luther's behaviour after he first saw Blaze had the gun," said Donnell. "He was suffering from shock and disappointment."

"Yes, but Luther's had plenty of time to calm down since then," said Machico. "He still threw that tantrum at breakfast, and now he's walked out of this meeting. None of the division leaders will miss the significance of his empty chair. If Luther doesn't see sense tomorrow, then you have to take action, Sean. You can't have one of your officers spitting defiance at you like a sulky two-year-old."

"I totally agree," said Vijay. "Chaos knows I'm biased in favour of any young man as good looking as Luther, but even I've had enough of his lordship's ego since he was made an officer."

"I suggest that Vijay, Aaron, Julien, and I have a little talk with Luther," said Weston. "We can take him up to the sixth floor of the Resistance wing, and explain that Donnell may be willing to put up with his behaviour but the rest of us have reached our limit."

"I'm totally in favour," said Machico. "Just don't let Julien be the one to do the punching, because he's bound to get over enthusiastic about it, and we don't want the bruises to be too visible."

I frowned. I'd never had any illusions about the Resistance being civilized, and it wasn't in my nature to become a pacifist like Braden, but I felt we should find better solutions to internal disputes than having our officers beat each other up.

Donnell shrugged. "If you four want to have a private chat with Luther, then that's none of my business. Just remember that losing Luther would mean I was short of one officer and with a second one still in an extremely debatable position."

He turned to Julien. "You didn't exactly help things there. I wish that..."

Donnell broke off as the door opened and Ice led in London

division. The other division groups gradually returned as well, and settled down at their tables.

"You've all had plenty of time to discuss this, so we'll move straight on to the vote." Donnell looked at the first table. "London division?"

"London votes yes," said Ice.

Donnell turned to the next table. "Queens Island?"

"Queens Island votes no," said Major. "We were willing to accept your daughter as an officer so long as she minded her manners, but we're not having a woman deputy."

He looked pointedly at Luther's empty chair. "I've no idea why you bothered proposing the girl as your deputy. You obviously can't even get your own officers to accept her."

I knew that Luther walking out on the meeting hadn't helped the situation, but I was sure Major would never have voted for me anyway. Another man might have been relieved that my victory against Cage had freed him from being blackmailed, but Major would be furious at a woman saving him.

Donnell turned to the third table. "Brooklyn division?"

Ghost turned to look defiantly at Major. "Brooklyn division votes yes. We welcome the idea of Blaze as deputy leader."

"Well, you already know you aren't getting her," said Major. "It takes three division leaders voting in favour to confirm a deputy leader appointment. We've voted against and so will Manhattan."

"Manhattan will cast our own vote," cut in Wall, "and we vote for Blaze."

Major gave him a disbelieving look. "But you said..."

"We have the required three to one majority," said Donnell. "Under the alliance rules, Queens Island must now either acknowledge the authority of the new deputy or withdraw from the alliance and leave Parliament House."

Major sat in silence for a couple of minutes. He had no choice but to accept the majority decision – he couldn't lead Queens Island off to find a new home in the middle of winter – but he was taking his time over it.

"Well?" prompted Donnell.

"We acknowledge Blaze as deputy," snapped Major.

Donnell nodded. "You'll all want to tell your people the news now. Please also tell them I'll be holding a general conclave of the whole alliance next week."

"To deal with the issue of Cage?" asked Major.

"Amongst other things, yes," said Donnell.

"Good," said Major. "Queens Island will have many questions to ask about the actions of Manhattan division in general, and particularly of its leader. This isn't the first time Manhattan has been involved in murders in Sanctuary!"

The Queens Island group stood and walked out of the room, followed by London. Wall stood up, but headed towards us rather than the door.

"Congratulations, Blaze," he said.

"Thank you."

"You had me worried, Wall," said Donnell. "In the closed session, you talked as if you were definitely voting against Blaze as deputy."

Wall smiled. "Blaze has convinced Manhattan that she will use her authority fairly, so she has our whole-hearted allegiance, but it's always enjoyable to raise the expectations of Queens Island before disappointing them."

Wall went back to his own group. Donnell turned to me, his eyebrows raised questioningly, but didn't have time to say anything before all eight of the Brooklyn division members came over to congratulate me.

"We're making true progress at last," said Ghost. "Donnell, if you're replacing Luther as an officer, then we'd like you to underline things by choosing Natsumi."

Donnell cringed. "I'm eager to have Natsumi as an officer too, but we have to let everyone calm down about Blaze's appointment as deputy before we stir up more trouble. Now I must get back and announce this to the Resistance before the rumours start spreading. I expect Blaze is eager to get back to her patients too."

I frowned. Tad was already upset about me being Armed. I had a feeling he wasn't going to react well to the news I was deputy alliance leader.

CHAPTER THIRTY-SIX

"You aren't just wearing a gun on your arm," said Tad gloomily. "It's a leadership symbol. You've taken on the responsibility for over seven hundred lives."

I paused halfway along the corridor to glare at him. "I've been deputy alliance leader for seven days now. You've said exactly the same thing on every one of those days."

"I keep saying the same thing, because I keep thinking the same thing," said Tad. "I go round and round the problem in my mind, but I can't find an answer. Even if I could find a way to get that gun off your arm, or to make Zeus accept an Armed scavenger girl, you wouldn't leave people who depend on you."

"No, I wouldn't." I started walking again. "Now please forget about it. I'm tired of having the same conversation over and over again."

Tad chased after me. "It's difficult to forget about the gun when it's right there on your arm with its lights flashing at me."

"I shouldn't take you to this meeting. I should take you up to the roof instead and throw you off it."

Tad sighed. "You're really worried about this meeting, aren't you?"

By now I'd learned a lot of things about Tad. His irritating endless questions were because he was used to having the local data net answer his every fleeting thought. His occasional unconscious arrogance was because of the way everyone had deferred to him on Adonis. His deep underlying insecurity was because

319

he'd grown up knowing the future of five hundred worlds depended on him doing something that was virtually impossible. I even knew something he'd never shared with anyone else; his secret feelings about Ellie and the debt he owed her for the second-hand web implanted in his brain.

Tad knew a lot of things about me too, like the way that stress could make me lash out at the very people who were trying to help me.

We'd reached the door at the end of the corridor now, so I stopped and turned to face him. "Yes. Sorry. I'm worried sick. I know the Resistance will follow Donnell out of New York, but the divisions will each make their own decision."

"You think some may want to stay?" Tad shook his head. "Donnell can't let them do that."

"Donnell can't force the divisions to leave New York," I said. "The leader of each division will decide what to do. If that leader doesn't believe the firestorm is coming, then they'll stay and make everyone else in their division stay with them. Today's meeting will decide who leaves New York and lives, and who burns to death in the firestorm."

I couldn't stop myself picturing those deaths, populating my old memories of the London firestorm with the people I knew in New York. I realized I was on the edge of crying, and scrubbed the back of my hand across my eyes. Crying would only make things worse.

Tad reached out to hold me. "Nobody is going to burn to death, Blaze. I promise it won't happen."

I let myself relax against the comforting warmth of him for a moment, before stepping away and shaking my head. "You must know what the division leaders are like by now, Tad. They won't all agree to come with us."

I put my hand on the security plate of the door in front of us, and it obediently slid open. As we went through it, I heard Tad gasp.

"I suppose I should have expected this," he said, in an awed voice, "but I didn't."

I was strangely impressed myself. This was a windowless

area of the building, and when I'd been here before we'd been saving power, so I'd only seen it as a dimly lit place of shadows. Now every single light was blazing, so I could see the full majesty of it. The dark wood and gold splendour, the curved banks of seats, and the raised platform where Donnell and his other officers were already standing.

"The United Earth Americas Parliament used to meet here," I said. "Now it's ours."

We walked down the nearest of the gently sloping aisles, and joined Donnell by the array of grand wooden seating on the platform. I noticed Luther giving me a painfully forced smile, and made myself smile back. Weston, Vijay, Aaron, and Julien had had their threatened chat with Luther after the vote on me being deputy. I'd asked Aaron what happened during it, and he claimed it really had been nothing more than a chat, with no punches thrown on either side.

I wasn't sure I believed that. Whether it was true or not, Luther had been carefully behaving himself since then.

"I want Blaze and Machico sitting on either side of me, so they've both got working microphones," said Donnell. "Tad, I've put a flexiplas chair behind the proper platform seating for you. You'll be hidden from view, but able to whisper information to us if anyone asks any awkward questions."

Tad vanished round the back of the seating, and I sat down in the place I still thought of as belonging to Kasim. I saw Luther frowning at me, and was worried that he'd throw another tantrum about me sitting in his father's seat, but he sat down without saying a word.

Everyone else sat down as well, and I heard Tad whisper from behind me. "Can you hear me?"

"Far too often," said Donnell.

People came streaming in through one of the six doors that linked this room to the wings of the building. I blinked in surprise. The Resistance were usually the first to arrive at a general conclave, but Brooklyn division had come in early. When they sat down, I understood why. Each division had their bank of seats, and the leaders of the other divisions always sat in the front row with their seven alliance representatives. The figures sitting in the front row of Brooklyn division with Ghost included three women.

Machico laughed. "Brooklyn have decided that a female deputy alliance leader means they can have female alliance representatives at last."

Donnell groaned. "I appreciate their reasons for doing that, but I really don't need extra complications in this meeting."

Natsumi led the Resistance in next, and there was an outbreak of startled conversation as everyone saw the seating arrangement of Brooklyn division. When the Resistance finally sat down, I heard a whisper from Tad.

"I see the Resistance sit in the middle bank of seats. Does that symbolize your political position?"

"The Resistance always sit between Manhattan division and Queens Island division to stop them trying to kill each other during the meetings," said Donnell, in a low voice. "You're here to answer questions not ask them, so hush."

Manhattan division came in next. They were halfway down their aisle when Wall saw the front row of Brooklyn division. He stopped so abruptly that a couple of his men bumped into him.

"And now the trouble starts," muttered Donnell.

Wall stood perfectly still for about ten seconds, then shouted a single word. "Mist!"

There was some hasty shuffling of the crowd behind him to let through a girl with a more feminine version of Wall's dark features and tightly curled black hair. Manhattan started moving again, and I watched in awe as Mist sat next to Wall in the front row.

"Chaos weeping," said Donnell. "Why is Wall putting his favourite niece in the front row with him?"

"Wall has a long history of opposing women having power, but he voted in support of Blaze becoming deputy," said Machico. "Now he's following Brooklyn's lead, and signalling Manhattan will be having female alliance representatives in future too. I'd love to know how Blaze talked the man into shifting his position like this."

"I didn't," I said. "At least, I didn't do it deliberately."

I scanned the faces of Manhattan division, and winced as I saw Hannah sitting at the back, her right eye purple and swollen shut from where someone had punched her. Wall was working hard to unite his division after the recent events, generously treating most of those caught up in Cage's plots as being victims rather than guilty parties, so I doubted Hannah had been punished for her past actions. Did that mean she'd already done something new to upset people in Manhattan?

Hannah saw me looking at her, and her depressed expression changed to something alert and calculating. I could tell she was hoping to use her bruises as emotional blackmail, to make me change my mind about having her back in the Resistance.

I met Hannah's gaze and pointedly shook my head. She slumped down into her seat and I knew she'd got my message. I remembered all the times we'd played together as small children, and felt a stab of sadness mixed with guilt, but thrust it aside. I had far more important things to worry about today than Hannah having an uncomfortable time settling into Manhattan division.

Queens Island division were the next to arrive. Major didn't seem to notice the women sitting in the front row until he was about to sit down himself. Like Wall, he reacted by shouting a single word, but this one was obscene.

"Do you have a problem, Major?" called Wall. "Unrequited love, perhaps? I'm sure there are plenty of lonely falling stars in New York that would be eager to cuddle you."

Major glared at him, threw himself down in his seat, and folded his arms.

Ice had led in London division just in time to witness the exchange. He paused for a second, before carrying on down the aisle and turning to wave at someone. There was a moment of confusion, then a burst of laughter from London division, as a bewildered woman went to sit next to Ice in the front row.

"Isn't that London's washerwoman?" asked Donnell. "If she's secretly part of London's power hierarchy, I'll eat an uncooked falling star."

Machico laughed. "Ice must think this is another vote about

Blaze. He's responded by putting a woman in London division's front row, but he's deliberately made a joke of it by picking someone no one can possibly believe has any real power."

Major stood up. "Can we start this meeting now?" he asked, in aggressive tones. "I want to know why Manhattan has stopped searching for Cage."

Donnell groaned, and turned on the microphone in front of him. "I ordered Manhattan to stop searching for Cage," he said, in a voice that echoed round the huge room. "Their search parties were obsessively hunting for him from dawn to dusk, even in heavy snow. It was only a question of time before someone was hurt or killed."

"You can't just abandon the hunt for Cage," said Major.

"Cage may already be dead," said Donnell. "We've found the spot where a falling star feasted on something large, but it's impossible to be sure if the prey was a man or a deer, since falling star saliva liquefies everything including bones and teeth. If Cage isn't dead, then he could be anywhere in New York by now."

"Or he could be hiding nearby, even sneaking into this building," said Major.

"Machico has spent three days working on the security system," said Donnell. "If Cage tries to enter this building through any door or window, then alarms will start screaming. If we find any unexplained tracks in the snow when we're hunting, then we'll resume the search for Cage. Until that happens, we just have to accept it's impossible to search a whole city."

Major made a noise of disgust. "Since Wall has failed in his duty to present his man for trial, Wall should stand trial in Cage's place. When Cage attempted to commit murder in Sanctuary, Wall was there with him."

I turned on my microphone, leaned forward to speak into it, and was startled by the volume of my voice. "I've repeatedly explained that Wall discovered Cage had escaped from his prison cell, and followed him to Sanctuary to stop the murder attempt."

I switched off my microphone again.

"Wall should still stand a formal trial so we can hear all the evidence against him," said Major.

"You've already tried calling general justice against Wall, and failed to get support from any alliance representatives outside your own division," said Donnell. "My daughter has stated that Wall went to Sanctuary that night to defend her, not to murder her. I'm fully satisfied that's true, and I don't want to waste any more time on this issue. I didn't call this general conclave to discuss Cage, but something far more important."

"What could be more important than a murder attempt in Sanctuary?" asked Major.

"The Resistance held a meeting last night," said Donnell. "We will be leaving New York this spring."

There was a shocked reaction from all sides of the room. All four division leaders were on their feet now and shouting questions. Donnell waited a moment for people to settle down, but they didn't, so he resorted to yelling into his microphone.

"Shut up and listen to me!"

Everyone finally went quiet.

"Six years ago, London was destroyed by a massive fire-storm," said Donnell. "The same thing is going to happen to New York this summer. I know you all thought it was a good thing when we got the power working again, but it wasn't. We could only manage it because the power grid is overloading and all its control systems are breaking down."

That wasn't entirely true, but I thought it was a plausible explanation that didn't involve admitting things about Tad that could get him killed.

"Once the long summer days begin," Donnell continued, "and more solar power floods into the power grid, it will explode and trigger a firestorm."

I expected more frantic questions, but instead there was a deathly silence.

"The Resistance will be leaving New York this spring," repeated Donnell. "I hope the whole alliance will come with us. Our plan is to head to Fence and trade the off-worlders in exchange for safe passage alongside the defences. That will allow us to take the shortest route to working portals in Philadelphia."

There was a murmur at the mention of working portals, but

Donnell kept talking. "The plan is to use the portals in Philadelphia to reach one of several, carefully selected, small towns. They're all good places where we'll be able to fish, hunt, and grow crops, with the added benefits of warmer winters and no falling stars."

"I thought it was bad enough when you foisted your daughter on us as deputy leader," shouted Major, "but now you're ordering us to start a settlement and become farmers!"

"I'm *offering* you the option of coming with the Resistance to start a settlement," said Donnell. "If you preferred to make a new home in Philadelphia, then you could. That city has a different, simpler type of power grid that shouldn't cause problems."

"I'm sure Philadelphia's streets are paved with gold too." Major's voice was heavy with sarcasm. "Do you expect us to...?"

Ice's voice drowned Major out. "Blaze, is there really going to be a firestorm this summer?"

I turned on my microphone. "Yes. There were far more fires last summer than in previous years because of power surges."

"Power surges caused by what exactly?" asked Ice.

A whisper from Tad prompted me. "Sections of the power grid safety overflow system breaking down."

"They were caused by sections of the power grid safety overflow system breaking down," I repeated. "Next summer it will fail entirely, and there'll be a firestorm."

"I might take that seriously if there had been five or ten times the number of fires," said Major, "but there weren't. We'd be fools to run screaming from a good home on the basis of an extra fire or two. I..."

Ice interrupted him again. "I never understood what happened in London, why the whole city erupted in flames that summer, but the power grid exploding would explain it."

He turned to glance at the faces of his people, before nodding and facing forward again. "London division will leave New York with the Resistance."

Major laughed. "So easily persuaded, Ice? Donnell just had to whistle and you obediently follow."

Ice swung round to glare at him. "My people were in London

when it burned. We all remember the buildings bursting into flames. We all remember the screams of family and friends who were trapped in those buildings. We all remember how the walls around us were smouldering as we fought to get a portal working and escape."

He paused. "If you'd lived through that, Major, you wouldn't be making remarks about being easily convinced, but packing your bags ready to leave right now. If there's a firestorm in New York, there'll be no way to make a last minute escape, because there are no working portals here."

"There are no working portals here because of *his* son's betrayal." Major jerked a thumb at Donnell. "A demonstration that we can't trust Donnell's judgement."

"Whether there's a firestorm coming or not," said Ghost, "a move could have advantages. I like the sound of warmer winters and no falling stars. I like the sound of a proper settlement and crops too."

Wall joined in the argument. "You weren't old enough to be in the battles on the barricades, Ghost, but I was there. The citizens had weapons and numbers on their side, but we drove them out. We fought like heroes for this city, and we won, but now you want us to give it up and walk away for the sake of warmer winters."

I looked at the four division leaders, each standing in front of their people. Ice had announced his decision that London division would leave with the Resistance. The others hadn't made a formal announcement yet, but I could already see they'd made their decisions too. Ghost would lead Brooklyn out of New York. Wall would keep Manhattan here for the sake of old glory. Major would keep Queens Island here out of pride and egotism. There was every chance that Manhattan and Queens Island divisions wouldn't die in the firestorm, because they'd kill each other the moment the rest of us left.

I stood up. I knew I couldn't say anything to change Major's mind, but Wall might listen to me. I remembered what Cage had said about me being the weak point in Donnell's armour. Wall's weak point was his nephews and nieces, and all the other children of Manhattan division.

"Many of you sitting here were at the barricades," I said. "I wasn't born then, but I've heard all the proud tales about how you fought like heroes. You won a glorious battle, but there's nothing glorious about the life we lead here now. You conquered a city, but that city is falling apart."

I waved my arms to gesture round the room. "Look at all the children here. They never knew the glory of your battles. All they have is a life of hunger, cold, and hardship. Their lives are ruled by fear. Fear of falling stars, fear that something will happen to the one or two adults they can trust to protect them, fear that one day there'll be nothing to eat."

Major started to say something, but I had a microphone and he didn't. I used that advantage and kept talking over the top of him.

"I know the lives those children have, because I was one of them. I've lived with their fear. I've watched my best friend betray me because of that fear. No one can change the past, but I want the children in this room to have a different future. If we leave New York and make a new start, we can give them security and replace their fear with hope."

I continued in a bleak voice. "Staying in New York will end the children's fear too. Permanently. I know what the New York firestorm will be like, because I've seen it in London. The children may die the kind death from smoke, or the agonizing death from burns, but they'll die. I'd rather give them hope than death, but it's your decision not mine."

I turned off my microphone and sat down.

There was a long silence before Ghost spoke. "Brooklyn will leave New York with the Resistance."

There was a still longer silence before Wall called out. "Manhattan will leave New York with the Resistance too."

I had one brief second to rejoice before Major said the inevitable words. "The cowards will flee from shadows, but Queens Island will stay in New York."

I bit my lip as I looked at the anxious faces of the people in Queens Island division. They were all going to die.

Donnell sighed. "If Queens Island change their minds before

the spring, they're welcome to come with us. We'll end this meeting now and have dinner. Those of us who're leaving New York will meet here again tomorrow evening to discuss details of possible new homes."

There was the usual end of meeting chaos as all the divisions tried to leave at once. Machico turned to smile at me. "You talked Wall into bringing Manhattan division with us, Blaze. You fought with words and won."

I shook my head. "I fought with words and lost. Queens Island will be staying. I know most of their women from days fishing and working in the gardens. I know every single one of the babies and children from my time working with the crèche and the school. I nursed some of them through the winter fever, stopped them dying of that, but now they're going to burn to death."

Luther's voice startled me. "You can't blame yourself for that, Blaze. You got Wall to listen to you. I admit that Machico was right about you being a better deputy leader than me. I could never have said all that soppy stuff."

Oddly enough, it was the grudging way he said it that convinced me this was a genuine offer of peace. "Thank you," I said.

"It wasn't easy for me being Kasim's son," he added. "People would never believe I'd achieved anything on my own merit, they always assumed it was because of favouritism, and kept comparing me to the impossibly high standard of my father. When he died, I was torn between grief at losing him, and relief that I'd be judged on my own merits at last. Everyone still kept comparing me to my father though, and deciding I'd never match up to him. The worst thing about it was that I knew they were right."

"Is that whining self-justification your idea of an apology, Luther?" asked Julien. "Do you imagine Blaze had an easy time being compared to her traitor brother?"

"Don't cause trouble!" I pointed my right forefinger at Julien, wondered why Luther was laughing, and then realized Julien was staring at my flashing gun in panic. I hastily lowered my hand. "Sorry, I'd forgotten about my gun."

"Please try to remember it in future," said Julien, in a slightly higher pitched voice than usual.

Luther patted him on the shoulder. "Calm down, Julien. If you'd paid more attention to what the gun's flashing lights mean, you'd know Blaze has the gun in safety mode."

"Don't patronize me!" snapped Julien.

"Luther, Julien, go and argue somewhere else," said Donnell, in a depressed voice. "Blaze and I are too worried about what's going to happen to the Queens Island people to bother with you now."

Tad appeared from behind us. "Is there any chance Major will change his mind?"

"No." I stood up. "Once a division leader takes a position on something, changing his mind is seen as a sign of weakness. Wall has the courage to do it anyway, but not Major. I'll take you back to the hospital room now, Tad."

He pulled a face. "Can't I eat in Reception with you and Braden tonight, instead of staying in the hospital room with Phoenix? I'm feeling much better now, and I'm tired of Nadira fussing over me."

"Nadira is being careful because you've had the winter fever very badly," I said. "Are you sure you aren't tired after the meeting?"

"I'm fine," said Tad.

Tad and I fetched Braden from the hospital room and then went to Reception. We sat with Donnell and Machico at one of the Resistance tables, and ate a silent meal. Donnell and I were depressed, Machico was deep in thought, Braden never said much anyway, and even Tad wasn't talking for once.

We'd just finished eating, when there was a shout from the London division area. "What's that?"

I looked round and saw Ice was pointing at the front glass wall of the building. It was past sunset, so it should be fully dark out there except for the lights of New York, but there was an ominous red glow in the sky. Donnell stood up and hurried towards the glass wall.

"Stay here," I told Tad and Braden, and joined the mob

rushing towards the windows. I pushed my way through to stand next to Donnell, and gazed in horror at the view. That was definitely a fire. A massive fire. I tried to hold back a sob of panic, smothering it to a faint squeak.

The four division leaders had fought their way through the crowd to reach Donnell too. "Is that fire in Newark?" asked Ice tensely.

"It's hard to tell," said Donnell, "but it's definitely over the other side of the Passaic River."

"That fire's covering a huge area," said Ghost. "Is the firestorm starting already?"

"I don't think so," said Ice. "If it was a firestorm like in London, we'd see chains of fires exploding all across the city. What we're seeing must be just another warning sign of what's to come."

"That's a pretty big warning sign," said Wall. "I'm starting to believe you're right about this firestorm, Donnell."

Major shrugged. "That's just an unusually large random fire. If it's across the Passaic River, then it's no danger to us."

A woman's voice called out from behind us. "Queens Island, gather on me!"

I turned and saw Raeni running towards the Queens Island area. Rogue met her and put his hands round her waist, lifting her up to stand on a table. Major cursed, and thrust people aside as he strode across to stand looking up at her.

"Get down from there!" he ordered. "I'm the leader of Queens Island, Raeni, not an arrogant, loud-mouthed girl who doesn't know her place."

"Really?" Raeni looked at the Queens Island members crowding round to watch the confrontation. "Newark is burning already. The whole of this city will burn this summer. Major would keep you here to die in the flames. I'd take you with the Resistance to a new home."

She paused before shouting at the top of her voice. "Make your decision now. Die with Major or live with me. Queens Island, gather on me!"

Major climbed on another table. "Let the other divisions run like cowards, and we will rule New York alone. Queens Island, gather on me!"

I held my breath as the crowd shifted position. A few went to stand by Major, but the rest were clustering around Raeni's table. Rogue climbed up to join her, and gave her a triumphant hug.

"I lead Queens Island division now," cried Raeni, "and we will go with the Resistance in the spring."

I heard myself make an odd, sobbing sound of relief. The whole alliance would leave New York in the spring.

Raeni turned to nod to Donnell. "I deeply appreciate you giving me a safe haven, Donnell, but you've always allowed your Resistance members the freedom to leave, so I'm sure you won't object to me returning to my own people now."

Donnell gave a dazed wave in acknowledgement, and went back to our table. Once we'd all sat down again, he turned to raise his eyebrows at Machico.

"Did you see that coming, Mac? I certainly didn't. I thought it was Rogue bidding to take the leadership from Major, but it must have been Raeni all along."

Machico gave a bewildered laugh. "I leapt to the wrong conclusion too. We were both feeling sorry for poor Raeni, being discarded by Major just because she was Rogue's girlfriend. In fact, we should have been sympathizing with Rogue. Major was pressuring Raeni to behave by setting up her boyfriend to be punished."

I remembered when Rogue was being dragged to the punishment post. Raeni had called out his name in an odd way, and he'd shaken his head in return. She'd been asking if she should surrender to Major, and Rogue had been telling her that she shouldn't.

Donnell abruptly buried his face in his hands. I gazed anxiously at him.

"What's wrong?"

He lifted his head again. "There's nothing wrong," he said, in a shaky voice. "Nothing wrong at all. I was just suffering a bit of reaction."

Machico smiled at him. "You told me you could never get

them all to leave with us, Sean, but you managed to convince them after all."

"I didn't convince anyone," said Donnell. "Ice and Ghost didn't need convincing. Blaze convinced Wall, and the freak luck of that fire starting convinced Queens Island to overthrow Major."

"The fire wasn't entirely luck," said Tad.

"What do you mean?" asked Donnell.

I turned to stare at Tad. "He means that he started the fire. I thought he was unnaturally quiet during dinner."

Donnell gave Tad a stunned look. "You set Newark on fire? Chaos take it, Tad!"

"I was very careful," said Tad. "I couldn't be sure exactly where a power surge would cause a fire, only the rough area, so I picked somewhere well away from us and on the other side of a river. You have to admit it worked beautifully."

"Oh, it did work beautifully," said Donnell, in a strained voice. "I'm even grateful to you, but I wish you'd warn me before doing these drastic things. First you light up New York, and now you set fire to it. What are you planning to do next, Thaddeus Wallam-Crane the Eighth?"

"I don't know." Tad turned to frown at me. "I'm still trying to work that out."

CHAPTER THIRTY-SEVEN

The next morning, I stood on the roof of the Americas Parliament House. The eastern horizon was streaked with red and orange harbingers of dawn, but elsewhere was still dark enough for the lights of New York to make a dazzling display. I looked up at the Earth Resistance flag and saluted it.

"I like your hand on heart salute," said Tad, from behind me.

I turned to face his shadowy figure and smiled. "Donnell says that the Military salute points to the head, but the important things come from the heart."

"That's true," said Tad. "Especially things like loyalty. Is it Earth you're swearing allegiance to, or is it your father?"

I shrugged. "There isn't really a difference, is there?"

"I suppose not," said Tad. "I've been thinking about our situation. I can't possibly stay on Earth, but when the alliance leaves New York, I want to go with you as far as your new home. I can spend a day or two helping out with things before I portal to America Off-world."

"Things like turning the power on for us?" I asked.

"Yes. It's not just that I want to make sure you have a good home for the future though. I need to know exactly where I can find you, because..." He paused for a second. "When I was ill, I kept having strange dreams about you and the Rosetta component. I've finally worked out the meaning of those dreams."

I remembered Tad rambling about components when he was

delirious, but I didn't see what his Rosetta component had to do with me. "I'm not sure what you're talking about."

"It's impossible for me to build the more advanced Rosetta component, so I'll have to make the simpler prototype instead. That isn't ideal, but I can make it work. It's the same with our relationship, Blaze. It's not possible for me to take you to Zeus, but there's another solution. One that isn't ideal, but we can make it work."

"What solution is this?"

"I have to go to Zeus, there's no way to avoid that, but I don't have to stay there forever. It will take me a year or two to get the Fidelis Project well established, but then I'll start coming back to Earth for a few months of each year, and finally settle down to live here permanently. It's not an ideal arrangement, it's going to be a difficult first few years for both of us, but I think we can make it work."

"Donnell kept meaning to come back to London," I said, "but he never managed to do it because there was always another problem that only he could solve. There's always going to be another problem for you too."

"I'm not Donnell," said Tad. "Chaos knows I'm worse than him in most ways, but I intend to do better than him in this. The Fidelis Project got its name because it's based on faith and loyalty. Every Betan world is sending precious experts and resources to Zeus and trusting them to recreate interstellar portal technology. I wouldn't do very well leading a project like that if I couldn't keep faith myself."

He solemnly gave me the hand on heart salute of the Earth Resistance. "Fidelis, Blaze."

I laughed, and studied Tad's face as he lowered his hand again. Having a relationship with him would be a huge risk, because there were so many things that could force us apart. We might have a lifetime together or only a couple of months, but that was true of all relationships, and my life had always been full of risks.

Tad seemed to be studying me too at first, but then his eyes started their rapid focusing on a multitude of invisible images.

"Thaddeus Wallam-Crane the Eighth," I said, "are you checking the Earth data net for instructions on how to kiss a girl?"

He gave me a startled, apprehensive look. "Yes, but I'm not finding anything useful."

"I think kissing is the sort of thing everyone has to research for themselves."

He hesitated, then took a step towards me and waited expectantly. I took my own step forward in turn, there was a pause as we exchanged the nods of two musicians poised ready to begin playing a duet, and then we both made the final movement to close the gap between us.

We were better at the timing than the actions. There was a clumsy moment or two as we worked out how to hold each other, then the awkwardness slowly faded as our lips bridged the gap between different worlds and opposing loyalties.

About a minute later, Tad pulled away a fraction. "You're right. We definitely have to research this for ourselves, but your father will be expecting you downstairs."

"I think he'll guess what's delaying me," I said.

Our lips met again, and the sun rose over New York as I kissed the last of the magicians.

Message From Janet Edwards

Thank you for reading Scavenger Alliance. This is the first book in the Scavenger Exodus series, and set in the twenty-fifth century of the Portal Future. I also have books set in the twenty-eighth century of the same future, as well as books set in two very different future universes. The Hive Future where humanity lives in vast hive cities. The Game Future where people no longer grow old and die, their bodies are frozen and they live their lives in virtual worlds.

Please visit my website, www.janetedwards.com, to see the current list of my books. You can also make sure you don't miss future books by signing up to get an email alert when there's a new release.

I'd like to thank Andrew Angel and Juliet for Beta reading Scavenger Alliance, and fact checking its New York setting. Any remaining problems are entirely my fault.

Best wishes from Janet Edwards

Printed in Great Britain
by Amazon